In Praise of *The Tubman Command*

"Cobbs's lively narrative fleshes out our understanding of Tubman as a woman while offering vivid portrayals of life in bondage, war-time strategies and America's knotty racial legacy."
—*Atlanta Journal-Constitution*

"I sped through it... Not able to put it down. *The Tubman Command* is a great mix of history and heart. Don't miss this page-turning tribute to Harriet and her cause."
—*Post Independent*

"Meticulously researched and carefully written, *The Tubman Command* is a true story with the pacing and suspense of a mystery novel."
—*Historical Novel Society*

"If you think you know all about Harriet Tubman, think again—this novel brings her alive as only fiction can."
—Kate Manning, author, *My Notorious Life*

"Cobbs is that rare writer who possesses both the uncanny eye of the historian and the dynamism of a natural storyteller."
—Fiona Davis, national best-selling author of *The Masterpiece*

"A phenomenal piece of writing which humanizes one of America's most beloved icons and shows a different side of a woman whom many think they already know."
—Edda L. Fields-Black, Author of
'Combee': Harriet Tubman and the Combahee River Raid

"The heroic and brilliant Tubman is brought vividly to life as a flesh-and-blood woman and a strong and cunning leader in this compelling and instructive fictional tribute."
—*Booklist*

"[A] terrific portrait of Tubman."
—*Publishers Weekly*

"A stirring fictional tribute."
—*Kirkus*

The
TUBMAN
Command

Books by Elizabeth COBBS

Fiction:
The Hamilton Affair: A Novel
Broken Promises: A Novel of the Civil War

Nonfiction:
The Hello Girls: American's First Women Soldiers
American Umpire
All You Need is Love: The Peace Corps and the 1960s
The Rich Neighbor Policy: Rockefeller and Kaiser in Brazil
Major Problems in American History

The

TUBMAN

Command

A NOVEL

ELIZABETH
COBBS

Arcade Publishing · New York

Arcade Publishing books may be purchased in bulk at special discounts for sales promotion, corporate gifts, fund-raising, or educational purposes. Special editions can also be created to specifications. For details, contact the Special Sales Department, Arcade Publishing, 307 West 36th Street, 11th Floor, New York, NY 10018 or arcade@skyhorsepublishing.com.

Arcade Publishing® is a registered trademark of Skyhorse Publishing, Inc.®, a Delaware corporation.

Visit our website at www.arcadepub.com

10 9 8 7 6 5 4 3 2 1

Library of Congress Cataloging-in-Publication Data is available on file.

Map from the Official Records of the War of the Rebellion, Courtesy of Stanford University Special Collections.
Cover design by Brian Peterson

Print ISBN: 978-1-950691-68-5
Ebook ISBN: 978-1-948924-35-1

Printed in the United States of America

For Myra Frances Burton,
Student, Teacher, and Friend

Then we saw the lightening, and that was the guns; and then we heard the thunder, and that was the big guns; and then we heard the rain falling, and that was drops of blood falling; and when we came to get in the crops, it was dead men that we reaped.

Harriet Tubman on the War Between the States

Chapter One

~May 1863~

Another woman today, just from "de main," said to me that she had hard work to escape, sleeping in "de ma'sh" and hiding all day. She brought away her two little children, and said her master had just "licked" her eldest son almost to death because he was suspected of wanting to join the Yankees. "They does it to spite us, ma'am, 'cause you come here. They spites us now, 'cause de Yankees come."

Laura Towne, Teacher, St. Helena Island

HARRIET'S EYES FLEW OPEN AT THE cock's crow. Her mouth was dry, and her heart pounded. In the early morning light, she still sensed her husband's solid hip against hers, as if all she had to do to take him in her arms again was roll over. Instead, she pulled the sheet across her face; John Tubman was gone for good.

Their marriage had been a sturdy one. John's timber business thrived in the five years they lived next to the plantation where Harriet grew up, rented to one sour-tempered mistress after another until she was strong enough for fieldwork outside slapping range. Her master, Edward Brodess, hadn't objected to the union. As she recalled, he even smiled when she asked permission. If a free man wanted to waste his seed on a slave wife, Brodess was happy to reap the fruit. Free people of color like John Tubman often loved the

1

wrong person. It was an easy mistake in a Maryland county where half the black population was enslaved and the other half was not. And John had been smitten ever since he spied Harriet felling a hickory all by herself—one tiny woman against the forest, he'd said, singing like an angel and swinging an axe like the devil.

Daylight filtered through the thin fabric. Harriet lowered the sheet in the stuffy boardinghouse on Port Royal Island and gently pressed two fingers against her lips, as John had done in her dream. She breathed slowly and deeply through her nostrils, filling her lungs. She could almost smell him.

His voice still sounded in her ears. "You know I can't, sweet baby," he'd whispered. Tracing a line down her cheek, his fingers had come to rest on her lips, quieting her objections. Then he'd lifted his head and kissed the dent above her left eyebrow—she felt it even now—in that tender way he once had. The gesture never failed to soothe her, though she couldn't abide a kiss on the back of her neck where the whip scars of childhood still tingled and shied at any touch.

Why wouldn't he go with her? She'd tried so many different ways to phrase the question, this way and that, though she knew all of them made him feel weak. If she wanted to be his woman, she needed to let him be a man. Or so Mama said, and she had been married to Harriet's father nearly three decades. They'd brought nine babies into the world despite seeing each other only on the Saturday nights that Daddy's owner let him visit. Mama cried and begged whenever Harriet talked about running away and told her to obey John. Mama thought that's how matrimony worked, or so she pretended. If she was a good wife, and Daddy a strong man, they would be together always. But Harriet knew that marriage was like a bizarre children's game. One cruel tap on the shoulder by the master and you were gone.

John had promised again and again that he would earn enough money to free her. In the dream, now fading so quickly she couldn't recall how it ended, his voice hadn't been much louder than the cicada that used to hide in the corner of their one-room cabin. But he must have said—as he had many times in person—that she shouldn't worry. That he'd saved nearly half the cost. That she'd see. But Harriet had never seen. She wanted to believe her husband was right, yet she also knew Brodess would sell her the minute he felt like it. And when she'd become pregnant, she decided she couldn't fool herself any longer. From then on, as her belly got bigger, it squeezed against her love for John Tubman.

Harriet sat up in bed. The limb of a live oak tree outside her window swayed in the sea breeze, trailing gray Spanish moss like an old man's beard. A cart passed on the street below, and a dog barked. The occupied town was stirring. Somewhere on the far side of Beaufort, an army bugle piped reveille.

She thought about the morning ahead. If she and Septima finished their baking before noon, Harriet would make it to Hilton Head Island on time. General David Hunter needed to know what they'd found on yesterday's scout of the Combahee, stealing past Rebel soldiers on picket duty who guarded the mouth of the river against Yankee warships. Though she felt scarcely rested, Harriet threw off the sheet and swung her feet onto the cool floorboards. It had been fifteen years since she left John Tubman and joined the Underground Railroad. If that no-good, no-account ever dreamed about her, which he probably didn't, he wouldn't imagine she'd become a spy for the Union army.

The woman on the far side of the whitewashed kitchen looked up brightly from her mixing bowl as Harriet entered the small outbuilding and took an apron from a hook on the back of the door. Harriet looped the strings behind her. "Morning, Septima. Thanks for starting without me," she said. "Felt like the sun climbed out a bed early today."

The apron tied high on Septima's swollen abdomen was dusty with flour and looked ready to come undone. Her green turban was smoothly wrapped, though, and a necklace of tiny seashells indicated a resolve to preserve appearances despite the big belly. Behind the worktable stood a brick fireplace with a beehive oven. Nearer the door sat a weathered sideboard from which the finer crockery had disappeared early in the war. Something sweet bubbled in an enamel pot on a stove against the far wall while a tortoiseshell cat supervised from a windowsill that overlooked an orange tree spangled with white blossoms.

It was a southern kitchen like any other except for the absence of slaves, which gave it a cheerful air, as if there was extra breathing room. Set back from the main house to prevent the spread of grease fires, it possessed windows on three walls, another feature that put Harriet's mind at rest, as she instinctively preferred as many escapes as possible.

"Morning, Miz Harriet," Septima said with a smile, her slim fingers kneading continuously. "Don't you worry on it. De beer is on t' bile, and I got de biscuits jest bout confangled."

Harriet walked over to look in the mixing bowl. It had taken a year to accustom her ear to the local Gullah dialect that combined African expressions with an English so retooled that it sometimes constituted a secret language. She saw that Septima had nearly finished the biscuits. Clumps of gingerbread stuck to the back of her hands. "That looks a bit wet," Harriet said. "May I fetch up more flour?"

"Yes'm. I might a added too much 'lasses. But we almos' out a flour, I b'lieve."

Harriet took the limp sack from the sideboard. From the weight, there might be a cup or two. She carefully tipped the large, floppy bag and a small amount of pale flour dusted the tacky dough. "That enough?"

"Maybe jest a bit more."

Harriet jiggled harder. The flour was stuck in the folds, so she gave the bottom seam a good, strong shake. The remainder dumped into the bowl, and a puff flew up into her face. She straightened and sneezed. Then sneezed again.

Septima's eyes widened. She burst into laughter. Her apron came loose, and the strings flapped down altogether.

"Ki! You done turned white, Miz Harriet. Now you one a dem high-falutin' Buckra. Don' have to work no more."

Harriet put her hands on her hips—she hadn't time to waste—but she pinched back a smile. Sometimes she did want to play. Lay down her burdens for a spell. Septima looked so pretty with her seashell necklace and catlike eyes that Harriet wondered if she ought to bead a necklace for herself even though she couldn't picture wasting time on such folderol. Septima grabbed the edges of her apron with sticky hands and sashayed around the table. She was nimble for a woman seven months gone.

"Play whenevuh you want!"

"Septima, I got to catch the packet for—" Harriet said.

"*Dance* whenevuh you want! No more cooking, no how. Mm-mm." Enjoying herself, Septima began humming a tune. She snatched up Harriet's hands. "Come on!"

Harriet saw Septima wasn't going to give up. She shook her head, then laughed and squeezed Septima's hands in return. Motes of flour flew upward as Harriet batted her lashes in her best imitation of a Baltimore belle. "All right, baby girl. Turn your partner."

The two women dipped and swung one another, humming, breaking into song, smiles bigger at each turn. Harriet ducked easily under the bridge of Septima's uplifted arms. The Sea Islander towered over her like an egret twirling a sandpiper. Harriet finally stopped. She brushed the flour from her nose with the hem of her apron and slipped behind Septima to retie the apron strings. "But don't you lay that burden on me, or I'll never get to heaven," she said. "Most white folk topple clean off Jacob's ladder. Shouldering too much guilt, poor sinners." Harriet turned back to the table. The dough looked firm. "Ready to roll that?"

Without awaiting an answer, she fetched a wooden pin from the shelf to start the task herself. Septima tended to give the dough a heavier workout than advisable, and Harriet didn't feel like making a lesson out of the afternoon. The day's biscuits needed to get done—and a soft crumb kept customers coming back.

Septima wiped her hands on her apron before taking up a wooden spatula. She scraped the contents of the bowl onto the work surface. Harriet shaped the dough into a ball that she rolled flat with the pin while Septima followed behind, cutting biscuit shapes with a tin cup. "Why you never marry, Miz Harriet?" Septima asked. "Pretty ooman like you."

Since Harriet had hired Septima three months earlier, she'd avoided topics she didn't care to discuss. The curious Sea Islander must have assumed that the abolitionist everyone called "Moses" had never had much of a personal life. "I did," Harriet said as she gathered the last remnants into a couple of lumpier biscuits for Septima's two boys and wondered what she'd done that morning to rile John Tubman's ghost.

"What happened?" Deep lines furrowed Septima's brow. A corner of her mouth quavered, and she looked like she regretted the question. "He git sold?"

Harriet wrestled a baking sheet from a crate of jumbled pots and pans and placed it on the table. She began arranging the cut rounds. "No. He was already free. I went without him."

"By yo'self? Like me?"

"Uh-huh."

Septima heaved a sigh. "'Clare to Gawd, I thought I seeing Angel Gabrul when you and Mistah Plowden chanced on we last fall. Don't know how much longer de boys could a held out. Famembuh?"

"I remember thinking the Lord marked you out special," Harriet said.

She and two other scouts had plucked Septima from a marsh along the Combahee on a moonless night, four miles south of the plantation from which she had escaped with her children. Although most of the Gullah lived on the Sea Islands, planters moved servants around as it pleased them and the Gullah dialect—whose origins time had obscured—had spread across the Low Country. Septima was born on St. Helena, called *Sa'leenuh* by folk on Port Royal, before being sent to the main. Harriet guessed she was around twenty-five. The father of Kofi and Jack, Septima's two boys, had been traded away long before as a down payment on a racehorse.

Septima placed the last row of gingerbread rounds on the sheet. She set the tin cup on a shelf next to the windowsill on which the cat slept and folded her hands atop her high belly. "Chillun, what bout dem? You and Mistah Tubman have any chillun?" she said after a cautious pause.

It was a question women often hesitated to ask. Seven-year-olds sent to auction instead of school. Harriet picked up a dishcloth to avoid Septima's eyes, folded it into a potholder, and told the lie that haunted her. "Thank the Lord, no."

A dodger might call it the truth. She had never possessed a child. John's younger sister, Mary—a free seamstress married to a timberman named Isaac—lived across the yawning Chesapeake in Baltimore. Mary had been expecting around the same time as Harriet and agreed to pass off the newborn as a twin. John and Harriet's child would come back later as their free "nephew" or "niece." Harriet had recognized the plan's merit. The baby didn't belong to her anyway; it belonged to Master Brodess. But if the child went to Mary, that was different. Free mother, free baby.

Even so, a terrible foreboding swelled along with the belly that Harriet hid under bulkier and bulkier coats that winter. Her arms actually cramped at the idea of never holding the child that tumbled and kicked just below her ribs. And even if they smuggled the infant safely to Baltimore, what if Brodess took it into his cussed head to peddle Harriet before John finished saving up? It had happened before.

As if he had taken a cleaver and removed her mother's fingers one at a time, Brodess sold Harriet's three older sisters a year apart. The frigid November that traders showed up for Linah, Harriet had been but twelve. Hauling water from the creek in pails, she'd heard a child scream on the far side of the Big House. Although her hands were frozen stiff, something in that wail caused them to fly open, and she dropped both buckets. One tipped over. She didn't stop to right it but rushed around the building to find her mother restraining a grandbaby. Linah, the child's mother, clutched her skirt to her thighs while a man in a beaver hat rudely pushed up her cotton petticoat to get his cuff around her ankle.

Master Brodess just stood there counting his money. "You said $400," he told the man, whose partner grunted and pulled out another $10 bill in response.

Harriet ran to Linah and grabbed her arm. "No," she yelled. "No!"

The man with the money tried to push her aside, but she clung for dear life. Linah almost tripped on the chain since his partner had by then secured the band around the other ankle. The trader had broad arms, and he shoved Harriet so hard the second time that both she and Linah stumbled. A button popped off her sister's sleeve as Harriet fell onto the rough gravel.

There was no uglier sight under Heaven than one human locking chains on another, or a mother looking at a child for the last time, as both Linah and Mama did when the traders' wagon rolled past the white Methodist church and turned into the forest. Ashamed, Harriet felt she should have done something more to save her sister. But her grip hadn't been strong enough, her voice not powerful enough. So gentle Linah—who knew how to nudge a comb through Harriet's stubborn hair in a way that never hurt—vanished into Georgia, leaving behind two children and the button that Harriet picked up off the ground.

John just didn't understand. He sometimes ribbed her for being too serious. "Always last to get the joke," he once said in annoyance, when she'd fretted so much during a Saturday supper with Isaac and Mary that she failed to smile the whole evening. This time, though, she thought he was the slow one. If history repeated itself, as was its tendency, she might be separated from her baby forever. Still, John wouldn't hear of making a break for Pennsylvania. It would mean pulling up roots sunk by his grandparents a generation earlier and abandoning the business. And she could hardly go alone or take a newborn. What sort of woman exposed her infant to patrollers if she didn't have to or deserted her husband to live on the run? In nightmares, she heard hounds baying. When she awoke, John held her to his chest until she stopped shaking.

"You asking too much, Hattie. You my woman, and you staying put," he said in sterner moments—one moment humble as a kitten, the next angry as a bear—when the sun came up over Cambridge, and it was time to face the day. So Harriet prayed instead for Brodess to change his ways. But then he took $350 for her cousin when he got a notion to buy some acreage, and she pleaded with God to let scrawny old Edward Brodess sicken and die. The wish became a chant in her head as she chopped firewood on the plantation, slaying one stump at a time, though she knew the prayer wasn't Christian. Each morning, Harriet scrubbed her face in the horse-trough with extra vigor, trying to wash her soul clean, trying not to forfeit God's grace.

A bang interrupted Harriet's troubled reverie. The tin mug bounced across the floor as a black and tan blur leaped from the windowsill and dashed through the open doorway. Bits of dough flew off the lip of the cup. Harriet threw the dishcloth over her shoulder, snatched a broom, and ran to the threshold. "Shoo!" she said, though all she spied was a swaying clump of ferns near the stable. She shook her head with disgust.

Harriet whisked the debris out the door and returned the broom to its corner. She picked up the fallen mug since Septima couldn't touch the floor any longer and handed it to the tall Sea Islander, who stowed the object on a shelf too high for the cat. Even Harriet would need a crate to stand on.

"Evuh see your man again?" Septima asked.

"I went back for him the next year," Harriet said. "By then, I knew folk on the Railroad. I bought John a suit a clothes, thinking he could pretend to travel north for a funeral in case anyone asked why he wasn't hauling his usual load. We'd pass through Bal'more. I got as close as I could, but he'd found already himself another wife."

Hurt thickened Harriet's throat as she lifted the tray. Anger and sorrow, braided tight as a pigtail, yanked her back to that instant when everything that made life sweet turned sour, and her heart broke beyond repair. The messenger she'd paid to find John had had to restrain her. She'd wanted to raise Cain. Bang on her husband's door and make him explain, regardless of who heard. Even now, she couldn't get over the way John had cast her aside. He wouldn't even talk to her, as if she were lower than the path down to the swamp and deserved nothing at all for the years they'd been married. She'd thought of him as the answer to her prayers. Then he betrayed her.

No man could do that ever again.

"He married a free woman," Harriet added. She reminded herself that he had found someone of greater value. That's what happened when you reckoned a wife in dollars.

Septima's mouth fell open. "Ki! A free lady? To replace you? I's sorry, Miz Harriet. You deserve bettuh. Dat man gafa!"

Harriet shook her head. "Not evil. Jest weak."

Most people were. A friend claimed that the blow to Harriet's forehead at thirteen had knocked a higher moral sense into her that others didn't possess. But she'd been able to see the right and do it even before an overseer brained her for defending another child. As Daddy said, "Hattie come with gumption for two." Others accepted how things were. Harriet asked how in the world they could be.

The future would be better. She resolved to keep that thought foremost for the rest of the day as she gestured with the metal tray toward the oven. "Get the door?"

Septima took the rag from Harriet's shoulder and held the cast iron handle as Harriet slid in the pan.

"Why don' you find yourself a new man? A bettuh one," Septima said as she closed the oven. "Alfred sho make me an my boys happy. I made my X, and now I's a lawfully lady. Married right under de Union flag. Wish you had someone like him, Miz Harriet."

But Harriet knew she was best off relying only on herself, so she shook her head and smiled. "A new man? Why, I get new men all the time. I got six right now. Hunter's scouts keep me plenty busy. I'd find jest one man boring."

Septima laughed and laid an arm across Harriet's shoulders. "You always got an ansuh. Dat must be why folk listen."

Harriet slipped her arm around Septima's waist. She didn't always have the answer—half the time she didn't know which way to jump—but she knew that a husband made life complicated. And Harriet had no use for that kind of trouble.

CHAPTER TWO

Go Down, Moses, way down in Egypt's land,
Tell old Pharaoh, "Let my People go."
Spiritual

"CONTRABANDS BELONG IN BACK," THE SOLDIER repeated with a scowl that cottoned no sass. He tilted the barrel of his long-shanked musket to indicate the path leading around the porch to the refugee camp and beyond it, the rows of silky white cotton for which Hilton Head was famous. There were dark half circles under the sentry's armpits. Summer came early to the islands that hugged South Carolina's coast. May was August on a low boil.

Being female wasn't particularly useful, except as a disguise, which was another reason Harriet had mostly given it up. Frustrated, she gazed up at the blue-uniformed sentry who blocked the entrance to army headquarters. Here was her chance to free more people in a day than she had in a decade. Raise an army. Turn the war around. Make up for all she'd sacrificed. This man stood in her way, and he wasn't the first. Harriet drew herself as tall as five-foot-zero would allow. She knew she looked no different from other former slave women in her gingham dress and yellow headscarf, despite the regulation musket.

The soldier tilted his barrel toward the path again—and slapped a mosquito on his neck with his free hand. "Damn!" he cursed in a brassy Boston accent. "Off the porch, I said. Now."

13

Harriet guessed he was another collegian come south to serve as an officer and assigned guard duty to learn the business of soldiering. Sunburn glowed on his cheeks where his blond beard still grew in patches, somewhere between the full whiskers fashionable among white soldiers and the smooth shave preferred by colored ones. She saw he was only a handful of years older than Margaret and it mitigated her impulse to kick him in the shins. His mother must worry about him, too. She had probably woken alongside the boy's father year upon year. They'd seen him take his first step, say his first word, jump his first puddle. Everything Harriet and John had missed and could never get back.

"The general's expecting me," she said in the confident, storyteller's tone she used with people who must be convinced to mark her words despite believing she could have nothing to say. In Boston years before, crowds curious about the Underground Railroad had pressed into theaters to hear thrilling tales of midnight raids and brazen reconnaissance missions from someone they would not have noticed folding their laundry. Northerners listened more attentively after the gentlemen of Charleston set fire to the Constitution and eleven states bolted the Union.

The sentry's expression toward Harriet wasn't hostile—she was only a woman after all—but his gray eyes narrowed. "General Hunter's in a meeting."

"Uh-huh. I supposed to be there," Harriet said.

The sentry leaned forward, casting a shadow across her face. "Orders are no interruptions. Except for a scout named Moses."

"That's me," she said.

He snorted. "You're Moses? Well, if you're Moses, I'm God Almighty, and I'm telling you, get your fanny off this porch. Field workers started five hours ago, mammy." Before Harriet could reply, he snatched her musket with his free hand, quick as a copperhead in slack water. "And I don't know what you're doing with this," he said, "but you'd best let go before you hurt somebody."

Harriet couldn't believe she hadn't seen him coming. She must be wearier than she realized. No Massachusetts toy soldier, no matter his height, could compete for grip with a woman who could pull a hysterical runaway from a swamp after dark.

Most assumed the scout everyone called Moses was a man. When strangers met her, they saw a woman. Once they knew she was Harriet Tubman, they saw a neuter without personal needs or soft spots. Saintly John Brown had called Harriet *him*. He meant it as a compliment. "I want *him*—General Tubman—leading my right flank," Brown had told a meeting of their supporters in Boston before he got himself killed. His comment stung, but she knew better than to disturb a notion that allowed her to do things otherwise unseemly. On the Underground Railroad, the name Moses had kept bounty hunters looking for a man.

The soldier rested the butt of Harriet's musket on the porch with a hand around the barrel. He appeared to relax now that he had the gun and eyed her with dawning recognition. "Hey, aren't you the one who sells gingerbread? I saw you last week, when we came off the steamer in Beaufort. Your helper ran out before I got to the head of the line."

"Sho am, sah," Harriet said, sliding into her deepest Maryland drawl to humor his expectations. She had always known how to stir men's interest or pass beneath notice, depending on need. When to look them in the eye, when to study her bootlaces. A generous smile cut dimples in her high cheeks and turned a plain face into an attractive one, despite the gap where she'd fixed a troublesome tooth with the butt of her pistol. Harriet had an unexpected, animated beauty. "Fine looking," said the advertisement offering a reward for her capture. With her lithe movements, minute waistline, and musical voice, no man would guess Harriet Tubman was close to forty. When she wanted to disappear, she simply let her inner light wink out.

Harriet's expression warmed. She lifted her small, pointed chin. "You partial to gingerbread, lieutenant? I add orange peel. Folk say mine the finest on Port Royal."

"Partial I am, indeed," the sentry said. "And I haven't tasted anything edible since we sailed from Boston two weeks ago." His nose wrinkled like he'd gotten a whiff of vinegar. "Hominy, peas, and salt pork is about it."

"You like some, sah?"

The youth's lips parted. Harriet pictured him at one of the pastry shops on Boston Common where students mobbed the counters and lady abolitionists had taken her for tea and apple cake. The boy was a long way from home.

"Why, I got some right here. Made mo' this morning," Harriet said sympathetically and lifted down the leather satchel she carried over one shoulder. She hitched up her dusty hem and bent over to search the heavy bag. She prayed he didn't have a hair trigger. The Rebels had taken down their artillery. Lucky breaks wouldn't hold still. The thought made her fingers clumsy, and she fumbled with the buckle before flipping it open.

Harriet dug around a small package wrapped in sailcloth, a leather pouch of gunpowder, a filigreed but practical pair of sewing scissors received as a parting gift from the Anti-Slavery Society when she'd sailed for South Carolina, and the button that had belonged to Linah. Harriet hesitated. Fear washed over her. Then she slipped her hand around the wooden butt and her finger through the cool brass loop.

"Here you go," Harriet said as she drew out the Colt revolver, straightened swiftly, and aimed it at the boy's chest. "Now let me in. I need to see General Hunter."

Chapter Three

To the [Congressman's] first question I therefore reply that no regiment of fugitive slaves has been or is being organized . . . There is, however, a fine regiment of persons whose late masters are fugitive rebels, men who everywhere fly before the appearance of the national flag . . . So far indeed are the loyal persons composing this regiment from seeking to avoid the presence of their late owners that they are now one and all working . . . to go in full and effective pursuit.

Major General David Hunter to Secretary of War Edwin Stanton

THE DOOR BURST OPEN. THE STARTLED sentry jumped sideways, and the heavy muskets clattered together. The youth dropped Harriet's on the porch. She swept up the gun with one hand.

"Moses. I thought I heard you," Colonel Thomas Wentworth Higginson said. "Where the hell have you been?"

The commander of America's first colored regiment—and Harriet's old friend—stopped short. He looked from her, holding two weapons, to the rattled sentry. "Is everything in order, Lieutenant Nickeson?"

With a poet's high forehead, Colonel Higginson was born looking heroic. Although he had thickened around the waist and acquired a dash of gray at his temples since they'd first met in Boston—where Thomas adopted every humanitarian cause from abolitionism to women's rights—he still glowed with youthful idealism. Like most

17

Northerners, he had a limited notion of all they were up against, yet he had done what few white officers would even consider. When the war started, he became first to lead former slaves into battle. By way of thanks, Confederate President Jefferson Davis signed a death warrant for any white man caught doing so.

"I been showing the lieutenant the new Colt that Uncle Sam sent us," Harriet said, her heart still thumping. She tipped the barrel of her musket skyward and leaned it toward the soldier. No sense making a fresh enemy when they had so many, or letting Thomas know she'd pointed a gun. "Watch my musket whilst I join the meeting?" she asked the sentry. "I'd be obliged, sir."

The youth's sunburn became general, reddening his neck and ears, and he answered the Massachusetts officer without looking at him. "Yes, Colonel Higginson. Everything's well." Not taking his eyes off Harriet, he took the gun and stacked it against the wall. "I'll keep it here, mam—Moses."

Harriet stooped for her satchel, tucked the pistol back in the main compartment, and pulled out the item wrapped in sailcloth. She handed her provisions to the sentry. "Welcome to South Carolina. Hope you like my gingerbread."

Thomas waved Harriet through the door, and she passed close enough to catch the fragrance of lemon verbena on his clean skin. It had been his favorite tonic as long as Harriet could recall, and she'd come to think of it as the smell of righteous indignation. "Did you get some rest?" he asked as they crossed the anteroom. A clerk stood and saluted, and Thomas returned the gesture without giving the man his full attention.

"Plenty," she fibbed as Thomas opened the door to the general's office, through which blue cigar smoke curled.

Major General David Hunter sat at the end of a long conference table. An older man with two stars on his shoulder and six decades of experience under his belt, Hunter stared gloomily at the map of South Carolina's coastline. Someone had pinned it to the wall when the Union wrested the Sea Islands from the Rebels a year and a half earlier, after the dust-up few expected to outlast the summer of '61 settled into civil war. Looming beside the map was tall James Montgomery, a pious and lethal Kansas Jayhawker who had ridden with John Brown himself. Light from a window touched the back of Colonel Montgomery's head and turned his unruly hair into a burning bush. A second window faced the alley, which Harriet automatically noted as a getaway if she needed one.

"With respect, General Hunter, your timidity confounds me," Colonel Montgomery said. "All we had to show for the Jacksonville raid was thirteen bales of cotton and a couple dozen contrabands. Not worth *spit*." The hawk-nosed former preacher avoided the cuss word many white soldiers would have chosen. He angled his head aggressively at the faded chart. "What are we waiting for when the prize is right here?"

The Southern sun had glared at the map so long that it looked like it had gone through the wash. Harriet recognized South Carolina's serrated coastline and the adjoining Sea Islands. Hilton Head, Port Royal, Lady's, St. Helena, and a handful of smaller lily pads were the Union's refuge from Confederate forces on the mainland. As the chart indicated, and gunshot occasionally proved, much of their turf lay within musket range of the Rebels. When Harriet first arrived, she'd been astonished to learn they were hardly islands at all. More like clumps of green that had broken off, leaving watery cracks between them and the main. Hunter and his officers had puzzled endlessly over the map that showed the isles they must defend and the coastal positions they might attack if they could avoid being trapped.

Listening for cues, Harriet took a chair against the wall. If a woman hoped to convince a roomful of men of anything, she must pick her moment.

An older soldier with heavy eyebrows and a coarse mustache dyed black, General Hunter showed his age that morning despite efforts to hide it. Lines ran down his cheeks. The wig that covered his bald spot rested awkwardly. While men elsewhere waged

Armageddon, General Hunter guarded the last federal foothold on the Confederate coast. His troops had fought a few remote, backwater skirmishes in Florida, but every one of them yearned to do something bigger—something that burned a hole in history and scattered Dixie's ashes. Unfortunately, the catastrophe in Charleston Harbor the month before showed they had little idea how. They'd spent weeks preparing to attack the birthplace of the Rebellion, only to be smashed within minutes. Underwater mines called torpedoes had trapped their ships right in Fort Sumter's line of fire. It was another humiliating defeat in the long line of disasters that had begun two years earlier in the very same spot.

Hunter shoved aside a stack of telegrams and stubbed out his cigar in a chipped teacup. "What makes you think your men can do what our navy can't?"

"We don't have to prevail against Sumter, just circle around and bushwhack the Secesh from behind. Attack some plantations. Get crackers on the defensive," Colonel Montgomery argued. The Kansan balanced his lean weight on the balls of his feet. His rumpled blue uniform hadn't seen the flat side of an iron in a week. "They want their fill of war? We'll give it to them. Now!"

Harriet knitted her hands tightly. They were her feelings exactly. The Secessionists had dominated from the start. It was time to turn the war around.

Thomas Wentworth Higginson pulled his chair close to the table. He straightened a notepad, took up a pencil in front of him, and studied his rival. Each of the former preachers hoped to cover his regiment with a little more glory than the other—as everyone with eyes in their head knew. Thomas had assumed command of the 1st South Carolina Volunteers three months before Colonel Montgomery took up the 2nd.

"This isn't Indian-fighting," Thomas said. He sat erectly, which made him seem taller than he was, and his fine locks brushed his starched collar. "Congress doesn't think colored men can learn discipline. We need to prove they can fight."

Montgomery's chin jutted out. "What we need is to win."

Harriet caught herself leaning forward and drew back with her face cautiously blank.

"Not at the price of dishonor," Thomas retorted. "You gave your troops too much license in Florida. We're training soldiers, not bushwhackers. Damaging civilian property breaks every rule of civilized warfare."

"No idea what you mean," Montgomery said, though his eyes gleamed at the reference to his first raid, when his men confiscated local foodstuffs to fill out their scanty rations. "I make it a point not to interfere with private property. I just reminded the boys they have a right to defend themselves if attacked by Rebel pigs and turkeys."

General Hunter withdrew another cigar from his top pocket and bit off the end. "I'd order our colored troops to burn every goddamn mansion in Charleston to the ground if I could, but we have barely enough men to hold the Sea Islands, much less attack overland," he said. The general took up a box of locofocos, struck one against a small piece of iron, and puffed on his cigar to light it. He blew out the smoke, turning the air around his head a deeper blue. "And conscription just won't work on people used to being swooped up like chickens whenever their masters needed cash."

Harriet knew exactly where they could get more volunteers. Hundreds. Maybe a thousand. She burned to speak up, but Hunter would listen better if he asked the question. Men always did.

The debate over how to recruit colored troops had simmered ever since the navy's invasion sent planters fleeing from the islands off South Carolina's coastline a year and a half earlier. The day they attacked Port Royal, one white family had abandoned a steaming pork roast, a full pitcher of mint julep, and over five hundred slaves. The poor four-year-old operating the fan over their dining table wasn't unstrapped from his perch for an hour.

Yet there had been switchbacks on the path to freedom for those accidentally liberated. The Union declared the Rebels' property forfeit, but when Hunter freed the human portion of the Confederate "contraband," Lincoln canceled the order. When Hunter turned slaves into soldiers, Congress pitched a fit and refused to pay them. And when the president issued his Emancipation Proclamation, he took aim only at states in rebellion. Plantation owners in Harriet's home state of Maryland could keep all the slaves they wanted, so long as they didn't backtalk the federal government.

When the proclamation was at last read aloud under Port Royal's biggest shade tree on Emancipation Day—that blessed January 1, 1863—a thousand contraband surprised the Northerners with a raw, heartfelt version of "My Country, 'Tis of Thee." Harriet asked one old Gullah man how he knew the song, and he said with a smile, "Dat de first ting I larn aftah freedom." The government finally approved colored units, but hardly a man didn't worry about being double-crossed once the white gentlemen of the United States patched up their spat. Despite ten thousand freed slaves on the Sea Islands, colored regiments lacked sufficient volunteers.

Colonel Montgomery glowered at Hunter. "I didn't join up to twiddle my thumbs."

"And the president didn't assign me command over our first colored regiments to watch them commit suicide," Hunter said. "God rest John Brown, but I'm not presiding over another Harper's Ferry. We need more men in uniform to have a hope of taking Charleston, and Lincoln isn't sending them anytime soon. The president's barely holding Washington."

Now was the moment. Harriet scuffed her shoe against the plank floor as if shifting to get more comfortable. Colonel Montgomery's head flicked toward her. General Hunter followed his glance.

"Moses," Hunter said. "What's your report?"

Harriet nodded at the map. "May I, sir?"

"I'm waiting," Hunter said.

Harriet strode to the map across the room while Colonel Montgomery took a seat and tipped back in his chair, scratching his armpit in contemplation of the worn chart. The Jayhawker appeared blind to everything except how to destroy the Secesh. Harriet liked him more all the time. Some beanpole had pinned the map, so she reached as high as she could to tap a squiggly line that burrowed deep into the mainland. The Combahee River watered South Carolina's richest rice plantations before flowing to the sea.

"We can recruit right here, General," she said, pointing to the river. "Y'all keep twisting the arms a men that got freedom right now on the islands. They ain't sure a Lincoln's plan and whether he gone stick to it, but they safe for the moment. The men over here," she said, and again tapped the squiggle of the Combahee, "live in a special kind a hell. They gone do anything to get out."

The grooves in Hunter's face deepened. "Our troops can't just sail up there, Moses."

"Yes, they can," she said.

The room grew quiet. Harriet waited.

Hunter flicked fresh ash into the chipped teacup. "There's artillery and pickets around every bend."

"Artillery's gone, sir."

"Gone? How do you know?"

"A man who escaped the Nichols place told us they drew the cannons away from Fields Point, where the river meets the Sound. Took the cannons off Tar Bluff, too. Hauled em up Stocks Road and onto the Savannah railway last week. I checked his story yesterday with my own eyes."

"Perhaps the guns are in the trench," Hunter said. He drew again on his cigar. The tip glowed red.

"Don't reckon so, sir," Harriet said. "Cannons been on top a them guard posts all year. We spotted em from the river." She had seen the Confederate earthworks numerous times, slithering on her stomach through stubby cordgrass wherever the marsh hardened, slipping through the mouth of the Combahee in a dugout when the first inklings of sunrise cast the guns in silhouette.

"Why would the Rebels remove their artillery?" Hunter said.

"Don't know, sir. Contraband say their owners head to high ground during the sickly season. Maybe Beauregard pulling his crews back ahead a the vapors. Whatever he's thinking, the cannons are gone, along with their crews. Ain't nobody there except a handful of guards on picket duty."

Harriet paused. Snares took patience.

"That ain't all," she said.

"What else?" said James Montgomery.

Harriet looked at the Kansan whose gnarled hands gripped the arms of his chair as if ready to bare-knuckle fight the next man who walked through the door. This was the subject where every officer conceded her authority. What slaves knew. It was the reason she was there. The fly in the buttermilk and only Southerner in the room. Governor Andrews of Massachusetts, Harriet's old acquaintance, had promised she would be useful. Desperate as he was, General Hunter had asked her to spy behind enemy lines, more or less as she had done on the Underground Railroad. With the Union courting extinction as each defeat knocked the wedge between the states deeper, Hunter apparently decided her sex didn't matter.

Harriet glanced around the table. Thomas wielded his pencil, and his hazel eyes darted back and forth from his notepad to the map on the wall as he sketched a diagram. She'd hooked him, too. Now she needed General Hunter. It was his decision.

"A new Rebel unit took over jest a couple months ago," Harriet said. "One a our men has a cousin who sweeps the tents. He overheard the new commander being chided for false alarms. Beauregard told him, drill more. Get to know the roads. It appears the commander allowed his troops to go to seed once they moved up and can't find his own pillow in the dark. We can slip past em."

"Up Stocks Road?" Hunter said.

"Up the Cum'bee. If our ships enter the river fore sunrise, we'll reach them rice fields jest after slaves start work. More'n a thousand be dressed for the day and ready to run."

Hunter drew meditatively on his cigar. He looked skeptical. "And a Confederate army less than a dozen miles away, up Stocks Road," he said. "Even if their commander isn't the sharpest, those pickets on the river are his eyes and ears, and he's got two thousand troops camped behind them." Hunter squinted against the fresh plume of smoke. "What about the torpedoes? Surely the Rebs didn't withdraw those, too."

Harriet knew this was the weak spot. Slaves had likely tethered the explosive barrels since alligators infested the waterways, and the Confederates relied on bondsmen for disagreeable tasks. She guessed the labor had come off the Lowndes Plantation. It was the only nearby estate that had not leaked runaways. Fugitives from elsewhere said the Lowndes overseer had horns and a forked tail. They quaked at his name.

"We looking for someone to tell us where they been put," she said.

Hunter's caterpillar eyebrows inched together. "So you don't know where they are," he stated flatly. The commander shook his head. "If I wanted to hazard the remainder of our navy, I'd send it back to Charleston."

James Montgomery shoved a hand through his wild hair and leaned toward Hunter. The front legs of his chair banged the floor. "We went all the way to Florida for thirty measly recruits, General. It's time to smite the big rice plantations. Fill our regiments with men trapped there. It's the only way to get enough troops to take Charleston."

The general tapped his cigar into the teacup. "I'm as eager to subdue Charleston as you, Colonel Montgomery," he said, "but not without an adequate plan. This isn't a prairie raid."

A blue vein throbbed in Montgomery's high forehead. "Those raids woke the nation."

"The Cum'bee ain't no Charleston Harbor, General Hunter," Harriet observed. "The Rebs took down their big guns on the river."

Hunter grimaced. He spoke sharply now. "Every fool knows that artillery's only half the problem. Torpedoes trapped us right under Fort Sumter's guns last month. Almost cost us the fleet."

Harriet felt her dander rise at his words. She wasn't a fool. "This is the time and place to strike," she said. "'Fore the Rebs haul the cannons back to Fields Point and the commander gets off his duff. I got a good feeling, deep in my bones. I see it in my dreams. The good Lord's looking down. He's telling us, make our move. We can get around them torpedoes."

"Around five thousand pounds of powder?" Hunter said. "Around a keg you don't see until you're on top of it? The *Cairo* sank in ten minutes. A feeling isn't a plan, Harriet. Unless you know where the torpedoes are, our ships will end up at the bottom of the Combahee."

Thomas stopped writing. He looked up from the opposite side of the table. A change had overtaken the room. From the corner of her eye, Harriet saw Colonel Montgomery glance at General Hunter, then drop his gaze to his chapped hands. Hunter's expression was severe, as if he'd witnessed similar displays too many times. The only career soldier in the room, Hunter had a bullet slash across his neck from the disaster at Bull Run. The scar turned livid as a flush climbed his throat. Harriet's gut tightened. Perhaps she shouldn't have brought up the Almighty. Hunter might consider her religion-addled. There was a slim line, regularly crossed by reformers, between faith and folly. Yet she was sure He would have warned her if the plan were flawed. She'd seen it plainly in her mind—men and women streaming toward Jordan's shore.

"A military assault isn't like smuggling a few people on the Underground Railroad, Moses," Thomas said, "as dangerous as that is." He tapped the tip of his pencil on the paper, and the light from the window winked off his Harvard class ring. Harriet knew he was trying to let her down easy. "Whole regiments are at risk."

She trained her gaze on Hunter. "I know we need a plan, sir. You don't have to tell me—"

"Well, I am telling you," the general snapped. "Unless you've got intelligence on the torpedoes—coordinates on a map—we're focusing elsewhere. Like on the defense of these goddamn islands." He collected the correspondence in front of him. A moment later, he glanced up. "Gentlemen? Dismissed."

Colonels Higginson and Montgomery rose to attention. General Hunter straightened his papers as if she'd wasted his time. Harriet walked back to her chair, so exhausted that her shoes scraped the floor. The excitement that had driven her had evaporated like brandy dashed in a pan. She felt unsure about everything of which she'd been convinced moments before.

Hunter might be old, but he was experienced and canny. The officers under him were responsible for hundreds of men. Although John Brown had called her General Tubman, she'd always operated alone. A civilian—and a woman, at that—she didn't know the first thing about an armed assault. She'd never loaded a cannon or drilled a regiment. She couldn't write an order or read a telegram. In a dozen missions on the Underground Railroad, Harriet had freed at best a hundred people under cover of darkness in terrain she knew like her mother's voice. Steal a thousand slaves in broad daylight up a strange river studded with mines? No chance. That would take a magician, not a Moses.

Harriet retrieved her satchel from the back of the chair. As she lifted the strap over her shoulders, she recalled the heckler with a drunkard's purple nose who had slandered her at the Melodeon lecture hall in Boston. "*Trickster!*" he'd shouted from the back of the mobbed auditorium. The insult had upset her abolitionist companions, but Harriet had been proud that day. She'd bamboozled the planters of Maryland again and again—to her boundless satisfaction. Slaveholders underestimated her. No man ever suspected what one puny woman could do. That had been the secret to her success.

The corner of her mouth twitched. Trickster, sure enough. If she took down the rice plantations of the Combahee, it would be the greatest trick of her whole career. With the Lord's help, the best thing she ever did. It would prove black troops could fight. Help Hunter recruit enough men to subdue Charleston, symbol of the Rebellion. Give other mothers a chance to keep their babies.

Her mood flipped like the boom on a boat. Ambition lifted her sails. Let them try to stop her. Men studied their maps and chomped their cigars and made their plans and told women to wait. Yet she knew what lifetimes of safety didn't allow most officers to see, just as soldiers afraid to get their feet wet couldn't find the paths in the trackless marsh. The signs added up: the guns, the new Secesh regiment, their lazy commander, the turn of the season. Years before, God had told her to go back one more time, then another, then another, to set His people free. He'd shown her the way every time. Running wasn't wrong if you brought others with you.

Harriet sucked in her breath. But it would not be easy. It might not even be possible.

The welts on the back of her neck prickled. Goosebumps chilled her arms. She drew the strap of the satchel tightly across her breast as she made her way to the door, comforted by the revolver's bulk. To persuade Major General Hunter, she would have to get onto the Lowndes Plantation even if the devil did live there and find someone to reveal the location of the torpedoes.

The thought made her head hurt. She had been in Satan's house before. If he caught her, she wouldn't get out alive.

Chapter Four

The sun has just gone down in Charleston Harbor. . . In half an hour, five out of the nine [Union] ships, were wholly or partially disabled! Such is the ghastly fact in its naked proportions . . . Stretching from a point close to . . . Fort Sumter, completely across the channel to Fort Moultrie, is a stout hauser, floating on lager-beer casks . . . strung with torpedoes.
                                                    New York Times, April 1863

THE UNIFORMED CLERK AT THE COMMISSARY near Major Hunter's headquarters reached for the pencil behind his ear and leaned a spindly forearm on the counter. The edges of his government logbook curled with humidity, and a molasses thumbprint obscured the pre-stamped page number at the top. A thin man with a receding hairline, Private John Webster glanced over the cheap wire spectacles balanced on the tip of his bony nose. His gaze shifted to some hazy point behind Harriet, then back again, eyes not quite on her. "How much do ye want this time?" he asked with an immigrant's lilt, possibly Scottish.

"I'll take thirty a the brown sugar and forty a the flour," Harriet said.

"Thirty o' the sugar, tis," Webster said to an assistant in ragged trousers who took up the burlap sacks that Harriet had placed on the counter. "Take the flour from yesterday's shipment."

"Dose barrels empty, boss," the contraband said. He was a short Gullah man with ears that stuck out like clamshells and a crooked

29

nose that had been broken more than once. "You wan' me get it from de other barrels you set aside?"

"What do ye think?" Webster said abruptly, as if the answer was obvious. He returned his attention to the logbook.

"Sugar still fourteen cents a pound?" Harriet asked as he wrote.

"Tis," he said. "Best bargain on Hilton Head."

"If you call prices twice those a Boston a bargain."

Webster looked up. "John Lilly over in Beaufort, why he'd charge ye sixteen cents."

"That's why I'm here," Harriet said.

She leaned over to examine the ledger as Private Webster resumed writing. Most letters looked like broken twigs to her, but she'd recognize an "H" anytime. Harriet considered it fitting that the first letter of her name mimicked a rung on a ladder, helping people up. "T" resembled a tree: strong, tall, and reliable—as her husband had been until he wasn't—though Harriet didn't blame the alphabet for John Tubman. "H" and "T" were her letters. She didn't need more, regardless of what some people thought. She had plenty on her brain already.

The clerk wrote "30" in the fourth column to the right of her name, and "40" several columns over. Numbers were clearer to Harriet, who had learned to substitute them for the marks she once made on a tally stick for Master Brodess. The clerk's pencil dragged slow gray tracks behind it like the ones snails left on the doorstep each morning, gone by afternoon.

"I'd like that in ink," she said.

Webster straightened. He pushed his spectacles higher and waved a hand at the counter, empty save for a grimy canister of corncob pipes. "Ye see a fountain pen, Tubman? Some thieving black stole it."

Harriet stiffened at the accusation and pointed to the entries above her name. "Why them in ink?"

Webster frowned. "That pass Hunter gave ye tisn't a license for impudence."

"It do make me accountable."

The clerk shoved his pencil behind his ear and slammed the book. His poorly fitted glasses slipped again. "Then come back on the morrow. When I've nothing better to do than hunt up me bloody quill."

Harriet leaned closer, her gaze fixed like a cat on a cricket. The name of Rufus Saxton, the general in charge of civilians on the Sea Islands, ought to make matters plain. Saxton had welcomed her into his Port Royal office more than once to discuss contraband concerns. An abolitionist, he had recently married the prettiest missionary in a hoop skirt.

"I'm in Hilton Head today, Private Webster. You gone sell me that flour now. You hear how much General Saxton's new wife likes my gingerbread? A regular, she is."

He looked down his narrow nose. "Ye can't be the only colored selling gingerbread."

"No, but Mrs. Saxton likes mine best," she said. "And don't think you doing me some favor calling me colored. I'm as proud a being black as you is a being white."

The stubble on Webster's unshaven chin bristled. Without another word he opened a crowded drawer beneath the counter and pawed around until he came up with a quill. His assistant, who slung the full sacks on the counter, fetched an inkwell from a cupboard behind the worktop. As the colored man did so, he gave Harriet a wink and a smile that brightened his homeliness. Webster opened the ledger and traced over the penciled numbers.

Once they'd completed the transaction, Webster's big-eared helper loaded Harriet's purchases into a wheelbarrow and followed her to the dock. There she gave the helpful man a penny and boarded the return packet for Port Royal Island as the steam whistle startled an osprey from the flagpole. She propped herself against her full sacks to nap. Rest kept the blackouts that had plagued her since childhood at bay. Stay calm, eat enough, get plenty of shuteye, and "don' tetch likker," a root doctor had advised long ago.

Even so, the fits that had begun after an overseer cracked her skull still came regularly, often at the worst times. Harriet closed her eyes and dozed to the lull of the ship's engine.

What seemed moments later, a jarring blow startled her from a deep sleep. She opened her eyes to find herself back in Beaufort. The steam packet had bumped the village dock.

Harriet straightened her dress, shouldered her sacks, satchel, and gun, and proceeded down the gangplank into the town that was the pride of the Sea Islands. Imposing homes shaded by glossy magnolia trees lined the main boulevard, called Bay Street for its dazzling views of the water. The army had renamed it "A Street," but no one paid heed.

Beaufort hadn't a patch on Auburn, where every dwelling bore the stamp of decency and liberty that marked upstate New York, from the picket fences of small homes to the sober portals of brick mansions that could have stood for courthouses. Yet Beaufort's columned white clapboards, pink palazzos, and yellow stone villas were nonetheless handsome in an extravagant, lazy sort of way, even with their curling paint. Harriet admired the immense homes as she walked. God had preserved her thus far, and she sent Him a word of thanks as her nerves settled from the tense meeting.

A clutch of barn swallow chicks chirped from a nest under the scrolled pillars of one mansion that was as pretty as a two-pound box of candy. English roses climbed to the second floor, interlaced with flowering jasmine that perfumed the soft air. Peonies hung their heavy heads over a fence. Port Royal Island's main town looked nearly untouched by the occupation—except for the blacks who moved about freely, going wherever they wanted. It was a good thing the planters had skedaddled, Harriet thought. They would have died of heart attack.

"Ma'am!"

She turned slowly, careful not to upset her precarious load.

A tall, well-built man hurried forward with hands outstretched. "Let me take those," said Samuel Heyward. "They look heavy."

Harriet squinted up at her newest recruit. The scout's wide-brimmed hat was pushed low on his brow to stave off the late-afternoon heat, but it didn't obscure his sharp eyes. Three months earlier, Samuel had escaped the Heyward Plantation, upriver from Lowndes on the northern bank of the Combahee. He'd since grown a handsome, pointed beard that gave him a rakish aspect, a quality worrisome in a scout, as hotheads were worse than useless. Yet she'd observed with approval that Samuel generally turned somber before a mission.

Around Harriet's own age, he'd become valuable for his experience on the water. Samuel recognized every local inlet and could thread most any marsh. Unlike men she'd had to chastise for splashing their oars near Confederate pickets—such as Walter Plowden, a good waterman but prey to jitters—Samuel pulled ten-foot sweeps through brass oarlocks without a whisper. He could even swim, a rare skill that had proved handy when another scout dropped an oar in the Sound. Harriet thought more rather than less of Samuel when he flopped back into the boat as if chased by a shark and confessed a horror of deep water. Most of what they did would terrify anyone with working survival instincts. She preferred men who would do what was necessary despite their fears.

"I got em, Samuel," Harriet said and turned back to her walk. One bag slipped an inch, and she jogged a shoulder to reposition it. The heavy weight propelled her feet, and she was proud of the strength that had earned nods of admiration when she used to log with her husband. It was only two blocks more to the cookhouse. Harriet wondered what Samuel wanted, yet she was glad to see him. He might save her some time.

"Sure I can't lighten your load, ma'am?" he asked.

A bead of sweat escaped Harriet's kerchief. He'd called her ma'am again. The last thing she needed was a scout fussing over her. Then he would stop taking her seriously—or taking orders.

"That's kindly, but you can best help by making a beeline for the soldier's camp. Find our men for a meeting. I gone need Plowden and Simmons. The others, too. Any time after dark should work jest fine."

Samuel continued at her side. "Yes, ma'am. Soon as I deliver the message Colonel Higginson gave me for the harbormaster."

A metallic groan drew Harriet's attention as they turned into a side street. Laden high with firewood, an unpainted mule cart approached on the opposite side of the lane. One of its wheels complained about a lack of oil, though the bells of the nearby Baptist Church, tolling four o'clock, drowned the sound a moment later. A white man held the reins of the cart. His unshaven jaw worked a cud of tobacco.

Samuel lowered his voice. "Can I ask what the meeting's about? Anything to do with our last . . . trip?"

The stranger across the street slowed his balky cart. Harriet expected him to bend to the complaining wheel with a can of grease, but he merely stopped as the bell's last toll reverberated across the sweltering town. A resentful look colored the man's sallow countenance. Still holding the reins, he folded his arms and, after a moment's rumination, hawked brown juice in their direction. A bad tingle climbed Harriet's neck. The man must be one of the few poor whites who hadn't fled the island along with the planters. She wondered if he rowed to the mainland after dark to pass intelligence. Port Royal had been evacuated twice when Confederates threatened to invade, alerted to setbacks in troop strength. Harriet cast down her gaze and kept walking. Samuel followed her example, though she saw his fists ball from the corner of her eye.

"Hey, nigger gal," the man called at their backs as they passed by. "Boy," he added, raising his voice a notch, "that's right. Keep walking."

The mule cart was soon well behind them. Harriet was relieved to hear its rusty whine as the man started again on his way.

"Jackass," Samuel murmured.

Harriet kept her voice low and spoke in code. "Overseer says our row could stand some hoeing. Harvest ain't ripe."

"Been hoeing my whole life. Time seems plenty ripe to me. Hunter worried bout weeds?"

"Uh-huh. We don't pull em, there goes the crop."

Samuel nodded. "I brushed against one the other day. Near Lowndes. Not close enough to catch a briar—but something bigger might."

Harriet thought of the barrel she'd seen hauled into Beaufort a few months earlier. Sealed with tar, the enormous cask looked innocent enough until a colored sailor pried off the lid and showed her the deadly gunpowder inside. Harriet wondered if Samuel's comment meant he'd spotted a torpedo from his dugout and could plot the mine's location on a map. Charting them was the only way to navigate the Combahee without getting blown up—and to convince Hunter that she knew what she was talking about.

As they approached the pink mansion where she rented a cookhouse, Harriet stuck out her foot to push open the gate in a low picket fence covered with creeping vines. At the same instant, a small dog dashed under her skirt, tangled with the petticoat, and escaped through the opening. Harriet's shoe caught on her hem, and she stumbled backward. The gunnysack slipped from her shoulder.

Samuel caught the bag with one arm and placed a steadying hand on Harriet's waist. "Whoa," he said.

The weight of the second bag pulled Harriet even farther as she fought to regain her balance. It slipped, too. The momentum carried her against Samuel. The waterman dropped the first sack and clasped Harriet around the middle as the second bag landed on the gate, unbroken but trailing sugar from the corner.

Solid on his feet, Samuel absorbed her fall without moving. The sensation of a man's torso behind her was jarring. Samuel's arm held her securely, despite her satchel and musket.

Harriet pulled away and bent to reclaim the flour, in time to knock heads with Samuel as he reached for it, too. They came up laughing. Samuel rubbed his forehead. "Y'all right, ma'am? You got a noggin like a nut."

Harriet smiled. "So I been told."

"Sure I can't help with them bags?"

"How bout you get one, and I get the other?" she said.

With a flash of white teeth, Samuel hoisted the full gunnysack to his shoulder. The size of shovels, his hands made the sack look small. They were nicked and callused, yet efficient.

Harriet picked up the bag of sugar and carried it through the vegetable garden to the kitchen. Weeds grew on the short path between the mansion and the cookhouse that once fed a planter's family. A steamy fragrance of sassafras, ginger, juniper, and sarsaparilla root wafted through the open door along with the sound of humming. Septima must be finishing the day's root beer. Harriet nodded to the stone slab where they kept an ash bucket. "Thank you. Jest put it there."

The scout set down the flour. "Glad to help. I'll rustle up Plowden and Simmons."

"Any time after dark is fine. Meet me at the Savan House, and we'll head to the usual place."

Samuel nodded. "Yes, ma'am."

That word again. She didn't want him getting a single idea. "Moses is fine," she said and brushed her hands to remove stray granules of sugar. "Jest call me Moses."

"Uh-huh. Yes, Moses." Samuel paused. The muscles in his neck bunched, and his lips tightened. She had the impression that he intended to confront her about something, though she couldn't imagine what. He cleared his throat. "One more thing."

Harriet realized then that it wasn't the sight of her laboring under a heavy load that had brought him running. Although she wouldn't tolerate scouts treating her like a female—and none tried—she felt oddly disappointed. Samuel seemed headed in that direction for an instant. She couldn't figure him out.

He glanced around the deserted yard, then toward the empty lane. He turned his eyes back. "I got family on the Cum'bee. They in a misery."

"That's why we meeting tonight."

"You sure Hunter ain't stalling? I never met a single reliable white man," he said.

"You never met John Brown," Harriet retorted, though she sounded more certain than she felt. In a decade on the Underground Railroad, no one had told her when to strike or lie low. She had picked every battle. Now she awaited orders from a government that hadn't freed a single person until it started losing the war.

Samuel nodded at the name contraband recognized like a cross around the neck. "Well, there best be a plan," he said. "Cause I ain't leaving folk behind. I ain't gone do that." He sounded like he was hammering a placard to a post.

"I don't leave people behind," Harriet said, irritated. The man ought to know better. "Not if they willing to run."

Samuel crossed his arms. "You can't get everybody."

Harriet's face flushed with anger. No one needed to tell her that. "Look here," she said. "This our chance to free a thousand and more. That ain't everybody, but it's as many as the Railroad ever did in a year. And that's jest the start. I ain't never gone quit."

A smile curled the corners of Samuel's mouth. "So I been told. Jest wanted to hear you say it. That's why I'm with you, Moses. No matter what." He tipped his hat. "See you tonight."

Harriet watched him walk up the path and through the gate. She shook her head in exasperation. Was he testing her? She didn't know him well enough to tell. Most men hoped merely to escape, but Samuel seemed resolved to go back. And why had he grown that rakish beard? Unaccountably, she wished she had broken away first. He needed to learn who was boss.

Harriet mounted the steps to the cookhouse behind the mansion. The humming had died. In the doorway, she glanced back over her shoulder. Samuel had vanished up the street. She ran her tongue over the gap in her teeth, of which his smile had reminded her. Too bad he was so attractive, she thought. Spies shouldn't warrant a second glance.

"You busy, Septima?" Harriet asked as she turned into the room. "I could use a hand."

Septima was scrubbing the worktable with a boar bristle brush. Her wet forearms glistened, and her eyes were trained on the task. "Give me jest a minute, Miz Harriet."

"That's all right," Harriet said as she deposited her satchel and musket in a corner and stepped back into the fading heat to retrieve the sack of sugar. "I got us some supplies. But the neighbor's terrier done tripped me," she said as she laid it on the hearth. "Nearly busted the bag."

"Who dat fellah he'ping you?" Septima asked. She rubbed an itchy nose with an upper arm. "Dere a fine-looking man."

"Jest one a Hunter's scouts."

"Uh-huh. I see he a scout," Septima said. "His eye tied up on you, for true."

Harriet shook her head. "He had something else on his mind. And how you know what he looked like?"

"Dat doorway awful wide, Miz Harriet."

Harriet glanced across the room. "You'd need the neck of a goose to see from here."

Smiling down, Septima brushed the wet wood vigorously. "Jest checking de cupboard to make sho we wasn't out a cinnamon, too," she said, and then she broke into a giggle. "I know you likes yo gingerbread dark 'n spicy."

Harriet rolled her eyes, amused. "What makes you think I'm hungry?"

Septima looked up, her smile bolder. "Every lady git hungry."

Harriet recalled her empty sheets. John Tubman had met her

needs once—and she'd been a fly trapped in honey. That was a mistake she didn't need to make twice. "I'm not every lady."

Septima blinked, startled by Harriet's vehemence.

"If you looking for supper, best not count on a man to feed you," Harriet added.

"Yes'm," Septima said apologetically. "I spose you right."

CHAPTER FIVE

We have had the greatest heroine of the age here, Harriet Tubman, a black woman, and a fugitive slave . . . She has a reward of twelve thousand dollars offered for her in Maryland and will probably be burned alive whenever she is caught.

Colonel Thomas Wentworth Higginson

HARRIET PULLED HER SHAWL CLOSE AROUND her shoulders in the chill evening air. The crackling fire made the clearing in the woods on the edge of town feel like a cabin with dark just outside the windows. She and five other scouts huddled around a diagram that Samuel had scratched in the dirt. His younger brother Jacob had been sold to the Lowndes estate six months earlier. Samuel suggested that Jacob might have the information they needed. Resting on his haunches, Samuel pointed out the features of the plantation on which his brother lived.

"The first cabins set here, jest shy a the Big House. Jacob's is second from the end, past the jail and smokehouse," he said. "The rest of the quarters is on the far side. Lowndes owns bout five hundred head. Same as Colonel Heyward."

"Where's the overseer live?" Harriet asked.

Samuel pointed to a small square with his stick. Light from the fire trembled in the grooves of the diagram. "His place is right here, between the quarters and the Big House."

41

"Tell us bout him," Harriet said, wondering about the man whom everyone appeared to fear.

"Goes by the name a Pipkin," Samuel said. "Old man Lowndes hired him a long time ago. Thinks he owns the place. Pipkin picks the angriest niggers to drive the hands. Bribes em with tobacco and food. He's outlasted every other overseer on the Cum'bee."

"When's the last time you talked to Jacob?" she said.

"Not since Colonel Heyward traded him. Colonel said he wouldn't sell a dog to Lowndes, knowing Pipkin, but his London buyer came upon a set a rare books. Said they too good to pass up. Always hankered after a library." Samuel spat on the ground. "That's when I decided to make a break, soon as I could. Might be me next."

The small knot of scouts flinched subtly, as if Samuel had brandished a torch from the campfire. Harriet recognized the reaction. Every refugee had a story that he'd rather not remember about mothers and fathers, brothers and sisters never seen again. Runaways, mostly male, chewed off their families like a fox chewed off a leg in a trap. It was a good thing there were so few mirrors on Port Royal. If men could see themselves, they'd cut their throats from guilt.

Harriet recalled the looking glass in the Philadelphia hotel where she'd gotten her first job. Gentlemen and ladies passed behind her while she polished the mirror in the elegant lobby. It was like a picture book in the stationer's window on Walnut Street come to life, folks looked so grand with their top hats and lace bonnets. However, when a flyspeck in the middle of the glass resisted her rag one day, and she leaned closer to rub it off, Harriet noticed something wrong with the picture. Her own reflection. There she was, with her familiar chin, mouth, and eyes—scar over her left eyebrow and hair pulled into a bun—yet nobody saw her. Guests walked by as if she was a ghost.

What was a life worth when all the people who met your eye and made you feel real were gone? And how could she ever rest, knowing they were captive? It was then she knew she had to go back. Being a ghost would allow her to do so. Once John was out of her life, she'd wed herself to the mission. After she got her family north, she went back for people she didn't know.

The sea breeze picked up, and Harriet tucked her hands into the shawl. She returned to the rock on which she'd been sitting, shoved against a loblolly pine. The men took the stumps they had pulled around the campfire. Samuel rubbed out the diagram with his boot heel to hide their plan from prying eyes and sat on a boulder across from Harriet.

"How you know the layout?" she asked.

"I delivered messages for Mas'r Heyward sometimes," Samuel said. "Him and Lowndes belonged to the Charleston Jockey Club. They bet against each other on the races."

"What your brother do for Pipkin?" Harriet said.

"He minds the rice trunks—them the water gates on the river. If Lowndes loaned anyone to lay torpedoes, he sent Jacob."

"What do rice trunks have to do with torpedoes?" Harriet said.

"The gates are one a the most valuable machines on any plantation. Only the smartest men work em. My brother's trained up to fix most anything." A note of pride crept into Samuel's voice. "They ain't gone use no common field nigger to lay a mine."

Harriet wondered how Samuel had escaped, and why Jacob hadn't come with him. Samuel had probably stolen a dugout. Watermen who ran errands on the river had more range than other slaves, and after the Union occupied the Sea Islands, they had somewhere to go. Yet Samuel didn't possess a Sea Island accent. More similar to Virginia or Delaware, though he'd come off the nearby Heyward Plantation.

Walter Plowden leaned forward. "We heard Jacob's opened his door t-t-twice to men trying to make it to the islands," he said.

A short, scrawny runaway held together with wire, Walter was Harriet's unofficial second-in-command. They had met a year earlier when General Hunter asked Harriet to cultivate men who otherwise wouldn't confide in the Buckra. Walter had helped her recruit their small band of volunteers. Like her, he had fled Maryland before the war and hadn't waited for President Lincoln to grant permission before heading south. He, too, drew no wages, and he made ends meet selling coffee, lemonade, and a weak beer near Camp Saxton, the army base for colored men. "They'd have to pay me to stay home," Walter once said. Harriet understood him better than she did her four brothers sitting out the war in New York and Canada. It had taken her years to steal them out of Maryland, followed by her parents. They refused to go south ever again.

Samuel reached for a sack at his feet, drew out some boiled peanuts, and passed the bag to the next man. Although the night was balmy, he wore an old canvas coat with large pockets for carrying odds and ends. One burning log collapsed into another as he cracked a nut, ate the meat, and pitched the shell into the flames. The campfire flickered in his black eyes, which were concentrated only on Harriet. "I know you want onto that plantation, but Pipkin, he got second sight. He gets ahold a you—" Samuel shook his head.

The group grew quiet as the warning sank in, and the peanuts went around the campfire. They had all heard stories about Pipkin.

Harriet leaned against the tree trunk. She suddenly felt exhausted. Her brief nap had been hours earlier, and she hadn't eaten since late afternoon when Septima pressed a bowl of pork stew on her. The hollow feeling in the pit of her stomach had grown into a general unease. She needed to be careful. Needed to get some food into herself. Across the circle, Walter accepted the goobers without taking any. He jiggled the sack. In Harriet's experience, the lean scout ate only when reminded, unlike Samuel, who must have gone hungry while enslaved, as he always seemed to have something in his pocket.

Harriet had a slight metallic taste in her mouth. She felt woolly and wished Walter would pass the peanuts. She put out her hand shakily. "Send those along," she started to say but never did. The glow of the fire vanished. All was darkness. The only sound she heard was a faint hum.

Someone jiggled her shoulder.

"Moses, you okay?" a man said. His voice was far away.

"She okay j-j-jest awhile ago," someone said. This man seemed closer.

"'Pears de debbil done took her," a boyish voice offered. "Bet she seen a haint."

"Naw. She jest sleeping."

"Dey say she got de charm," the younger man said in an awed tone. "Dem Johnny Rebs can't tetch her. Buckra never even know she dere."

He was wrong, Harriet thought sleepily. Daddy had been the one with the charm, not her. Able to see the future. "War's coming," he had told them in '46, right before President Polk invaded Mexico to grab more land for slavery.

"Moses jest brave, is all," someone protested. "Got a man's courage."

"N-n-nobody brought more slaves north," a different voice agreed.

Harriet recognized Walter's stutter. An uneasy feeling crept over her—as if she'd bumped over the refreshments at a public meeting or slipped in manure on the way to church—and she forced her eyes open. The scouts loomed above her, all except Samuel, who squatted with a hand on her arm as if to keep her from falling. Charles Simmons, a younger scout with a round face and buckteeth, stood next to Samuel. His mouth hung open, and he looked like he'd seen a specter. Charles fingered a lucky rabbit's foot on a string around his neck.

Walter stood in front, still holding the sack of peanuts. Three other scouts—Joseph Sellers, Atticus Blake, and John Chisholm—ranged behind him. Walter leaned forward and licked his chapped lips. "Hey there, M-M-Moses. You had one a them spells."

It seemed no time had passed, but Harriet knew from their faces that she must have been out awhile. She sensed the rough tree bark against her spine and reached down to touch the rock underneath. She was still upright, fortunately. Had her mouth flopped open like a dimwit's? Harriet flicked her hand over her chin. No drool, thank the Lord. She felt relieved and then angry. Why had He given her this curse? She threw off Samuel's steadying hand.

"I'm fine," she said. "Y'all give me some air."

Samuel rose. Walter and the others backed up.

Harriet swallowed hard against the metallic aftertaste and checked the kerchief on her head. She waved the men back to their seats. Samuel edged away but didn't sit. Walter took his stump and tugged on the tail of Charles Simmons's frayed shirt. The boy dropped down beside him. Harriet knew that if she pretended she had merely fallen asleep, the others wouldn't challenge her, though they would believe she wasn't the strongest timber in the tabernacle. That was useful when a bounty hunter took her for a feeble-minded field hand sleeping against a fence, but not when she needed to convince six men that she could lead them to hell and back. They needed to know they could depend on her, which was hard since she couldn't always depend on herself.

"We all brought something with us out a slavery," Harriet said. She tapped the scar above her left eyebrow. "This here is mine." Her mouth twisted in a rueful smile. Better to smile than weep, she knew. Her shawl had slipped down her arms, and she drew it back over her shoulders, feeling exposed. "I can run, and I can fight. And with the Lord's help, I done freed more than a hundred folk. Never lost a one. But I got my spells. Walter can tell you I don't miss much when they happen. Sounds come through like a whistle in fog. And I never missed a station on the Underground Railroad. Not many conductors can say that, not even on the old B&O."

Harriet wouldn't mention that the sounds she sometimes heard were ones others did not. Strange singing, loud buzzing, God speaking. The men didn't need to know that.

Charles Simmons glanced around at the woods outside the circle of light. He nervously fastened the open neck of his shirt. "Thought you seen a haint," he said. "Sure you d'int?"

"No, I did not see a haint. I jest had one a my fits. You want to worry on something, worry on Rebel spies." Harriet looked up at Samuel, still standing. "None a you need to fret bout me."

"Okay, then, Moses. Glad you all right," the waterman said and retook his seat.

Like thunderstorms, seizures scrubbed her mind clean once they broke. Harriet returned to the question of Samuel's brother. She wondered what kept him on the Lowndes Plantation. "Why hasn't Jacob tried to escape?" she said.

"He got a woman," Samuel replied. "Pipkin give him one."

"It's the overseer's way a tying men down—and breeding the workforce," Walter explained. He shot Samuel a critical look that Harriet didn't know how to interpret, then passed the bag of peanuts to the next scout without taking any.

No wonder Walter looked like a broomstick, she thought. The man didn't eat. Slavery must have killed his appetite.

"Now he got a child on the way," Walter continued. "If Jacob runs, Pipkin gone m-m-murder him if he catches him. He can't catch him, he'll finish off the woman instead."

"Won't Lowndes complain bout property being destroyed?" Harriet said.

Samuel shook his head. His voice was as flat as the Combahee. "Pipkin too good at his work. Best on the river. Meaner than a sack a rattlesnakes."

"So how does Jacob help other runaways?" she asked.

"They don't belong to Lowndes," Walter said. "P-P-Pipkin only hunts his own. A contraband from the Middleton Plantation told us Jacob hangs a rag on his door to wipe his hands. When Pipkin's in a 'specially bad mood, Jacob takes it down to warn folk trying to sneak by. Them days, Pipkin will take the hide off runaways from other p-p-plantations if they cross his path."

"Well, let's hope he's having a good day. Cause if Jacob helped lay those mines, we got to get to him," Harriet said, returning to the matter with which they had started the meeting.

Walter frowned. "Why you?"

"You know why," she said.

"It's too dangerous," he protested. "Pipkin catches you, Moses, the whole mission goes in the ditch. Who gone talk to the white folk then? General Hunter won't listen to us. And if Pipkin spots you, your old life in Maryland gone seem like a church p-p-picnic."

"Let us watermen find the torpedoes," Samuel agreed. "I already spotted one. We get two boats working on it, we gone find em all, sooner or later."

"Ain't no better disguise than fishing," Walter said. "Always someone on the river for the big houses."

Harriet shook her head. "It ain't enough. You can poke along only so fast on a twenty-five-mile stretch and still fool anybody you jest fishing."

Refusing to give up, Walter folded his arms across the buttoned vest he had brought with him from New York. "How bout we send someone who knows the Lowndes Plantation real g-g-good? Someone who can get on and off quick?"

The bag of peanuts finally made its way to Harriet. She drew out a handful, crushed the shells in her palm, picked out the meat, and popped the salty goobers in her mouth all at once. Relief washed over her. They tasted like manna. Harriet threw the empty shells onto the smoldering coals of the fire pit. The papery edges lit like fuses before turning red and bursting into flame. "We can't use anyone the patrollers might know," she said. "That means Samuel and Charles is out."

The younger man leaned forward at his name. His lucky rabbit foot dangled into the light. Charles usually hung back in conversation with the older scouts but was first on his feet once they were underway. Like Samuel, he had escaped only recently.

"I can give it a try, Moses," Charles said. He rubbed one hand over the other. "Better me getting ketched dan you. Dey jest send me on back to Heyward's place."

Harriet studied Charles, who couldn't be more than sixteen. Boys always wanted to face down giants. The bigger the odds, the more excited they got. Trouble was, giants hit harder than they knew. And the mission was too important to trust to any boy. She shook her head. "I got the best chance, Charles. Them patrollers don't know my face. They gone be on the watch for you, and they won't look too close at a harmless old woman, especially one that ain't missing." She made eye contact with each scout one by one. "Only I can hide in plain sight, and y'all know it."

Reluctant nods followed. Samuel changed the subject to the question of who was going to bring the fishing poles. They had the Sabbath to get ready. Harriet thought about her own disguise and alibi. A small amount of foot traffic between plantations wasn't unusual, but she would need a signed pass and legitimate errand.

She listened absently while the men debated whether to make rods from tupelo or willow branches. Joseph Sellers and John Chisholm had strong opinions, having fished regularly for their masters. Chisholm, a barrel-chested man who looked as if he could lift a mule yet had an anxious habit of biting his fingernails, argued for the flexibility of willow. Sellers insisted that tupelo's rigidity allowed a man to fight the current, giving him a better chance with the fish. Atticus Blake, a scout who generally listened more than he spoke, suggested they borrow poles from the army's confiscated loot to make it seem their masters had sent them. Store-bought poles would give the ruse an air of greater authenticity.

Samuel stroked his pointed beard. "No mas'r gone let a nigger use his good gear," he said.

"My mas'r did once when the neighbors dropped by for dinner unexpected," said Blake, who kept his hands busy rotating an old slouch hat by the brim. "Say he never did see a nigger wrestle catfish like me."

"Loaned his gear jest once?" Samuel said. "Ain't that the point?"

Harriet wondered what the waterman thought of her as the conversation shifted back to the attributes of willows and tupelos. Explaining her defect never got easier. Samuel hadn't been part of the team long enough to witness one of her fits. Did he think less of her? Would he balk at her command?

As if he sensed what she was thinking, Samuel glanced across the circle. The embers cast a glow across his cheekbones, though his beard disappeared in the shadows. He gave her a smile as he warmed his hands over the dying coals, but it did not reach his eyes. They were watchful.

CHAPTER SIX

They'd send for a man that had hounds to track you, if you run away.
They'd run you and bay you, and a white man would ride up there and
say, "If you hit one of them hounds, I'll blow your brains out." He'd
say "your damn brains." Them hounds would worry you and bite you
and have you bloody as a beef, but you dassen't to hit one of them. They
would tell you to stand still and put your hands over your privates.

Henry Waldon, Slave

Two nights later, Harriet pushed aside the fishing poles in the bottom of the boat, took a hemp scarf from her pocket, and tucked her good shoes under a plank that served as a seat in Walter's trus-me-Gawd, a Gullah dugout hollowed from cypress. Her hair had finally dried from the soapy gray ash she'd applied. As Harriet wound the rough scarf into a turban, she felt for the braids above her forehead to make sure the gray was visible and tried not to worry about going back into the land of the Pharaohs. She was doing God's work.

Walter held the covered cage on his lap while Samuel pinned the boat against the bank with a long pole in the shallows. The flood tide that had sped them twenty miles up the Combahee under cover of darkness was slowing. Young Charles Simmons and nervous John Chisholm had stopped their boat farther downriver.

The moon had recently set, which made it around one in the morning according to the almanac. Sweet water would start pushing back shortly in the old struggle for dominance, and salt water would ebb toward St. Helena Sound and the sea. Harriet had approximately three hours before the gong sounded on the Lowndes Plantation. As she waited for the dugout to steady against the north bank of the river, she looked over the side with eyes accustomed to the dark.

Harriet reached into a box of gravel in the bottom of the trus-me-Gawd and threw a handful into the slack shallows and onto the bank to scare away snakes. She sent up a prayer against alligators. Walter Plowden said the immense beasts avoided people, yet they nonetheless terrified her with their giant teeth and unholy stealth. Snakes, spiders, and bloodhounds didn't alarm her overmuch, but she'd never seen alligators before coming to South Carolina. Contrabands sold the pink meat in the market. Not long before, she'd seen one drag a dog into a creek when the unsuspecting pup lowered its snout to drink.

Even so, Harriet knew that mud was the principal danger as she balanced on the edge of the craft and knotted her skirt above the petticoat that covered her legs. "You sure bout this spot?" she asked.

Samuel's reply came softly in the dark. "Yes'm. Shore hard right here."

Holding fast to the side of the boat, prepared to claw her way back in, Harriet lowered her bare feet into the murky water that came up to her knees. She ignored the chilly shock to concentrate on the river bottom. Sticky goo bloomed through her toes, but the bank felt solid. Not the hideous pluff mud that swallowed a woman to the armpits and trapped her worse than quicksand. Relieved, she stood upright and reached back into the boat for her oldest shawl.

Walter leaned toward her. A slouch hat obscured his face, but Harriet knew he was agitated. His slim fingers had drummed the wooden cage the entire voyage along the salty ribbons that separated Port Royal Island from the South Carolina mainland. "I still don't like this plan," he hissed.

"Dang it to heck, we'll find the rest a the torpedoes if you give us a chance," Samuel echoed.

Harriet wrapped the shabby knit around her shoulders. She appreciated their concern but wasn't going to let her cold feet, or theirs, stop her. "When you gone stop saying that? You know the Secesh can bring back their big guns any time," she said. "We got to try this."

"Well, just remember that Jacob's cabin is second from the end," Walter said in a resigned tone. "And if his rag ain't there, don't stop, hear? Pass on by and find somewhere to hide. We'll p-p-pick you up downriver on the tide. Where Samuel sh-sh-showed us."

Harriet nodded. Walter was her bravest scout, but he repeated himself when anxious, and his stutter grew worse.

"If anyone asks, you headed to the Nichols p-p-place to see Sally," Walter said. He turned to Samuel. "Sally?"

Samuel's correction came softly in the dark. "Sadie."

Harriet hoped Walter's nerves didn't get the best of him. A precise man, he didn't usually mix up names. Samuel had described his cousin, known up and down the Combahee as the area's best midwife, at length. Her name was an important piece of the alibi Harriet had worked out with his help. "Sadie," she repeated to calm him down. "And Jacob's wife is Mayline."

"Mayline," Samuel confirmed.

"All right then," Harriet said and put out her hands. "Give em to me."

Walter slipped the cloth off the cage. The first chicken ruffled its feathers at being awakened but made no protest when handed over. Wrapping her thumb and pinkie finger securely around its scaly ankle, Harriet tucked the bird under one arm. Walter passed her the second chicken, which remained asleep with its head nestled deep in its feathers.

"Good luck fishing. Catch us a torpedo or two," Harriet said and turned to climb the earthen levee that kept the tidal river out of the fields except when summoned through the trunks in the bank. She pushed upward with straining thighs, careful not to squeeze the chickens. When she reached the top of the slope, she turned eastward to retrace the river toward the Atlantic. Ahead, causeways ran toward the plantation, dividing flat lowlands into squares of rice. Planters had reclaimed most of the marshes, cultivating every foot of the rich, black earth right up to the river. Wild blackberries sometimes attached themselves to the levee, and an occasional tree made a brave stand, but the bank was mostly unobstructed. In daylight, one could see for miles from the high levee. Harriet mustn't be caught on it. She quickened her stride.

The rice fields were immense. Harriet walked fast, yet the embankment seemed to go on forever. Without moonlight, the brackish river rustling below on her right could be heard but not seen. Silent as a house robber, she finally came to a causeway that allowed her to head inland.

Sounds carried alarmingly with the ricebirds and bullfrogs asleep. Cold gravel bit her callused feet. An owl hooted faintly in the distance, prompting the chicken under Harriet's right arm to lift its head. She jiggled the bird reassuringly and picked up speed. If anyone spotted her on the raised divide between the fields, they would know she had approached from the Combahee.

Time was against her. She broke into a jog. Her knotted skirt loosened and spilled over her wet petticoat. Growing winded, she switched to two breaths in, two out, which was a trick of endurance learned years earlier. Anxious to get there quickly—afraid to go at all—Harriet forced herself to see only the beaten path, one foot in front of the other. After another mile or so, the causeway tilted upward, and she reached a narrow avenue that skirted a towering pine forest at the back of the rice fields. At least an hour had passed, but she was safely off the dike.

Nothing made one look more like a runaway than running, so

Harriet slowed to a walk as she turned east toward the Lowndes Plantation, two miles or so downriver. Her heartbeat gradually slowed. Lines materialized in her brow, and the dirt of the road caked on her feet. Her petticoat dried as she walked the lane dividing the forest from the rice fields. She elbowed the birds close for company, hunched under her shawl, and focused on the rheumatism in her left hip. She didn't have rheumatism, but her mother did, and she found it easier to mimic the slow, pained limp if she devoted her attention to what the sensation must feel like. Anyone on the road would see an old woman up early, as old women tended to be, on a birthing errand.

Harriet hummed to herself, and then she put words to the tune. "Swing low, sweet chariot," she began softly as she shuffled along, savoring the hopeful notes. The hymn called to mind all the refugees she had brought to freedom in Canada. Once again, she was coming to carry more home. Next time, if she found the torpedoes, she'd bring a "band of angels," she thought, as the verse crossed her lips. Blue-coated angels with guns.

Harriet polished the rich, jubilant notes until the sound grew bigger than the empty road and bounced back from the resinous trees to strengthen her courage. *Heavenly Father*, she prayed even as she sang, *Thy will be done*.

A rosy glow peeped above the eastern horizon just as the hollow clop of hooves sounded behind her. Her heart fluttered. She forced herself to maintain the same pace as before, though fear twitched in her calf muscles. *I've come to do your work*, she reminded Him. Two—perhaps three—horses were coming down the river road that ran between estates. Must be patrollers. No planter would ride for pleasure at that hour. With dawn breaking, it had to be close to five in the morning, and gongs would have sounded on local plantations. She had hoped the local guards would have retired for the night.

The horses now trotted. They must have spotted her. She trudged doggedly despite a rash impulse to duck behind the pine trees. Her urge to run gathered strength until it was like white-water rushing toward Niagara Falls under the last train bridge to Canada. "Swing low, sweet chariot," she began again, closing her ears to their pursuit. The dirt lane vibrated under her bare feet. The throbbing gathered fury in the gloom. They were galloping.

"Coming for to carry me home," she sang at full volume, pushing toward a crescendo to stop her throat from strangling the sound. *Please Lord*, she prayed. *Don't let them take me. Not today.*

"Swing low—ahh!" A spray of dust and pebbles attacked Harriet's scarred neck, shooting starbursts of pain into her skull. The road swam before her eyes.

Two patrollers pounded up on either side in the dim light. Both pointed guns. One wielded a coiled rope. The other had a set of horse pistols across his pommel and handcuffs on his thick belt. In the instant they swung around her, saddlebacks clanking with chains, Harriet squinted hard against the dark mist at the edges of her sight and twisted the leg of a bird. "Lawd above!" she cried, stumbling backward. "Land sakes!"

The chicken cackled and winged its way over the head of the nearer horse, roosting on the hind end. The stallion tossed its mane and bucked. Its rider, a grizzled man of fifty or so, brought his horse under control as the bird fluttered to the ground in a blur of speckled feathers that sounded like a gambler shuffling his deck.

"Sorry, sah!" Harriet proclaimed. "You done spooked me. I hard a hearin'!" She crouched and shuffled clumsily back and forth on bare feet to snatch up the chicken, inches from the horse's sharp hooves. "My missus gone snatch my head if I lose her bird. She be all cut up."

"What you doing on the road?" the second patroller demanded. He was a younger man with close-set eyes, somewhere around thirty, with an ugly purple welt that crawled the length of his jaw and drew one side of his mouth into a humorless grin. The scar looked like an old burn injury.

Harriet hitched the bird under her arm and clucked soothingly.

She stroked the plumage with her cheek, relieved not to look at the man's shocking visage for an instant and aware that it gave an impression of calmness. It fooled her brain, too.

She opened her eyes as wide as a child's, boosted her arms to show off the birds, and loosened her tongue so that a honeyed Maryland slur rounded the edges of her words. "They missy's favorites, sah. Betsy and Bitsy. I dassen't lose em, or she gone have a conniption."

The older man's horse shied sideways again, and he patted its dusty neck. "Why you have your mistress's chickens, mammy? You sure you ain't stealing them?"

"No, sah! No how. I keep em with me so nobody can 'propriate em. Niggers have em in a pot 'fo you can whistle Dixie. Missus Heyward told me never turn my back, and I ain't yet. Sleeps with em at night. Keeps em on my lap when I use the necessary."

The older man chuckled. He holstered his pistol.

"Why you on the road?" the dour young patroller asked again, though with less enthusiasm than before. He rested the rope on his pommel and yawned, revealing stained teeth. His knuckles were bruised and scraped. "Where you going?"

"I headed to Nichols' place, sah. That Sadie gal struggling with a mammy what jest birthed twins. Missy give me leave to he'p, so long as I back 'fo dark. Poor mammy's titties swelled so bad she can't nurse mas'rs new baby, much lessen her own. Youngins' can't grab hold a the nipple. Milk won't let down."

The young man winced at the details. "Where's your pass?"

"Right here in my pocket, sah." Harriet glanced about for a spot to perch the chickens. She looked up. "Gives me a second, mas'r."

At that moment, a whistle sounded. Harriet glanced at the pine forest, grateful for the reprieve, and saw a horseman picking his way down the rise. Behind him walked a short man with a heavy rope around his neck. The prisoner's hands were tied, and his dark face shined with sweat.

"I'll be damned. Mason Lee," the young patroller said.

The newcomer's perspiring red sorrel paused at a ditch and then cantered onto the path. The prisoner's leash grew taut, and he broke into a run to keep from being dragged. His damp shirt clung to his chest.

"Mornin', Carter," the new patroller said as he drew to a halt. "Sir," he said to the older man and tipped his hat respectfully, though both had gray in their full beards.

"Seems you had a good night," said the young patroller, whose name was apparently Carter.

Harriet stared at the ground, as she was expected to do, though she saw the slave's face from the corner of her eye. Her stomach turned over. The man's swollen nose bled freely, and one eye was a pulpy mess. The rope across his gullet was tied so as not to close the windpipe, though his heavy breathing had a strangled sound. She'd seen his face before. Something about the ears, which stuck out straight from his head. Then she placed him. The man at the commissary. Private Webster's assistant. Her stomach knotted harder. She wished she could get to her Colt, though she knew better than to move an inch.

The new patroller shrugged off the compliment. A smile flickered across his face. He was still handsome, with a strong nose that deflected attention from his sagging jowls. "Doing my bit," he said.

"Not bad for an old man," Carter said with a touch of envy.

The horseman didn't respond. "Got any water?" he asked. "Lost mine in the chase."

Carter slipped a canteen from his saddlebag. He threw it to the patroller, who uncapped the container and drank deeply.

The slave put up his hands. "Watuh, boss?" he croaked. "Please, sah?"

The patroller ignored the request. He capped the canteen, guided his horse forward, and handed back the container. "Thank you," he said. "I best get this nigger home. It's slow going on foot back, and the overseer's itching to get ahold of him."

"Throw him across the horse," Carter suggested.

The new man shrugged. "Think I'd rather have a polecat at my back."

"You know this one?" the older patroller inquired.

"Since he was a pickaninny," the man said. "Can't miss those ears. He made off a few months ago and was dumb enough to sneak back for some gal at the Nichols place."

His wife, Harriet guessed.

Perplexed, the three men gazed down at the prisoner. The older patroller shook his head like he'd seen everything under the sun yet still could be amazed. He shifted his tired bones in the saddle. "You'd think there'd be plenty of gals on Port Royal."

The unscarred half of Carter's face turned upward to join the other in a grin. "Honeypots ready for dipping," he said.

The new man turned his horse upriver. "Well, I b'lieve the overseer is going to give this nigger something else to think about."

Carter lifted his hat. "You tell your sister I send my regards, Mason Lee," he said. "Hear?"

"Will do," the patroller called back.

As Lee moved away, the rope tied to his pommel jerked, and the prisoner ran past Harriet on his bloody, briar-torn feet, trailing a sour smell of defeat. The prisoner didn't glance Harriet's way, nor did she look up, but the air hummed with their awareness of one another.

The older patroller consulted a pocket watch. "No sense wasting what's left of the morning," he told his companion.

The younger patroller turned again to Harriet. He nudged his mount closer. The mare stopped just shy of Harriet. He'd want the pass now, she thought. The forgery was still in her pocket.

"You ain't from these parts," the young man said. "You talk different."

His horse neighed and stamped a forefoot, perhaps sensing that the other animals were headed for the barn. Inches from Harriet's bare feet, its iron shoes cut gingerbread biscuits in the sandy road. Harriet's toes curled. A sweat broke out between her breasts. She kept her eyes down. "No, sah, I ain't. Mas'rs sistah sent me down from Mar'land."

"Maryland? I don't recall him having kin there."

"Miz Heyward was visitin' a friend," she said. The patroller's stare burned on her bent neck. He wouldn't want to go home empty-handed now that he'd seen Mason Lee's catch. "Mas'r had more niggers than he could use, sah," she added. "Sold me cheap."

The patroller's leather saddle creaked. Harriet sensed him reaching for the rope on his pommel. It would be the work of an instant to tie her around the neck. If he ran her back to the Heyward Plantation, the overseer would be happy to claim her. Permanently.

She looked up with a wide smile that showed off the gap in her teeth. "Sho was lucky. That plantation had no good men a'tall. My old man, he so weak, a baby chile chop firewood faster. I scoutin' a better man this time. Down here, they thick as fleas. Handsome bucks. Carolina grows em good."

The young man leered and shifted back in the saddle. "Ain't you a mite long in the tooth for such nonsense, granny?"

"Why, I got more sap than a cherry tree in July." Harriet shifted her weight onto her left hip. "If I din't have this here rheumatism, I be skipping 'stead a walking."

The rider looked her up and down. His eyes rested on her bosom, to which she held the chickens. Her stomach knotted. Harriet let her left hip sag farther, worse than Mama's, and stared back.

An unreadable but somehow petulant expression crossed his face. She dropped her gaze again to the road. As if he'd been waiting, the man jerked his reins. The mare shied. Its powerful flank bumped Harriet, knocking her to the ground. The chickens protested loudly against her convulsive grip as she fell onto her side. Dust filled her mouth.

Harriet rolled to a knee and stumbled awkwardly onto her feet. Humiliation and helplessness rose in her, but she kept them from her face. Fear raised the hair on the back of her neck. She brushed her gritty lips against the feathers of a squirming bird and fixed her gaze on the road, praying he didn't have more in him.

The man guffawed. "Watch your step, Granny."

"Yes, mas'r," Harriet replied, impassive.

He lifted his reins and turned toward his partner. "Damn Mason Lee has all the luck."

The older man just shook his head with disgust at the boorish antics. "That's enough, Carter," he said. He turned shrewd gray eyes on Harriet. "Just be back on the Heyward Plantation afore dark, mammy," he said.

She met his gaze. The double-barreled shotgun across his saddle looked older than him, yet its burnished action gleamed from polishing. Harriet guessed that he was the deadlier of the two.

"You don't want no Yankee Buckra sneaking across the water to steal you," the man continued. "They'll sell you to Cuba sure as night follows day. You'll have spiders crawling down your neck in a cane field fore you know it."

"Yes, sah," Harriet said, and she nodded vigorously.

The man swung his horse around in the direction from which he had come, and the two patrollers trotted off. Harriet continued down the road. She spit sand until her mouth was clean. Her body trembled as if she'd taken ill, and she clasped the chickens tighter. A forged pass guaranteed nothing against the whim of a patroller who would lasso a woman if he didn't like the look of a signature. Though her feet stayed in motion, her eyes flicked closed. The image of the roped prisoner burned in her mind. He'd been kind to her at Webster's store. Harriet took a deep breath and opened her eyes as a whippoorwill announced the arrival of another day.

In the far distance, the sun had cleared the horizon, dispelling fog that clung like wisps of cotton to the forest hollows. Sparkling rice fields stretched down to the Combahee. Dark heads—too many to count—were bent over their work, ankle-deep in water. The morning rays cast gold splinters in the swaying grass. A white overseer on his horse watched from a causeway with a shotgun across his lap. On the next causeway down, sunrise glowed on the face of a black driver who stood with a coiled whip.

The road wound another half mile before she finally reached the outbuildings of the plantation, where the aroma of smoked ham told Harriet she was in the right place and reminded her she hadn't eaten since midnight. She wondered where Pipkin might be as she shambled past the smokehouse and neighboring jail toward a double row of unpainted cabins elevated by bricks on each corner. *Deliver us from evil*, she prayed silently.

Few of the shanties had windows. Those that did were bare of glass. Gray moss skulked up the bricks and onto the faded boards. A few had steps but most doorways dropped straight to clay earth dotted with beaten clumps of weed. At the end of the long lane, on a slight incline, stood a large house with blue double-sash windows that overlooked the quarters. Beyond it, higher on the hill and with an expansive view of the snaking river, there rose a two-story mansion with square pillars that supported verandas on the first and second stories. A brass weather vane in the shape of a dove turned atop a green copper cupola.

Harriet heard the bright tambourine of children's voices somewhere behind the cabins. She picked up speed, trying to sustain the limp. When the cry of a toddler broke into the lane, she glanced around, and seeing no one in sight yet, she dashed to the second cabin beyond the smokehouse. Harriet pushed the door open with her hip, ducked inside, and nudged the door closed with her foot. With their unbridled curiosity, young children—black or white— were the worst about calling attention to a stranger. She heaved a sigh in the dank room. Safe.

"Who there?" a voice rasped.

Ice water flooded Harriet's veins. She hadn't seen a rag on the door.

Chapter Seven

*When a girl became a woman, she was required to go to a man and
become a mother . . . Master would sometimes go and get a large, hale,
hearty Negro man from some other plantation to go to his Negro woman.
He would ask the other master to let this man come over to his place to
go to his slave girls. A slave girl was expected to have children as soon as
she became a woman. Some of them had children at the age of twelve or
thirteen.*

Hilliard Yellerday, Slave

HARRIET SPUN AROUND, TAKING IN THE room at a glance. One
window. A reclining figure in a bed struggled to sit. The man
started to say something, but a raspy cough strangled him, and he
fell back.

Harriet set the chickens on the floor on either side of her full
skirt. She reached down and snapped the neck of one and then the
other in quick succession. Harriet placed the poultry in a cold pot
on the cabin's stone hearth. The family would burn rags to disguise
the scent, but they would eat well.

The man groaned as his choking subsided. Harriet sidled up
to the window, which looked toward the last cabin and smokehouse beyond. The path between the buildings led down to the
rice fields, now whitish in the morning haze. She listened for the
children. All was quiet. They must have turned in a different

direction. She ducked under the window and crossed to the pallet lined with dried moss.

"Hey," Harriet said softly. She knelt and placed a hand on the man's brow. He burned with fever.

"Why you here?" he rasped. "You got to—" The words triggered a string of hacking coughs.

Harriet glanced around for water. A jug stood atop a crate near the door. She scooted under the window again to fetch it. Returning, she lifted the man's shoulders and placed the spout to his lips. He took a sip and sprayed water over the blanket. After a few tries, his respiration calmed, and he drank. She laid him back on the bed and arranged the cover around his waist. "Jacob, right?"

The man closed his eyes. "Go away."

"I'm looking for Jacob. You him?"

The man nodded. His lids looked too heavy to open. His nostrils flared, and he panted shallowly. "What you want?" he asked without opening his eyes.

"I need help."

Jacob mumbled something Harriet couldn't make out. She leaned closer.

"Can't help nobody," he whispered.

Harriet clenched her jaw. He'd assisted others in the past, so something must have happened. Perhaps it was the fever talking.

"I gone listen to your chest, all right?" she said in her nurse's voice. "You hold steady on me. Hold steady on the Lord."

Jacob wore a vest cut from old carpet. Harriet parted the garment and lifted his coarse shirt. She placed her ear on his chest to listen for the hiss that Doctor Durant called wheezing. Harriet wished she had the ear trumpet Durant used at the contraband hospital. Jacob's heart beat more rapidly than normal, but she couldn't tell if he had pneumonia. The man certainly had the cough and telltale fever. A bad catarrh, if not worse.

Harriet reached for a pouch she wore around her neck and took out the phials she always carried. Countless runaways had come down ill on midnight treks through rain and snow. She dumped cayenne, ginger, and powdered bloodroot into the water jug, planted her palm on the spout, and swirled the vessel vigorously. "Here," she said and lifted the patient's shoulders. "This gone loosen your chest."

Jacob drank greedily without coughing but still kept his eyes closed. He must not have had water all morning. His wife would have gone to the field.

Harriet lowered him to the pallet. She stroked his brow to ease him toward sleep. Rest would calm the fever. Then they could talk. She was prepared to wait—indeed, she had planned to hide in the cabin until he returned from the fields.

As the man's breathing evened, Harriet found herself studying him in the quiet of the plain room. Jacob looked younger than Samuel, but he had the same square chin and straight eyebrows. Both had generous foreheads. The bridge of Jacob's nose was raised rather than flat, however, and his color wasn't as rich as Samuel's. White people had little to discuss compared with colored people, she reflected, who debated shades of brown and yellow like farmers discussing the morning sky and whether it suggested rain. *Adu,* the Gullah said. *Very black.* Harriet was grateful the Lord had made her as dark as he had.

Jacob coughed in his sleep. Sweat beaded along his hairline. Harriet felt his brow again for fever, though the perspiration indicated it was breaking. Jacob had probably suffered for his tawny shade, she thought as she wiped his forehead with the blanket. Slaveholders watched lighter blacks with extra vigilance, suspicious of attempts to rise above their station; darker blacks sometimes mocked lighter ones, disdainful of the impurity.

Like Margaret, Harriet thought with the rush of joy and anxiety her daughter's face always conjured. Harriet hadn't realized the infant possessed her father's medium complexion when she gave Margaret to Mary in a patchwork quilt sewn from dresses bought off a Cambridge rag picker. It sometimes took a few weeks for the skin of colored babies to deepen to its natural hue, and Harriet had had but one night before John spirited away the mewling lump of Harriet's own flesh.

When she saw the child years later, miraculously grown and holding Mary's hand in the Baltimore fish market, the four-year-old shone so brightly in Harriet's eyes—as if the sun touched her alone—that her complexion again escaped Harriet's notice. All she saw were the curious eyes, snub nose, high cheekbones, and generous smile that looked just like Harriet's. A real little girl, wearing a red straw hat with an upturned brim and standing in a puddle of light. Free. Harriet had cried herself to sleep that evening, miles away in yet another safe house.

It was then that she developed the fixation that could wake her from a sound sleep, kill her appetite on an empty stomach, and cause her to break off in the middle of a conversation. After giving Margaret up all those years before, the refrain cycled over and over in Harriet's head. *The time had come. A mother deserves her child. Her only child.*

Sometimes she fretted she was just being selfish. It would be hard on the girl and Mary. Then she reminded herself that Mary had promised to give Harriet's "niece" back one day. Of course, the child couldn't be told the real reason, at least not for a long time. If word ever leaked out that Margaret wasn't Mary's by birth, she'd be clamped into chains instantly. Even free people of color had to fend off bogus attempts to enslave them. The South was unsafe, which was one reason Harriet had borrowed a cart and driven her own aged parents north a few years earlier at great personal risk, even though Daddy had by then saved enough to buy their freedom. Old and alone, Daddy and Mama just wouldn't go unless she came and got them, and she certainly wasn't going to leave them in Dixie by themselves. Nor would she leave Margaret there. John Tubman might object to the child's removal, but he had a new family, and Harriet had no one. Surely God wouldn't deprive her of that consolation after all the troubles He'd heaped on her head.

And so five years later, when Senator Seward sold Harriet some land as a kindness to a fellow abolitionist, she slipped back to Baltimore for Margaret. Even then, she hadn't noted Margaret's complexion until she overheard a black woman criticize the girl as "pumpkin-faced" after they returned to New York.

Footsteps crunched on the gravel path outside the window. Harriet quickly scooted against the wall to hide.

Two voices approached, though Harriet heard only a single pair of shoes. Boots, perhaps. One voice had the timbre of a bull, the other a bird. A man seemed to be addressing a child. Harriet's heart beat loudly in her ears. Why had Jacob taken down the rag? How had she forgotten to look? She edged farther along the wall so anyone who glanced in the window wouldn't spot her.

"Leave the bedding," the man ordered. "I don't need the vermin."

"Yes, sah," a girl replied. "Where . . . Where we going, sah?" Her voice wobbled.

"My house."

"You need he'p with de washing and cooking, Mistah Pipkin?"

"I got Callie for that."

The boots moved past the window. Harriet rose cautiously. She made out the speakers in the narrow slip of daylight. The man wore a dented bowler hat. Streaked gray hair showed on a sun-soaked neck, though he had an irregular bald patch behind his ear, as if a gear had snatched a chunk of scalp long ago. A bull-whip swung from his belt. The gun that extended from every white Southerner's arm rested on his shoulder. Harriet couldn't see his face, but his flat tone raised goose bumps on her arms.

The girl was nearly Harriet's height and coming into woman-hood, a child of thirteen or fourteen. The swinging hem of her dress was wet, and she walked barefoot. Two braids were gathered together at the base of her neck. The pair must have come from the rice field.

"I never done inside chores, Mistah Pipkin. But I real good wit' weeding. I . . . I git dem by dey roots, and I ain't afraid a snakes. I's good in the field, sah. But I don't know nothing bout being a house nigger. Mama call me cl-cl-clumsy."

The girl spoke breathlessly, words tripping over one another. She turned in profile until Harriet saw her better. She had curly eyelashes and lips as delicately drawn as any the hand of God could manage. Her skin was coffee with a dash of milk, and new breasts sat high on her chest. She was Margaret's age, Harriet decided. Thirteen. Old enough to be a mother.

"You'll learn," Pipkin said.

He turned the corner of the last cabin a step ahead of the girl, who glanced back down the lane as if looking for help—and spotted Harriet in the sidelong rectangle. Their gazes met. The girl aged before Harriet's eyes as an awful knowledge took hold. She seemed carved from cypress, that sorrowful hardwood that grew with its feet in the swamp.

Harriet poured all her courage into a look and raised a finger to her mouth.

The girl nodded almost without moving her head, and then she followed the overseer around the corner. Rusty hinges shrieked on the door of the neighboring cabin.

Harriet slumped against the wall. Knowledge of what was coming—and that she and every other man and woman on the plantation must stand by and watch—sent a bolt of pain across her brow. There weren't two ways to understand what it meant for an overseer to take a girl on the verge of womanhood into his house. "Getting the first slice a pie," she'd heard one man brag to another when she passed the auction block in Cambridge.

Harriet pressed her palms against her temples to stop the awful throbbing. She slowly filled her lungs with air and then breathed out even more slowly. Her mouth tasted as if she had a penny under her tongue. She must remain calm. *Away, Devil*, she prayed.

The door of the nearby cabin banged shut a few moments later. She flinched. The child must not have much in the way of possessions. Harriet slid down the wall until her buttocks rested on her callused heels.

"Mama's poorly, Mistah Pipkin. She need a hand wit' my brudduhs," the girl said. "Maybe I could he'p you during de day, sah. Rest here nights."

The man didn't reply, perhaps thinking an answer would suggest she was due one. Harriet held her breath, waiting for the danger to pass. The one spot on Earth she couldn't explain her presence was a cabin on a strange plantation.

"I ain't being hankty, sah," the girl said. "Mama jest need de he'p."

The slats of Jacob's bed creaked loudly. The ill man sputtered, then broke into a cough that rebounded in the small room. The boots outside stopped. They pivoted on the gravel. Harriet froze. The yard went quiet.

A swift blow rattled the old boards under the window. Harriet's head jerked back, hitting the wall. The butt of Pipkin's gun pounded mercilessly. His coarse roar was almost in her ear. "Jacob! Still faking it?"

The man on the bed stirred but didn't wake.

"Do I need to haul you out a there, nigger?"

Harriet's eyes darted to the stack of firewood next to the hearth—not high enough—and to the bed. Jacob's narrow pallet rested on the ground. No space underneath. The chimney? No, the chimney was too tight to climb into. The only door emptied onto the exposed yard. No escape. Harriet grabbed Jacob's foot and shook it. He didn't move. She shook harder, but he just groaned.

"Answer me!" Pipkin hollered.

Panicked, Harriet twisted Jacob's foot toward the edge of the bed to roll him off. The sick man broke into a cough so ragged that Harriet heard his throat tear. He started up upright. "Yes, boss—" he said, but hacking seized him before he could finish the sentence. He swung his feet onto the floor and dropped his head between his bent knees.

Pipkin stuck his face in the window. Harriet shriveled against the planks.

"He sho sick, Mistah Pipkin," the girl said.

The overseer looked over his shoulder. "How would you know, Kizzy?"

"Mama say he real bad. Got de lung fevuh again."

Jacob gasped for air and hacked again, bringing up the lungs in question. Harriet didn't stir.

"Mama say it de ketchin' kind," Kizzy added more urgently.

Pipkin withdrew his head. He gave the wall another bang with the butt of his gun, one so hard that dust swirled up from the crevices and made plumes in a shaft of light just beyond the bed. "This is the second time in two months, nigger," he said. "Be at the rice trunks tomorrow or I'll use my bullwhip to make you better. I paid good money for your hide."

Harriet listened as the boots moved away and faded. She took a shuddering breath. Helplessness caused tears to start in her eyes. Kizzy had saved her, and Harriet couldn't return the favor.

Poor girl. Like all the others. Like Harriet's older sisters Linah, Mariah, and Sophie, all sold south. Like Harriet's younger sister, Rachel, who wouldn't leave without her boys, rented out to other Cambridge slave masters. Harriet had gone back three times to convince Rachel that she must rescue herself first—and trust in God to rescue the children later.

"We going next time, Hattie," Rachel promised when Harriet slipped onto the plantation one dark January night. Her sister was mending a shirt for the eight-year-old who worked fifteen miles away. But next time never came. When Harriet made her final raid south on the Underground Railroad—the year Lincoln was elected—a logger who worked for John Tubman told her that pneumonia had come for Rachel two months earlier. Knowledge of the boys' whereabouts perished as well. Her younger sister had waited for nothing at all.

Harriet was now her parents' only daughter. Nothing remained of Linah, Sophie, Mariah, and Rachel except their names. Pieces of Harriet had disappeared with each of them. No matter how many trips she made, someone was always left behind, and every year new babies were added to their number. If Harriet had a torch big enough, she would burn every plantation to the ground. Stamp the cinders into ash. Magically corral every man like Pipkin in some vast pen with others who had committed the same crime. They'd turn to one another and ask, "What are you doing here?" Guilt would rise to their shocked faces like scum on a pond. God's vengeance would be swift.

Squeaking planks interrupted Harriet's reverie as Jacob fell back on the slats and pulled up the blanket. His eyes were shut.

Harriet wiped her tears on her sleeve and crawled to the man's side. He needed to drink. Needed to cough up the mucus. If his fever didn't break, he would die without giving Harriet the information she needed. The baby his wife carried would live the same half-life as every other slave. Harriet fetched the jug, lifted his shoulders, and placed it to his lips. "Drink," she ordered. "Come on. Let the good Lord heal you."

Jacob pursed his mouth.

Her voice grew steely. "Don't you quit on me. You gone drink this water, or I'll make you a swamp to lie in."

He opened his lips and took a few sips, but he writhed when she adjusted her grip to hold him more securely. There was a fetid smell Harriet hadn't noticed before. It came from the moss on the pallet. No, it came from his clothing. "Let's get these off," Harriet said and slipped the rough vest from one shoulder, then the other. Jacob cried out when she inched the shirt over his head and rolled him onto his side.

Scars crisscrossed his muscled back. Most were old. The salt water poured into wounds to make suffering livelier had also done its job of cauterizing the broken flesh. The long lumpy welts looked like ship's rigging splayed on a Maryland wharf. Some of the damage was fresher. A gash from shoulder to tailbone had reopened, ruptured by coughing. Pus seeped along his spine.

Harriet glanced around the bare room for a clean cloth. He needed bandages to protect the wound. A sheet, perhaps. Spying nothing that would work, she stood with a cautious glance at the window, reached under her skirt, untied her cotton petticoat, and tugged it down her hips. She hesitated a second at the lace edging, then tore the undergarment into strips. As Harriet dribbled water on Jacob's back, she recalled the gray-haired benefactress who had pressed the petticoat into her hands when she sailed from Boston a year earlier. Harriet had never had so feminine an article. She washed it every day. Dingy from its earlier bath in the Combahee, the fine fabric nonetheless took up the sticky pus cleanly. She laid long strips across Jacob's back and tied them around his stomach. He fell asleep as she wrestled on his shirt to hide the unusual dressing.

Harriet resumed her post against the wall and dropped her head onto her knees. She needed rest. A short nap at least. Before she had a fit when she couldn't afford one.

A faraway bark woke her sometime later. She lifted her head to see Jacob studying her. He'd propped himself on one elbow. "What your name?" he asked hoarsely.

Harriet hesitated. If Pipkin questioned him in his weakened state, he might give her away. Yet she needed to earn his trust. "Moses," she said simply. "Folk call me Moses."

He nodded without expression, seemingly prepared to accept any name she gave him. "What you doing here?"

"Samuel sent me," she said.

Pained recognition showed in his eyes. "Must be alive, then. I heard he ran. You running from Heyward, too?"

"No. I'm with the Yankees. On Port Royal. We looking for someone to tell us bout the torpedoes in the river."

Jacob started to answer but coughed instead. He collapsed back on the bed.

Harriet moved to his side, put a careful arm under him, and lifted his shoulders. This was her chance. He seemed stronger, ready to rally. "Bring it on up," she urged him.

He struggled to sit again, coughed roughly, and finally spat into the hand she held out. Harriet wiped the mucus on her skirt.

Jacob pulled away and lay back down with his eyes shut. "The barrels, right?"

"Yep. The barrels with gunpowder. Secesh call em torpedoes."

He tugged the blanket fretfully. "We anchored em with chains a few months back. They was four. No, five."

Gunships could navigate around five mines, she thought. And they would have to. No way could her crew dismantle chained torpedoes without being spied. "Men from other plantations lay em, too?" she asked.

Jacob answered with his eyes closed. "No. Secesh took us from Fields Point clear up to the ferry landing. We would a seen em doing it, if they was." His voice drifted to a lower register. "I got an eye on the river most a the time. A trunk minder—" He trailed off.

Harriet unbuttoned the collar of her dress and reached for the paper she'd tucked into the band supporting her breasts. "Can you look at this?" she said.

The man didn't answer. His breathing had slowed. Harriet shook his shoulder. "Wake up."

Jacob blinked and rocked his head.

Harriet unfolded the sketch of the river and held it to his face. "Show me where you put them barrels."

Jacob squinted and reached a hand above the blanket. "There," he said, and his finger pointed to a small island across from Fields Point that divided the broad river into two channels. "We put the first one there. You sail up their blind side, pickets ain't gone see you—but you'll hit the torpedo."

Harriet nodded. The Secesh would count on the Yankees trying to avoid the lookout.

Jacob scrunched his eyebrows. He seemed uncertain. His finger swayed, and he pointed to a spot near Tar Bluff. "We put a second one here. And another there," he said, tapping a stretch on the approach to the Nichols Plantation. "I . . . I think another there," he said as he rested a finger on the bend just before the Heyward estate, near the ferry landing that served the plantations on the upper Combahee. The Confederates had a reinforced contingent there.

"Jest a second," said Harriet. She took a nail from her pocket and poked tiny holes in the spots he had indicated. The torpedo near the Heyward Plantation must be the one Samuel had spotted from his boat. They had marked it on their map in Beaufort. She held the paper up again. "Where you put the fifth one?"

Jacob had become more ashen, and his eyes were sunken. He didn't answer. Harriet shook the sick man's shoulder. "Jacob, wake up." She placed a hand on his forehead, now dry and hot. The fever had spiked again. She set aside the map, reached for the jug, and lifted the man's dead weight. "Come on, Jacob."

Harriet placed the spout to his lips, but he was unresponsive. Water trickling down his chin failed to rouse him. His lips were shut tight. A hound barked close by. Harriet shifted back against the wall, still holding the vessel.

Boots approached. It was the same tread as before, now accompanied by an animal, its nails clicking against gravel. They bypassed the window.

Harriet heard a dog whine. The boots turned back toward Jacob's cabin. Harriet stopped breathing.

"What is it?" Pipkin said.

The hound bayed under the window.

"That's Jacob," the overseer told the dog, which bayed and then whined again. A distant gong clanged.

"Hear that, boy? Chow time," Pipkin said. He walked away.

The dog whimpered. It pawed the wall under the window. Harriet braced herself. Bloodhounds would track a runaway across three counties. They wouldn't stop to eat or drink. They'd run themselves to death to get their man. The gong sounded again. Pipkin whistled from afar, but the dog scratched harder.

"Come on, now," the overseer called. He whistled again, and then he turned back, walking quickly.

The hound barked more ferociously. Harriet shut her eyes. She felt him close in. A thud, then a sharp yelp, filled her ears. A second kick produced whimpering. "Damn dog. I said *now!*"

Harriet heard the boots pivot. The crunch of gravel faded. She opened her eyes. Blood thrummed in her temples. Pipkin must have some task near the cabins or smokehouse. He'd return after supper—and Kizzy wouldn't be there to distract him. Harriet must leave and hope the noontime bustle covered her movements. If only Jacob could tell her the location of the last mine. She looked at him again. His face was slack.

Harriet set aside the jug, tucked the map into her bosom, and stood to find a new prop. A small crock on the hearth caught her eye. She quickly swept up a handful of ashes, dropped the powder into the vessel, and poured some water over it to mimic a midwife's poultice. A square of white fabric, tied around the neck of the crock with the last strip of her petticoat, served for a lid.

Harriet tightened her headscarf and fumbled for her gray braids. She bent over to tuck Jacob's blanket more securely, then placed her hand on his brow. On impulse, she knelt. The hard floor dug into her knees, but she closed her eyes and put her hands together. *Keep Jacob safe*, she prayed. *Safeguard him from sickness, dear Lord. And don't let Pipkin hurt the girl too bad. Keep her heart strong. Tell her your servant is coming for her.*

Harriet drew a deep breath. The air of the cabin seemed less foul than before. She knew He was present. "Amen," she whispered, and then she patted Jacob's hand. "Hold tight," she said to the sleeping man as she stood. "I'm coming back. I always come back."

Chapter Eight

Yes, you are fighting for liberty—liberty to keep 4,000,000 of your fellow beings in ignorance and degradation; liberty to separate parents and children, husband and wife, brother and sister; . . . Liberty to seduce their wives and daughters, and to sell your own children into bondage; liberty to kill these children with impunity. . . This is the kind of liberty—the liberty to do wrong—which Satan . . . was contending for when he was cast into hell.

Major General David Hunter to President Jefferson Davis

Samuel withdrew a packet from the folds of his coat. The night was breezy.

The trio sat in the bottom of the dugout on their way back to Beaufort, anchored in an inlet where an unusually high sandbar topped with salt grass hid them from view. The tidal pull toward the sea had slowed, and they had an hour or so before the Combahee reversed itself and nudged them back upriver. The trus-me-Gawd was maneuverable enough to battle the current once it turned, but it was better not to pick a fight with the tide, which could be both friend and enemy.

Harriet watched Samuel unwrap their provisions on the plank seat. Famished, she considered devouring the canvas in which he had packed the pork. She had eaten two biscuits and some peanuts hours earlier under a stand of pines a mile past the Nichols Plantation, but it wasn't much. When the moon disappeared over the horizon around midnight, Harriet had slipped down to the river to find Samuel and Walter.

"Five, he say?" Walter murmured. His eyes followed Samuel's hands, too. Walter must have the same hard yearning in his gut as she did, his appetite wakened at last.

"Yep," Harriet said. "Wish he could a told me bout the fifth, but he was in a fix, and Pipkin didn't give us time."

She had sketched Jacob's illness without revealing its seriousness. She realized what kin meant to Samuel and didn't want to tempt him into something rash. There was nothing they could do that wouldn't jeopardize the mission and the safety of others. The only solution was to convince Major General Hunter to raid upriver as soon as possible, though she knew how agonizing it was to wait. It had taken her two precarious years to get her own brothers out of Maryland, and Rachel had died before Harriet could save her. Harriet had been the middle child, the one her overworked parents didn't take much notice of, but she'd seen from her quiet spot what had happened to the four older children, and what might happen to the four younger ones if she didn't act. Samuel must have the same sense of urgency.

He looked up from his task. "But he ain't coughing blood, right?"

Harriet shook her head.

"Fever?"

"Some. But it gone come down with rest," she said, conscious that it was a half-truth. No one knew whether a fever would come down or not, though she felt the Lord would watch over the man.

Samuel's mouth tightened. "Not much chance a that." He stared down at the dried pork. "Jacob always been first to get sick in winter. Never could learn that boy to swim. Say it make his ears hurt."

"He was coughing up the catarrh," Harriet said. "That's a good sign."

From his pocket Samuel had taken a fisherman's knife that looked like a toy in his outsized hands, making nicks with his knife to size the portions of their skimpy meal. The meat was thicker on one end. He waved away a mosquito that dove for his hand and turned the meat over to make certain the pieces were equal.

Harriet's stomach grumbled.

Samuel looked up with a half-smile. "Got anything more to say?"

"Nothing other than hurry up."

Samuel placed his knife on the first cut and sawed through the salt pork. He repeated the task and handed each of them a slice. She noted that he kept the thinner end for himself. "Keep the smallest piece if you can't size something right," Mama had taught her. "That's only fair." Harriet wondered if Samuel's mother had told him the same.

They ate in silence, working their jaws on the leathery flesh. A surge of strength washed over Harriet as she ate. When she finished the last gamey bite, she closed her eyes and heaved a sigh. She had rested behind a fallen tree during the afternoon to get off the road, but it had been a long journey across a terrible day. Food tasted good.

"You okay, Moses?" Samuel said.

Harriet darted him a look. Why was he asking? What did he think she was—some kind of weakling? Who would put such a question to his commander?

"A course," she said curtly. "Jest waiting on y'all." Harriet looked at Walter. "Time to go."

Walter nodded. "Yes, Moses."

Samuel sheathed his knife and shoved it in his pocket. He leaned forward. "Want to play a trick first?"

"A trick?" Walter said. "What you talking bout?"

They were anchored across from Fields Point. Samuel nodded toward the earthworks in the far distance. He stroked his pointed beard. The rakish look appeared. "This," he said, and he pulled a jar of spiny cockleburs out of yet another pocket. "We know them pickets been chided for false alarms. How bout making em jumpier?"

Harriet turned the plan over in her head as Samuel laid it out. His idea for spooking the Confederates' horses was clever. Keeping the pickets off-balance was desirable. Yet she wasn't used to altering her route—literally midstream—once she'd finished a mission. Improvisation meant delay. Delay was risky.

Walter stuck his fingertip in a small phial that he took from his knapsack. He applied liniment to his dry lips. "What you think, Moses?" he asked as he corked the phial, rubbed his lips together, and put the salve away. "I don't know it worth another day in the marsh, waiting out the tide and hoping the skeeters don't pick us apart."

Harriet knew he was joking. Rebels were the problem, not bugs.

Samuel cocked his head.

Harriet studied his face. She sensed bitterness behind the mischief. Was he a hothead, after all? His lips were seamed tight. He must be upset about Jacob. That wasn't a reason for running risks. "No," she said. "We got what we come for. This ain't no time for pranks."

Samuel frowned. "It ain't a prank. If those pickets send another report upriver that makes em look like fools, it gone help us."

Walter's eyebrows lifted, and he gave a shrug. "Ain't a bad idea, Moses."

Harriet realized that Rebel commanders in the field might be slow to heed a warning if they thought the guards on the river prone to false alarms. Anything that bought Union gunships more time during a raid was invaluable, yet Harriet hesitated at taking another risk when they were almost clear of danger.

Samuel might have read her mind. "Ain't much farther to the Sound," he said. "We can be in open water in fifteen minutes, well before the tide turns. Secesh ain't got no navy there. Won't be nothing to fear."

Harriet recalled the runaway tied behind the patroller's horse, which now seemed a year earlier. This was her last chance to improve the odds of men like him—their last scouting expedition before the raid itself. The man's feet looked as if he'd run across knives. Harriet reminded herself that a plan could be smart even if she hadn't hatched it. She brushed a hand over her lips, reminded of the mouthful of sand. She was tired of eating their dirt.

Harriet nodded. "All right. I'll give you five minutes. That's all."

Walter poled them out of the inlet. Samuel took over the sweeps. He rowed like a pantomime in a minstrel show, the quietest oarsman Harriet had ever observed. A gentle wind ruffled the water, which lapped the bluff as they approached. Dawn was at least an hour away, judging from the hint of gray in the sky, and Harriet could see that the outpost remained unfortified. She listened for any noise beyond the rhythmic wash of river against rock, yet the fort was as quiet as if it had been deserted for a month or everyone inside had taken a dram of opium. She knew not to hope for either.

When the dugout reached the black shore a hundred yards beyond the landing, Walter stood and grabbed the limb of an oak tree that hung well over the water. He tethered the boat to keep it from knocking against the rocks. Samuel leaned forward and put his lips to Harriet's ear. His breath tickled her neck. She caught the masculine tang of his sweat and flinched away.

"Your life's worth more 'n ours," he whispered. "You hear shots, or we don't come back, row on home. Get to General Hunter."

Samuel reached up after Walter, and the two shimmied along the branch like circus performers, before they dropped soundlessly to the ground. A second later, they vanished.

The shore fell silent. Harriet strained her ears for any alarm from the pickets, but the only sound was the moan of the rope. She clasped her knees to her chest. The air was sharp on the water. Without a petticoat, the dress provided scant warmth. Five minutes turned into ten on her internal clock. She shook her head, confirmed in her opinion of men. Always promising more than they delivered. Slower than molasses in January.

A few more minutes passed, and the eastern horizon turned a

softer gray. Harriet's disquiet grew. She had never liked waiting on someone else's plan. Not on John Tubman's, no one's. On the Underground Railroad, runaways wanted her to call the shots. It made them feel safe. Over the years, she'd gotten used to walking in front. Felt right. Harriet rubbed her chilled hands together and put them under her armpits. She wished she hadn't listened to Samuel. He'd concocted the plan in anger. And she didn't like it when he said her life was worth more than theirs. He was patronizing her. She'd put a stop to that.

The breeze picked up. Harriet looked over the waterway. The mouth of the river had the sloppy, inky quality of slack water getting ready to run in the opposite direction. A log bobbed not twenty feet away and looked as indecisive as Harriet felt, as it was moving neither upriver nor down. In the quiet, a horse snorted from the direction of the fort and fell silent again. Harriet stood and placed a hand to her brow, trying to penetrate the underbrush on the bank, yet the deserted shore was too dark and, still standing, she turned again to examine the open water.

The log had drifted. The stern of the dugout swiveled in the eddy. Harriet reached for Walter's pole to dig into the shallows in case the current began tugging upriver. It was difficult to tell how much time had passed. What had happened to the men? They hadn't much longer before the tide began pushing toward the plantations. Harriet shivered at the thought of Pipkin.

She peered again at the river. The log had picked up speed. Its yellow eyes opened.

Harriet gasped. She lifted the pole high, transfixed. The alligator that was studying her appeared to be nearly twelve feet long. The scaled monster glided toward Harriet, closing the distance without effort. Her grip tightened.

The alligator flipped downward and disappeared in the inky water. Harriet's cramped grip relaxed. It wasn't interested in her. The animal must be fishing.

The dugout took a sudden blow from behind and jerked sideways. Harriet's knees bent in the swaying craft, and she swallowed a yelp. She stabbed the water, unsure where the beast was, trying to scare it with her pole without hitting the boat's drumlike hull.

The dugout finally stabilized in the empty water. Harriet's knees quaked. Where was Samuel? She looked down, then around the perimeter of the trus-me-Gawd. No alligator. A stand of grass waved at the river's edge. The reptile must have hit the boat by accident. "Thank you, Jesus," she whispered.

The next blow came directly underneath, lifting the dugout clean out of the water. Harriet lost her balance. The pole hit the edge of the craft and almost slipped from her grasp as she fell backward onto the seat with an involuntary cry. Harriet glanced frantically around the bottom of the dugout for a decoy. If only she had the pork.

The heavy boat rocked, and then it quieted. She looked again at the dark river. Two diamonds of light caught her attention. The alligator bobbed five lengths away. Its eyes glowed malevolently. Water rippled away from its snout as it swam toward her, horrible jaws agape.

Harriet stood again and raised her arms above her head. The heavy pole weighed nothing. She must aim for the dark gap behind the glistening teeth to stop its attack. Her heart felt ready to burst through her chest.

A roaring pierced the dark. Horses squealed and thrashed somewhere on shore. Men yelled. The alligator dove under the boat. An instant later, the tree limb above Harriet's head shook. Walter, then Samuel, swung into the trus-me-Gawd. Samuel took the pole from Harriet as she dropped heavily onto the bench. Walter pulled at the rope's slipknot, snatched up the oars, and rowed swiftly toward the sea.

Samuel's shoulders heaved with quiet laughter. "You should a seen them suckers run out a the fort at our rocks! Two were thrown to kingdom come when they jumped on their mounts. Ain't nothing like cockleburs under a saddle."

"Where the hell were you?" Harriet snapped.

Samuel's grin died. "What's wrong?"

Harriet glanced back at the rippling, but vacant water near the shore as the boat reentered the ocean-bound current. The beast had vanished in the murk. "A gator come at the boat," she said. "I'll face down any man, but I can't abide gators."

Samuel hesitated, and then he placed a callused hand over hers. "He must a wanted to see the famous General Tubman."

She snorted. "I think he wanted to eat the famous General Tubman."

Samuel withdrew his hand and tucked the pole into the bottom of the dugout. "I would a liked odds on that. No question who'd win."

Harriet let out her breath. The wind brushed her cheeks as Walter rowed them toward the Sound and away from the horrors of the Combahee. "You should taste my alligator stew," she said to the two scouts. "Lots a pepper."

"I could eat a bucket bout now," Walter said.

Samuel chuckled. He spoke to Walter. "Don't know. Bet she makes it pretty spicy."

You have no idea, Harriet thought. *It would light up your mouth.*

Chapter Nine

When we entered where she [Harriet Tubman] was at work ironing some clothes . . . she no sooner saw me than she recognized me at once and instantly threw her arms around me and gave me quite an affectionate embrace.

   Lt. George Garrison, son of William Lloyd Garrison, in South Carolina

"GENERAL HUNTER ISN'T IN," THE SANDY-HAIRED clerk said, squinting up from his cluttered desk. Numbers crowded the pages of an open ledger, and the knife edge of his hand was blue with ink. The man blinked twice.

Louvered shutters cast stripes across the soldier's freckled face. The afternoon sun appeared to hit him in the eyes. Harriet stepped nearer to give him the benefit of her shadow and the lines around his eyes eased, though his dry manner didn't become any more welcoming.

"When he coming back?" she said.

"Who's asking?" the man said, as if he wasn't authorized to utter a whole sentence.

"I am," she said crossly. "That's who."

Harriet didn't feel like arm wrestling another Yankee at the moment. It had taken much of the day to get to Hilton Head, following a long night in the dugout with Walter and Samuel and a meeting with Simmons and Chisholm, who'd come up empty-handed on the lower Combahee. She had been awake most of the past twenty-four hours and was entirely out of patience. What was wrong with white soldiers? When would they realize what the war was about? That people like her had done more than their share to build the infernal country, taking all of its punishments and enjoying none of its rewards? The only thing whites had given blacks was a hard time. She felt like slapping the man's face.

He squinted again. Harriet saw the gesture was habitual. Perhaps he had myopia. Needed glasses.

"And you are?"

"Moses."

The man stood up behind his desk and gave a bow out of character in a soldier. He smiled. "I thought you might be. If I had a hat, I'd tip it, ma'am. I heard you were in these parts. I hail from Boston, Missus Tubman. It's a real honor."

Harriet pressed her lips in a hard line to keep them from trembling—and suddenly realized how frayed her nerves were. It was so easy for people to treat one another as human beings, but at low moments, it caught her off guard when a stranger actually did so. She stuck out her hand. The man shook it.

"I'm pleased to meet you, Moses," he said in words that now crowded together. "My Aunt Zilfa—that's Zilfa Bodfish, she's married to Thankful Bodfish of Concord—perhaps you know them— told me if I ever saw you down here, I was to remind you of your abolitionist friends in Massachusetts."

"Thank you, sir," she said. "I don't recall your people, but there's a host of righteous folk up north. Right now I'm scouting General Hunter. You know when he's coming back?"

The man glanced down at his desk and shoved aside the ledger to reveal a diary underneath. He flipped open the pages. "I wasn't here when he left—my shift started an hour ago—but it says he's headed to Lady's Island for the day—a meeting, I suppose. He probably won't return 'til tomorrow." He looked up. "May I give him a message?"

"No," Harriet said emphatically. "No, thank you, sir," she repeated more quietly. "I'll stop on by tomorrow."

"Yes, ma'am. And may I write my Aunt Zilfa that you send your regards? Her congregation in Concord prays for your safe return. She thinks of you as a hero—her hero, truth be told."

"A course. Please thank her for her prayers."

The man nodded eagerly, and Harriet took her leave. When she stepped back into the dirt lane that bordered headquarters, she glanced in both directions, unsure where to turn. With General Hunter on Lady's Island and Colonels Montgomery and Higginson on Port Royal, Harriet felt the strange slump that sometimes came upon her when thwarted. Septima must have started the blackberry hand pies, Doctor Durant would have assigned another nurse to wash patients, and Harriet's scouts were circulating in the refugee camps. She could undertake any of these tasks, but none held a candle to seeing David Hunter.

Harriet idly wondered if Septima had set out milk for the cat.

A wagon loaded with wooden casks clattered up the road, its wheels spitting sand. The driver pulled up his reins. It was John Webster. She wondered if he knew his assistant was missing, though she couldn't report where she'd seen the man. A flash of impatience made her grip the strap of her satchel. She just had to see Hunter.

"Tubman," Private Webster said as he rolled to a stop in front of Hunter's headquarters. The commissary clerk shifted the reins to one hand and pushed his wire spectacles higher on his nose. "How are ye for sugar?"

"Don't think I need any right yet," she said.

"An extra shipment just came in. I can let it go at a special price since it's the end o' the month."

Harriet thought it over. Root beer required large quantities of sugar to cut the bitterness of the sassafras, and hand pies were popular. Soldiers liked to hold the turnovers by the rippled crust

Harriet had learned at the Philly hotel where she once earned money for raids south. Pies fetched a higher price than ginger-bread—and Margaret was growing into a young lady in the Sewards' Auburn household. Distinguished guests frequently came to the home of Lincoln's new secretary of state, and the girl might need a dress. Harriet and Septima weren't out of sugar, but extra supplies wouldn't hurt.

"I'll take it," she said. "Sixty pounds."

Webster glanced down the road. He nodded and lifted the reins. "I'll mark ye down when I get back. One of my fellows will deliver it on the morrow."

"The man I saw at your office a few days ago?"

"Which one? Contraband come and go. Shiftless, they are."

Harriet held a hand a few inches above her head. "Not real tall. Funny ears."

Webster shrugged. "Cudjo, likely. I'll send him if he's around. Don't worry. The sugar will get there." He clucked at his mules, which pulled toward the port.

So Cudjo was the man's name. Shading her eyes with her hand, Harriet watched Webster's cart roll away. Would he even care if he knew what had happened? Harriet drew a breath to calm her nerves. She must get Hunter to agree to go upriver—for Cudjo, Kizzy, Jacob, and countless others.

Webster's cart turned right at the next corner, where a gang of young contrabands in patched dungarees filled ruts in the harbor road. Beyond that, a smaller gunship sailed out of the port while another took on supplies at the army wharf. Admiral Du Pont's flagship, pockmarked from the failed assault on Charleston, under-went repairs alongside the smaller boats.

The Union's blockading squadron was such a pitiful force, con-sidering all it had to do. Keep the devil from the door. Patrol a coast a thousand miles long. Carry the assault against Charleston. Harriet recalled the men's smoke-stained faces when they came down the gangplank after their defeat the month before. Many had been wounded. A white man with a crushed leg writhed on a stretcher. He'd died that evening. Of the nine ironclads that had sailed out of Port Royal to attack the Rebel stronghold, five came back disabled. Broken masts, torn sails, and holes near the waterline. Word around town was that some had taken as many as ninety hits. Admiral Du Pont had been forced to scuttle the new USS *Keokuk*.

The memory depressed her. How would she persuade Hunter to risk more ships? Torpedoes at Charleston had thwarted their entire force. Was there some key to Hunter's thinking she had yet to discover? She must find it before the Secesh restored their artillery. *Give us time, dear Lord*, she thought.

At last, the heat drove Harriet from the porch to a bench under a massive oak draped with Spanish moss. She felt tempted to camp there until Hunter returned the next day, but that was nonsense. She would rest a moment, and then she would head for the dock and the next packet to Port Royal.

Harriet tucked her feet under the seat in the deep shade. She sighed, steeling herself to ignore the troublesome feelings she'd been suppressing since the night before. When people told her she was a hero, they didn't think of her as a woman. Yet she was one. Not a stone statue or a rag doll stuffed with straw. Despite John Tubman's failings as a husband, the yearnings he had awakened in her had never died away, even though she tried not to think on them. Alone at night, or during quiet hours when nothing else vied for attention, desire still sometimes tugged. And why not? Her body kept living. She had the same heartbeat, as Samuel's warm breath on her neck had reminded her the night before on the Combahee.

The waterman's determination to rescue his family prompted her respect. His forcefulness intrigued her, and she admired his ingenuity. But the supple muscles that worked in his round forearms when he rowed were a distraction that reminded her of old pleasures that had no place in her new life. She was on a mission. God's mission.

Harriet smiled as she recalled how daintily Samuel's big hands had cut the dried pork. Then she frowned and shook her head. She didn't need any man. Her husband had been good with his hands, too. Harriet poked at the smoldering ashes in her heart and waited for the anger that reliably protected her against sentimental mistakes. Yet the fire was cold. Instead, she felt a different kind of warmth that began in her thighs and spread seductively upwards.

No, she thought. Harriet bit her lower lip against the traitorous impulses. Plumb tired, she closed her eyes.

Time abruptly stopped.

Someone placed a hand on her shoulder. She shrugged it off. Someone shook her shoulder again.

"General Tubman. May I get you some water?" said a distant voice.

Wake up, Harriet thought, yet she was tired, and a weight as tenacious as pluff mud seemed to have hold of her, tugging her down.

"You all right, Moses?" someone said.

The weight grew lighter. Harriet opened her eyes to the puzzled face of Robert Smalls. The young naval hero sat next to her on the bench with a hand on her shoulder.

"Oh. Howdy, Robert," she said, relieved it was not a white person or one of her scouts. She wondered how long she'd been asleep. Then she recollected what she'd been dreaming about and felt awkward anyway.

"You was so still," he said. "I thought something happened."

"Bless you," she replied. "Jest resting my eyes and getting some shade. Today's a hot one."

He shifted back on the bench and took off his felt derby. Harriet noted that he wasn't in uniform. She yawned and sat up straighter.

"It's a beatdown, for true," he said.

Harriet saw that he hadn't shaved in a day or so. He had a red rash on his jaw, as if the razor had irritated his skin. "How you find yourself this afternoon, Robert?"

Robert fanned his face with the hat. "Enjoying every day a freedom. Plotting tomorrow's insurrection."

Harriet smiled. "Good rules."

"What brings you to Hilton Head?" he asked.

"General Hunter. Pity is, he ain't around."

The sailor leaned closer. "Got something for us?" He clearly expected an interesting answer from the renowned Harriet Tubman. "Something to bring down the bastards?"

She examined his face. The fewer who knew any secret, the better. Yet Robert was quick and might be of help. A slave at the start of the war, he had nicked the Confederate gunship CSS *Planter* from the Charleston dock and run it past Fort Sumter, stealing the gunship and six contraband. Afterward, Secretary of War Edwin Stanton had pumped Robert's hand personally. Since then, the twenty-four-year-old war hero had piloted ships for the Sea Islands squadron. He'd been at the recently failed assault on Charleston.

"We looking at the Cum'bee," she said. "I got information on the artillery there."

Robert placed his palms on his knees and glanced up and down the road. Seeing only the men filling ruts, he said, "What you find?"

"Secesh took down their guns at Fields Point. Tar Bluff, too," she said.

Robert's eyebrows shot up. "No artillery? That's a sight different from what we found last month in Charleston."

"Which ship was you on?"

"The *Keokuk*. A crack vessel, she was, too, fore we had to scuttle her."

Surprised, Harriet clasped her hands around one knee and leaned forward. "Not the *Keokuk*. How'd she take so many hits?"

"Commander told me to steer within nine hundred yards a Sumter to avoid the torpedoes. Damn fort erupted like a volcano."

Harriet shook her head with wonder. "Praise God you still alive. But the Cum'bee's a different story. No artillery there."

Robert rubbed a hand over his pimply jaw. "What bout the torpedoes?"

"There's only five, and we can chart four of em."

Robert whistled softly. "Damn. You got someone working on the fifth?"

Harriet sighed and spread her empty hands. "That's where we weak."

Robert looked thoughtful. He scratched the part in his hair, then bent over and took a twig from the ground. He traced two squiggly parallel lines in the dirt. Harriet recognized the oxbow curves of the Combahee. "Where are the ones you found?" he said.

Harriet pictured the map she had hidden in her bodice. She took Robert's twig and made scratches at the four spots Jacob had indicated, including the one Samuel originally located.

Robert studied the marks on the road. A long moment passed. The heat was stifling even in the shade. Harriet forced her eyes to stay open. A scattered rain started to fall just beyond the tree's dense canopy. It sparkled in the sunshine. The perfume of wet dirt bloomed on the dry road, and Harriet drew a full breath, expanding her lungs to take in the good smell.

Robert pointed to the drawing. "There," he said. "The upper reaches a the river. You said they put a torpedo near the ferry. I bet they put another one opposite. They aiming to protect the ferry and the rail line to Savannah. That's the most important spot on the river. We done that on the Stono, too."

The warm air became thicker. Harriet wiped her brow with her sleeve. "You laid torpedoes on the Stono?"

"Yep."

"How you anchor em?"

"Waited til dead low tide to fasten the chains," he said. "That way, you see what you're doing better."

"We won't be there at low tide. We gone be upriver at full flood," she said.

Robert nodded. "Can't breach the bar unless the tide rising. Too shallow."

"So how do we spot mines at high tide?" Harriet hoped he had a good answer. Hunter wouldn't go forward without one.

"Make a damn good guess?"

She exhaled, disappointed. "That all?"

The young sailor shrugged. "Take it slow. Look for snags. The Cum'bee flows steady near the ferry. No rocks or sandbars. You see a ripple out a the ordinary, it gone be a torpedo. Either that, a gator."

Harriet recalled the ripples in the water from the night before. In view of the swarming wildlife on the Combahee, Robert's advice wasn't especially useful. The thought of submerged alligators gave her the shivers. Of all God's creatures, why this one? Still, she noted his advice. Look for snags.

The boat pilot pushed his hands against his thighs and stood. "I best mosey along. My missus gone be waiting. Always glad to see you, Moses."

"You taking the packet to Beaufort?"

"Yes'm. You, too?"

Harriet felt as if her shoes had taken root under the bench. "I planned on heading back, but I'm worried about missing Hunter."

"Why don't you talk with Colonel Montgomery? See what he thinks?"

Harriet straightened. "He around?"

"I jest saw him at the quartermaster's—"

Robert Smalls hadn't finished his sentence before Harriet was on her feet. She would catch a later packet or find a corner in the refugee camp overnight, if necessary. Montgomery could help her with Hunter.

Robert clapped his hat on his head. "Should I save you a seat on the packet?"

"No, and don't you tarry none," Harriet said. She leaned forward to hug the lithe young sailor, and then she reached for her satchel. "Get on home to your missus. I got an insurrection to plan. You understand."

Robert smiled. "Yes, ma'am. That I do."

The thought of Robert's family gave Harriet pause. She had never asked him, but she wondered now how he'd done it. Why he'd done it. Whisking six slaves and a gunship past Fort Sumter. Most people couldn't muster the nerve to fight back. Even when opportunity banged on the door, they were too scared to open it.

"Robert, tell me. How you get the gumption to steal the *Planter*? They might a blown you sky high, sailing right under their noses."

He laughed and slapped his hands together. "I tell you, Moses, I saw my chance right off."

She smiled. "Just like that?"

"Yes, ma'am. The captain took his officers to the grog shop. 'Round midnight. The rest a the crew was conked out below decks, half of em drunk, the other half enjoying a night off. Nobody noticed a thing til we fired up the boiler, and by then, it was too late. We'd locked the hatch. Nobody could hear em hollering over the engine."

"You come on the idea then?"

"No, ma'am. I been figgering on it for months. Every time the *Planter* made port, I told my Hannah to be ready. When I saw the opportunity, I got her and the chil'ren aboard."

"How y'all get past Sumter?" Harriet asked. "Don't they stop every ship?"

Robert rubbed his hands. He clearly relished the story. "That they do, that they do," he said.

"So how you trick em?"

"Well, first I got me a fine-looking uniform from the captain's chest." Robert tugged at his lapels and sleeves, as if to smarten them. "Then," he said as he adjusted the tilt of his old derby, "I fetched up his favorite straw boater. You see, most captains wear

navy headgear, but not Captain Relay. He got a particular fond-
ness for his old straw hat. The Confederate lookouts all knew that,
you see."

"So the hat got you past Sumter?" Harriet asked admiringly. She
loved a good disguise.

"Oh, Sumter wasn't half the problem. I had to get us past *five*
lookouts. Charleston's a door with five bolts. Locked tight."

"Nobody recognized you that whole time?"

"If you believe a man's a man, why then, he is. Nobody sees
color in the dark. They spotted that old straw boater and the brass
buttons, and I give the right signal at each lookout. So the bat-
teries waved us on. Any a them could a sunk us with a couple a
rounds."

Harriet shook her head with amazement. "Most folks would be
scared stiff. No amount a praying would set them on that road."

Robert paused. His expression went vacant, and he rubbed the
irritated skin of his jaw. At last, he said, "I believe it was Charlotte.
She asked if she could call me daddy. Poor little mite so scared, she
hardly got the question out." His eyes cleared. "Yep. That was it."

Harriet recalled Robert's stepdaughter, who had recently lost
her two front teeth. From the child's coloring, Harriet guessed her
natural father might have been white. "Why's that?" she asked.

"I knew a real daddy had to get her safe if he could. Charlotte
couldn't help not having none." He smiled and scratched the part
in his hair again. "It worked on me. Made me feel I had to try.
Every chile needs a daddy."

Reminded of her own daughter boarded out to the Sewards
while she was away, Harriet reached out to squeeze Robert's hands.
"Charlotte sure is lucky. The good Lord looking down on you
both."

Chapter Ten

I was a house servant—a situation preferable to that of a field hand . . .
My mother was a field hand, and one morning was ten or fifteen minutes
late behind the others . . . As soon as she reached the spot where they
were at work, the overseer commenced whipping her . . . I heard her
voice, and knew it, and jumped out of my bunk, and went to the door.
Though the house was some distance from the field, I could hear every
crack of the whip, and every groan and cry of my mother. I wept aloud.

William W. Brown, Slave

WHEN SHE ARRIVED AT THE QUARTERMASTER's office a few minutes later, Harriet found Colonel Montgomery reading a newspaper with his feet on a desk. He sat in a far corner of the hall that served as an exchange for foreign buyers of the rare variety of cotton for which the Sea Islands were famous. Officers examined ledgers while soldiers unpacked crates of supplies imported for the war. A man with a crowbar attacked an unhappy nail somewhere in the back of the building, though no one took notice of the nail's protest.

The Jayhawker removed his feet from the desk as she approached and combed his fingers through tangled hair. Tight across the shoulders and short on the wrists, his blue uniform looked as if had been sewn for someone else, though dusty elbows and a missing collar button suggested he didn't much care. Montgomery's beard showed a day's growth. "Moses," he said. "Take a seat."

Harriet felt too anxious to sit still, but she pulled out the chair opposite his desk. "Afternoon, Colonel. Thank you, sir."

"What brings you down to Hilton Head?"

"Looking for General Hunter," she said.

Montgomery's face wrinkled like he'd bitten on a bad tooth. "You might want to give that up. The man's as useful as a teat on a bull. Too cautious. Seems I'm here every other day to beg for a mission."

"I got one for you," Harriet said.

Montgomery hunched forward. His eyes glittered. "Tell me about it."

"I been back up the Cum'bee, sir." Harriet clasped her hands in her lap. She waited for the next question.

"Looking for the torpedoes?" he asked. Montgomery's directness suggested he hadn't stopped thinking about their last conversation.

"Yes, sir," she said.

"What did you find?" His voice acquired an edge.

Harriet took no offense at his impatience. She felt the same. "There's five torpedoes between Fields Point and the ferry landing," she said. "The Johnnies laid a pontoon across the river there."

"Five mines? You sure?" he asked.

"Five," she said, though she wondered if illness might have prevented Jacob from spotting a second crew from another plantation. Harriet gripped her hands more tightly. "Five," she repeated.

Montgomery glanced at two men carrying a crate through a side door, then down at a defect on his desktop. He moved aside a worn pocket Bible and worried the blemish on the table with his thumbnail. "That's a lot of explosives to sail around."

"Not when you know where they is, sir."

Montgomery looked up with a frown. "Like John Brown knew the defenses at Harper's Ferry?"

Harriet raised her chin. "Brown was Joshua at Jericho. His music still tumbling walls. But he wasn't no military man. He wasn't even much of a soldier. We both know that."

Guilt shot across Montgomery's rugged face so fast that Harriet wasn't sure she'd glimpsed it. She wondered how he felt about not being at Brown's side when Robert E. Lee cornered the old abolitionist at Harper's Ferry in Virginia. Harriet knew how sorry she was. John Brown had wanted her to help him start the slave rebellion, but the Lord gave her a fever that had prevented her from joining him and forced her to accept a friend's hospitality for two weeks. It was true He worked in mysterious ways.

"Brown wasn't a planner," the colonel admitted, "but I would've followed him anywhere."

"You followed him here," she said. "John Brown's looking down right now. This is your chance to finish his work. Get General Hunter off his duff."

Montgomery didn't answer. He thumbed the scratch on the desk some more. Then, with a decisive grunt, he drew a map from the drawer and unrolled it on the tabletop. He spun the paper to face Harriet. She gazed down at the tangled yarn ball of rivers, creeks, inlets, and sandbars, and pointed to the split in the channel at Fields Point. "There," she said, tapping the map. "That's where they put the first torpedo, thinking we'd sneak through on their blind side."

Montgomery made a mark on the map with a small pencil. "Where else?"

Harriet hesitated. If she revealed all, she might not be of further use. She might not see Hunter. "The chart's back in Beaufort," she said. "Don't want to tell you one thing now and something else later."

Montgomery looked up from the map in irritation. "Five torpedoes aren't that many. Surely you remember?"

Harriet passed a hand over her brow. "Sorry, sir. Been a long night."

Montgomery studied the map, calculating. "But you have all the locations figured?"

"Yes, sir," she said despite an inner tremor.

He glanced up again, perhaps noting something unusual in her voice. Harriet looked him in the eye and switched subjects. "If Hunter gives the go-ahead, will he ask you or Colonel Higginson to lead the raid?"

"I don't know. But I do know outcomes will differ depending on his choice."

"Differ?" she said.

Montgomery's mouth thinned. He rolled up the map. "Higginson and I don't see eye to eye on how to bring war home to the Secesh."

She sensed it was he who was now evasive. "How's that, sir?"

Montgomery slipped the chart back in the drawer. He didn't answer.

"Something to do with Rebel pigs and turkeys?" she asked, recalling Thomas's criticism about attacks on civilian property.

That drew a smile. Montgomery tipped back his chair until his shoulders rested against the wall. His blue eyes were keen. "You could say that."

"I reckon General Hunter favors sterner measures than Colonel Higginson," Harriet said. She hoped Montgomery did, too. She thought he did—everything pointed to it—but she needed to be sure.

"He and I both do. I'm probably the most notorious on that account. So long as the planters have the luxury of their slaves, and the fruits of their sins, they're going to continue this rebellion. You can't get anywhere with a warlike people by treating them like church deacons."

Harriet nodded. The Union had pussyfooted long enough around the armed half of the South's population, ignoring the other half at gunpoint.

"In Florida, you took men and cotton," she said. "How this gone be different, Colonel?"

"We wouldn't just be looking for recruits. I mean to get women and children, too. Free as many people as we can," he said. Montgomery rocked, balancing on the back legs of the chair. "Every slave we liberate is one the Secesh can't use."

The children's voices on the Lowndes Plantation came back to Harriet as clearly as if they were playing in the lane outside the office. She pictured Kizzy with her armful of clothing following Pipkin back to the house with blue sash windows.

"Anything else?" she said.

Montgomery leaned forward until his chair legs touched the floor. Since he didn't indulge in tobacco, Harriet was surprised when he took a small tin of locofocos from his top pocket and struck one against the corner of the wooden desk. The sulfur flared. The teetotaler watched the flame and then blew it out. He flicked the matchstick back and forth to cool it.

"Ever see how easily these new ones spark?" he said. "It's time to let the Secesh know what this war's going to cost if they keep it up. Every crop we burn makes it harder for the Rebels to feed their army."

Harriet was silent. Most Northern officers—even abolitionists like Thomas Wentworth Higginson—believed the South must be treated according to the rules of civilized warfare. Private property mustn't be intentionally destroyed, even if colored people were chained to it. There would be no burning of Southern estates.

Harriet considered plantations hell on earth yet wasn't sure God had elected her to put them to the torch. Hadn't she dreamed of it, though? Razing those scenes of despair even if they were the only shelter some people had ever known, where their children had been born and parents were buried? Harriet's own mother still wept for her old cabin whenever the unfamiliar weighed too heavily. Mama hadn't a good word for New York peaches or Canadian winters. She sometimes acted as if gaining her freedom had cost her a leg.

"Them cabins are all some folk got," she said.

Montgomery shrugged. "I'd think they wouldn't mind starting over somewhere else." He pitched the matchstick at a trash barrel a few feet away. "But we can spare the negro quarters, if you think best. The barns and mills are the structures with real value. But mind you, this isn't some friendly boxing match, Moses. We're fighting this to the death. And we need to do it differently if we're going to win. Right now, we're going nowhere."

Harriet's hands curled tight. Montgomery was the man they needed.

A grandfather clock stolen from an elegant foyer somewhere struck the hour in the bustling office. She counted the chimes. Four o'clock. Perhaps she could catch the last packet. Let Montgomery approach Hunter first. Prepare the general for what she had to say.

"I best head to the dock, if you'll excuse me, colonel," Harriet said. She stood. "Knowing bout them torpedoes changes things, don't it?"

"It does," he said. "I expect Hunter's going to give us a different answer." Montgomery's fingers lightly tapped the desk, as if he itched to pull out the map again. "Sure you can't remember where they are?"

Harriet shook her head.

"Well, bring that chart tomorrow."

"Yes, sir. Thank you, sir," she said.

Harriet wended her way to the door, hardly seeing the desks and chairs, grazing objects she passed with the tips of her long fingers like a blind woman.

The raid roared up in her imagination. She saw South Carolina's richest plantations burst into flame, crackling and smoking. Thousands of women, children, and men flocked to Jordan's shore. The ranks of the colored infantry swelled. Shots resounded across America like the one that the ladies in Concord described with such shining eyes. Thomas Wentworth Higginson would be alarmed at Montgomery's destructive intentions, she knew. He'd object that colored troops would be called barbaric.

Harriet doubted that the Kansas Jayhawker would show Thomas his locofocos ahead of time.

Her own evasions might have even graver consequences, Harriet realized. Colonel Montgomery plotted against property. If she proceeded with her plan, not knowing the precise location of the fifth torpedo—or if there were others—she might doom the first colored regiments of the United States. The Combahee would suck them into its depths. The Lord might forgive her come Judgment Day, but no one else would.

Chapter Eleven

Some masters were kind to their slaves, and some was cruel, just like some folks treat their horses and mules—some like them, and are good to them, and some ain't.

Foster Weathersby, Slave

HARRIET SLEPT SO DEEPLY THAT IT wasn't until around noon the next day that she awoke to the realization that it was too late to do her work and still catch the ferry to distant Hilton Head before Hunter's office closed. She was only half sorry as the thought of moving forward with limited information nagged at her. A day to ponder their strategy might be useful. "Act in haste, repent at leisure," Mama said.

Pressure against her head had stirred her from a bottomless slumber. Without opening her eyes, Harriet felt for her crown, only to discover a large, purring lump that was definitely not part of her. She cocked her head and looked up.

The tortoiseshell cat was curled on the mattress. It must have crept through the open window in the night. "Shoo!" she said.

The cat didn't move so she pushed it away from her head. The animal glared and arched upward into a half-moon with a tail. When the cat reversed direction and turned its rump to Harriet's face, she gave it a stronger push, and the animal jumped to the floor. It gave her a sulky look before leaping to the windowsill, where it licked a black paw and washed its face in the shade cast by an oak.

"I gone call you Trouble," she said. Lying on her side, Harriet studied the animal. The cat possessed an independent streak as wide as the Chesapeake—a trait she admired. Ignoring her, the cat was just pretending not to want to cuddle. A week earlier, it had placed a dead mouse on Harriet's pillow when she wasn't home, repaid with a bit of chicken broth in a bowl.

A muffled voice on the street below, then another, reminded her that the day was well underway. She rolled from bed and reached for her petticoat on the empty chair. When she recalled she didn't have one, she slipped a dress from the nail on the door and buttoned it over her cotton drawers.

The long hallway outside her room was empty, though she caught the fading fragrance of hoecakes as she passed the parlor of the confiscated mansion that the army had given a local spinster to run. A thread of brown molasses trickled down the side of a jug next to an empty platter on the sideboard. Breakfast had come and gone. Harriet hoped Septima had gotten an early start on the gingerbread so they could roll it out immediately. A biscuit or two would hold her until suppertime, after which she would take a shift at the contraband hospital, which was always woefully shorthanded.

When Harriet arrived at the cookhouse after a quick walk across town, she noticed a sack of sugar on the stoop. Webster's delivery had arrived. Entering the kitchen, she found Septima perched against a stool with her back to the doorway. A savory aroma of sausage and onion indicated that she had started the dish she called "bog." Rice for their afternoon meal bubbled on the stove.

"Don't know you can fight it, ma'am," Septima said doubtfully. "Mas'r Lincoln done proclamated it."

Two white women stood next to the worktable on which, Harriet noticed with chagrin, a tray of gingerbread biscuits already sat cooling. The older of the visitors appeared around sixty. Dressed in black widow's weeds, her pendulous bosom adorned with a cameo brooch made of white ivory and orange coral, the still handsome dowager supported her weight with a cane parasol that had a handle that was shiny from use. A torso of considerable bulk gave her the dimensions of a well-dressed bureau. Behind her stood a much younger woman, perhaps a granddaughter, whose pale cheeks and lace bonnet indicated a sheltered upbringing, though she could have taken to the stage with her brilliant green eyes. The two women looked over as Harriet entered, which caused Septima to turn around, too.

Septima pushed up from the stool with one hand on her lower back. "Afternoon, Moses. I awful glad to see you. These ladies done brought a tangle I cain't pick."

"Miz Tubman," the older visitor said in a peevish tone, and she then glanced reprovingly around the cookhouse as if to note deficiencies in their housekeeping. "I hear you are an authority of some sort. I cannot believe I am standing here, large as life, asking niggers for advice, but such are the circumstances into which this unprovoked war has cast us."

Harriet's lips tightened. "Uh-huh," she said. "What you need?"

"My family has owned two homes on Bay Street—Bay Street, you hear?—for five generations. On that terrible day last year, that day no one in our fair city shall ever forget, when the finest families were driven from their ancestral homes, beggared by those upstart Yankees, I was forced to hightail to New York where my brother's connections took us in. I could bring only one nigger with me, my girl here, and now that I'm back, those damn Yankees say they . . . want . . . her . . . *too!*"

The widow punctuated her last words with raps of the parasol.

Her blue eyes watered with indignation. "It's intolerable," she continued. "After all I have done for my niggers. 'Specially Edda."

The young white woman stared at the floor. She rolled one hand over the other as if wringing the wash, and Harriet noticed that the girl didn't wear gloves, as a proper debutante normally would. Her lips, the heartbreaking color of a ripe peach, held back emotion. Apparently not a grandchild after all—unless she was. Harriet recalled Charles Nalle, the runaway she had busted out of the courthouse in Troy, New York, before the war. Nalle's fair countenance had been the same as his owner—Nalle's own half-brother—who had tracked him north. Folk called such pale-faced slaves "white niggers."

"What I do not understand," the dowager said, "is why in the world I am perfectly entitled to keep my servant in Manhattan yet forced to give her up when I return to my very own home."

"That the law," Harriet said.

"Fiddlesticks. I'm a Barnwell. I know all about the law," the woman retorted. Blue veins stood out on her knobby hand, flaunting their prominent bloodline. "The Barnwells of South Carolina wrote the laws. Back when the people had a voice in making them. Now it seems that *man*, that tyrant in Washington, has simply declared, has *proclaimed* from on high, the end of our way of life."

Harriet felt her anger mount. She'd heard it before. When would Southerners stop acting as if slaver Thomas Jefferson had anointed them personally to carry the torch of liberty?

"Yes, Miz Barnwell, he has," Harriet said, as her voice rose, too. "And what exactly would you like me to do bout that, ma'am? 'Cause we ain't going back to when half the people weren't people." She burned to eject the woman but clenched her fists instead. A deserved kick in the rear would only incite a lecture from Colonel Higginson or General Hunter or some other cautious white man in authority about keeping the peace with landowners who trickled back. Harriet must remember her place or lose it. No momentary satisfaction was worth that risk. Though it was tempting. Devilishly tempting. Harriet couldn't let her head dwell on it.

"Would you have me hand Edda over to that teeming refugee camp, men and women all jumbled together like hogs?" the dowager asked. "To live in squalor and wake up with some contraband's hands wandering all over her? Or to find a Yankee soldier who will give her protection in exchange for you know what?"

The older woman shifted her parasol to the other hand and nodded at the gingerbread on the table. "Edda," she said. "Those look cool now."

"Yes, ma'am," the girl replied. She brought forth an ironed handkerchief from her reticule, took up a biscuit with it, and handed the gingerbread to her mistress, who bit into the pastry with the aplomb of one entitled to anything made by black hands—colored people having but second call on the results of their labor.

The dowager examined the biscuit curiously. "Orange peel?" she asked, as she ate the other half.

Harriet nodded silently.

Mrs. Barnwell put out her handkerchief for another piece. Septima and Harriet exchanged glances.

"The contraband ain't your concern, ma'am," Harriet said. "Slavery done gone from Port Royal forever."

"We'll see about that," the woman said. She finished the second biscuit, handed the girl her umbrella to hold, and brushed the crumbs from her fingers with the linen. "For the time being, I'll allow it's a heavy burden lifted, thank the Lord."

"So why you here, if your burden is lifted?"

"I've gone to great trouble for Edda. Taking her North, keeping her from that uppity riff-raff in New York, making sure she knows her needlework. Edda's a good nigger. I hate to see all my efforts go to waste. And I simply can't do without a lady's maid."

"So you need someone to do your work for you," Harriet said. She might not be able to eject the woman, but she didn't have to lick anyone's boots in the middle of Beaufort, under the protection of the Union army. "Well, so far as I can see, ma'am, you gone have to get used to ironing your own unmentionables."

The Barnwell woman inhaled sharply, but before she could retort, Septima put up a hand to stay the debate. "Hush a minute, ma'am. Please."

She turned to the young woman. "Tell we, chile. What you want?"

"I . . . I don't know," the girl said. Her voice was timid, and she looked from Septima to Harriet. Her tender skin was the color of cream, though its silky texture reminded Harriet of a Congolese beauty she'd once met. The girl appeared unconscious of her looks and, with lips slightly parted, immature for her age. "My white folk take good care a me," she said. "I never done nothing 'cept house chores, ma'am. Miz Barnwell tell me all measure a evil go on in them refugee camps. I scared to go by m'self."

"She's right to be frightened," the old woman interrupted. "An octoroon like Edda will be soiled before sunup around all those loose men. They say there's more than six hundred runaways in the barracks on Hilton Head."

Harriet knew the awful dowager was correct—though she refused to agree. Without family, the girl courted a dire fate. Edda's fair complexion and naïve air would attract stares from men of all colors. Let loose to fend for herself, washing or cooking for Yankee soldiers and sleeping in any corner she could find, she would be fair game the moment night fell. The thought made Harriet's empty stomach churn.

Septima took the girl's hand and gave it a consoling pat. "Maybe yo' missus right. She got a nice house. Dat bettuh dan camp. Jest common sense." The pregnant Sea Islander looked at Harriet. "Don't you tink so, Miz Tubman? Fo' now?"

The dowager interrupted. "If I am to shelter this poor unfortunate, I want to be sure no military man beats down my door. I refuse to be hounded for doing my Christian duty."

Harriet hated the Barnwell woman's insistence on an exemption from the law. Keeping a slave was wrong, pure wrong. But could Septima be right? Life was full of compromises that must be endured.

Harriet sighed. "That what you want, Edda?" she asked. "Your choices are your own now."

The girl glanced at her mistress. The wrinkled dowager, with her neck gone to strings and wattles, bobbed her head like an aged tortoise. Perhaps Edda was just simple-minded, Harriet thought.

Some people didn't have the sense they were born with. Fed a diet of honey-flavored lies—how lucky they were, how much better off than field hands—house servants often had more difficulty grasping their situation than slaves at a farther remove. The girl might not understand this could be her only chance for freedom, lost forever if the rich woman took her north again, where the law still protected the property rights of slaveholders who hadn't joined the Rebellion.

Edda turned to her. "Yes, Miz Tubman. That's what I want. To stay with my missus. For now. Can you fix that up, ma'am?"

Harriet caught the words. *For now.* Edda had repeated Septima's phrase. Perhaps she wasn't witless after all.

"Yes, Edda," Harriet said slowly, though her mind raced forward. "I'll talk to General Rufus Saxton. He's in charge a civilians in Beaufort."

"That's settled, then," the Barnwell woman said. "And it's a good thing, as I am this child's only bulwark against a life of shame." She glanced around the cookhouse a last time, patently displeased to find herself still there. Her eyes fell on the Franklin stove, where a glossy spill bore witness to a batch of root beer that had boiled over. "My word," she said. "You best clean that up. Left to your own devices, you'll have this place down around your ears in no time." Then, without a nod to Harriet or Septima, she stumped over the vestibule with her parasol.

Edda followed her mistress toward the open door. She paused to look back. "Miz Barnwell ain't so bad. She never whipped me. I know I got it good."

Harriet stepped forward to lay a hand on the girl's sleeve. "You go with her now," Harriet said under her breath. "But this ain't the end a it. I gone talk to the missionary ladies. Find some folks up North, take you in."

A smile dawned on the young woman's face, as if an angel had entered the room, and a pretty flush colored her cheeks. "Really?" she said in a hushed voice.

"I done it before," Harriet said, and she thought of her own daughter, whom Missus Seward treated like a member of the family. "I can do it again."

"Thank you, ma'am," Edda said and followed her mistress with her eyes lowered to dim their light.

Septima gazed at the empty doorway. She rested her hands atop her belly and shook her head. "Ki! Poor chile tink she a nigger."

"Ain't she?"

Septima turned to Harriet. "Dat gal don't look a ting like we."

Harriet sat down on the stool Septima had abandoned. "Color don't make a nigger. That's jest a word for someone folk think they can use—and who thinks she deserves it somehow."

Septima sighed. "Whatever she be, I don't know if we done de right ting or de wrong ting by dat chile. 'Clare to Gawd, I not sure de Buckra know how to be good. Dey proud as Lucifer. Dat no-manners ma'magole preach like she gone help, but you can't git straight planks from crooked trees."

Ma'magole. Gullah for old woman. "Amen," Harriet said.

Septima shook her head. "I thought Miz Barnwell gone poke a hole in de flo' with dat parrysol. I keep hoping it snap in two."

"I kept hoping to bust it across her head," Harriet said as reached for a piece of gingerbread and bit into her breakfast, which had the softness of a macaroon. "How'd you make these?" she asked. "They so light."

Septima smiled. "If you wasn't set on doing every'ting yo'self, Miz Harriet, you would a seen two months ago that I learnt to handle dat dough like a baby's bottom. Mind you, other folk can do stuff. Take all the 'sponsibility and you gone find yo'self wearing it like a millstone 'round yo' neck."

A crumb lodged in Harriet's throat. She coughed and hiccupped so strenuously that Septima finally clapped her on the back. *Not do everything,* Harriet thought as she waited for the tickle to settle. *Hard to imagine how that would work out.*

Chapter Twelve

Tonight I have been to a "shout," which seems to me certainly the remnants of some old idol worship. The negroes sing a kind of chorus— three standing aside to lead and clap—and then all the others go shuffling around in a circle . . . and stamping so that the whole floor swings. I never saw anything so savage.

Laura Towne, Port Royal Missionary

THE LITTLE BOY HELD HARRIET'S FINGER later that evening as they trailed a crowd toward the Praise House after the twilight burial of an elderly member of the community whom Harriet had not known, but everyone called Uncle Henry in accordance with the custom that all adult males were "uncle," provided they hadn't been slave drivers or some other type of scoundrel.

"How Uncle Henry gone git to heaven, Auntie?" Septima's youngest son asked her.

"Why, he go straight on up, Kofi," she said.

The boy looked doubtful. "It raining."

Harriet nodded. "I know, baby, but the Lord brings you home no matter how thick the clouds. Uncle Henry got a through ticket on the gospel train to glory."

Kofi's round cheeks were wet, and raindrops glistened in his curls. Despite the sprinkle, they kept to a sedate pace in keeping with the occasion. The Praise House was a short distance from the

113

graveyard along the river road, and their blouses would dry quickly in the warm building.

Voices and laughter drifted up from the purplish water, where dugouts and small rafts discharged friends and neighbors from nearby islands who had finished work too late to make the service yet in time for the shout. The twilight revealed forms but not faces as men threw lines to shore, clambered over low gunwales, and lifted women from the boats. One stripling took the opportunity to kiss a girl's cheek as he swung her from a dugout, and she cuffed the back of his head. Harriet smiled when the youth pretended to lose his footing in the shallows, and the girl squealed, wrapping her arms around him more tightly. It lifted her heart to see people living lives without fear—falling in love—and made her glad that she had come along for once instead of working into the night at the hospital, as she'd planned.

"What de preacher mean, Auntie?" the somber five-year-old continued after a pause in which he appeared to ponder the idea of a gospel train, though the island possessed no such modern contraptions. Kofi looked up at her as if she'd hung the moon. "Friends might forgit you, but death won't?"

With an arm crooked through her husband's and her younger son on her hip, Septima darted a look over her shoulder. "Dat ragamuffin gone talk yo' ear off, Miz Harriet. He got a question a minute."

"It mean you got to pray every night, baby," Harriet said. "Jest in case."

Kofi squeezed her finger harder. "In case a what?"

"In case it's your time."

He stopped short. "Is death gone git me like he done Uncle Henry?" Kofi's eyes were wide. When Harriet didn't immediately answer, he put up his hands as if hoping to be carried.

Harriet looked away. She hadn't carried her own baby. It wouldn't hurt the boy to walk.

"Everybody die sometime," she said and tugged on Kofi's hand to get him going again. "But you ain't gone go for a long time yet."

They continued walking, though the boy's feet dragged, and he studied the path with his chin down. "How long?" he asked after a while. His voice was small.

The rest of the family was well ahead. The rain had picked up. Harriet sighed, steeled herself, and reached down. Kofi lifted his hands, and she hoisted the boy onto her hip. His spindly legs bumped against her knees. He was a slight child for his height, hardly heavier than her satchel, and he smelled of tadpoles and cornbread.

"The good Lord will decide, but He gone watch over you til then," she said. "Jest like He do me and your mama and papa." Kofi laid his head sleepily on her shoulder, as if she was his most trusted friend. Harriet felt a thrill of tenderness, then a pang of sorrow. She stared straight ahead.

"And my brudduh, too?"

"And your brother, too," she agreed, and she moderated her pace to encourage the boy to nod off. The Gullah practice of burying kin at night meant weepy children in the morning.

He lifted his head. "And Mama's new baby?"

"Uh-huh. And the baby."

When they reached the makeshift church, kerosene lanterns cast a ruddy glow over the mourners. Sea Islanders marked death by hugging life close, and a shout in the family's cabin typically followed a funeral. On this occasion, due to the renown of the old man, the preacher had lent his Praise House in anticipation of a large crowd. Harriet laid the sleeping boy on a bench just inside the front door. She tucked her shawl around his shoulders with a vow not to forget it later.

She turned to find Septima in the crowd, which had swollen to fifty or sixty friends of the deceased chatting eagerly, ready to shake off the sadness of the funeral and weariness of the day. Most were strangers to Harriet, though they seemed to know her, which made her feel oddly apart. Men doffed their hats. Their wives nodded in shy greeting. A girl dipped into a clumsy curtsy when her mother commanded, "Make yo mannuhs," as Harriet looked for a corner to stand in. "Berry pleased t'meet you, Moses," the girl said under her mother's stern eye. "We glad you come," her mother added with a smile as she clasped Harriet's hands.

"Wouldn't miss Uncle Henry's big night for anything," Harriet said, warmed by the stranger's touch, and continued across the room where she found an inconspicuous place against the wall. Most people had a partner. She didn't need one but also didn't want to stand out as alone.

Lanterns illuminated familiar faces that Harriet hadn't previously spotted in the dim burial ground or coming off the boats. Robert Smalls and Walter Plowden talked near a window. Samuel Heyward placed a bench against the wall for two missionary ladies who appeared determined to sit out the festivities. Harriet recognized Philadelphia spinster Laura Towne when she waved an embroidered handkerchief. Harriet recalled Samuel saying that Miz Towne was teaching him to read. The ladies were members of the small band of northern missionaries—white, with the exception of young Lottie Forten—who had come south to help the abruptly liberated Sea Islanders.

Samuel glanced over, catching Harriet's eye as she returned Laura Towne's wave. He gave a pleased smile, as if he thought she had meant to signal him. Harriet felt her face flush when Samuel returned the gesture.

"Take yo' brudduh's hand," a deep bass boomed over the crowd.

"Take yo' sistah's hand!" another person called out.

Septima appeared on Harriet's right and grasped her palm with a happy smile. An elderly man Harriet didn't know took her other hand in a fist as rough as tree bark when they joined a circle that grew larger as congregants took their places. The gray-haired old soul closed his eyes and swayed in anticipation. People around the room hummed different melodies like members of an orchestra tuning their instruments. When the circle grew too wide for the cramped space, parishioners formed a second circle inside the first.

Harriet usually avoided shouts. Sea Islanders packed a room tight, and their singing rushed toward a Gullah so fast and exotic that Harriet struggled to decipher the words. Septima aimed at regular English, as did most of the contraband who worked in town, but men and women from the fields could be hard to understand.

Shouts reminded Harriet that she was an outsider with a strange accent and fractured family. Yet Septima had pleaded while they crimped crusts on a tray of hand pies that afternoon. She'd even strung a necklace for Harriet out of tiny pink-and-white shells. Only Septima's children had escaped with her from the mainland. "Be my sistah tonight?" she'd asked with a plaintive expression, and then she added, "You bossy 'nuf!"

Harriet replied with a swat of the dishtowel in her hand and a promise to attend.

Two younger men and an ancient woman in a tattered dress made their way inside the circle as congregants briefly dropped their hands to admit the singers. The two men began with a deep hum that drew the random melodies into one broad stream. The tiny crone, whose back was so crooked that one shoulder sagged three inches below the other, took up a slow beat, clapping with hands whose nails were scarred and broken. Life had plowed deep furrows down her cheeks, and one filmy eye drooped below the other. Harriet realized with a stab of kinship that the woman must have taken a blow to the head in some distant age that had damaged her left side.

Conversations fell away, the humming deepened, and the circles slowly rotated around the two men and the decrepit old soloist as she closed her eyes

She began in a soft, pure alto that sounded like honey poured over butter. "John Brown's body is a'mold'rin in its grave," she sang quietly. "John Brown's body is a'mold'rin in its grave," she continued more warmly as the circles picked up speed and her accompanists increased their tempo. "John Brown's body is a'mold'rin in its grave," she belted in a voice that made the light shimmer and a finer, higher, more glorious place open above their heads, "and his *soul* is marching on!"

The crowd joined in on the chorus of the abolitionist anthem beloved from Beaufort to Boston. *"Glory, glory, hallelujah,"* people sang as they circled, stamping faster and faster. When they came to *"soul,"* everyone dropped hands, clapped, and shouted out the precious word that expressed the dignity, worth, and eternal life of all God's children. Then the circles wheeled in the opposite direction, and the old woman and her troubadours added more verses, each embellished with unexpected harmonies and strange Gullah phrases until *"soul"* became the only word Harriet felt confident shouting during the chorus.

No sooner had the trio finished their song than they began another, keeping the dancers in constant motion. Harriet's palms became so sweaty that she felt the old man's dry calluses soften. When she accidentally stamped on his foot, he gave her a radiant, toothless grin and squeezed her hand tighter. "Hang on, sistah," he said.

Harriet felt surrounded by friends. While the gray-haired man kept up his warm pressure, Septima gripped her other hand. Walter waved from across the room. Harriet caught herself looking for Samuel and saw him smiling back like they'd known one another all their lives. She felt part of a living chain that would pull them to safety through all the tragedy. At the end of a breathless hour, the singers stopped for a short recess. Septima went to check on Kofi.

Harriet made her way through the crowd to a stone well outside where people took turns lowering and raising a bucket in the dark. The rain had stopped. When someone near the front of the line brought up the pail, Harriet recognized Samuel's silhouette as he offered the dipper to a woman next to him. Moonlight caught the flash of his smile.

Harriet turned around. She didn't want the waterman to think she was following him. "Go on ahead," she said to a man behind her, who held a child's hand. "That youngin' looks parched."

The father's eyebrows went up in recognition, reminding her again of her reputation in the crowd. "Yes, Moses," he said and pressed forward with a grateful nod.

Harriet drifted across the open grounds to a magnolia whose upper branches were lost in the silvery night. She leaned against the trunk and closed her eyes, grateful just to drink the air refreshed by the storm. A barn owl hooted in a nearby tree, sounding as solitary as she suddenly felt. Why did she feel so connected one moment and apart the next? A visitor wherever she went, not fully belonging North or South, not with men, not with women.

She'd never forget the first night she'd been alone, which was when she'd walked out on John without saying goodbye. She'd been afraid he would try to prevent her, or that his angry voice might alert someone who would trade their secret for food or mercy. So when her husband left for Baltimore with his loaded wagon one ordinary morning, she merely called from the doorway, "See you tomorrow."

She'd been a fool for thinking she could make it up to him later and that he'd wait for a wife who hadn't mentioned she was leaving him. Deep down, she'd known John would never get over the hurt of her wordless disappearance. No one would. The rupture wasn't only his fault. It was hers, too.

She had also betrayed their only child. First by giving Margaret away at birth, and then by taking her back. The girl had lost her family twice. Although Margaret accepted the story that Aunt Harriet could offer her a better life than any colored girl would have in the South, the "niece" Harriet took from Baltimore at ten whimpered in her sleep for a month for the woman she thought was her mama. Over the years, Margaret had become fond of her eccentric aunt, who wanted nothing more than a child of her own to love—and who then abandoned her again to fight the war.

Harriet had never mustered the courage to tell Margaret who she really was, even though the girl was now old enough to keep a secret. It would mean admitting her shame: that she'd given away that bundle in a quilt not just for the child's sake, but also for her own. Everyone thought Harriet was so unselfish. It was partly true, which meant it was also partly a lie.

She wondered if she had sacrificed *for* her child or just sacrificed the child. No real mother turned her back. Rachel hadn't. And then she'd died. In the end, her boys had been lost anyway.

A tear escaped down Harriet's cheek, and she brushed it away quickly, though no one would see in the dark. People were returning to the building. The thud of feet had picked up again. She wondered if she could slip away, then reminded herself that she'd sworn never again to leave without a farewell. A sad half-smile flickered across her face. The brain was so fickle, always ready to forget promises made in contrition, when regrets briefly cowed selfishness. She would stay for another song, she decided, and then she would make her excuses.

Harriet stepped from the lee of the trunk in time to collide with someone returning from the well. The dipper in Samuel Heyward's hand flew upward. Water drenched his shirt.

"Oh, my!" she cried. Harriet started to reach for the utensil on the ground but remembered the last time they had butted heads, and she hesitated.

He apparently had the same thought because he glanced at her warily before leaning sideways to snatch the dipper. "You a hard lady to help," he said.

"I don't need help," she said instinctively.

"Maybe you jest don't want it," he retorted.

"I do fine on my own."

"I see that. But I ain't the enemy. Folk who dish out help ought to be able to take it."

His observation brought her up short, and for a second, she didn't know what to say. Why was it so hard to let anyone take care of her when she spent so much time taking care of others? He was right. Harriet smiled, and then she burst into a laugh at her own pigheadedness.

Samuel grinned. "Saw you give up your spot in line. Thought you could use some water. Didn't realize you needed something stronger."

"I hope you don't take me for a drinking woman," she said.

"Nope. Though I myself wouldn't say no to a drop a 'shine."

Harriet laughed again. "I might jest join you. Feel like I'm at sixes and sevens tonight."

"With respect, it looks like you being jest Harriet for once."

Harriet felt her face grow rigid. Like most folk, Samuel must believe that a real woman wasn't a serious person. A *real* Harriet wouldn't act like a man among men, ordering them around. Let him think what he wanted. "Don't know why you say that," she said stiffly.

"You got a big job," he replied in an easy tone. "Glad to see you let down. A shout's s'posed to make folk laugh and cry. This your first?"

Harriet relaxed at his answer. She touched the necklace Septima had given her—proof that she wasn't "Moses" all the time. She was glad she'd worn the pretty strand along with her better dress.

"First shout in a while," she admitted. "My friend Septima twisted my arm. Made me come."

Samuel put his hand under her elbow, leaning closer in the moonlight. "'Pears she falling down in her duty. Mind if I take over? You don't want to miss the next dance."

Harriet looked up into his eyes, which held more than one question. She sensed the warmth of his body. He had unbuttoned the collar of his shirt to cool off, revealing the light pulse in his neck.

His hand tightened on her elbow when she didn't answer. Instead of guiding her toward the hall, he drew her closer. "Anyone ever let you know you the brightest star in God's sky, Harriet Tubman?" Samuel spoke so softly that the breeze seemed to scatter his words, though he clearly meant her to hear each one.

Harriet's elbow felt as if it was melting. She ached to reach up and touch the beating of his heart. If she did, would he take her in his arms?

Maybe she didn't have to be alone. Maybe life could start over. She'd never understood if John Tubman's new marriage meant she was divorced. Was she free to remarry? The law ignored the tangled obligations of black people.

Too much was happening at once. Harriet turned her gaze to the Praise House and willed her feet to move. The arm Samuel held was the only part of her body that seemed to possess nerve endings. "Music's starting up," she said. "We best go in."

Neither of them spoke as they started toward the harmonies that tumbled through the open door and mounted the steps that shook with the rhythmic pounding of a hundred feet. Samuel hung the dipper on a nail as they came inside. Harriet hooked the hand on her elbow closer for an instant—an intimate gesture that felt daring yet natural—before letting go and taking his hand as they joined the circle. One of the male singers now performed the solo role in a spiritual that spoke to all their hopes and dreams. The room resounded with music.

The shout ended an hour later when the female soloist led them in a song that reminded Harriet of all the people she had urged into creeks and streams to hide their footprints. "Wade in de watuh, chillun," the singer began, her warm voice rising. "God's gone a trouble de watuh!"

Samuel and Harriet looked at one another. The song was meant for Moses. Meant for her. Harriet glanced around the room and caught Septima grinning back. Across the circle, Harriet saw a man and woman she didn't know nod in her direction. They reminded her of others she had smuggled across the swamps of Maryland, kin to those now wheeling in the lamplight. God had troubled the waters for them all, covering their tracks and sparing their lives.

When the song was over, Harriet found her hand still in Samuel's as the crowd jostled toward the exit and emerged into the balmy night. Now the back of his shirt was damp from the evening's exertions rather than the front. The missionaries preceded them down the steps, tying their bonnets. Their words drifted back.

". . . Heathenish," Laura Towne said in a low voice to the other woman. "I shall never get used to it."

Harriet darted a glance at Samuel, who was looking over the heads of the crowd. He seemed not to hear the women in the hubbub.

"I've only ever seen quiet prayer at the Praise House," said her companion, dressed in brown Quaker garb. "The better negroes come here on Sundays. Why, a shout hardly looks Christian."

Harriet stepped aside at the foot of the stairs to allow others to stream past. If her hand weren't in Samuel's, she would cover her ears. It hurt to hear the contrabands' white supporters react with disdain to their unabashed fervor. Colored people had the same problem in reverse. A local preacher had told her, "The Buckra, they know the Bible's reasons and rules, but they ain't never caught the feeling. I'm not sure God have much respect for that." To Sea Islanders, the missionaries' relationship to the divine felt dry. Perhaps whites had less need for a passionate God, ready to take their side, ready to inspire a faith mighty enough to counter the worst evils. Could black and white ever be one, as they must— as they truly were, if Christ's injunction to love thy brother meant anything?

Someone bumped into Harriet as she paused in distress, nearly dislodging her shoe. She pressed down into the heel and turned to see Walter Plowden. The joyful expression she'd glimpsed on his face during the shout had vanished. His eyes were hard, unforgiving slits. Perhaps he'd overheard the unkind comments. Yet he wasn't looking at the Northern spinsters retreating down the path. Instead, the wiry scout scowled at Harriet and Samuel's joined hands.

Walter lifted his chin to stare straight at Samuel. He didn't look at her, and she had the distinct impression Walter was avoiding her gaze. He spoke each word like it cost a dollar. He didn't stutter one bit. "Too bad your missus ain't here, Samuel. Must be awful hard on her, left behind on the plantation with your boys."

The warm night went cold. Time stopped and then sped back to that moment when Harriet first learned of John Tubman's new wife. Her face flamed red.

Samuel glared at Walter. "We talked bout this." He turned toward her. "Harriet, it ain't—" he started to say.

But she dropped his hand faster than a hot pan. Without a good-bye, without hearing the rest of the conversation other than its brusque tone, she strode furiously down the road toward the river. When she spotted a man lifting a woman into a boat anchored in the shallows, Harriet spun on her heel in the opposite direction. There was more than one way home.

CHAPTER THIRTEEN

Two particular traits of the black troops grew out of their former state of servitude. When serving on their own soil, or even on a soil or under conditions resembling their own, they had the great advantage of local knowledge. They were not only ready to serve as guides, but they were virtually their own guides . . . They could find their way in the dark, guess at the position of an enemy, follow a trail, extract knowledge from others of their own race; and all this in a way no white man could rival.

Colonel Thomas Wentworth Higginson

"NANSI!" SEPTIMA YELPED THE NEXT MORNING as they took stock of their supplies. She dropped her end of the heavy sack on the cookhouse floor.

"Where?" Harriet said. She plucked the entire bag off the ground and swung it rapidly onto the counter. Expensive sugar must be handled with care, but she also didn't want to get bit.

"Dere! It run'd under de bag."

Harriet lifted one end. A large spider scrambled into the canvas folds of the opposite corner, though not before Harriet spied the red hourglass on its black abdomen. She grimaced, mad at a world overrun by spiders and troublesome men. She had no time to waste on either.

"How'd a black widow get under there?" she said, angry at her own foolishness. "I shouldn't have taken that sugar off Webster.

We don't have enough cupboards to keep it up off the gol'dang dirt."

Harriet took a wooden spoon from a container of utensils on the counter. She flipped the bag over and gave the spider a whack hard enough to kill a mouse. The crumpled body tumbled into her spoon, and she threw it out the front door onto the ground.

"Think I'll see if John Lilly will take it off our hands," she told Septima. "Maybe he'll give us a penny more a pound."

"I can handle de work here," Septima said.

Harriet nodded. "I 'spose four dozen biscuits gone be enough."

Septima tilted her head sideways. "Why, I b'lieve you ready to trust me with dat dere gingerbread, Miz Harriet."

Harriet cracked a smile but merely lifted the bag to her shoulder by way of answer. She must get going. Today she would see General Hunter. Nothing else mattered. "I'll stop at the store, then the hospital," she said. "From there, I'm off to Hilton Head."

Septima looked curious. "Seem you jump dat packet near every day. What keep taking you dere?"

Harriet nudged the cat's bowl under the table with her shoe to keep Septima from tripping on it. "There's new contraband," she said, fudging the truth.

New runaways often did slip through the lines, but Harriet didn't know if any had arrived recently. Most people believed Harriet's job on Port Royal was to nurse contraband and help Hunter recruit new scouts. Few knew she went behind the lines.

"I hope General Hunter paying you for de trouble," Septima said. "Dem teachers told my husband make sure he gets paid for extra work. De guv'ment giving some folk close on twelve dollar a month."

The comment reminded Harriet that she had taken Septima's earnings from under her mattress that morning. She set the bag down one more time, drew the money from her satchel, and handed over two greenbacks. "Almost forgot," she said.

Septima pocketed the money gratefully. "Dat remind me. Yo'

shawl. You left it with Kofi last night." She fished the article from a sweetgrass basket on the floor. "Dat chile sho do mind you. Don't know how you git him to quiet down so quick. You gone have to tell me yo' secret."

Harriet recalled the morning Septima had arrived late because Kofi had wandered to the riverside looking for frogs. "What if a gator got him?" Septima had said, horrified. "'Clare to Gawd, I roping him to his bed tonight!"

Harriet smiled at the idea that the child favored her. "I ain't done nothing special."

"Well, he think you special." Septima handed her the shawl. "Here."

Harriet put the item in her satchel. "Good thing my head's attached," she said as she lifted the bag of sugar to her shoulder once more.

"Famembuh," Septima said. "Make sho de guv'ment pay you."

Fifteen minutes later, Harriet trudged up the front steps to John Lilly's store on Bay Street. Men crowded the entrance. A colored soldier stepped aside when he recognized her. He tipped his blue kepi cap but didn't offer to take her load.

"A thousand. Maybe more," Harriet heard one man say to another as she pushed past a group standing around a white soldier who was reading aloud from a newspaper. Someone groaned.

"Troops under General William Tecumseh Sherman led the assault," the man read. He glanced up from the page. "That's the redheaded officer what refused to join the Louisiana secessionists," he explained.

"We don't care if his hair is blue," said a man with a burl pipe in his hand. "How'd he lose, goddammit?"

The tall soldier refocused on the cheap newsprint. "Flags unfurled, the troops of the 13th United States Infantry charged bravely along Graveyard Road," he read. "Despite Federal valor, the Rebels carried the day, firing over the abatis and inflicting considerable losses."

Another soldier spoke up. He was an older white man who gripped his long beard with a firm hand, as if he'd pull it off to win the war. "Valor, my ass. That's a load of crap. What the hell is Grant up to? Ain't Vicksburg been under siege a month?"

"Close on two months," the reader replied. "The army's been in Mississippi since April. Grant's circling around, or so the papers report."

"Bull," the bearded man said.

"Another thousand gone," came a gloomy observation from somewhere in the back.

"And don't forget Chancellorsville," the reader said. The tall man had the sharp cheekbones and prominent chin of the Scots-Irish. "Copperheads were right. Lincoln can't win. He should've given the South their terms to start with."

Someone hissed loudly. An angry murmur broke out near the doorway, where a group of colored troops stood with arms crossed. Everyone knew what terms meant to the Confederacy: a guarantee of slavery until the Second Coming. *If Judas had been a northerner, he'd be a copperhead Democrat,* Harriet thought.

She plumped her sack on the counter.

"What can I do for you, Tubman?" John Lilly asked. The stout, dark-haired shopkeeper ignored the arguing troops. Quarrels broke out whenever a new edition of *Harper's Weekly* or *The Soldier's Journal* arrived from up north. The news in recent months had been particularly disheartening. After two years of bloodshed, the North seemed less likely to prevail than ever. Talk was that the Rebels would win.

"I got sugar to sell, Mister Lilly. Bought more'n I can use."

The jowly storekeeper drew back his double chin. "You didn't buy it here."

"No, sir. But it's quality. Jest can't use it fast enough. I can give it to you at fifteen cents a pound."

"That's hardly giving it to me. I earn barely a penny above that."

Harriet tried to recollect what Webster had charged her, but all she recalled was that he said it was a cut rate. She didn't have much head for bargaining. "What if I lower the price a penny?" she asked.

John Lilly looked beyond Harriet. "What's that you got?" he said as another customer dropped a sack on the long wooden counter.

"Afternoon, Mister Lilly, sir," Walter Plowden said. "Wondering if you can use some sugar. T-t-turns out I have t-t-too much on my hands." The skinny scout glanced at Harriet and tipped his hat. "Moses," he said cautiously and took a small phial from his pocket to apply salve to his lips.

"Walter," she replied with a cool nod. After the preceding night, Walter was one of the two men in the world she felt least like seeing.

The merchant crooked his thumbs under the straps of his apron. "Now that's something," he said. "This is wartime, and both of you have more supplies than you can use. I don't know the last time I saw that."

Harriet looked at him sharply. "What you saying?"

Lilly stared right back. His blue eyes narrowed. "I'm saying it's curious. Contraband are in here every other day begging for credit, complaining that they're waiting on rations because a ship from New York's been delayed, and here you two have more than you know what to do with."

"I bought this sugar from the commissary," Harriet said.

"That's where I got it, t-t-too," Walter said. "It's jest more'n I need for my business, sir."

"So you hope to turn a profit," Lilly said. "Off the Union that's helping you people."

Harriet pressed her hands into the counter until her knuckles wrinkled. "You accusing us?"

Walter shifted. Harriet felt the toe of his boot against her foot.

"We all trying to make ends m-m-meet, Mister Lilly," Walter

said. "I know you are, too. But I promise you, Miz Harriet and me got these stores fair and square. I don't know why Private Webster had extra, but he did. You can ask him."

"I'll do that," the shopkeeper said. "Because I can't accept stolen goods. If they're stolen," he added without looking at Harriet.

"And I'll talk to General Saxton," she snapped. "He gone be interested to know how you treat people he trusts."

She picked up the sack and perched it on her shoulder. "Walter?"

Walter nodded at the shopkeeper and hoisted his bag. As they made their way toward the screen door, John Lilly's voice drifted back. "Biggity niggers," he told the next customer. "Never know when they're telling the truth."

Walter and Harriet exited the crowded store and walked down the steps into the bustling street as a wagon loaded with bricks rumbled by. Two women clothed in old flour sacks and carrying water jugs on their head waved to Harriet from the other side of the street. She nodded back, careful not to lose her grip on the heavy bag of sugar.

"Don't that beat all?" she said.

"Seems that happened every t-t-time I walked into a store in New York, once I got free."

"But when we laying down our lives for the Union?"

Walter shrugged. "People used to stealing from others believe everyone else a thief. White folks took so much from us, they convinced we trying to get it back."

"Think Webster's crooked?"

"Hard to know. He sure got a lot of supplies coming down from the North for the refugees, that's for true."

"He better not be filching their rations," Harriet said and pursed her lips tightly. The idea infuriated her. New runaways got little more than a few cups of flour along with meager handfuls of beans, hominy, and sugar.

"Either way, I sure ain't gone t-t-truck with Lilly again," Walter said.

"That might not be enough. He could turn Saxton against us. Hunter, too."

"No one gone doubt you, Moses," Walter said.

"Doubts are like skeeters. You got to swat em quick." Harriet shifted the sack to her other shoulder and glanced at him, irritated. "Wish you would a let me give him a bigger piece a my mind. I would a taken his head clean off if you hadn't been kicking me."

"And have Lilly throw us out? Or get them white soldiers mad? You know how it is." He shook his head. "Someone got to w-w-watch out for you, Moses."

Harriet started up the street. That's what Walter had been doing last night. It wasn't something she wanted to talk about.

"I need to get this sugar back to the cookhouse," she said. "Least it's on the way to Saxton's."

"Didn't you hear? Saxton just sailed for Washington. Folk saying he might replace Hunter."

Harriet stopped short, causing the bag to slip slightly. She jiggled it more squarely onto her shoulder. She hadn't known that Hunter's head was on the chopping block. She'd spent months cultivating his trust. If Hunter was reassigned, she would have to start over. The delay would cost them the raid. "Replace Hunter? Where you hear this?"

"Last night at the shout. Robert Smalls told me word's all over Hilton Head that Hunter's gone be relieved soon."

"Why?"

"His failure to take Charleston or much a anything, I reckon. The Union's drowning in blood. Saxton hopes to get the job. Wants to do more than b-b-babysit contraband." Walter looked around and lowered his voice. "What did Hunter say bout the map?"

"I missed him. Gone try him again this afternoon," Harriet said.

"You missed him?" Walter's eyebrows shot up. "Those Rebs could put back their artillery any t-t-time."

"I know that. But Hunter's not some hound dog waiting for me on the front porch. He ain't there all the time. Tell you what. I owe Doc Durant a few hours at the hospital, and then I'm headed straight to Hilton Head. You grab Heyward and meet me at army headquarters 'round four o'clock."

Walter's gaze shifted to the road ahead. "Samuel?"

"Yes," Harriet said impatiently. "He knows the river better than either a us." Determined to put the mission ahead of personal feelings, she ignored the flush creeping up her neck. "I don't care what a man's situation is. I need all the backup I can get, and three voices is louder than one. We need Hunter to shake his head north-south 'stead a east-west fore it's too late."

Walter hesitated. He gave her a searching look, as if there was something he wanted to say. "Harriet, you deserve—"

"I don't want to talk about it, Walter."

He tried again. "I should explain—"

"No explanations," she said. "Be on Hilton Head by four."

"Yes, ma'am," he said, and he fell back as she continued up the street.

Walter had used her Christian name. And he'd called her *ma'am*. That surprised Harriet some, but she found she didn't mind so long as those words didn't roll off the lying tongue of Samuel Heyward.

CHAPTER FOURTEEN

The first expedition undertaken by this regiment left Beaufort somewhere around the middle of November [1862] . . . Several of the men were wounded. While the Surgeon Dr. H. was dressing the wounds of one of the men—another came up with his arm badly shattered—when the first man stepped back saying, "Fix him, boss, he's worse than I is." How few are the men of any color who could have been more unselfish.

Esther Hawks, MD

HARRIET REMOVED A CLEAN APRON FROM the hospital closet, tied it around her waist, and carried her broom and dustpan into the main ward. The repetitive duties of nursing would allow her to collect her thoughts. Walter's information meant she must find some way to convince General Hunter without further delay.

Doctor Henry Durant stood near a window at the far end of the long room, formerly a salon in the opulent mansion. The Northern volunteer leaned against the wall for support while writing on a chart. A small man with red hair and jug ears, Durant tended to favor one leg over the other due to an old injury. He walked with a limp when he was tired.

Two long rows of iron beds held the hospital's worst cases. Other patients lay on mattresses in the walkway. Someone had opened windows overlooking a veranda to dispel the odor of urine and gangrene, though black flies flew in on the sprightly breeze. A man in the middle of the room thrashed on his cot. "Fuck!" he shouted in his delirium. Harriet started her work in the near corner and proceeded down the row.

General Hunter must be warier than ever of making a mistake, Harriet reflected as she dipped her broom under a bed and circled round a chamber pot. She knew from camp gossip that the West Pointer had spent decades as a paymaster and pressed for a frontline command after the war broke out. Nearing the end of his career, Hunter must itch to make his mark. Any man who dyed his mustache clearly felt a need to prove he wasn't a has-been. Hunter had promoted colored units but done little with them. With the War Department breathing down his neck, budging him would be even harder.

The problem consumed Harriet's attention so thoroughly that she hardly saw the floorboards as she wielded her broom.

"Who dat?" someone asked. "Dat you, Harriet?"

She looked up to see a patient with a bandage over his eyes and the outline of only one leg under the covers. He waved a hand in front of his face to shoo away the flies that crawled under his blindfold. An especially big one hummed noisily before landing on a plate that rested on the windowsill. Harriet had just edged her broom under the man's bed, coming away with a pile of mouse droppings and human hair.

"It's me, Uncle Romulus," she said. "Can I get you something?"

"Yo' voice medicine enough, sugar, though I wouldn't turn down a cup a water," he said. "It taste bettuh coming from you."

"Yes, Uncle. I'll get that now," she said as she leaned her broom against the windowsill. Romulus always wanted the same thing.

Harriet picked her way across the room, stepping over patients until she reached the water urn under a large fresco of a bucolic plantation scene. The artist, likely a slave, had painted handsome men hoeing green fields at the edge of a river, overlooked by a mansion on a hill. Tiny women in colorful headscarves carried sheaves of rice to a brick mill in the distance while a liveried servant drove a gaily dressed white couple in a barouche toward a church at the edge of the picture. Billowy clouds scudded across the blue sky.

Everyone looked so healthy, Harriet reflected as she held a cup under the tin spout. From such a picture, one would never expect the disease that was rampant among the Sea Islanders in the civilian hospital. Since Doctor Durant's arrival, the confiscated mansion had been constantly full. Most patients had only ever had root doctoring. They presented an array of swamp fevers, typhoid, worms, abscessed teeth, and old injuries. The wall mural made bygone days look good, though; it was as if God was smiling down.

"Moses," a woman called.

Harriet turned around to see Doctor Durant limp across the room with his hand under the elbow of Esther Hawks, the physician whom the army had assigned to a schoolhouse. Esther had arrived with other missionaries after the Union invaded the islands. Most of them served as teachers, but Harriet thought it a shame that one as qualified as Esther was not assigned more specialized duties. Her husband, also a physician, had started Beaufort's new hospital for black soldiers. General Saxton had insisted on two facilities for colored folk—one for civilians, and another for the military.

"How you find yourself this morning, Doctor Hawks?" Harriet asked.

"The day finds me well, Harriet, thank you." The tall young woman reached for Harriet's hands and leaned down to kiss her cheeks. "My spirits are higher—and hearing better—since I shifted to the hospital. You wouldn't imagine the din occasioned by three hundred pupils reciting their ABCs. They nearly drove me deaf."

Harriet smiled. "Didn't realize you was freed up from teaching, ma'am. How that happen?"

Doctor Durant wiped his brow with an ironed handkerchief that he then tucked back into his breast pocket. He had an unmistakably courtly air in the lady's presence even though he was married. "I suggested Missus Hawks take charge of Number 10 when

General Hunter sent her husband to Florida last month. The brass could hardly object since no other physician was available."

Esther was taller than the doctor and looked down at him with a benevolent smile. "I've been working night and day since," she said. "No trauma yet—unless you count the soldier whose ear was taken off last week by a Rebel picket across the river. 'A lucky shot,' he said, though it sounded more like good aim to me."

Harriet's attention sharpened. If Hunter approved the raid up the Combahee, colored troops would have casualties. "How does Number 10 stand for beds and chloroform?"

"We're finally ready for action," Esther said. "My husband spent so much time outfitting the Barnwell House that training unavoidably came second. Now every orderly can suture." The doctor pushed back the dark waves that framed her face. "Though we still beg for supplies. The army apparently isn't aware that colored patients bleed as copiously as white ones. I believe that's why I was allowed to take over. It doesn't bother them if colored soldiers have only a female doctor."

"The army letting you stay, then?" Harriet said.

"No," she said with a rueful shrug. "It's back to the schoolhouse now that Doctor Greenleaf has arrived. What a pity that men insist upon hogging all the glory."

A cough from the other side of the ward reminded Harriet of the cup in her hand. "Lordy," she said. "I clean forgot bout Romulus. Excuse me, Doctor Hawks."

"Don't let me interrupt. I just wanted to express my regards. My ears still ring with your speeches in Boston. Did you ever write them down?"

"No, ma'am. I wouldn't know how."

"Then I hope you'll come see me when I go back to teaching," Esther said.

"Thank you, ma'am. I'll think on it," Harriet said, though she'd given up the prospect long before. Her head ached whenever she stared too long at letters that spilled across the page, looking like someone had kicked over an anthill. Telling one word from another pressed against some scar deep in her brain.

Harriet continued across the room to the sightless patient. After he emptied the cup of water, she returned to her broom, turning over the problem of General David Hunter. When she was done sweeping, she took a basin from the cupboard, got ice from the icehouse, and filled the pan from a pump in the garden. Patients appreciated the cool bath water.

In her years on the Railroad, she'd helped people strong enough to run. The hospital, built for a family that didn't mind watching other families suffer, housed bodies too broken to make such journeys. Nursing was her amends for abandoning them all those years. Harriet sighed at the hardest part of her task and began with the old woman in the first bed.

"Morning, Auntie," she said as she sat down and waved away the flies on the patient's forehead. "How you doing this sunny day?"

"Well, de Lawd gib me another, so I like it jest fine," the old lady said with a smile that lifted the tumor on her cheek. "How bout you, nurse?"

"Sassy enough to pester poor Doc Durant."

The woman laughed. "Bless his soul," she said. "Dat white fella never miss a day. Laying on his hands like Jesus."

Harriet held up her rag. "He asked me to clean y'all up. Okay to start with your face?"

The woman closed her brown eyes, which made her easier to look at, even though Harriet focused on only one part of the face at a time. She wiped saliva from the chin and dabbed at the remains of soup on the upper lip. Then she moved her cloth around the tumors that bulged from the forehead and distorted the nose, and finally, she made a second pass at the drool on the chin. Its fine cut hinted at the beauty the woman must have possessed before contracting her master's French pox.

"How's the pain in your legs today?" Harriet asked as she dipped her cloth and washed the woman's right hand.

"If it feels as bad as I do, it sho has my sympathy."

Harriet laughed and started on the other hand.

"Tell me sumpin' cheerful," the woman said. "How yo man?"

"Oh, he all right," Harriet said.

"Bless you," the old lady said at the comforting fiction. "Dat nice."

Harriet returned her rag to the water. She stood and lifted the basin. "I'll let the doctor know to check on your legs, ma'am."

"Thank you, chile. P'haps he got a physic,'" she said and closed her eyes.

It took Harriet another two hours to wash every patient. When she finally threw her linen in the basket, she stretched her neck right and left to take out the kinks. Doctor Durant stopped by the cupboard for a clean towel at the same moment.

"Done for the day, Moses?" he said and leaned against the wall to take the weight off his bad leg.

"Done with this part a my day, sir. Now I'm on to the next."

"Always busy. What don't you do?"

Harriet thought for a moment. "Well, I don't insist on glory, sir. Like Miz Hawks, I mostly want to get things done."

The physician straightened. "Just like a woman," he said. "I'm afraid men need more motivation."

Harriet stared as Durant reentered the ward, and she then turned toward the front door. He had made her argument. She didn't need to convince General Hunter that the plan was foolproof. She just needed to convince the old paymaster that he had one last chance for glory.

Chapter Fifteen

Pass the bearer, Harriet Tubman, to Beaufort, and back to this place, and wherever she wishes to go, and give her passage at all times on all Government transports . . . Harriet was sent to me from Boston, by Governor Andrews, of Massachusetts, and is a valuable woman.

Major General David Hunter

A SEA BREEZE SEIZED THE OPEN DOOR behind Harriet as she entered the general's private office and slammed it shut with a loud bang. It was a terrible way to begin.

General Hunter looked over his newspaper. "You certainly know how to make an entrance," he said.

The commander's table was uncluttered. He sat in a chair that had lost one of its arms, reading the paper by the glare of an open window. The bent and fingerprinted glasses at the end of his hooked nose looked like they'd traveled with him all his sixty-plus years. It was hard to imagine he'd ever been young. His freshly combed wig blended more naturally than before with the hair that tickled his veiny ears, but he still looked like a man whose candle had burned low.

"Sorry, sir," Harriet said, relieved that he wasn't annoyed. "Must be the Lord making a point. Thank you for seeing me."

"Colonel Montgomery said you have new information. What is it?"

"I done what you asked, sir," Harriet said. She stood completely still and straight, hands at her side, saying nothing more. Harriet had often used silence to concentrate listeners' attention, especially in public forums. Chatter lulled people. Bursts of silence made them listen. From a woman, it was downright unnerving.

The general folded his newspaper and draped it over the remaining arm of the chair. He looked perplexed. "What I asked?"

"What you asked when I last reported, sir. When I brought the news bout Fields Point and Tar Bluff."

Hunter reached in his breast pocket for a cigar. "Oh. As I said, we can't launch against those torpedoes." He bit off the end of the cigar, spat it on the floor, and patted his other pocket for a match.

"I know, sir. You said we need to map em."

"That's correct." Hunter stood and walked to the wooden secretary in the corner to get a tin of locofocos next to a pitcher of water. He struck a match, took an experimental puff, and resumed his seat under the window.

"My men and I'd like to show you," Harriet said.

"Your men?" he said, as if confused by what she meant. The breeze coming through the window wafted the cigar's reek across the room.

"My scouts," she said. Hunter sometimes seemed to forget that he'd asked her to recruit them, as if he couldn't credit that he'd put a woman in charge, even the famous Harriet Tubman. But he had, and she'd recruited all of them with the exception of Walter, who had found her. "The contraband who help out. May I bring em in, General?"

"How many?"

"Jest Walter Plowden and Samuel Heyward, sir," Harriet said. "You met Plowden before. Heyward, he's new."

"Proceed," Hunter said, and he drew again on his weed.

Harriet opened the door, taking care to hold the knob tightly. She peered into the anteroom. Samuel read a farmer's almanac with a finger under the words while eating a hunk of bread. Walter examined the tips of his shoes. A bearded, sour-faced clerk watched the pair with folded arms. The two men looked up. Harriet nodded. Samuel put the bread in his pocket and brushed crumbs from his lap. He and Walter stood and followed her into the smoke-filled room.

Hunter had moved to the head of the conference table. "Men," he said and motioned to the chairs next to him.

Walter looked uncomfortable at the invitation, but Samuel sat down without any change of expression. Harriet gave the waterman a wide berth and took a chair on the opposite side of the table, next to the general. She placed her satchel on the floor. Walter joined her.

"Plowden and Heyward went with me up the Cum'bee four nights ago, General Hunter." Harriet nodded at Samuel. "Heyward here found the first torpedo."

Hunter examined Samuel's face as if scrutinizing a federal note for counterfeit. "Tell me about that, Mister Heyward," he said.

Samuel appeared untroubled by the long stare. He rested his large hands on the table and spoke calmly. "I was scouting the Cum'bee by myself a week ago, sir, when I spotted the barrel in the water near the Lowndes Plantation."

Hunter's eyes narrowed. "Alone? What were you doing that far upriver?"

"My missus and chil'ren are on the Heyward Plantation, sir."

"Surely you weren't visiting them?"

"I stash food in a hollow oak near the river when I can," Samuel said. "I took em a piece a salt pork."

Harriet stiffened. The image of Samuel portioning rations in the dugout sprang to mind. The rotten cheater.

"That's a long haul for one man," Hunter said. It was a statement of fact that could double for an accusation of lying.

"Master Heyward used to race me on the river, sir. Like his horses at the Jockey Club," Samuel replied. "I got fast. And good at timing the tide."

"So what did you see?"

"I was coming back on the ebb, when I spotted a snag jest in time to dodge it. Thought it was a gator. I seen the barrel below the surface as I nicked past."

Harriet spoke up. "We *confirmed* it, General."

Confirm was a word with the power to make doubts go away, she knew. Men in authority liked it.

"How?" Hunter asked.

"My brother Jacob done told us," Samuel answered for her.

"I got onto the Lowndes place," Harriet said. "Samuel's brother gave me the location a the torpedoes. He laid em."

"Did he say how many there are?" Hunter said.

Harriet reached down into her satchel. She withdrew the small map from the inside pocket and unfolded it on the table. "Jacob said there are five. I used a nail to mark the spots where the Secesh anchored the barrels." She pushed the pocked chart in Hunter's direction.

Hunter tapped the ash off his cigar into a tin can that looked as if it had come from the officers' mess. He took the paper and held it to the light coming in from the window. "I see only four holes."

Earlier that morning, Harriet had taken out her nail, then put it back in her satchel, unable to commit the lie to paper and certain that God Almighty was looking over her shoulder. She'd known it was Him by the way the sun slanted through the window.

Hunter set the paper on the table.

"Robert Smalls confirmed that the fifth bomb is across from the ferry," Harriet said. *Confirm* wasn't truthful, but it was close enough.

"Smalls? How does he know?" General Hunter asked.

Walter broke into a cough. The wiry scout placed a fist over his mouth and hacked until his narrow chest heaved. When Harriet reached behind to clap him on the back, he shook his head, unable to speak.

"Water?" she said.

Walter nodded vigorously. "Yes," he croaked.

The general pointed with his cigar to the pitcher atop the secretary. Harriet got up and poured a glass, which Walter downed in noisy gulps.

"Smalls said they done the same on the Stono," she said as she took her seat, thinking how best to phrase the information without lying outright. "They laid mines on either side a the ferry. He told me to watch for snags."

"You know what to look for, they plain as rice," Samuel added.

Hunter balanced his cigar across the tin can, took a pencil from his pocket, and placed a fifth mark near the ferry landing. "In a river that black?" he asked. "A man can't see to the bottom in five inches around here."

Samuel replied like he had a hand on the Bible. "Yes, sir. I'm sure. I done it once already."

General Hunter studied the map again. The room quieted, and someone opened and closed a door in the antechamber. Hunter nodded to himself. He pocketed the piece of paper and leaned back in his chair with his hands behind his head. His mouth twisted in an attempt at a smile. "Thank you. I'm sure my replacement will find the information useful."

Harriet's toes curled in her shoes, and her heart started thumping. She struggled to stay in her seat. The Rebs could refortify Fields Point any minute. The entrance to the Combahee would swing shut. If the Union didn't free people when it had the chance, what was its purpose? What did the abolitionists' fine words add up to? She pictured the last ship for the Promised Land sailing without them. Thousands left behind. When it came to morality, a woman could sometimes say things a man couldn't. Usually, she hoped Hunter would forget she was one, but now was the time to remind him.

"To everything, there is a season, General, and a time to every purpose under Heaven," she said. "A time to be born, a time to die." Harriet leaned forward. "This the time to do what you come

144

for, sir. What we all come for. This ain't the work of another man, General Hunter. The good Lord waiting on *you* to lead His chil'ren to freedom."

Hunter's jaw squared. "Lincoln appears to be waiting on someone else," the general muttered. But he took the map out of his pocket and looked at it again.

"No one but you believed in recruiting colored regiments til you went and done it, General Hunter," Harriet said. "You were the one man in America ready to give em a chance."

"You've got to treat men like men," Hunter said. "It's taken a year to get the 1st South Carolina close to a full complement, and the 2nd South Carolina has barely three hundred. We can't afford to lose a single soldier."

Harriet at last understood. Hunter had battled Congress, the War Department, and the president for his regiments. He couldn't bear to see them destroyed. "We can't afford not to lose em, sir. Your troops want to fight and die for something important—just like you," she said. "As you say, you got to treat men like men."

Hunter stared hard at her. Then he held the map to the light again. The old soldier took a deep breath.

"I'll consider what you've brought me." Hunter looked at Samuel and pointed a heavy finger. "If I decide to go forward, I'll want you on the lead vessel—where you can scout the torpedoes or be first to get your head blown off." He looked at Plowden. "You, too."

Walter had recovered his voice. "'Course, General. What bout M-M-Moses, sir?"

"What about her?" he said. "This is a military expedition, boys."

"Won't work without Moses, sir," Samuel said. His tone was respectful but definite. "The slaves gone be frightened. She knows best how to coax em."

"Once the t-t-tide turns, the river moves fast," Walter added. "Them Secesh reinforcements won't be far away. We ain't got much t-t-time to get everybody off."

"Who's everybody?" Hunter asked.

Walter and Samuel looked at Harriet.

General Hunter stared at her in puzzlement. "The plan is to recruit troops. Fill our regiments for an assault on Charleston."

"Men don't want to leave without their wives and chil'ren, sir," she said. "We gone get more recruits if we don't make em choose between family and freedom. And if we get all the planters' hands, rice fields won't pay. Secesh gone dry up."

Hunter picked up his cigar, which had gone out. He seemed not to notice and merely flicked cold ash into the tin can. "Thank you for coming by, men."

The three of them stood. Harriet leaned over for her satchel.

"No, Moses. Not you," Hunter said. He turned to her as Samuel and Walter left the room, closing the door behind them. "The space on the gunships is limited. What we need are soldiers, not civilians."

"Yes, sir. But it's bout impossible for a man to get on board without the woman standing next to him."

Hunter looked reluctant.

"With women and chil'ren, someone needs to let em know they gone be all right," Harriet continued. "The Secesh already filled their heads with every kind of nonsense. That you gone sell em to Cuba. That you gone break up their families. They got reason aplenty to figure any plan hatched by a white man is a trick. They need faces they trust."

"Aren't black soldiers enough?" Hunter said.

"Might be. Might not be," she said, recalling her sister Rachel, for whom the threat of being parted from her children served better than chains to keep her on the plantation. Convincing trapped and terrified people to make a leap of faith was never easy. A woman's voice—her voice—was calming in a way different from a man's.

Hunter stroked his dyed mustache, which had a rusty look that afternoon. "There'll be killing. No guarantee who comes back alive. Are you willing?"

"That depends," Harriet said.

"On what?"

Harriet sat back in her chair. She folded her hands in her lap. "On who you sending as commander."

Hunter looked at her quizzically. Then he shook his head in disbelief and burst into a laugh. She waited for him to explain, but he just laughed harder. He stood after a moment, still chuckling, and got another match to light his cigar.

"Harriet Tubman, you're some piece of work," he said as he retook his seat. He blew the smoke straight up. "Most days I ponder how a woman can do what you do, and then I recollect that only a woman would. You have a new job for me every other day and won't give up until you fix the whole damn world. Exactly who do you have in mind? Not that it's your decision."

"Colonel Montgomery."

Hunter raised his bushy eyebrows. "Not Higginson? Haven't you known him for years?"

Harriet nodded. "Yes, sir, I have. Colonel Higginson done as much for colored folk as anybody since John Brown."

"Then Higginson ought to have command. And he has seniority. So the question is, Moses"—and at this Hunter pointed at her with his cigar—"why are you standing in his way?"

Harriet hesitated. Hunter was right. The glory did belong to the 1st South Carolina Volunteers, the regiment Thomas Wentworth Higginson had drilled until they paraded like an armed ballet. Thomas had been one of John Brown's most ardent supporters, risking imprisonment for abetting Brown's insurrection. Leading colored troops into heroic action was Thomas's dearest wish, and a friend wouldn't rob him of that honor. But Montgomery prized fighting over drilling, and the Kansas Jayhawker's men showed more dash than discipline. While his prairie methods raised the hackles of New Englanders, they were exactly what was needed.

"This a bushwhacking operation, sir. Colonel Montgomery's the fightingest man we have. If he goes, I will."

Hunter looked displeased. "Are you saying you won't unless I give him the command?"

Harriet stared out the back window. In the distance, beyond the sandy alleys dividing the refugee camp, she spied men and women hoeing cotton in the hot sun. A child wearing only a slip-like shirt carried drinking pails on a yoke across his shoulders. Harriet thought of Kizzy under Pipkin's roof, a memory that pained her like a splinter burrowing deeper every day.

Harriet turned back to the general. "Yes, sir, that's right."

"Why?"

She nodded at the window. "Cause a them. The minute this operation gets botched, every slave on the Carolina coast gone be marched inland where we'll never see em again. We get only one try."

Hunter flicked fresh ash into the can. "Those Western fighters do have a certain grit. More dirt under their fingernails."

"A man told me afore the war that our grandbabies gone be free one day, but not us. I don't want to prove him right."

"Perhaps I will appoint Montgomery." Hunter pondered the ash can, and then he glanced up. "But I have my doubts about you, too, Moses."

Harriet drew back, puzzled. "Doubts?"

"I'm thinking it might be better if both you and Higginson stay back. What with your condition."

"I don't know what you're talking bout," she said, though she stiffened. She knew exactly what he was talking about.

"You've got that problem." Hunter tapped his forehead. "Don't think I don't know. I keep track. On a raid as chancy as this, every man must be ready for duty. Consider what might happen if you had a fit at the wrong moment. We can't take that risk."

Harriet's long fingers dug into the arms of the chair. For once, instead of feeling humiliated by her condition, all she could think about was what she'd done despite it. "You know how I got that, don't you?" she said. If Hunter insisted on bringing it up, he was going to hear the whole story. "That *problem?*"

Hunter shook his head. "No, but it doesn't—"

"I got it fighting a white man. When I was jest a sprout. The things that happened on that plantation would make your flesh creep. Would make your hair stand on end. My mama sent me to the store one day for some bicarb a soda for the Big House. An overseer from down the road came in hollering for a child who'd run inside, fearing for his life."

Harriet pushed up from her chair. "That man told me—'*Hold onto that nigger! Don't you let him get away! Help me tie him up.*' Well, I wasn't much older than the boy. Maybe twelve or thirteen." She held her hand at shoulder height to indicate someone small. "But I *felt* older. That child looked so pitiful and scared, dancing and ducking to avoid that overseer's bullwhip. That man, he was a bad one."

David Hunter stared up at her. "Harriet, you don't—"

She opened her arms wide, hands back, as if to shield someone behind her. "So I told him, '*No.*' I wouldn't do it. I blocked the door, and that child—he flew right around me, onto the porch, and down the steps. That overseer, he mad as a hornet! So he took up an iron weight next to the storekeeper's scale and chucked it at that boy. Hard as he could. The child got clean away, but that man, he dropped me like a tree. Broke my skull."

Harriet fell back into her seat, perfectly composed on the outside, though her hands shook slightly, and her tongue tasted of wire at the memory. "Montgomery needs men who gone fight with everything they got," she said. "You can count on me, sir. I done this before. I been there, bringing folks home to freedom past bloodhounds and patrollers. Plenty a times. And I'm one a the few in this whole country that can say that. So I ain't the one you got to worry about."

Hunter's face flushed. The scar on his neck turned liver colored. "Well, I do worry. I know your record on the Underground Railroad, but this is war. Are you ready to end up like Shields Green?"

Harriet blinked at the reference to John Brown's colored lieutenant. She had met Green only once, before the attack on Harper's Ferry. The Charleston native hadn't said much beyond, "I gone stick with de ole man" when someone questioned John Brown's military strategy. Newspapers later reported that Shields Green declined to say anything more when he stood under the noose a week after John Brown's more celebrated hanging.

"I been facing that possibility more'n a dozen years," Harriet said.

Hunter seemed almost angry. "You know they dug Green up?" he said with a scowl. "Dissected his body at a Virginia medical college? Think how they'd treat a woman."

Harriet lifted her chin. "Think how they treat women now, sir. If Shields Green could die with Brown, I can die with Montgomery."

Hunter studied her silently.

Harriet stared back.

"It ain't a choice, General Hunter," she said after a moment. "If someone stole your ma and pa, would you go back for em? They took your sister and sent her to some man to use however he want, wouldn't you do ever last thing you could to save her?"

Harriet rubbed the back of her scarred neck. As long as she could remember, she'd been both praised and hunted for sticking it out. Of course she was scared. Anyone would be. Thomas Wentworth Higginson once speculated that her old injury might have addled her brain. "Knocked the fear right out of you, thank the Lord," he'd said in his small office off the church entrance. "I enjoyed the danger of running guns to Brown," Higginson said. "But feminine sensibilities are different from masculine ones. Why, you're just a tiny thing, Harriet."

"So you saying I'm brave only cause the Lord hit me upside the head?" Harriet waved at the books on Thomas's shelves. "Jest last week you preached that girls should learn the alphabet. If they learn that alphabet, maybe they gone write books, too. Like men. That mean they got masculine sensibilities? I've had to fight my whole life. Can a woman stand up for herself only if her head is broken?"

General Hunter now stared at her much as Thomas had done. Maybe bravery was strange in a woman, but she didn't think so. White gentlemen tended to revere womenfolk who were limp-wristed and lily-livered. Black people didn't hold with that. They reserved their respect for those who fought back against a world trying to take down their families. A woman like that was a prize.

The old soldier sighed and reached for a match to relight his cigar. "Saxton returns next week," he said after a few puffs. "My authority will be at an end after that. So I can give you until then. I'll send orders for Montgomery and tell him you're to go along."

Relief washed over Harriet as if poured from a bucket. They had a plan. "Thank you, sir," she said. "Thank you."

"But keep Plowden and Heyward quiet," he said. "If Colonel Montgomery's troops learn they're readying for an assault nearby rather than on Florida, spies will get ahold of it, and you'll have guns instead of gators waiting for you on the Combahee. You can count on that."

"Yes, sir." *Dismiss me*, she thought. *Dismiss me*—she repeated silently, afraid he might change his mind. Her hand crept toward the satchel.

"And make sure you obey every goddamn order he gives you, like it or not."

"A course, sir," she said.

"No going off on your own," he lectured.

"Yes, General Hunter."

Hunter looked as though there were other warnings he wanted to lard on but couldn't think of any. "Dismissed," he finally said.

"Thank you, sir," Harriet said, and she reached swiftly for her bag.

"Careful, hear?" he called as she hurried from the room before he could think up another objection.

CHAPTER SIXTEEN

More slaves were born than died. Old [John] Pinchback would see to that himself . . . because it meant money for him. He chose the wife for every man on the place. No one had no say as to who he was going to get for a wife. All the wedding ceremony we had was Pinchback's finger pointing out who was whose wife.

James Green, Slave

WALTER STOOD WITH ARMS CROSSED TALKING to Samuel at the bottom of the porch outside. The men fell in step once Harriet descended the stairs and turned onto the street. The trio walked a block without speaking until they entered a busier thoroughfare where horse-drawn wagons coming from the port dominated the afternoon traffic.

Samuel looked straight ahead. "What the devil you up to, Moses?" His voice hummed with anger.

Walter walked on her other side as they navigated the pedestrian strip. "Robert Smalls never told me n-n-nothing bout going up the Cum'bee," he hissed.

Harriet nodded at a white-haired old man who stopped his wheelbarrow for them as he approached with a precarious load of rocks. "Thank you, Uncle," Harriet said as she sidled past—and took the opportunity to put Walter between herself and Samuel. It made her mad just looking at him, especially now that they were finished with Hunter.

The contraband tipped his hat and grinned. "I know'd it was you a mile off, Moses. Watch yo step now. Cain't have you gitting runned over."

"I surely will, Uncle."

The man clamped his hat back on his head and squinted suspiciously at Samuel and Walter as they passed.

"Getting runned over is right, Moses," Samuel said once they were out of earshot. "Except you barreling over us. You making up information we don't have, without letting us in on the plan."

"Smalls never said nothing to me," Walter said, repeating himself. "When did he tell you bout—"

"You gone get us killed," Samuel interrupted.

Harriet held the strap of her satchel tight across her breast to prevent the bag from knocking against her companions. She carried herself as calmly as if going to the market for a hair ribbon, but doubts troubled her. She felt certain she had done the right thing—yet what if she hadn't? The fifth torpedo must be where Robert Smalls suggested. It made sense.

"Hunter needed a push," she said defensively. "He understands you can't figure every angle fore a mission."

"Don't you sweetmouth us," Samuel said. "He was asking bout that fifth hole on the map. Wanted to be sure you knew what the heck you was talking about. And you don't."

"I did speak with Robert," she said.

"What he t-t-tell you?" Walter asked.

"He said they put torpedoes on either side a the Stono ferry. Figures they did the same here."

"So Smalls hasn't been up the Cum'bee. You was lying through your teeth," Samuel said.

Walter shook his head. "Thought you was. That's why I stalled. Figured you was mincing the truth pretty fine."

Samuel looked at Walter, ignoring Harriet. "That's why I said the torpedoes in the river are plain as rice. Dang it to heck. Cum'bee is more like mud soup."

"M-m-mud stew," Walter said. "With a helping a alligator on the side."

Amusement crept into their voices.

Harriet kept her eyes forward. They were almost to the dock. She wondered if they could get upriver again before the raid. General Hunter would now pass the initiative from the scouts to Colonel Montgomery, who might want them to lie low. Scouts usually stepped aside once troops came forward. It had surprised her when Walter and Samuel insisted she was still essential to the mission. And she'd been grateful. It would save her the trouble of stowing aboard.

"Thanks for sticking by me," she said. "And for telling Hunter I should come along."

Walter looked at Samuel. "Hear that? She saying she needed our help."

Samuel smiled and stroked his beard. "Oh, you know how she hates that."

"I don't mind help," she protested.

"Like cats don't mind getting wet," Samuel said.

As they approached the wharf, she wondered if her own cat had turned up at the kitchen on Port Royal. She hadn't seen Trouble in at least a day. At the head of the dock, a contraband in a straw hat ladled molasses-water into a cup for a line of customers. Someone had written "1¢" on a broken slate shingle. A buyer at the head of the line downed his drink and passed the cup to the next man.

"Want to wet your whistle?" Samuel asked Harriet and then Walter. "My nickel."

"Sure thing," Walter said. "I've been working up a thirst ever since Hunter say he gone p-p-put us on point."

Samuel's mouth curled into a smile as they stopped. The hollow of his neck shone with sweat. An urge to accept his offer stole over Harriet. She tasted the molasses—nectar in a bottle to a Southerner. She wondered if he had stashed a jug for his family along with the pork he left them. Anger immediately prickled her skin. She pinched her lips tight. As if all it took was a smile to make things right.

"No," Harriet said, and she drew her satchel closer. "I got business with the captain. I'll see y'all back in Beaufort."

"Suit yourself," Samuel said without missing a beat.

Harriet made her way down the wooden dock to the boat. She was thirsty from the hot day, but no libation was worth more time in Samuel Heyward's company. Though he had helped with Hunter, his notion of loyalty and hers could never be the same.

A raucous squall blew over Port Royal Sound during the crossing from Hilton Head, which caused Harriet to spend most of the voyage holding the hand of a contraband woman convinced they were all going to die. When she arrived at her boarding house well after dark, she opened the door to her room and lit the oil lamp expecting to see Trouble shedding black and tan fur on the clean mattress. Yet the scoundrel was nowhere to be found. Harriet searched under the bed and even carried a wooden crate up from the storage room to look on top the wardrobe in case the cat had decided to nap there while waiting for mice foolish enough to venture indoors.

Harriet finally gave up and took off her shoes to get ready for bed. She never tired of the luxury of a feather tick after all the floors on which she had slept. On impulse, just as she started to unbutton her collar, she went to the window and pushed up the sash. Propped on her elbows, she leaned into the muggy night. "Here, kitty, kitty," she called. "Trouble!"

The wind answered in the oaks, and a cicada soloist sawed a tinny melody somewhere nearby, but the only creature she spied was a mutt trotting down the street that glanced over its shoulder in the moonlight before continuing on its lonely way. Perhaps the cat had wandered under the house, she thought, into the arched breezeway that constituted the first floor of most Beaufort mansions, with their crinolines lifted above seasonal floodwaters.

"Trouble!" she sang out again.

Hearing no response, Harriet reached for the sash to close the window against mosquitoes but stopped when a tiny whimper sounded above the cicada. She held her breath. A small meow. Then silence.

"Trouble," she called. "Kitty cat!"

The weak meowing grew more insistent. Harriet scrutinized the street until the sound drew her attention to the oak tree that shaded the house by day. On a bough that looked a considerable jump from the windowsill, a pair of glowing eyes begged for rescue.

"Dang-blame cat," she said. "How did you get yourself over there?" She leaned out of the second-floor window as far as she could and held out her hands. "Come on. Come back, kitty." Settled deep into its haunches, Trouble answered only with a plaintive cry, so Harriet laced up her shoes once more.

When she descended the front steps of the sleeping house, she was relieved to see the lane deserted except for a dark form strolling up the opposite side of the street. An audience would make the indignity only more absurd. Harriet walked under the oak and gazed up. The limbs seemed higher than they had from the window. The topmost branches towered over the house. The cat peered down, watching her. Harriet circled the trunk looking for a place to begin. But although the corrugated bark offered ample handholds, no branch hung low enough to provide a foothold.

The cat cried even more pitifully. "Ain't no way up," she called. "You earned your name yet again. Trouble! That's what you are."

"Why ain't I surprised?" said a deep voice. "Harriet Tubman's got a cat named Trouble." Samuel Heyward stepped around the tree and into the moonlight that filtered through the branches. "I'd help, but I know it riles you."

Harriet doubted he could see the severity of her glare in the darkness, so she burned two holes into him without holding back. "This ain't about me. It's bout the cat."

"Maybe I can help the cat," he said.

Harriet didn't answer.

Samuel edged a rucksack off his broad shoulder and placed it on the ground. Harriet spotted a hammer and an adze as he rummaged inside. She wondered what he was building. The man had mysterious interests. Always packing something. A moment later, he pulled out a rope.

The waterman looped the line around the wide oak and tied it about his hips. With his feet against the trunk, he threw the loop high on the far side of the tree and, leaning back into the rope, walked his way up—leveraging the line higher every few paces—until he reached a branch to climb. With one hand and then the other, he pulled himself free and onto the limb. He grabbed awkwardly for the rope at the last moment, but it fell to the ground. Harriet thought she heard him mumble a cuss word as she snatched it up, untied the knot, and stood back to watch.

The sturdy tree didn't move with his weight until he reached the branch on which Trouble turned around to evaluate the progress of her rescuer. Samuel edged onto the limb on his belly, distributing his bulk along the branch. It sagged as he inched forward, though he stopped every foot or so to quiet the swaying.

He was too heavy, Harriet thought. She ought to be up there. The limb would support her, not him. "Samuel, come down," she called.

"Here, cat," he crooned high above her head. With one arm around the limb, Samuel reached out his other hand. "Come on, Trouble. Come on, stupid cat."

The animal watched him without moving. Samuel crept closer. "Kitty, kitty," he said.

A crack split the night. The end of the tree branch sagged toward the ground far below. The cat hissed angrily. Samuel froze. His head was lower than his feet.

Harriet stopped breathing. *Dear Lord, dear Lord,* she prayed. *Don't let that fool break his neck.* Her own head whirled at the downward tilt of the branch. "Come down," she called. "Dang cat ain't worth it!"

Samuel edged cautiously back toward the trunk. The limb leveled. He called down. "Find a rock. Throw it at her."

Harriet dropped to her knees in the dark and groped around until she found a couple of pebbles. She pitched one. It sailed below the branch. Trouble meowed but didn't move. Harriet cursed her aim. She studied the limb and threw the second rock harder, grazing the cat's rump. Trouble yelped and ran down the branch. Samuel snatched it under his arm and scooted backward into a seated position against the trunk. Gripping the animal against his chest, he climbed down the trunk until he finally got to the lowest limb. There he leaned over.

"You take it now," he said.

Harriet stretched as high as she could. Samuel let go. The cat dropped into her arms and then sprang away with a loud complaint at the rough handling. It dashed through the dark, up the stairs, and into the house.

"Damn cat," Samuel said.

"Infernal ingrate," she said with a grin.

"How do I get down?" he said.

"Should I throw up the rope?"

"No," he said. "I think I can make it."

Samuel slipped over the branch again. Hand by hand, he worked his weight toward the middle of the limb. He paused a safe distance from the trunk, then dropped a sickening fifteen feet to the ground. Harriet rushed to help him up, brushing the dirt from his shirt. He looked down at her, which reminded her of the man underneath the clothing.

She stepped back. "You okay?"

"Seem in one piece." He took an experimental step but quickly laid a hand on her shoulder. He inhaled sharply. "Think I twisted the ankle."

Harriet picked up his rucksack and wrapped an arm around his waist. "Lean on me," she said. "Let's make you a bandage for that."

They hobbled up the stairs of the house and down the dark hallway of the boarding house. "This way," she said with a whisper. "But quiet. My landlady has a tongue on her."

Harriet showed him into her room, where he dropped onto the bed. She took a clean rag from a basket, folded it into a long bandage, and removed his shoe and sock. The sprain had started to swell. She wrapped it tightly. "Lay back," she said and then got a blanket from her wardrobe. She rolled it into a pillow. "Put that foot up."

Samuel looked reluctant, but he reclined backward as instructed. "Don't want to put you out, Moses. I know you're mad at me."

"It ain't no bother. We don't want this to get worse." She doubled the pillow-roll and propped his ankle on top. "Stay here whilst I fetch up some ice."

Harriet took a cup from another shelf in the wardrobe and went outside. When she returned from the icehouse, she packed the chips around his ankle with a second rag. By morning, the swelling should be reduced or gone. She would sleep on the couch in the parlor.

"You stay here tonight," she said. She put her hands on his chest when he tried to sit up. "No walking. We need you right as rain. Can't take no chances with the raid coming."

"Where will you sleep?"

"Don't you worry none. I got a spot," she said. Harriet stood to get a shawl and walked to the side table to turn off the oil lamp.

"Stay a minute," Samuel said. "I wasn't just passing. I come here to talk to you."

Harriet held the knob of the lamp. She was glad he couldn't see her face. He's an injured man like any other, she reminded herself. "We ain't got nothing to talk about," she said.

"I need to say this," he said. "Please."

Something in his voice reached her. She turned around. Samuel had propped himself against the wall. The lamplight caught the tip of a broken oak leaf in his hair. She resisted the urge to remove it and instead sat on the edge of the bed. Harriet folded her hands over the shawl in her lap. "Say your piece," she said.

He waited a long moment, as if searching for words that didn't exist. "What Walter said, that's true," he said. "I have a wife. Should've told you. Mas'r sent her to my cabin years ago. She didn't know why—she was that young. Fourteen, maybe."

Trouble jumped to the bed. Harriet let the cat climb onto the shawl, glad to have something to hold.

"Lucy had no interest in me. And I had my eye on another gal. But that didn't matter. Heyward decided it was time for Lucy to breed, and I was the one. He'd bought me and my brother from a Virginia trader. Liked our size."

Harriet stroked the cat, which stood and turned around to find a more comfortable position. Samuel leaned forward. He pinched the wisp of the cat's tail. When the animal settled, Samuel fell against the wall again.

"I didn't do nothing when Lucy first came," he said. "But when I finally told her what Heyward wanted, she thought I was behind it. Got so mad, she threw a frying pan. Took a chunk out a the door." Samuel smiled. "Luce is known to speak her mind," he said, using what must be her nickname. He stared down at the cat on Harriet's lap as if looking at the past rather than the animal. He doled out the facts in a low voice.

"So we decided I'd sleep on the floor. Wouldn't tell no one," he said. "That worked for a spell. Then Heyward's driver told me that mas'r planned to sell Lucy to the next trader. Didn't want no woman who wasn't a breeder. Said a barren gal wasn't worth her grub. Mas'r Heyward, he had a new one in mind for me."

Samuel looked up. "I couldn't do that to Luce. So I told her what he said. We decided we'd best get to it." His voice roughened. "Think South Carolina is bad? In Cuba, they grind niggers up with the sugar. Never heard tell of anybody coming back."

Harriet studied his resolute, purposeful face. Despite the turned ankle, nothing about him was weak. His wide shoulders and long legs filled her bed.

"We didn't have no choice," Samuel said.

Harriet nodded. "I know."

"So we took up with each other," he said. "Now we have three boys. I told her I'd come back for em. And I will."

"You miss her?" Harriet asked.

"I miss my boys. Lucy and me, we get along alright, but she thick with her mama and sisters. Say she can't leave without em. I think she needs them more'n me."

Harriet gazed down at the sleeping cat and ruffled the fur behind its ears. She wondered what Lucy felt for Samuel, then and now. Perhaps she loved him. Or maybe she resented him. Harriet's own years in Maryland hadn't been lucky ones, but at least she and John had chosen one another. Turned out, some parts of hell were hotter than others. That wasn't something preachers talked much about, perhaps because each person's suffering was different and incomparable and designed just to torture them.

"Why is Walter mad at you, then?" she said, her gaze still trained on the cat. She recalled the yearning, conflicted look on Walter's face earlier that day.

Samuel gave a mirthless laugh. "Jest when you think you got a raw deal, you learn someone else got it worse," he said. "Mas'r Heyward gave me a woman to sire big youngins'. Walter, he's a runt. Never had nobody. His mas'r kept breeders for prime hands. Walter thinks I ought to be grateful."

Samuel leaned toward the cat again, but this time, he caught Harriet's sleeve instead of its tail. "And I did accept my lot," he said softly. "Until now."

Harriet glanced up. Their eyes met. She couldn't look away. Didn't want to look away.

"God made you, Harriet Tubman. So I expect He gone forgive me for being awed," Samuel said. "I never seen anything finer in all my years than that first meeting when you lit into Walter for splashing his oars near a Rebel picket."

Harriet leaned forward and picked the golden leaf from his dark curls. "That's what you remember? My hollering at Walter?" she scoffed.

"Made a better waterman a me," he said with a grin. Then his smile vanished. He reached for her hand. Samuel slipped his rough fingers between hers. "It changed me. I never knew there was this," he said. He withdrew his fingers and wrapped his hand around her slim wrist. "All this fire and glory in one woman."

It was as if the cuff of her blouse had vanished and her skin was bare. She felt the warmth of his palm as his hand slid up her sleeve, cupped her elbow, and came to rest on her bare neck, where the scars of childhood didn't rebel for once. A finger caressed her earlobe. Although his hand was calloused, he touched her tenderly. Samuel looked for reassurance in her eyes, and then he drew her down. She came toward him until their lips met like the halves of a locket closing on itself.

Samuel's tongue found hers. Eyes shut, Harriet sensed only the tremor in his lips and the irresistible pull of his hand on her neck. She felt his eager body through his clothing. She wanted him on top of her. Wanted to weave her legs with his. Nothing else mattered. Not even saving the world.

Harriet crushed her mouth against Samuel's and pushed away the cat. Trouble fell to the floor along with her shawl.

Chapter Seventeen

*I traveled all that day and night, up the river in the day and followed
the North Star that night. . . . I was hoping and praying all the time that
I could meet up with that Harriet Tubman woman. She's a colored
woman, they say, that comes down here next to us and gets a man and his
wife and takes them out and they don't get ketched, either.*

Thomas Cole, Slave

THE FAMILIAR *rat-a-tat* OF A WOODPECKER summoned Harriet from a profound sleep. The murmur of the town filled her ears like any other morning. Then she remembered. Wonder flooded her. She'd almost forgotten that being held felt as good as breathing. Harriet rolled over and put out her hand to touch him.

The sheet gaped. Only a few odd lumps in the feather tick, shaken smooth each morning, indicated that someone had lain beside her through the night. Harriet ran her hand over the depressions sculpted by his head, shoulder, and hip. A short strand of hair clung to the sheet. The room he had filled with his presence suddenly seemed hollow. She pressed her face into the mattress. Only a wisp of his scent remained. She twisted a handful of sheet and pushed herself up.

Voices argued somewhere in the boarding house. Harriet thought she heard the landlady say something about a broken dish, or perhaps a broken desk. Harriet swiveled toward the window. The sun's rays burned the empty sill, indicating that dawn had passed an hour earlier and not even the cat had stayed to greet her. Samuel had slunk out like a thief. Disappeared. Like John Tubman.

Harriet pushed back the covers and then realized that her drawers were somewhere in the bed. She felt around in the tangled linens, suddenly desperate to cover up, and found her pantaloons wedged at the bottom of the tick. She pulled them on, sprang from the bed, and jerked her dress from the nail, snagging the collar in her haste. Harriet buttoned the bodice to her chin, wrapped her hair tightly with a kerchief, pulled on her stockings, and tied her shoes. Still, she felt naked.

Then she spied the abandoned ankle wrap, swirled on the floor in front of the door, with loops and bends like those of the Combahee. Was the rag arranged in a pattern? Peering down, she thought it might be an "S." The young poet Louisa May had shown her a grammar school template years earlier when Harriet stayed with the Alcotts in Concord, shepherding a fugitive along the Underground Railroad. The letter "S" looked and sounded like a snake, the chatterbox had said as she pointed to the reptile twined around the curvy letter. Its red forked tongue darted at a bird that wasn't there.

"Snake," Harriet said scornfully, "snake in the grass."

But her heart ignored the criticism. Instead, she recalled the poem on the first robin of spring that Louisa May had recited for Harriet's frightened companion. "Welcome, welcome, little stranger," Harriet whispered as she picked up the rag. "Fear no harm, fear no danger."

Harriet tested the letter between her tongue and teeth. She smiled at the hiss. Samuel's name began with an S, she realized. He had left the cloth to say he would return. With a flush of lightheadedness, she recalled his chest and hips against her. His hands had found and unlocked every intimate part of her. They'd both been spellbound. But why hadn't he just woken her up to say he was leaving? He knew she couldn't read, as she'd admitted when he told them about his lessons with Miz Towne.

A flush of embarrassment swept Harriet as she recalled the times when even the youngest children opened their hymnals in northern churches while she just sat there holding her Bible as if it was a block of wood. Samuel could read. She was illiterate. He was also married and under her command. Harriet wadded up the rag and threw it onto the floor. She had her own life. Her own mission. That was all she needed. What had she been thinking? A fool, she was.

A rattle at the doorknob scattered her thoughts, and her frown vanished. Samuel must have stepped out to relieve himself. Or went to find something for breakfast. The man was always hungry. Harriet reached for the knob and flung open the door.

Two soldiers on the other side stepped back at the suddenness with which she appeared. The white officer in front had a sergeant's stripes and a Colt revolver at his waist. The taller man behind the first wore a musket over his shoulder.

"What is it?" she snapped.

The sergeant's chin jutted forward at her tone. He waved a paper with an official stamp, then shoved it in his breast pocket. "I'm Marshal Clyde Granville. Captain Louis Lambert orders you to army headquarters. That is, if you're Harriet Tubman, the gal what markets baked goods."

Now Harriet saw the guns. And white faces. Really saw them. She resisted the impulse to back up and stood taller instead. These men weren't her allies. She stuck out her hand. "That's me, and I want to see them orders," she said.

The marshal looked displeased but took out the piece of paper. Harriet accepted the document, unfolded it, and turned the blue masthead upright. She pretended to read, playing for time.

"What this about?" she said coolly, though she felt the start of sweat in her armpits. The forward cast of the officers' shoulders gave her a bad feeling. She irrationally wished she had made the bed, as if they might deduce what had gone on.

"I don't know what Captain Lambert wants, but I got a pair of handcuffs if you need further explanation," the man said. "I ain't got time for your guff."

"Course not, Marshal." She nodded at her satchel slung across the chair. "May I get my bag, sir?"

The man nodded at her meek request, though he took the precaution of placing her between himself and his partner as they marched down the steps of the boardinghouse and across town to the imposing Verdier House on Bay Street, where sentinels guarded the entrance to the confiscated residence that served as army headquarters on Port Royal.

Harriet took the empty seat shown to her outside the second-floor office of the adjutant general, flanked by the two soldiers. The handcuffs on the sergeant's belt were the same as those of a slave trader's. Had she been summoned to face justice for some arbitrary reason? Justice for blacks was usually short work.

Although the windows facing Port Royal Sound stood open, the breeze had not yet come up, and the air in the corridor was stale. Minutes passed. She hadn't had even a sip of water since waking. The experience with Samuel seemed a lifetime earlier. They'd slept little. Harriet's mouth felt dry and tasted like a tin spoon. Thirst, exhaustion, and dread vied for attention. Her nerves were stretched like catgut. She felt the trap close around her and shut her eyes to brace herself.

The room quieted and vanished. Everything went dark.

"Jest a nip," she whispered to a tall runaway as she handed him a jug of water. The man sat with a four-year-old on his lap, his shoulders tipped against the slanted eaves. "And don't let that baby spill none."

They had traveled over one hundred miles since leaving

Cambridge the week before. Stray beams of candlelight from cracks in the floorboards gleamed on the sweat-streaked faces of the runaways in the attic of a Delaware farmhouse. A woman with twin ten-year-olds, a married couple, and a teenager with a brand burned into his cheek all slumped in awkward postures on the rough planks. Only Harriet, the man, and the boy remained awake. She'd been thankful when the free colored woman opened the door of her home just as sunrise turned trees the color of ghosts.

"Patrollers posted rewards for your capture all over Baltimore and Wilmington," the last conductor had told her. "Don't stop for nothing, but don't get caught in daylight neither."

The isolated farmhouse wasn't Harriet's usual stop, but it was close to the border of Pennsylvania, where train tickets to Canada awaited them at the headquarters of the Anti-Slavery Society, and she had been told the family was friendly. It was Harriet's seventh trip bringing runaways north. She'd gone with the intent of rescuing Rachel, but Harriet had been unable to convince her.

The young father took the jug and gave a sip to his boy, whose solemn gaze was fixed on Harriet. Somewhere below, a door opened and closed. Harriet put her finger to her lips. Muffled voices suggested that the woman's husband had finally come home. The farmer had already left for market when the refugees arrived around daybreak. A thump and then a clank sounded, as if someone in the kitchen underneath had placed a plate and some other item—a tankard, or perhaps a metal spoon—on the table.

"Rice and collards?" a querulous male voice said. "How I sposed to keep up my strength if these vittles are all you feed me? Where's that rabbit from yesterday?"

"Runaways stopped by," the woman said. "I had to give em something." Another dull thump, followed by the shriek of a chair, indicated that the wife had placed another plate on the table and taken her own seat.

"Why my meat? We live close enough to the bone already,

woman. Couldn't you just give em a taste of sorghum fore sending them on their way?"

"They had chil'ren with em, Hank. Little ones. And they were with that Tubman woman. The one they call Moses. Can't move again til after midnight, she said."

"They still here?" He sounded surprised. "The Tubman woman? The one they offering a reward for?"

"So she say. Seemed in charge, though she ain't no bigger than a girl."

"Where you put em? The barn?"

"No. The gal said it ain't safe. I put em in the attic. Ain't heard a peep since."

Harriet didn't catch the next thing the husband said. He spoke quietly, though with greater intensity. The back of her neck tingled, and she leaned forward as his voice dropped.

"We ain't that hard up," the woman said. "Please, Hank."

The man replied in a low buzz, definite and commanding.

"They jest like us," the woman said.

The man's voice rose. Harriet caught the words "—*ain't* like us. They slaves."

A chair scraped the floor again. Harriet peered between her shoes, trying to see through the cracks in the boards, but all she could make out was a wobble in the light, as if someone had walked around the candlestick. The man's voice sounded from a different part of the room, and the front door creaked. It seemed he was saying goodbye.

Harriet looked at the runaway across from her. The man drew his child tighter. Sensing a change, the boy shrunk against his father's chest. "What is it, Pa?" he whispered. The child looked up when the man didn't answer and reached a hand to brush off dirt that had fallen from the rafters onto his father's nose. The pair appeared to have the same jumpy nerves. Neither had slept much.

"We got to go," Harriet said as she reached for her satchel, heavy with her pistol. She would never be able to hold off a determined posse, but the gun would motivate any runaway who panicked. The last bullet was for her. No patroller would ever take her alive.

An unquenchable resolve filled Harriet. She would get them out. She would entertain no other outcome. If it took every last drop of blood in her veins, this boy in this attic on this night would not grow up a slave. That was her mission. It made everything worthwhile. Running wasn't lonely if you took others with you.

"We got to get out ahead a the patrollers," she told the man.

A door opened. Harriet felt someone tap her foot. She wished she'd taken a drink before handing off the jug. Her mouth was truly parched. A loud buzzing started up, filling her head. Someone kicked her foot harder.

"Sit up, hear?" a faraway voice said. "What's wrong with you?"

The buzz in her head faded, as Harriet regained consciousness. She forced her eyes open in time to see Walter Plowden come out of the adjutant's office. The soldier shook her shoulder, but she saw past him to the scout. Walter gave her a meaningful look as a pair of guards escorted him down the hall. His face was grim, and the wire that held him together appeared to have been tightened, but he wasn't handcuffed. His eyes conveyed a warning as he passed her chair and headed for the staircase under escort.

The marshal prodded her again. "Okay, mammy. Captain Lambert's ready."

Harriet pushed to her feet. The day was hardly two hours old yet felt like an eternity.

The captain didn't look up at Harriet's entrance. She stood a long moment in front of his desk as he made notes on a pad and shifted documents from one pile to another. His motionless face was dispassionate. At last, he gave her his attention.

"Take a seat, Miz Tubman," Lambert said, and he indicated the straight-backed chair that faced his desk like the witness box in a courtroom. A swarthy man, he had a low forehead and deep eye sockets. His hair was plastered flat with pomade, in which the teeth of his comb had left deep grooves.

"Yes, Captain," she said and sat down.

"I understand you volunteer at the hospital. I hope my officers weren't rough." Lambert said mechanically, as if reciting army protocol about fair treatment of contraband.

"No, sir. They was gentlemen," she replied, as it was the only allowable answer and close enough.

"I asked you here because John Lilly over at the General Mercantile has reported some stolen supplies. You appreciate the seriousness."

Captain Lambert said the words without preliminaries, perhaps to test her. He looked at her without expression, which itself was an expression. Cold. Would she deflect or start making excuses?

"Yes, sir, I do appreciate that." Harriet looked into his eyes and allowed her shoulders to soften. Inside, she could hardly catch her wind, but he couldn't see that. "Men who steal from the Union, why, they the lowest of the low," she continued. "I told Mister Lilly that very thing when he asked bout the sack a sugar I tried to sell him yesterday."

Captain Lambert sat back. A faint flicker of his nostrils indicated surprise. His uncallused, well-groomed hands relaxed on the wooden armrests. "Mister Lilly shared his suspicions with you?"

"Yes, sir, he did. And I tell you, it tested my faith in mankind. Who would take food out a the mouths a black men and women struggling for freedom—or from the brave white men risking their lives to defend em?"

Lambert's steady gaze was appraising. Harriet sensed he might have been a banker or circuit judge before the war. Someone used to excuses. "Humans are morally frail, Miz Tubman. Most are prey to temptation." His voice hardened. "Can you tell me how you came in possession of these supplies?"

"I was in Hilton Head a few days ago, sir. I stopped by General Hunter's office to pay my respects."

Lambert's eyebrows drew together. He must wonder why she would have occasion to know Hunter. "I knew Colonel Higginson fore the war," Harriet said, "when he helped me get some a my kin to Canada. He introduced me to General Hunter. I help the general when he needs someone to talk to new contraband."

Lambert jotted a note on a paper in front of him. "So a contraband sold you these supplies?"

"No, sir. No how. It was Private Webster from the commissary. I chanced upon him that same afternoon. He stopped me coming out a the general's office and asked if I'd like to buy some sugar. I said yes, thinking I was low, but realized later I had too much. That's when I offered it up to John Lilly."

Lambert's blank expression was unsympathetic. He must be one of those officers who blamed blacks for the war that had split the alumni of West Point. Few men were like Hunter, Saxton, Higginson, and Montgomery, in the tiny abolitionist wing of the army. Draftees sometimes expressed contempt even more forcefully, like the New Yorkers liquored up on Cuban rum who had recently torched the cabins on the nearby Jenkins Plantation. Afterward, General Saxton sent Harriet to reassure the inhabitants that not all Yankee Buckra were evil. Captain Lambert needed someone to blame for the pilfering that was common when men had access to government stores, and John Lilly had given him a name. Hers.

The officer made another note. "Did Private Webster give you a receipt for the purchase?"

"No, sir. I thought he'd write it in his register. He usually does," she said.

Lambert looked up again. "Usually?"

"Yes, sir," she said. "That's how he keeps track a what I owe. I pay up at the end a the month."

"You have no receipt, then? Nothing to prove Private Webster sold you these supplies?"

"I give you my word, Captain. Anyone who knows me knows my word is good."

Lambert leaned forward. "The last contraband I spoke to said the same thing. Are you acquainted with Walter Plowden? Did you discuss your story with him?" His bland tone had turned accusatory.

"Yes, sir. I mean, I-I-I knows him." Harriet tripped over the words. She hadn't meant to agree with the second question. "But we didn't talk on this. I jest happened to see him at Mister Lilly's place. Plowden had extra supplies, too."

Lambert's features hardened. "You realize the penalty for defrauding the US government, Miz Tubman? You may think you've got some special status on account—"

"Sir—" Harriet started to say.

"On account of your activities before the war," he continued, "but it's best to admit your mistake right off. Things go easier that way. Five years hard labor is a long time."

Harriet sat as still as she could, hardly breathing. She didn't flinch or blink or shuffle her feet. "I'm telling you God's honest truth, Captain Lambert. I did not volunteer to come south, where I got a price on my head, jest to steal a sack a sugar."

Lambert picked up his pen again. "Well, we can't have contraband spreading stolen supplies about town. I'm holding you until General Rufus Saxton returns next week, when I can speak to him about court-martial proceedings. That may prompt your memory."

Harriet gripped her seat. Colonel Montgomery mustn't sail without her. For all his tenacity, Harriet trusted no man like she trusted herself. She had to be on that gunship. "Next week, sir? But you can't—"

"I can, and I shall." He signed the document before him. "This thievery ends right now." He reached for a bell on his desk to ring for the marshal. Before he could do so, the door opened. Lambert glanced over Harriet's shoulder. "Yes?"

"Captain Lambert, if you will—" a familiar voice began.

Harriet turned to see Colonel Thomas Wentworth Higginson. He gazed over her head.

"May I help you, Colonel?" the adjutant general asked.

Thomas entered the room until he stood alongside Harriet, and she breathed in the clean scent of lemon verbena. Shoulders back and chin lifted, he looked like a *Harper's Weekly* drawing of the gallant reformer he had been before the war. One hand rested lightly on the hilt of his sword. "I'm sorry to interrupt, Captain," he said, "but I happened to arrive just as a man who sells coffee near my camp passed by. Walter Plowden informed me of your conversation. Plowden is absolutely trustworthy. I vouch for him without hesitation."

Lambert's jaw tightened. "Thank you, Colonel. I'll take your testimony under advisement."

Thomas didn't move to withdraw. Instead, the former preacher remained as still as a statue. "You most certainly should, sir," he said. "I have grave doubts about the veracity of Private Webster's records and no doubt whatsoever about either Walter Plowden or Harriet Tubman."

Thomas laid his free hand on Harriet's shoulder. It felt like an anchor. "You may not be aware of Miz Tubman's prior record, sir," he continued, "but there is no more noble person in our forces. She freed nearly a hundred slaves before the war, at great personal risk. Miz Tubman would no more steal from the Union than a mother would rob her child of milk."

"Are you suggesting Private Webster is behind this?" Lambert said. "On the word of some coloreds?"

"I do not see what role color plays, Captain. Private Webster should be next on your list of people to interview." Thomas's tone was genteel, but there was no mistaking who was the superior officer.

Captain Lambert gazed down at his signature, then at the papers he had been arranging when Harriet entered the room. He moved the arrest warrant from one pile to the other and looked up.

"You may go now, Miz Tubman," Lambert said. "But do not go far. I'll need to interview you and Mister Plowden again for further details. I intend to get to the bottom of this."

"Yes, sir, Captain Lambert," she said and rose.

Thomas reached out to shake her hand. "It's good to see you again, Miz Tubman," he said, as if they had been casual acquaintances before the war, not fugitive co-conspirators who had plotted with John Brown. "Would you mind if I take that chair? Captain Lambert and I have matters to discuss."

"Yes, sir. Thank you, sir," she said and made her way to the door.

At the threshold, Harriet glanced over her shoulder. Lambert stared back with cold dislike, then slipped the signed warrant under the blotter on his desk for apparent safekeeping. The captain would be coming for her. Harriet realized it was only a matter of when. He'd been thwarted in front of a superior officer and wouldn't forget. Now it was personal.

The corridor outside the door was empty. Thomas must have dismissed the guards to spare Harriet's feelings and defend her honor—something that apparently required constant vigilance no matter her sacrifices. Even in Beaufort, she must watch her back. Harriet gripped the newel post at the top of the stairs and started down.

She wished she could be as loyal a friend as Thomas Wentworth Higginson, but she just didn't have that luxury.

CHAPTER EIGHTEEN

I would go along the picket line, and I could see the rebels on the opposite side of the river.. . . . Sometimes one or two would desert to us, saying, they "had no negroes to fight for." . . . I learned to handle a musket very well while in the regiment, and could shoot straight and often hit the target.

Susie King Taylor, Nurse, 1st South Carolina Volunteers

HARRIET SPOTTED WALTER WHEN HE STEPPED out of an alley a short distance from the Verdier House. His lips were pinched so tight they looked gray.

"What you tell him?" he asked.

"The truth. But I sure wish General Saxton was around," Harriet said.

Walter shook his head in disgust. "I can't tell if we safer with the Johnnies or the Union."

"We ain't safe anywhere," Harriet said, "but in one we're slaves, the other free."

Walter spat onto a dandelion growing between the paving stones as if to insult both sides personally. He changed the subject. "I got to get back to camp. What you gone do?"

Harriet considered her choices. The brush with Lambert changed everything. They must improve their odds. If they mapped the last torpedo and alerted at least one key person on every plantation, the plan would be more secure, even if Lambert arrested her. The thought was horrifying, but she must face it and do everything possible to become less indispensable. As to Samuel and his rude disappearance, the morning proved she needed no further complications. The war presented more than enough challenges.

Her stomach knotted and growled. "I'll come with you," she said, "so long as we stop by the cookhouse first. I need to eat." Harriet glanced around and lowered her voice. "After that, we gone find Montgomery—and head back up the Cum'bee."

Harriet shook the reins of a wagon from a stable owned by an enterprising contraband and urged her mule across a muddy rut in the road that flanked the parade ground at Camp Saxton. Walter had climbed down earlier. The tents of the 1st South Carolina stood in rows on one side of the parade ground while the tents of the 2nd South Carolina were arrayed on the other. The army had billeted its colored regiments four miles from town to avoid conflict with units from Connecticut, Rhode Island, Pennsylvania, and New York quartered closer to civilization. Some white draftees resented blacks in uniform and the equality it implied.

Camp Saxton overlooked the Beaufort River and, across its shimmering waters, the low wooded shoreline of Lady's Island. The mule pulled Harriet's wagon imperturbably through the military base despite the clamor of men shoeing horses, hammering structures, and practicing firearms. An instructor drilled his platoon in bayonet techniques. He apparently found much to criticize.

"Not like that! Double-quick!" the colored officer yelled at infantry soldiers abusing hay bales. Harriet stopped to watch as he waved the group of soldiers, faces streaming with sweat, back to their starting point on the parade ground. From there the men ran the length of the immense field with bulging knapsacks and fixed bayonets before spearing the inoffensive horse fodder. The officer waved them back again. "Faster! *Double-quick.* Goddammit! What it is bout them two words you don't understand?" he yelled as Harriet flicked the reins of her mule.

Her wagon finally rolled up to a large canvas tent in the middle of the camp. A tall man with sergeant's stripes brushed aside the flaps and stepped out. Dressed in the dark blue of the Volunteers, the colored officer carried a tablet. He paused to make a mark and then handed the pad to an orderly. His dignified carriage was unmistakable. Harriet was surprised to see Colonel Higginson's chief assistant on Colonel Montgomery's side of the camp. Sergeant Prince Rivers looked up as Harriet halted her rig and climbed down.

"Miz Tubman, how may I help you?" Rivers said with the formality and educated phrasing that had earned him a reputation as the proudest coachman in Beaufort prior to the war. Rivers had stolen books when still a slave and applied himself to reading despite the threat of whipping. He had been one of General Hunter's first recruits, back when Congress still wouldn't pay colored men. Rivers famously faced down a mob that had ripped the chevrons from his sleeve as he and General David Hunter passed through New York on their way to petition the War Department. Copperheads wouldn't abide black men carrying arms or courting heroism.

Harriet ignored the impatient set of Rivers's shoulders. She smiled across the rope that surrounded the colonel's quarters. "Afternoon, Sergeant. How you find yourself today?"

"I'm well, Miz Tubman," he said, but he declined to return the small talk. "What do you need?"

"I'm looking for Colonel Montgomery, sir."

Rivers read her face as if he knew exactly what she and every man in the camp had in the bank. Harriet wondered if he knew about her wider responsibilities. As provost marshal in charge of troop discipline, Prince Rivers must make it his business to chase down rumors.

The tall sergeant appeared to make a swift decision. "The Colonel is with someone at the moment, but you may belong in this meeting." Rivers lifted the rope to admit her, then held up a hand. He paced to the tent and peered through the flaps. "With your permission, sir. Harriet Tubman is here." He nodded to someone inside. "Yes, Colonel," Rivers said. He held open the canvas and motioned her forward.

Montgomery leaned over a map that spilled across a small camp table. As Harriet entered the tent, he put up a finger to signal patience, and then he reached for a pencil behind his ear. He placed the lead on some feature of the scroll.

"—the dikes, then," Montgomery said to the man standing next to him. "How easy is it to flood the fields?"

Samuel Heyward glanced up briefly, catching Harriet's look of surprise. He refocused his attention on the map. "The trunks are spaced regular along the river bank." Samuel traced the curves of the Combahee with his broad finger. "They made a cypress. The gates are heavy, but they got long handles. Two men can lift em."

"Does it take long?" Montgomery asked.

"No. But breaking em takes even less time. And they ain't easy to replace, sir, especially if you get em all. Then the tide comes in."

Montgomery nodded at the waterman's logic, just as if a white man had spoken. The commander's manner was perfectly natural. His good qualities registered in Harriet's brain at the same moment that she wondered if this was the first time Samuel had gone around her. She had no rank, but the colonel and every one of her scouts knew Hunter had placed her in charge.

"Salt water kills the new crop," Samuel explained.

Montgomery crossed his arms. His chestnut hair tumbled across his brow. "We'll need whatever rice they have stored. We have to feed those we can convince to join us."

"That's why we need to get word to a few folk that we coming, Colonel," Samuel said. "Make sure someone is pushing the hands toward the river. They afraid a the drivers. Got to persuade em quick. Grab the Buckras' stores, too."

Samuel finally looked at Harriet. A charge traveled across the room, and she felt like her drawers had disappeared once more. Colonel Montgomery followed his gaze.

"Moses, what do you think?" the Kansan said, as if she'd been standing there from the start.

But she hadn't. She'd walked in to find her subordinate hatching plans with their commander. Samuel had embraced her so fiercely the night before. Seeing him again, she felt his arms and wished she didn't. Harriet addressed herself to Montgomery. She couldn't look at Samuel for wanting to horsewhip him.

"I got a mission planned for tonight to do jest that—get word to a few a the slaves—with your permission, Colonel," she said, hoping neither man heard the wobble in her throat. "We need to get folk primed."

"Excellent." Montgomery gave a rare smile. It rusted over immediately, and he frowned. "Can you be sure they'll keep a secret?" he said. "We cannot afford a single slip. If word gets out, this mission is finished. We need the whole world to think we're headed to Florida again—not up the Combahee."

Samuel awkwardly cleared his throat, something Harriet hadn't heard him do before.

"I know a gal on the Heyward Plantation," he said. "She can rally the women, sir. And no man gone let himself be outrun by a gal."

The idea was brilliant, Harriet realized. A brave woman would shame reluctant men and give courage to mothers and girls. Samuel must be thinking of Lucy. That's why he had gone to Montgomery—to avoid talking with Harriet about putting his wife in charge. The conniver. The coward.

Yet he was correct. Slaves must decide in an instant whether to trust the Yankees or obey the tyrants who held guns to their backs. A respected woman could make all the difference. "Samuel's right," Harriet said without looking at him. "And I know a gal on the Lowndes Plantation. She's young, but she got grit."

"Can she keep quiet?" Montgomery said.

Harriet recalled Kizzy staring back wordlessly. The girl had shown courage in pulling Pipkin away from the window. The

experiences that must have followed would have fired her motivation to escape. Most people refused to think about problems they
couldn't remedy, but once they had hope, they couldn't think
about anything else. Harriet trusted Kizzy to keep a secret, especially if she got a whiff of freedom. Harriet prayed the Lord would
strengthen the girl to do more. He had made Harriet His servant
at a young age, too.

"Yes, sir. She gone keep quiet," Harriet said. "Samuel's brother
can help, too. He been sick, but folk will heed him."

"I want you to get word to them tonight, then," Montgomery
said. "We're taking advantage of the full moon two days from now.
These shallow waters are treacherous, and we need all the moonlight we can get."

Harriet cocked her head in Samuel's direction. "I'll take Heyward
here, along with Plowden and Simmons. We can't send anyone to
a plantation where they're known, so I'll assign em accordingly."

She turned at last to Samuel. He better not count on the night
before as anything special. It hadn't earned him a thing. No way
was she sending him to his wife. Would he think she was spiteful?
She didn't care, and she was boss. "You gone handle the boat,"
she said. "Plowden can meet up with your gal on the Heyward
Plantation."

Samuel ran a hand over his beard. "If that's how you want to
play it."

"I do. We'll meet up around four o'clock. You talk to the dock-
master bout a boat and bring that almanac a yours."

Montgomery rolled up his map. "All right, then, Mister
Heyward," he told Samuel. "I need a moment with Moses."

Harriet felt a warm glow. At least the Colonel appreciated her.
Samuel picked up his hat and left. Harriet noticed that he limped
only a little. The bandage had done its work.

Montgomery tapped the edge of the scrolled map on the table
to straighten it. He looked concerned. "You aren't going to get
caught, right? This isn't the time to get yourself killed."

"Absent from the body, present with the Lord," Harriet said.

He frowned. "That's not what I want to hear."

"No, sir. I won't get caught. Nobody knows how to fool patrollers like Harriet Tubman. I jest waltz right up to em. Asks em to dance."

"Well, don't do that this time," he said. "I don't want you or anyone else fouling this mission. Not with three hundred colored troops at stake. You get yourself and your scouts back here by tomorrow morning."

"Yes, sir. I will, sir," Harriet said, though she knew all she could promise was not to squeal if caught. She didn't know why she spoke so glibly—except that that troublesome man had knocked her world spinning.

She was glad that Samuel was gone when she exited the tent to study the encampment. An air of excitement pervaded the grounds, she noticed. The brisk movement gave an impression of hurriedness. Axes rang aggressively; harnesses jingled loudly; men half ran. Supplies accumulated in the center of the parade ground. A young black nurse Harriet knew rushed past with an armful of bandages. "Hey—" Harriet called, but Susie King Taylor just nodded and kept going. Harriet made a loop, pretending to look for a former hospital patient, though she had spotted him on her drive through the parade ground. An hour later she caught up with the cooper whose hand Doctor Durant had stitched when a faulty iron strap sprang loose from a cask. Swearing her to secrecy, the older man confided that they were preparing for a raid on Florida.

"We ain't got no orders yet. But de colonel sho gone make it hot for dem Johnnies." The Sea Islander tipped the heavy barrel on its side and slid his hands down the seams to check for imperfections. "Ki! Our cullud sojers make me so dern proud. I ready to quit the world all togedduh when I see dem marching with dey muskets."

"You headed to Florida, too?" she said.

The man shook his head. "Nope. I wit' the 1st South Carolina. Higginson's sojers. But I tell you, Moses, I'd give up gulu to go."

Harriet didn't believe that. Islanders parted as readily with their hogs as soldiers turned their backs on tobacco. "Even bacon?" she said with a smile.

"Down to de chitlins," he swore.

Like others she'd met on her walk, the cooper could give her no precise information about when the 2nd South Carolina might sail for Florida. His comments confirmed that he little suspected their target was much nearer. Busy with preparations, the man soon excused himself. By early afternoon, Harriet had seen eight supply wagons roll out of camp, headed for the Beaufort wharf.

She finally aimed her mule in the same direction. She needed ashes from the kitchen, a shawl, the older of her two dresses—the others having been lost during an emergency evacuation of Beaufort—and an hour alone to fortify her nerves against a long ride in a narrow dugout with Samuel Heyward. They had a job to do. She couldn't waste energy on anything else, especially a man she had welcomed into her bed like a blame fool.

Chapter Nineteen

In the middle of the door [of the jail] was a large staple with a rusty chain, like an ox-chain, for fastening the victim down.... We also found three pairs of stocks of various construction, two of which had smaller as well as larger holes, evidently for the feet of women or children.

Colonel Thomas Wentworth Higginson

THE AFTERNOON HEAT HAD DRIVEN EVERY dog into the shade and worn the edge off Harriet's anger by the time they gathered at the dock. The mission now crowded out all other thoughts, leaving her with a hard focus on what lay ahead. As she thought about each scout's assignment, she felt the same worry for each man—and the same painful awareness that she might be leading him to capture or death.

Upon arrival, she discovered that Samuel had cleated two trus-me-Gawds to the dock instead of one. The dugouts floated between two old ferryboats, now gunships, from which a toiling stream of soldiers came and went. Samuel suggested they split into two teams in order to travel up and back on a single tide.

He opened the farmer's almanac to the page that showed the phases of the moon and tides. Kneeling, he placed the open book across his broad knee and pointed to words that no one else could decipher. "The tide gone crest around midnight, and the moon set around three," Samuel said. "Sunrise is a couple hours after that, around low tide. We got twelve hours to get up and back fore daybreak."

"Can we make it?" Harriet asked.

"It gone be hard, but yes. Walter and I done it before. And the full moon helps. Tide moves faster when it's big."

"That means everybody got to do their job in under an hour," Harriet said.

She turned to Charles Simmons, who knew the river nearly as well as Samuel, having been a waterman on the same plantation. "Charles, you gone find Sadie at the Nichols place. After Samuel drops you there, he'll scout the torpedoes near the ferry," she said. "I don't want either a you anywhere near the Heyward Plantation."

She turned to Walter. "You gone take me to Lowndes, then row upriver to find Samuel's wife. After that, come on back for me fast as you can. We'll meet up with Samuel and Charles where the Cum'bee hits the Sound."

The men listened solemnly. No one said the obvious. Getting onto any plantation was perilous. Hurry heightened the danger. It was hard to say whose mission was chanciest. Walter had the farthest to row—all the way to the Heyward Plantation—but Lucy's cabin was close to the river, and Walter should be able to get in and out quickly. Harriet's target was closer, yet she had to walk farther and must contend with the worst overseer. Charles would infiltrate the Nichols Plantation, nearest to the Combahee's mouth, but he might have to search around for the midwife if she'd been called to attend a birth. Although Samuel should be relatively safe on the water, he must locate a bomb in the dark, which was no Sunday stroll either.

"What if I gets delayed?" Charles asked. He fingered the rabbit's foot around his neck.

"Don't," Samuel said. "We ain't waiting, and we ain't going back for you. We got one tide. Just one."

"That's right," Harriet said. She eyed each of the men in turn. "Y'all know this territory. We got a long way to go, but we been over it before, and we all coming home." Her tone was rough. "So don't let me down. Or I gone have your heads."

The afternoon sun beat on their faces as they rowed west toward the mainland. When night fell and the waxing moon rose, the dugouts lost sight of one another in the Coosaw River, a salty ribbon between the mainland and the Sea Islands. They met again as they crossed St. Helena Sound to enter the mouth of the Combahee when the tide turned. Just past the first Rebel post at Fields Point, Samuel raced ahead of Harriet and Walter on an oxbow bend where the river curved like the ring in a bull's nose. With their dark clothes and faces, Samuel and Charles vanished against the black water.

Walter and Harriet traveled on alone. He breathed heavily by the time they reached a short tributary that was the closest approach to the Lowndes Plantation. The moon was still high. It couldn't be much later than eleven o'clock.

"Careful," Walter whispered when he nosed the boat up to the landing. He leaned forward to touch her sleeve. She sensed the trembling of his hand. "You be careful, M-M-Moses."

Harriet nodded and stepped from the boat. She didn't wait for him to shove off. Eyes accustomed to the dim, she followed a path that ran below the dark mansion on the hill. No light shined from the windows of the overseer's house either. The sleeping slave quarters were equally quiet as she approached, and Harriet ran her hand along the back walls to stay within their protective lee until she came to the last two shacks.

Harriet crept around the corner and cautiously put her head into the black hole of Jacob's window to avoid alarming him or his pregnant wife. Mayline was the woman's name, Harriet reminded herself, listening for someone shifting on a pallet. Yet the cabin was quiet. Harriet stopped breathing to hear better. The profound silence was unbroken.

Her heart sank. The cabin was empty. She had counted on Jacob's help—at the very least to get a message to Kizzy. Just then,

Harriet heard the creak of the door to the last shack. She slid back behind Jacob's vacant cabin. A feathery tread approached on the gravel between the buildings. The person must be barefoot and couldn't weigh much.

Harriet peered around the side. A small form neared. The silhouette of a dress. The outline of braids swinging free. It was Kizzy. Harriet slid behind Jacob's cabin again.

She let out a hiss to avoid startling the girl. The footsteps stopped.

"Who dere?" came a whisper.

Harriet stepped around the corner. She put a finger to her mouth. Kizzy cocked her head but didn't speak. Harriet approached, took the girl by the hand, and led her behind Jacob's cabin. They slid down the wall and crouched close to the earth on their haunches.

The slave put her hand to Harriet's face, feeling the shape. Her clothing had a musty smell, as if the fabric had mildewed before it could dry fully. "What yo' name?" she asked.

Harriet waited as Kizzy satisfied her curiosity. Then she slipped an arm around the girl's shoulder. "Moses," she whispered.

"You was in Uncle Jacob's cabin," Kizzy said. "Fore Pipkin took 'im away."

"Took Jacob? Where?"

Kizzy pointed to the buildings beyond the cabins.

"The smokehouse?" Harriet said, wondering why Pipkin would send an ill man there.

"No, ma'am. De jail."

Harriet felt the young woman shudder. "Jail? Why?"

"Cause," Kizzy said in a whisper so faint and scared that Harriet felt she was dreaming, "Cause Jacob hit Pipkin."

"Lord help us." Harriet drew her closer. "Where's Jacob's wife?"

"She staying wit' my mama, cause a her baby coming. Didn't want to be alone." Kizzy leaned her head on Harriet's shoulder. "It's my fault, Moses, that Jacob got put away."

"How's that?"

"Uncle Jacob was feelin better. He come outside two nights ago to make his water, and seen Pipkin drag me by de hair." Kizzy ran a hand nervously down her braid. "I'd run back to Mama's."

"But why did Jacob hit Pipkin?"

"Uncle Jacob's head got take away. He asked Mistah Pipkin not to haul on me like dat, but Pipkin, he yanked my hair harder, and I tripped. Tol' me stop being clumsy. Kicked me. Dat when Jacob took a swing. It was me dat brought on de trouble." The girl again smoothed her braid, as it trying to put herself back to rights.

"No. It was Pipkin, not you."

Kizzy's head sagged. She didn't speak.

Harriet had a sick feeling and put a hand to the girl's face. Tears wetted Harriet's fingertips, and she brushed them away. "Listen. Nothing that man has ever done can make *you* bad," she said. "You the same good girl you always was. A slaver can take every last thing 'cept the most important thing you own."

A twig snapped in a nearby tree, and Harriet thought she heard the squeak of a possum. Kizzy still didn't say anything, but she raised her chin.

"Your spirit," Harriet continued sternly. "Who you are. That he can *never* have."

Kizzy finally nodded. "Yes, ma'am."

"So why you out here tonight?" Harriet asked.

The girl reached into the pocket of her dress and drew out a tin mug. "Pipkin, he sleep like a log mostly. I snuck out to get Uncle Jacob a drink."

"I'll go with you," Harriet said. "After that, I need you to do something."

Kizzy cocked her head. "What dat, ma'am?"

"Day after tomorrow, I'm coming back with the Yankees." Harriet felt the girl startle. She gripped Kizzy's knee. "They gone get y'all out a here. Take you to freedom."

The girl drew a deep breath, yet when she spoke her voice was tight. "Everybody get dey freedom? My mama and brudduhs, too?"

"Uh-huh. But we need help. We need someone that can tell folks when the moment's right that we coming for em—and to step lively. Think you can do that? Make em believe you?"

Kizzy pushed her braids back and squared her shoulders. "Yes, ma'am. I can, for true."

"Then you got to lead em. But nobody can get wind ahead a time. Not your mama, not your brothers, nobody. Anyone you tell might tell somebody else. That's how secrets fall apart."

"Don't you worry, ma'am," Kizzy said. "I won't tell a soul til de time come. But how I gone know?"

"I'll be on the Yankee gunship," Harriet said. "A big old boat with flags and colored soldiers. Can't miss us. We'll give a toot on our steam whistle. Then you got to holler to the treetops that the Yankees is coming to save y'all. Everybody got to hightail that very minute."

"Morning or night?"

"Sunup," Harriet said.

"Dayclean?" Kizzy said.

Harriet nodded, and the girl sprang to her feet with the impatience of youth.

Harriet stood. "But not for another day or two."

"Yes, ma'am. I heard you. I got to get Uncle Jacob his watuh now." Kizzy took Harriet's hand this time and led her silently past the last cabin. A windowless building squatted only a few yards beyond the smokehouse. The girl lifted the iron bar that locked the jail from the outside. Its hinges groaned. When Kizzy closed the door behind them, everything went black.

The stink of shit and sweat assaulted Harriet's nostrils. The air was thick and close. She recognized the splash of water being dipped from a barrel. Kizzy must be filling her mug. A rustle in a distant corner sounded like the scratch of a rat, though Harriet couldn't see anything. The dark had extinguished her vision. She could tell her eyes were open only because of the dry air on them—and she blinked to be sure.

Kizzy took Harriet's hand again. The girl must know the layout.

"Dis way, Moses. Listen for breathin'," Kizzy said as they walked forward.

Harriet strained her ears. A moment later, she heard a low sigh as they made their way cautiously across the chamber. Then the child dropped Harriet's hand and crouched down.

"Uncle Jacob," she said. "It me, Kizzy."

Harriet knelt beside the girl and put out her hands. Flesh. She felt flesh. A man's bare limb took shape under her hand, though Harriet couldn't tell if it was an arm or leg. The body was neither up nor down but instead angled sideways. She explored his form tentatively, unable to make out his position until she came to a shoulder suspended strangely. He seemed trussed in a harness of leather and iron, unable to stand or sit. The strain on his joints and muscles must be agonizing.

"Jacob," Harriet whispered. "I'm here, too. Moses."

"Help—" the man murmured, breathless. "Ah!" he exclaimed in pain when she tried to shift a strap that seemed to be cutting him.

"Water. Jest water," he said.

Samuel's face reared in Harriet's mind. Seeing this would torture him. She whispered to Kizzy in the dark, "What they got him in?"

"Pipkin call it de Teacher."

The girl made some kind of forward motion in the dark. Her youthful voice was fresh and encouraging. "Pipkin gone let you out tomorrow, Uncle Jacob. First ting. But I got you watuh for now."

Harriet wondered if the girl actually knew Pipkin's mind or was just keeping up Jacob's spirits. Her thoughts raced as she heard an animal-like slurp. Getting Jacob out during the raid might prove impossible. The quarters weren't close to the landing. Troops wouldn't have time to come looking. But at least she knew where he was. That might help.

An awful creak filled the dark room as the prison door suddenly swung open. Harriet snatched the bag from her shoulder, yanked out the Colt revolver, and whirled around to meet the intruder.

Chapter Twenty

I had a brother, Jim, who was sold to dress the young Missus for her wedding. The tree is still standing what I sat under to watch them sell Jim. I sat there and cried and cried, especially when they put the chains on him and carried him off. And I never felt so lonesome in my whole life.

Ben Johnson, Slave

KIZZY SEIZED HARRIET'S FREE HAND AS they faced the door together. Harriet hid the gun behind her skirt. A shaft of moonlight betrayed their location, lighting a path straight to them.

"Girl? You there, girl?"

Kizzy broke away. She ran toward the opening. Her toe caught on something, and she tripped.

A bent outline grabbed the child by the arm. "What you doing here?" It was a woman's voice, low and fearful. "You want to git us all kilt?"

"No, Mama. I leaving now," Kizzy said.

Worse than being spotted by a stranger was being trapped behind a bolted door. Harriet shoved her pistol back into the satchel and walked into the light. The landscape outside looked like noontime compared with the pitch-dark of the chamber.

The woman backed up. "Who dat?"

"I'm running from the Heyward place," Harriet said. "Thought Jacob could help me. Guess not."

191

"Keep running," the crippled woman said.

"Let's go home, Mama," Kizzy said as she took her mother's arm.

Harriet followed. When they reached the family shack, Kizzy allowed her mother to go ahead. Harriet reached for the girl's hand. "You done good to give Jacob water," she whispered. "But listen to your mama. Don't take no more risks. You can help most by staying alive."

"Yes, ma'am," Kizzy said.

"Pipkin really say he letting Jacob out tomorrow?" Harriet asked.

"Yes'm. Dey short a hands on de rice trunks. Fore he conked out, Pipkin say he calc'lated Jacob learnt his lesson."

Harriet's stomach revolted at the thought of Kizzy lying beside the overseer, and she fought the urge to take the girl back to Port Royal. Both Kizzy and Jacob must await the gunships. On impulse, Harriet reached under her collar and drew out Septima's shell necklace. She pressed it into Kizzy's hand. "This is to remind you a me."

Kizzy clutched the necklace tightly. "But you be back, right?"

"You can count on me like the sun coming up," Harriet said, and she slipped away as Kizzy followed her mother up the stairs. It was hard to tell how much time had passed. It must be short of an hour. Walter would be headed downriver.

She retraced her steps as quickly as she dared in the dim. The moon had sunk to just above the treetops. Once past the mansion, Harriet sprinted the final quarter-mile. Her breath came in gulps by the time she reached the rice trunk that held back the water of the tributary.

Harriet grabbed a handful of grass and climbed onto the high rice trunk. The tributary seemed soupy. Harriet threw the grass onto the water. The strands barely moved in the moonlight. The lazy inlet had gone slack. It couldn't be much past one in the morning. Walter would return soon. Samuel must have already rowed past to pick up Charles downriver. They would be proceeding toward the Sound, as ordered. They had but four hours before the sky lightened, after which the pickets at Field's Point and Tar Bluff would spot anyone on the river.

Time passed. Harriet's eyelids fluttered. She stood up on the wooden gate and pinched her arms to stay focused, drawing deep, calming breaths. She mustn't have a fit. Had it been ten minutes since she'd arrived at the tributary? Twenty? They risked being caught in daylight if they didn't leave immediately.

Harriet glanced over her shoulder toward the Lowndes Plantation. It remained quiet. When she gazed again at the water, she no longer saw the strands of grass on the smooth surface. She climbed off the trunk, caught up a stick, and pitched it as far as she could, past the eddy at the tributary's edge. The stick drifted downstream. The tide was turning.

Where was Walter? Harriet again looked over her shoulder. Where could she hide if he failed to appear? Low-lying rice fields offered no cover. She considered running back to the plantation or taking her chances in the forest behind. She peered anxiously at the river.

A whippoorwill announced the start of the day, though the sun still slept in the sea. The bird sang again. Harriet puckered her lips and trilled back. A boat came into view. Charles Simmons stood and threw Harriet a line. She caught the rope and tugged the balky dugout closer.

"Where's Walter?" she whispered. "What you two doing here?"

"Samuel and I was waiting for you and him to pass," Charles said in a low voice. "When you didn't show, Samuel decided we best come back for you."

"You was supposed to head for the Sound," she said.

Samuel's voice was low but distinct. "Change a plan," he said.

"You find the last torpedo?" she asked.

"Yes'm," Samuel said. "But this ain't no time for a meeting bout it."

Charles reached up. The tide was high enough that Harriet took his hand easily and jumped down into the dugout. The next instant, Samuel dug his oars into the water and swept them away. Harriet drew her shawl closer with shaking hands—thankful to hear about the torpedo but upset to learn about Walter. She sat in the deepest part of the craft, hugged her knees, and pushed the horrifying possibilities from her mind. The patrollers. The dogs. The Rebel pickets. She must believe he would be all right. They'd had narrow escapes before. *Lord a mercy, watch over him,* she prayed.

Samuel rowed with powerful, silent sweeps. Only his breath sounded above the rustle of the wind. The craft shot eastward toward the Sound as the tide picked up speed. His arms bunched and stretched like rods on a locomotive. Harriet heard a dog bark as they raced past the Nichols Plantation, and a rooster sounded on the other side of the river five or six miles later. Samuel shook his head without wasting a breath when she offered him a canteen, so she put the water to his lips, and he drank without breaking rhythm. When Charles leaned forward to switch places, Samuel again refused to stop.

The sky gradually turned a deep gray, and the bright stars dimmed. A gong sounded on some faraway plantation. It grew light enough for Harriet to glimpse slaves moving down a causeway toward the river, which meant the dugout was visible, too. She couldn't imagine how they would escape without being spotted.

The sun peeped above the horizon as they neared Tar Bluff. Harriet spotted the dirt breastworks from half a mile away. A bright ray tipped the blade of a bayonet poking above the wall, and she waited for the Secesh holding the musket to look over the side as they approached. A lump rose in her throat, but Samuel rowed ever more quietly, and the bayonet didn't move. Soon the river carried them past the picket station and into an oxbow turn where they couldn't be seen. Harriet let out the breath she didn't realize she'd been holding.

The river continued to ebb, though more slowly. Samuel was tiring as well. Sweat poured down his haggard face. As the river widened toward the sea, Fields Point, at last, appeared on a high

bluff a hundred yards or more to their left. Harriet saw no bayonets, and the big cannons were still missing. The Secesh hadn't
yet refortified the river. Luck hadn't abandoned them. They were
almost to the Sound. *Praise God.*

A gray Confederate kepi hat suddenly appeared above the
earthen fortification. Then another, and a tall guard peered over
the wall. Harriet saw a white face looking down. The unmistakable cock of a shotgun traveled over the water. "Halt! Who goes
there?" someone yelled.

Harriet slipped down in the dugout to make her body as small
as possible. She pressed against the floor. The faraway promontory
suddenly seemed right on top of them.

Another man called out. "Runaways!"

"Niggers! Halt, or I'll shoot," a voice cried.

The speed of the dugout increased. Harriet turned her head
away in the trus-me-Gawd. She closed her eyes. Didn't want to see.
It was hard to believe that He wanted her home so soon. *Please,
Lord. Not now, Lord.*

A shotgun boomed.

Charles lunged atop her, covering her body. The rabbit foot
around his neck struck her cheek. A crash in the side of the dugout let her know they had been hit. The boat veered sideways, and
the oars splashed sloppily. What had happened? Harriet pushed
against Charles's chest, all muscle and bone, but he pinned her.
The water underneath didn't hum as fast as before. Other shots
rang out, though more distantly, and the riverbank went quiet. A
seagull cried overhead.

Charles released her. He and Harriet sat up together. The dugout had entered the wide estuary into which the Combahee and
other rivers emptied on their way to the Atlantic. Samuel still
rowed, but his hat was gone. Shiny liquid coursed down his face.
He rowed with his eyes shut tight against the blood. Fragments of
wood clung to his coat. Buckshot had hit the gunwale right past
the oarlock and sent splinters flying.

Harriet dug her nails into her shoulder seam without thinking and tore the sleeve off her dress. The gingham ripped raggedly, exposing her shoulder to the stiff breeze. Charles shifted without a word to allow Harriet to get around him in the boat.

"Samuel," she said. "We cleared the Point. They behind us now. Stop."

The waterman slumped forward with his eyes closed. He rested his powerful forearms on his knees, oars dripping water into the sea. His hands trembled.

"I gone look at your forehead," she told him. Harriet blotted blood from his brow. A gash near the crown bled profusely, though she saw it was a surface wound, thank Jesus. A buckshot pellet had grazed his scalp. She tied the cotton around the laceration. The faded fabric blossomed bright red.

"You need to lie down," she told him. She took Samuel's hands and guided him into the middle of the boat as she scooted back. He stayed low so as not to upset the balance of the narrow craft. Charles climbed carefully around them and took up the oars.

Samuel lay on his back, knees bent. Harriet held his head in her lap, thankful that he was alive. She picked chips of wood from his coat and face.

Harriet recalled her mother doing something similar years before, the day Harriet was injured. She had been harvesting flax that morning, and dirt, broken seeds, and bits of fiber had turned her hair into a bush. Like any young girl, Harriet had been embarrassed about her appearance, so before entering the village store, she'd hid her filthy mane under a thick scarf tied low on her brow. That vanity saved her life. When the overseer told Harriet to seize the runaway boy, she saw him grab the iron weight the second before he threw it. The bulky scarf mitigated the blow to her head, but its strands had been driven into her skull. Harriet regained consciousness hours later to see Mama leaning over her in the cabin's dim light, teasing thread from flesh and bone.

Harriet now removed splinters from Samuel's hair and collar. The weight of his head, and the rise and fall of his chest, were all she asked of God. Tired as she was, she didn't dare close her eyes for fear of blacking out. Instead, she chanted under her breath, *I believe in God, the Father Almighty, maker of Heaven and Earth, and in Jesus Christ, His only son, our Lord.* The tang of iron was in her mouth. It seemed she would taste it to the end of her days.

The tide guided them toward Morgan's Island on the far side of the Sound, where they stopped to rest. All three of them slept for several hours on the warm sand of the deserted shore. When the afternoon was nearly spent, Charles rowed them up to the Beaufort wharf. He threw a line to a contraband cleaning fish on the dock. The man cleated their boat and gave his hand to Samuel, who clambered out of the dugout with Charles pushing from behind. Samuel staggered onto the floating dock as if his ankle troubled him anew.

"Montgomery," he muttered. "Got to see—"

"We got to clean you up first," Harriet said. "You don't need stitches, but you do need soap."

She took one arm while Charles supported the other. Harriet thought about the flies at the contraband hospital and the stench of Pipkin's jail. The latter information she must keep from Samuel for now. He'd had enough of a shock, and needed somewhere clean to lie down.

"We going to my place," she told him. "Or you ain't gone make it to Montgomery."

CHAPTER TWENTY-ONE

Thus passed my child.. . . I looked for the approach of another gang in which my wife was also loaded with chains. My eye soon caught her precious face, but, gracious heavens, that glance of agony may God spare me from ever again enduring! . . . I went with her for about four miles hand in hand, but . . . at last we were obliged to part.

Henry Box Brown, Slave

HARRIET CARRIED THE MUG OF HOT broth like a chalice, grateful for the stroke of good luck. The street vendor next to the arsenal had sold her the cloudy dregs of the soup he'd made in his steam digester from bone, marrow, and flank. Harriet knew that the last briny cup was the best, concentrated with the properties needed to rebuild blood. She walked it down the dark hallway of the boarding house. Samuel had fallen into a deep sleep after she and Charles laid him out, but she must rouse him soon. He needed fluids. Needed strength.

A door opened at the far end of the corridor, where the landlady lived. A reedy voice wafted through the opening even before the face appeared. Harriet felt her luck dissipate. Ruby Savan took every opportunity to express disapproval of the black tenants the army had forced her to accept.

"Harriet? That you?" Ruby stepped into the hall with a tatty shawl around her stooped shoulders and a nightcap tied under her chin. She carried a candle. "I heard a man's voice a while ago. You got a man in yo' room?"

Hot liquid from the brimming mug escaped through Harriet's fingers as she halted and splashed onto her shoes. "Evening, Miz Savan. A patient's resting there. You know I'm a nurse at the contraband hospital, ma'am."

"Why ain't he in the hospital?"

"Hospital's overcrowded. Colonel Montgomery needs this man to get better real soon."

Miz Savan pulled her wrap closer with a crabbed fist. A ringlet like the spring of a cracked pocket watch escaped her nightcap. "Then send him to the colored soldiers' hospital."

"I can't do that, ma'am," she said. "This man special."

"Special." Ruby's lips puckered into a prune around the word. "You nigger gals always got somebody special. I won't have it. I run a decent establishment. General Saxton may push colored officers off on me, but I ain't got to tolerate harlots, too."

Harriet ground her teeth. Slavers used black women as whores and then denounced them as loose. She felt like dashing the broth in the landlady's dried-up face, but Samuel needed every bit of the soup, and Harriet had nowhere else to live. Not in a town overrun with soldiers and refugees. She forced a polite smile. "I got a job to do, and you need to let me do it. I mean no disrespect, Miz Savan, but this is army business," she said as she brushed past the landlady and opened the bedroom door with her foot. "Thank you," she called as she bumped the door closed with her bottom.

Harriet leaned against the frame. After a long moment, the footsteps in the hallway shuffled toward the kitchen. Harriet silently nudged the iron rat-tail lock over the doorjamb with one hand and turned around.

Samuel slept on his side with an arm across his face like some mythical hero who'd thrown his last thunderbolt. The new bandage across his crown had only a small bloodstain, dry already, and his breathing was shallow and even. Harriet crossed the room, sat down next to him, and pushed off her shoes. To avoid kicking the mug over, she felt under the bed for the coiled rope she kept for going out the window in an emergency and set the cup against it.

"Samuel," she whispered. He slept without stirring.

She shook him again. "Samuel. You got to wake up." He didn't respond, as if dosed with morphine.

She patted his face. Concussions could turn into comas. "Samuel, come on. Wake up."

He moaned, and he then rolled onto his back. His arm lolled outward, and his eyelashes fluttered. Harriet retrieved the cup and slid under him, holding him against her bosom. She cautiously held up the mug. "Drink this," she said.

Samuel hoisted himself groggily. He took the broth, drank until it was finished, and handed back the cup. Harriet ran her tongue around the rim to catch the last drops of liquid and laid the vessel on the far side of the bed. Samuel turned over and nestled into her lap as if he'd forgotten where he was. He fell back to sleep.

Harriet studied the side of his lax face. A tiny white scar she hadn't noticed glimmered near his hairline. She touched the marred skin, then cupped the back of his head to avoid the bandage over the crown. Samuel had surprised her. He'd rowed upriver for her when she didn't appear. Not every man thought of himself first; not every man stomped on your heart. In all the years on the road, she'd made others safe, but this was the first time someone had done the same in return. Samuel had braved bullets for her.

Harriet tucked away the strange and precious memory, mentally placing it alongside Linah's button. She would always have it.

The quietness of the house deepened. Harriet thought about Walter and hoped he'd found a place to hide. Her eyelids felt so heavy that she could hardly keep them open, though, so she nudged Samuel aside and lay down next to him in her clothes. She needed rest.

Harriet didn't know what woke her a while later. A warm lump pressed against the back of her thigh. She reached around to shove away the cat, but a femur, not a feline, met her hand. Harriet's eyes opened. She rolled over to look at Samuel.

Moonlight from the window glimmered in his eyes. Samuel's expression indicated he had been waiting for her to wake up. He traced her mouth with his finger. "Hattie," he whispered. "You here."

Harriet's lips parted. Mama called her Hattie, and she found she liked the sound of it in Samuel's voice.

He leaned forward and, without asking, kissed her once. "Thank you," he said. As he shifted back, he grimaced with pain and closed his eyes briefly. Then, not lifting his head this time, he reached out for her.

But Harriet inched away.

Samuel breathed unevenly. He caught her hand without moving his head. "Where you going?"

"You're injured," she said. "You need rest."

He brought her palm to his lips and kissed it softly. "I need you."

Harriet curled her fist to shut him out.

Samuel sighed and let go. He touched the bandage on his crown. "You some nurse." He rested his palm on the mattress and extended his fingers toward her, just short of her breast. An inch closer and they would touch again.

They stared at one another. Harriet said nothing. Her heart drummed. His skin smelled of warm, yeasty bread and salty seawater. She dug her nails into her fist to stop herself from digging them into his back and pulling him toward her.

"When this is over," he said at last.

"We don't want that cut reopening," Harriet said to let him know she wished it were otherwise.

"I know."

"You gone have a heck of a scar at least. Something to brag on."

"Oh, I don't brag," Samuel said. "Never have. Not once. Not

even that time I beat the pants off Mas'r Nichols's fastest nigger in his new batteau."

Harriet broke into a smile and laid a finger across his mouth. His lower lip had the softness of butter. He opened his mouth to taste her finger, but she pulled back and laid her hand over his on the mattress. "Don't say that word," she said.

His brow wrinkled, which caused him to wince. He took a pained breath. "Nigger?"

She nodded. "I never want to hear that word again."

"Wish I could make that happen, sugar. But I promise you won't hear it from me." He touched her chin, then he gently tapped the tooth next to the missing one. "How you get your own badge a honor?"

Harriet's lips pinched together. The gap wasn't pretty. "We was on the trail in Delaware," she said. "I had such a bad toothache, I couldn't see straight. Patrollers were closing in, so I knocked it out with my pistol."

Samuel smiled, letting her know the defect didn't matter. "We'd win in a week if every soldier was a Harriet Tubman."

She edged closer, still keeping her torso several inches from his. Harriet tilted her head to see into his eyes. "We gone win. I don't know when—but I do know it."

"How?"

"The Lord told me."

Samuel stroked her back. Harriet couldn't tell if he believed her or not. That, too, didn't matter. God's will be done. Another thing she knew was that winning would not restore broken bodies and minds. And the South would reject the lesson. A man who loses his legs for a cause won't hear it wasn't worth fighting for. Northerners had no monopoly on righteousness either—though it would become easy for them to think so.

She settled into the mattress, bathing in Samuel's protective presence. His hand on her back felt like heaven. "That don't mean we won't have to scrape tooth and nail to get there," she said.

He snorted. "Let's hope Montgomery's up to it."

She recalled the day before, when Samuel had sought out their commander. "Why you head out afore me yesterday?" she asked.

Samuel stroked her again, and Harriet cuddled closer.

"I had something to do."

"What?" Harriet asked.

"Tell you later," he said.

Harriet thought about his brother. Samuel's evasiveness evened them up some. She'd tell him about Jacob in the morning. Best not to share bad news at night, when all one could do was lose sleep over it. Walter's face suddenly rose in her mind, and her eyes opened. She hadn't thought about him in hours. Remorse struck her, and her stomach knotted. "You got any idea what happened to Walter?" she asked. "There any good hiding spots on the Heyward Plantation?"

"Not many," he replied in a low voice that made his chest vibrate. "I'm worried about Luce, too. I hope no snitch saw em together."

Harriet thought about the woman Samuel trusted to rouse a plantation of five hundred people. The mother of his three boys. She wondered what Lucy looked like, and Harriet pictured a face like Kizzy's, only older. A good woman.

The room tilted on its axis. Harriet tasted the tin mug on her lips again and rolled onto her back. She hoisted herself up against the wall to stay alert. "Think the overseer might suspect her?" she asked.

Samuel cautiously scooted up alongside her. He was definitely mending.

"Don't know. He twitchy, what with the Yanks nearby. And me a runaway."

Harriet smoothed her tousled skirt. She thought of all the times she'd gone back to Maryland. "Why don't you jest get them? Steal your family in the dugout?"

"Lucy won't go without her sisters, so my boys is stuck. Her sisters got a passel of chil'ren. That's why I got to get everybody in one swoop."

Silence fell between them, peopled by those left behind. Harriet thought of Rachel, whom she had begged and begged. "Not without my boys. Not without Ben and Algerine," her sister said, arms folded, expression closed, life ended.

"What's your boys' names?" Harriet asked.

"Well, there's Sammy." He began slowly, as if telling a favorite bedtime tale. "Sam's our firstborn. Lucy named him for me. Day he showed up, nine years ago, my own name changed. Pa, Lucy called me after that. Sammy's tall, like me. And he got a level head—unlike Jake, our second boy. Jake's named for my brother Jacob. I gone make a waterman out a him. The boy ain't scared a nothing, but that lands him in a fix pretty regular. I've taken more'n one licking for something he broke or lost. Abe, he's the baby. So far, Abe ain't been a speck a trouble. Some old soul come back to Earth the day he showed up."

Harriet folded her arms and gripped her elbows. The tender words hurt. She pictured Samuel and Lucy under one roof, watching their children grow and keeping them safe against danger. It was a life she might have had, had she not left John. Samuel's boys depended on their father, as his words showed, and Lucy ought to have both her husband and her freedom—not one without the other.

Harriet mustn't get in their way. She wouldn't forgive herself if she did. Nor would the outside world, which expected and needed Harriet Tubman to be a saint, not someone who had abandoned her own child or busted up another family. No matter how much white folk said they understood the ways that slavery twisted people's lives, they didn't. They would look at her and her cause differently. And she mustn't let the cause be tarnished. No matter the cost.

"We gone get your family. Each one a them," Harriet said, as loneliness took its normal, rightful place in her heart.

A thump came from somewhere in the sleeping house. Harriet stopped breathing to listen for the landlady. Silence followed.

Samuel turned to her in the dark. He unfolded her arms and took her hands. "I want you to be my family. Maybe I can't have you tonight, but I won't spend my life without you. Don't you ask that."

Harriet didn't answer. Mustn't answer. It was all she wanted and couldn't have. She jerked her hands away and folded her arms again.

Samuel cupped her chin, then stroked her cheek with his broad thumb. "My boys always gone be my boys," he whispered. "Jacob and I never knew our daddy. It gone be different for my chil'ren. And I'll make sure Lucy's got a roof. I'm working on that. But my life's *mine* now. All mine. What's freedom if I ain't free to love who I want? Ain't free to love you?"

Harriet wondered what it would be like to have someone watching out for her, on her side always. Her throat swelled until she felt it would close. She forced out the words. "A child never gets over that kind a loss."

Samuel paused. She couldn't see his expression in the shadows. He drew back and cleared his throat. "I never even asked. You got chil'ren, sugar?"

"I was married once," she admitted. "But tell me more bout your boys. They got their daddy's coloring or their mama's?"

"They got their own coloring," he said dismissively. "But what—?"

She fended away the subject. She didn't want him any closer to her secret. "How old's the baby? He walking yet?"

Samuel placed a hand on her knee. He shook it gently. "Hattie. You got chil'ren?"

It was the question she refused to answer. What was her usual lie? It seemed inadequate. Yet the truth terrified her. The shame would swallow her whole. Harriet's throat tightened like a vise.

Samuel slipped his arm around her shoulders. He drew her close. "Tell me, sugar. You can tell me."

His voice was so kind, so patient, that a sob broke loose in her chest. A door she hadn't known was there suddenly opened, and Harriet saw she could walk through it. "I have a girl," she said. *There*, she thought. She'd said the words. Right out in the open. Exposed.

"A girl. What's her name?"

"Her name's Margaret." Tears rolled down Harriet's face. Her heart squeezed hard in her bosom. She struggled for breath. "She's my very own girl."

"Course she is. Where she now?"

"She with a white family up north. They watching her for me."

"She must miss her mama," he said encouragingly.

The tears rolled faster. The tightness in her chest was fierce. Harriet needed something to dry her eyes. Samuel wiped her cheek with his rough hand.

"She doesn't know I'm her mama. Poor baby thinks I'm her auntie."

Samuel nodded and wiped her other cheek. "Uh-huh."

The words now poured forth. Harriet couldn't stop them. "I'd die fore letting anyone know Margaret was born a slave and risking some bounty hunter thinking he can jest snatch her up and take her south. But I also can't tell her that I ran out on her. That I handed her over. Just gave her up." Harriet covered her face. Her shoulders shook.

Samuel didn't speak. When she finally calmed, he said, "Seems like you could tell her now, Hattie. You brave. No one braver than you."

"Won't I jest break her heart?" she said. "Knowing her own mama put freedom first? That she's been lied to every day since?"

"It might break her heart," he agreed. "But then she gone mend. And she'll know."

Harriet looked to the window, where the darkness was mellowing toward dawn. "I did go back for her."

"Course you did. That's Harriet Tubman right there." Samuel tugged her toward him until their foreheads met. She closed her eyes.

"Tell you what," Samuel whispered. "Let's get us some sleep, sugar. Day after tomorrow's the big day, right?"

Harriet nodded. Samuel kissed her cheek, slid back onto the mattress, and pulled her down beside him. He curled against her backside, wrapping his strong body around hers. Despite all the reasons they shouldn't be together, Harriet smiled as drowsiness claimed her limbs. She didn't have to carry the weight of the past alone anymore. She had Samuel.

"The raid's all you got to think about for now," he said. Samuel held her snugly. "But after that, Harriet Tubman, jest you try and wiggle away."

CHAPTER TWENTY-TWO

———

The New York Tribune *says that the Negro troops at Hilton Head, SC, will soon start upon an expedition, under the command of Colonel Montgomery, different in many respects from any heretofore planned.... Should any number of negroes cross our lines for such purpose, boldness and confidence will be sure of success against any disparity of force.*
Confederate Headquarters, McPhersonville, SC

HARRIET TOOK THE RUMPLED SLEEVE FROM the windowsill where she'd left it to dry and sat on her chair to thread her needle. Cold water had pulled the bloodstains from the gingham. One sleeve would always be shorter than the other, but the dress would still serve. She looked over at Samuel, sprawled on his lean stomach with an arm under his head. His sound sleep indicated that the superficial wound was healing quickly. If he didn't lift heavy objects that day, he should be fine to sail the next.

Harriet took a deep breath and let it out softly so as not to wake him while she joined the ends of the thread, looped them around her index finger, and rolled them off the tip to make a knot. She felt lighter than she had in years—ready to float to the ceiling—though she could hardly believe she'd told Samuel her darkest secret. Sharing a room with him, even if for only another hour, felt too wonderful to bring to an end.

Yet the scene was also oddly normal. Samuel dozed while she worked on a simple task, just like any woman with her man on a

Sunday morning. Free people did it all the time without thinking about it—married couples who didn't have to live on the run, who knew the vows they made could be kept. *What God has joined together let no man put asunder* instead of, *'til distance do you part*, as the preacher told her and John. Harriet rested her needle and closed her eyes. *Lord Almighty, hear my prayer*, she told Him, knowing His capacity for generosity.

A donkey brayed outside, and Harriet opened her eyes. A moment later, a cart rolled by, soon followed by the stamp of soldiers. She wondered what had happened to Walter. They must find him. Harriet poked her needle into the unattached sleeve and set it aside. "Samuel, wake up," she said, rising to shake his arm.

He opened his eyes halfway, then rolled onto his back and yawned. "Already?" He pointed at his bandage. "How's it look?"

Harriet sat beside him to examine the dressing. The bloodstain was brown. "Looks good," she said. "How you feeling?"

He reached up and stroked her cheek. "Ready for anything," he said with a mischievous smile.

She took his hand and placed it on the bed. "I need to see if Walter's turned up. I'm hoping he rowed back on the tide."

Samuel grew serious. His hand curled over hers. "'Clare to God, I don't know where he could a hid."

Harriet didn't either, not with the wide, exposed rice fields, but she wouldn't say so. Putting fear into words tempted fate. Samuel's anxiety for Walter must be compounded by worry for his children, and he didn't even know about his brother. The news would hold awhile longer, until she got back from the dock. But she did need to know what he'd found on the Combahee. Harriet felt a rush of impatience. "Tell me bout that last torpedo," she said. "Can you pinpoint it on Montgomery's map?"

He nodded. "Yes, but it won't be hard to spot neither. A stand a tupelos grows near the ferry landing. Both barrels are right there, on either side a the Cum'bee. The current is fast on that stretch, so if a pilot don't know better, he gone hug the inside bend. Can't do that."

"Not without getting blown up?"

"Not without getting blown to heck and gone." Samuel let go of her hand and sat up in bed. "I'll come with you to look for Walter."

"No need for you to get up. I can scout the situation pretty quick."

Samuel's jaw squared and he acquired a mulish look. "So can I."

"You ought get some rest. That wound still—"

"I'm rested plenty," he said.

Harriet sensed the arrival of an argument she'd rather avoid. No good came of stepping on a man's pride. "That decision's yours," she said, "but I hope you gone think on it. We need your help tomorrow to show us which tupelos you mean. I'd hate Montgomery to mix em up."

"I'm feeling fine," he said.

Harriet stood up. "Let's change that dressing then." She got the discarded sleeve from the chair. "I ain't got any more clean linen, but we can reuse this. The hospital has fresh bandages, but that's across town, and I'm not sure you can make it there without the bleeding starting up."

Samuel's eyes narrowed. "You told me a minute ago that my noggin looks okay. This one a your tricks, Hattie?"

She shook her head. "No, I'm giving it to you straight. The wound might open up if you walk around in the hot sun. It's up to you."

Samuel scooted down on the mattress. He folded his arms under his head and stretched out his legs. "I think I been out-generaled, General Tubman. Promise me you'll stop by the contraband hospital for a clean bandage?"

Harriet returned the sleeve to the chair. Relieved, she leaned over to kiss his forehead. "Yes, soldier, I will. So long as you promise to rest."

The morning was already hot. At the Union dock, a third gunship floated alongside the two paddle wheelers Harriet had seen before. Busy crews now swarmed the triple-deckers that once took families across the Hudson or traders down the Susquehanna. A line of men toted bundles of firewood for the boilers. Colored machinists with oilcans inspected the giant side-wheels. Yankee gunners from the 3rd Rhode Island Heavy Artillery positioned and sighted the guns on the upper decks. Officers carrying charts traipsed in and out of the tiny pilothouses while the Stars and Stripes flapped boldly from the jack staffs at the bow of each ship. The repurposed ferries looked like layer cakes with their flat decks and white railings.

Goosebumps swept Harriet's arms. The steamers that once delivered passengers on northern rivers were the most glorious sight she'd ever seen: a fleet to rescue Israelites from the land of bondage. They rose like a biblical armada. She felt sure no one had ever before launched a navy against slavery. Harriet noticed a painter touching up the gold letters on the bow of the middle gunboat, the smallest of the three, and felt she must learn their names. If all went well, she would teach them to Margaret one day. They would recite them like the names of the Apostles. And Samuel was right. She must tell her daughter the truth at last.

A white man walking down the dock stopped to tie his shoe.

"Excuse me, sir," Harriet said. "I don't know my letters. Can you please tell me the names a these ships?"

The man stood and shaded his eyes to peer down the long wharf. "The first one, she's the *John Adams*," he said. "The one in the middle is the *Harriet Weed*."

"The *Harriet*?" she said, delighted. She wondered how the ship had gotten its name.

"The *Harriet Weed*," he corrected her. The man paused and squinted. "The one at the far end, I believe that's the *Sentinel*."

"Where they headed?" Harriet asked.

"Florida, I hear," the man said, and lifted his hat without a trace of the casual venom she sometimes encountered from white

Northerners, with whom she'd found little middle ground between friend and foe. He continued on his way without further comment.

Harriet smiled to herself—their final destination still remained a secret—but an instant later frowned with alarm. Sergeant Prince Rivers, Thomas Wentworth Higginson's right-hand man, stood next to a crate of ammunition on the dock. Why was he there? Had Colonel Montgomery been pulled off the raid? General Hunter had promised her the Kansan, and here instead was Higginson's assistant.

Consulting a sheaf of notes, Sergeant Rivers spoke with two infantrymen who nodded at whatever he was saying. A moment later, the soldiers took either end of the crate and hauled it onto the *Harriet Weed*, disappearing into the hold.

Harriet strode down the dock before the imposing officer could follow his men. "Sergeant!"

Sergeant Rivers glanced at her as she approached and then back at his manifest. "Miz Tubman. How may I help you?" He took a pencil from his top pocket and crossed something off.

"You preparing to get underway?"

He grimaced but didn't look up as he crossed off another item. "Yes, that's why we're putting supplies on the ship. It's the general procedure."

Harriet ignored his sarcasm. She was ready to forgive outright rudeness from officers under pressure. But she needed to know whether command had been transferred. What in the world was General Hunter up to? Colonel Montgomery would be livid. She felt her dander rise. No way should Higginson—a just man, a kind man, and the wrong man—lead the expedition.

"I see you're busy," she said, sustaining a pleasant tone with effort. "Colonel Higginson around?"

The colored officer glanced up from his tablet. His lean frame radiated impatience. "No, he's back at camp."

"You expect him anytime soon?"

"No idea," he said.

"Colonel Higginson directing the work from camp?"

"Nope," Rivers said and turned away abruptly.

She could have hit him over the head with her satchel for his brusque answers. Instead, she stepped in front to cut him off. "You in charge, then, Sergeant Rivers?"

The tall sergeant glared down. "Ma'am, if you want a senior officer, you need to address Colonel Montgomery. I've been loaned to the 2nd South Carolina for the day. They're on their way to Florida." He flicked a thumb toward the ship at the end of the wharf. "I believe he's on the *Sentinel.*"

"Thank you, sir," Harriet said, and she continued down the dock. Sergeant Rivers apparently didn't know that the fleet's destination was a ruse—or was sticking to the official story. Either way, Colonel Montgomery remained in charge. *Thank you, Lord*, she thought.

A wide gangplank at the end of the wharf led onto the *Sentinel.* Harriet followed two muscular men pushing wheelbarrows filled with iron ballast up the walkway and onto the main deck. Colonel Montgomery stood a short distance away in conversation with the ship's captain, who frowned and shook his head. Montgomery noticed her approach and motioned her over. The captain signaled the stevedores to follow and disappeared into the engine room.

"Morning, Colonel," Harriet said.

Montgomery lifted his hat and wiped the sweat from his brow with the back of his hand. "What's your report?" he said, ignoring any preliminaries. "Did you accomplish the mission?"

"Yes, sir, in part."

"Which part?"

"Heyward confirmed the two torpedoes nearest the ferry, and we got onto the Lowndes and Nichols Plantations. But we—we lost touch with Walter Plowden, sir." Harriet forced herself to say the terrible words, which felt much like burying her friend. "He never come back."

Montgomery shook his head. "Plowden rowed in this morning.

Looked a sight. I guess he hid in a pigsty. Said he found the woman he needed to see but was delayed and missed the tide. One of the sutlers took him back to camp a few minutes ago."

A lump rose in her throat. "Lordy," she said. "Thank Jesus, he safe!"

The memory flashed upon her of the day she'd crawled into a pigpen to escape the whip. Still a child, she'd been terrified that the immense animals would crush her, and their putrid offal stayed under her fingernails for a week. But the hogs had accepted her, and now they'd saved Walter, too.

"Amen." Montgomery cast a troubled glance around him. "Now we need to pray for this ship."

"What's wrong?"

"Captain says she can't keep her head. Lists in a storm. I'm bringing extra ballast on board, but the draught is too deep as well. She draws nine feet, and the Combahee permits only ten at high tide. We'll have to drop the ballast at the bar in order to cross into the river, and count on the weight of the contraband to steady the ship on the way home."

Harriet considered the list of problems. "Sounds like a fair plan."

"You'd think so. But the captain isn't confident we should take her out at all. Says the boat needs a thorough refitting. These are all patches."

"What you think, sir?" she asked. Harriet wanted to tell him the answer, but he needed to ask the question. As always, he'd listen better.

Colonel Montgomery paused. His unshaven jaw flexed. "I think we have to risk it," he said. "What about you? You've been up the Combahee."

"There must be three, four thousand slaves on that sorry river. Each plantation has five hundred or more."

"We can't rescue them all."

Harriet nodded in agreement. Some estates were set too far back to raid easily. Others lay upriver, beyond the ferry landing. "How many folk can we take with three boats?" she asked.

Montgomery heaved a sigh. "With three ships, maybe a thousand. We also have to fit the men of the 2nd Carolina, plus the gun crews from the 3rd Rhode Island."

Harriet's eyes widened. Towering above the wharf, the boats seemed so large. "That all? Can we get more ships?"

"No. I had to beg for the *Sentinel*. The navy is still refitting after the disaster in Charleston. They don't want to risk more gunboats." Montgomery pulled his hat farther down over his brow, as if to hide his disappointment. "This is it."

Dismay filled Harriet. So many would be left behind. They always were. But this was the first battle, she reminded herself, and they would free a thousand in a day. Charleston was next. "Then we got to take the *Sentinel*, even if she ain't tip-top," she said. "Do we need so many Rhode Islanders?"

"Those Rhode Islanders are the ones who are going to get us home if Rebel artillery shows up," Montgomery said. "If the Secesh haul their field pieces down Stokes Road, and our men can't bay them, the Rebels will blow a hole in these boats and sink us all."

"Them Yankees ready to fight alongside colored troops?"

"Some are the very ones that Higginson's troops pulled off the *George Washington*," he said. "They feel they owe us."

Harriet nodded in recognition. The Confederates had sunk a Yankee gunship in the marsh off Port Royal the month before. Black troops had rescued Rhode Islander gunners from the burning wreck. The Rebels picked off seven, but more would have been lost if the colored troops hadn't rushed to help.

"But our men gone take the fight ashore, right?" Harriet asked. She knew she sounded defensive, but slaveholders pretended black people didn't care for freedom. Didn't even want it. That slaves thanked them morning, noon, and night. Colored troops would show the world otherwise.

"Yes. But don't forget the risk those Yankees are taking. We need every last one of them."

"I won't, sir. They John Brown's sons."

"Pray for them, then. Pray we all make it over the bar and back."

Harriet walked home from the contraband hospital with her satchel stuffed with bandages for Samuel and others who might need them on the morrow. For the first time in months, all she had to consider was how to spend a Sunday. Her steps quickened as she neared the boarding house. They could enjoy the Sabbath like a regular couple. Perhaps Samuel could read to her from his pocket Bible, since he wasn't well enough to go to church. First, she would tell him about Jacob, and then they would pray together.

A limp curtain twitched in a sidelight of the front entrance. Ruby Savan's nose was an inch from the pane. Ringlets hung on either side of her sallow face.

"Morning, Miz Tubman," the landlady said as she opened the front door.

Harriet knew she should inquire after the woman's health, but she had no patience. "Morning, Miz Savan."

"That man still in your room?"

"I'm bringing him bandages now," she said. "He'll be gone tomorrow, ma'am."

"Make sure of that," the landlady said. "I have a respectable name, my daddy's name—"

"Yes, ma'am, so everyone say," Harriet agreed. "I better change that dressing right away."

Harriet moved quickly down the hallway. She dreaded telling Samuel about Jacob but couldn't wait to report that Walter had made it back safe.

She pushed open the door, which stood slightly ajar. A wave of heat swept her face. The man with two women on a string had disappeared once again. "Fine," she told the empty room, and she slammed the door with a bang so loud that glass rattled in the window. "That's jest fine."

CHAPTER TWENTY-THREE

Let us examine together the Word of God, and then you will know what has moved me to sacrifice property and friendship, and home and reputation. With Christian patience and Christian love, give me your attention to the end of this letter, whilst I endeavor to show you that the Holy God disapproves American slavery.

William Brisbane, Abolitionist

WHEN HARRIET ENTERED THE DISPENSARY, HENRY Durant looked up from his desk, puzzled. "I thought you'd left," he said.

"I did. But I found myself with time on my hands. Figured I'd come back," she said.

"Don't you want to rest on the Lord's Day? Or go to church?"

Harriet shook her head. "Tell you the truth, doc, don't think I could sit still. Thought I'd praise the Lord by tending His flock, if you can use me."

"Always," he replied.

"Then I'll fetch up a broom, sir," she said and continued to the supply cabinet for a clean apron. She needed something to take her mind off Samuel Heyward. She'd sworn twelve years earlier never again to let a man get under her skin.

A nurse feeding a patient near the door gestured to the far corner when Harriet entered the ward. "Would you start over there? I don't want that dust flying up into my soup," the woman said.

"Yes, ma'am," Harriet replied. She walked to the far side of the large room where an old white man, seated between two cots with his head bent over a book, read to patients. Harriet began her chores in the opposite corner. She saw only the floor as she swept and did not realize that the reader was Preacher William Brisbane until she overheard the slurry accent of South Carolina aristocracy.

"Yes, sister," the Beaufort native explained, "that's exactly what Saint Paul meant. 'For freedom, Christ has set us free. Stand firm, therefore, and do not submit again to the yoke of slavery.'"

To Brisbane's right lay the sightless old patient who usually asked Harriet for water. She didn't know if the one-legged man just wanted attention, but she always fetched him a cup anyway.

"What he say bout de Buckra, preacher?" Romulus asked, his head turned blindly toward Brisbane. "What Saint Paul say to de Galatians bout dem?"

The former plantation owner looked over his reading glasses at the contraband who might have been born on Port Royal the same year as himself. Both men had gray beards and frayed collars. "They must mend their ways, every one of them, and stand firm against greed and false counsel," Brisbane said.

"De Buckra change?" a woman said from her pallet on the floor. She was young, about twenty, with close-cropped hair and a weary, dead expression, as if all inner light had gone out long before. "Dat ain't possible."

Romulus turned his face in the direction of the woman's voice. "Preacher Brisbane done it hisself. He slapped down dat false counsel long time ago."

Harriet rested her chin atop the broom.

"Dem other Buckra try to push de preacher off de path of righteousness, but he warn't having it," Romulus continued. "Took his slaves north better'n twenty years ago. Freed em all. Wouldn't truck with slavery no more. Give away ev'ry dime."

The young woman on the floor waved a bandaged hand to

dispel the flies that clustered on her wrist. Harriet hadn't seen her before. She must have been admitted while Harriet was on the Combahee. "Dem other Buckra is different from de preacher," the woman said.

The Baptist minister leaned forward with a paternal smile. Brisbane must find the hospital a congenial spot for a sermon, Harriet thought. Perhaps he'd courted his wife in this very ballroom as a young swain. Then, Romulus would have waited on him, and a banquet table with rum punch and pound cake might have stood where the hospital cot did now.

"George Washington, the founder of our country, freed his slaves," Brisbane said.

"When?" the woman asked.

"Upon his death," Brisbane answered.

The woman sat a little straighter and a glimmer of anger made her look more alive. "Figures," she said. "When dem slaves can't help him no mo'. Anybody else?"

The preacher looked down at his Bible.

Harriet spoke across the ward, causing heads to turn. "Plenty a folk," she said. "Ain't no more slaves in the North except ones Southerners bring in. None in Canada, neither. And the folks in England, across the ocean, they give it up, too. The British lion swept away them slavers thirty years ago. Freed everybody 'round the world. America jest catching up."

"Moses, I didn't see you there," the preacher said with a smile.

Harriet directed her words to the patients. She wanted them to see the bravery she had seen. Lift their hearts in this backwater and let them know they were on the right path with plenty of company. Share the hope that other abolitionists—black and white—had given her.

"White folks is jest folks," she said. "Some of the Buckra are sinful, and they now reaping the wages of sin. They bloodied and bowed and their end ain't yet in sight. Many is ignorant. They uneducated. But when I left my home, when I walked away from my family's sheltering arm and every last person on Earth who loved me, it was white ladies who stretched out their hands. I saw em in a dream. And I saw em again when I crossed that holy line into Pennsylvania."

"Glory, hallelujah," Brisbane said, as if preaching a sermon. "Amen."

"Amen," Romulus and other patients echoed, with the exception of the woman on the floor, who just stared at the flies that again swarmed her bandaged wrist.

On the other side of the ward, Harriet glimpsed Doctor Durant enter with someone she had hoped not to see a second time. The nurse held a spoon to the mouth of a young child, then she gestured with it across the room. The redheaded doctor caught Harriet's eye. He telegraphed caution as he limped toward her.

Sergeant Clyde Granville stepped around Doctor Durant to hand Harriet a folded document. "I'm here on orders of Captain Louis Lambert, Miz Tubman. He needs to speak with you."

"Can't it wait, Marshal? I'm in the middle of sweeping this here ward," she said calmly, though she fought an urge to throw down her broom and dodge around him.

The possibilities cascaded in her mind. She thanked the Lord that Samuel had located the torpedoes and Montgomery had sent Walter back to camp, where the marshal wouldn't readily find him. They had done the right thing going back up the Combahee. But what if there was something she hadn't anticipated? She knew more about rescuing slaves than any person alive. Montgomery needed her. She couldn't let Lambert arrest her. And the thought of jail frightened her, as black people often didn't come out in one piece. Harriet's hand tightened on the broom.

Granville touched the butt of his pistol. "No, it cannot wait. Captain Lambert is a busy man. I need to take you in."

Several patients gasped at "take you in."

Romulus sat up. "Who this Captain Lambert? He know General Hunter? Hunter gone have something to say bout this."

William Brisbane rose from his chair with a finger still in the Bible. "Why does the captain need Moses? May I help in some way, suh?"

"You can help by staying out of my way, old man," Granville said. "Why the captain wants Miz Tubman is none of your concern. This is government business."

The aged patrician smoothed his threadbare cravat. "You may not be aware that I am tax commissioner for Port Royal, Sergeant Granville, under Federal jurisdiction. My labors fund your pay warrant." He laid the Bible on the empty chair. "And I am coming with you, suh. Harriet Tubman is not seeing your Captain Lambert without me."

Leaning against a bedpost, Doctor Durant straightened with an impatient expression. "My patients need rest, gentlemen. Whatever you do, please do it outside the hospital."

Harriet set her broom against the wall with a cocky air to hide her fear. "Let's go," she said. "We gone take care a this nonsense right now."

An old man of fifty-six, Preacher Brisbane walked with a cane from gout. Harriet took an elbow to support him as they poked down New Street and turned onto Bay in the direction of the Verdier House. Harriet's mind raced. Lambert's trap was closing.

She stared angrily at the dusty windows of John Lilly's mercantile as they came abreast. A colored child swept the stairs and halted his broom when a customer traipsed down them to a horse tied up in front. Next to the horse stood a mule wagon. A wagon Harriet recognized. Webster's wagon. She squeezed Brisbane's arm and stopped walking. "Captain Lambert is investigating the theft of government stores, sir," she explained. She turned to Sergeant Granville and pointed at the emporium. "The man with the real information is Private John Webster. This is his wagon. He's inside a that store."

The marshal tugged at his blue collar as if the boiled wool had shrunk in the heat. "Miz Tubman, I don't know what you're up to, but you already have a preacher in tow. That's plenty."

Harriet dropped Brisbane's elbow and crossed her arms. "Webster's behind this mess. You need to bring him in."

"I don't need to do anything," Granville said.

Preacher Brisbane planted both hands atop his cane. "Treasury Secretary Salmon P. Chase appointed me personally, suh. If Harriet Tubman says there's a witness to theft inside this establishment, we are going in. Or I will hold you responsible for thwarting justice."

Granville's eyes shifted from Brisbane to Harriet and back. Again, he touched the pistol at his belt. "You have thirty seconds," he said and nodded for them to precede him up the stairs.

The colored boy stopped his broom as they passed by. The emporium was empty save for Private Webster and John Lilly, who shook hands in apparent farewell.

"—at the social, then," the stout storekeeper said to Webster. "Assuming you can get over to Port Royal for the day."

"Aye, sir," Webster replied. "I promised the pastor I would."

"And honorable Welshmen don't welsh," Lilly said with a grin that Webster returned, though he looked uncomfortable.

"Yorkshire born, sir. English, I am," he said, as if that was different.

Harriet approached the counter. "Afternoon, Mister Lilly, Private Webster. How you gentlemen find yourselves?"

Webster nodded. "I'm well. Thank ye, Miz Tubman." He touched his cap and turned to go.

Harriet put up her hand. "Private Webster, hold up a moment. I'm awful glad to see you. I need you to clear the air. Mister Lilly has questioned some sugar I hoped he'd take off a me. Turned out, I ordered too much from you. Can you tell him that I bought that sugar last week on Hilton Head?"

The pale-skinned commissary agent flushed to his sparse eyebrows. "Why, I help hundreds a month—and we've had any number o' dealings."

"I asking you to remember jest this one," she said. "I was coming out a General Hunter's office, and you stopped your wagon to see if I needed more sugar. Said you had extra."

He pushed his wire glasses closer as if trying to make out her point, though unable to do so. "I may have."

"You did," Harriet insisted.

Preacher Brisbane interrupted. "Mistah Webster, I take an official interest as tax commissioner for Beaufort. Our government is terribly short of funds to quell this rebellion. Can you please recount your business with Miz Tubman?"

Webster shook his head. "Sorry, commissioner," he said. "I just don't recall."

The portly storekeeper behind the counter watched the conversation with a perplexed expression. He drew back, and his double chin became a triple. "Private Webster, surely you recall a sale just last week," John Lilly said. "Tell Miz Tubman she's mistaken."

"Robert Smalls passed by 'round the same time," Harriet said, gauging how far the truth would stretch. "He saw your wagon, too."

Webster's large ears, rimmed with short blond hairs, reddened in accord with the rest of his face. He scratched his head. His gaze shifted to a point over her shoulder. "Now that ye mention it, I do recall. We received an unusually large shipment, and I was concerned about palmetto bugs. It seemed prudent to part with some o' the sugar before the roaches got into it."

Preacher Brisbane's face lost its normally benign expression. Hard lines bracketed his mouth, and the experience of five decades glittered in his eyes. "I expect you to share this information with Captain Lambert."

The screen door behind them slapped closed. Three white soldiers laughed at a joke, then separated to examine the store's wares.

John Lilly nodded agreement. His chins jiggled. "You best sort this out," he said to Webster, then he turned away as a customer approached the counter with a new jackknife.

Webster looked around without meeting Harriet's eyes or those of the marshal or preacher. "Of course. I'll see you at the social, then, Mister Lilly. Miz Tubman, if ye need anything—" he said and walked out the front door.

Harriet and Brisbane trailed the commissary agent down the stairs, with Harriet supporting the old preacher's elbow. Webster cracked a whip over the heads of his mules and rolled away before they reached the last step.

A sweet breeze came up Bay Street. Harriet smiled at the beauty of the day, in no hurry to pursue the cheating clerk. Time itself was going to catch up with Private John Webster. William Brisbane would tell Captain Louis Lambert what he had heard, and she'd be free to go. Lambert would be unable to indulge his animosity, and the army's investigation would grind in the correct direction while Harriet Tubman sailed up the Combahee at the bow of a gunship.

Chapter Twenty-Four

Light of dim mornings; shield from heat and cold;
Balm for all ailments; substitute for praise;
Comrade of those who plod in lonely ways . . .
Spell that knits friends, but yearning lovers parts.
                    "Duty," by Thomas Wentworth Higginson

HARRIET SPENT THE LAST HOURS OF the afternoon giving the cookhouse a final scrubbing. It seemed important to put things to rights for Septima in case she didn't return. So she filled two iron pots with water, heated them to boiling, rolled up her sleeves, and went to work with rags and a brush. The hot, soapy water felt good on her forearms. The sun declined in the red and inflamed sky while she scoured the last stains from the old stove.

As twilight turned into dark, she lit the kerosene lantern and uncovered the slice of pork pie Septima had left on the mixing table sometime earlier on the Sabbath. Montgomery had instructed them to be at the *John Adams* by noon the next day. The first of June. The beginning of slavery's end in South Carolina, Harriet prayed.

Perched on the cookhouse stool, Harriet applied herself to the cold supper. The food tasted like nothing. She ate because she needed sustenance, but she took little interest in the proceedings until a shadow appeared on the windowsill and then jumped to the table. "There you are, you ornery critter," Harriet said. She stroked the cat, which arched its back as she transferred it to the floor along with a large pinch of pie. Companionship made the pastry more interesting, and together they made short work of it. As she finished the homely meal, Harriet wondered if it would be her last supper. Considered that way, it was a feast.

Once she'd washed the plate, Harriet decided to walk off her restlessness. It was too hot for a shawl, so she splashed vinegar on her neck to ward off mosquitoes before shutting the window and closing the door behind her. The danger ahead loomed like thunder clouds that caused the air to crackle with electricity. Pickets awaited them at Fields Point, Tar Bluff, and the Combahee ferry landing. An army of two thousand men camped nearby. Confederate cannons were somewhere on the route to Savannah. Rebels had bled the Union for two years. Hundreds of thousands had died, and more would perish. Maybe Harriet Tubman.

She decided to return to the cookhouse to sleep. If this were her last night, she didn't want to spend it under Ruby Savan's roof. The times she had laid her head on the floors of strangers came back to her, and she felt close in spirit to the men and women who had followed her to Canada. They whispered encouragement now. She hadn't lost a single one. Perhaps Louisa May Alcott would put that in an epitaph.

Harriet walked along Bay Street until she passed the wharf. The stevedores had deserted it, but colored sentinels paced the length between bright torches. A shooting star streaked across the night sky and lost its way somewhere in the ocean. The moon was just short of full. Harriet came to the row of private jetties from which fishermen and other folk plied the waterways between Hilton Head, Port Royal, St. Helena, Lady's, Parris, Coosaw, and all the neighboring islands where the Gullah people were building lives outside slavery. A fresh breeze beckoned, and Harriet turned onto a dock to walk out over the water.

Hammering boomed from a small boathouse toward the end of the row. A carpenter on a ladder nailed the roof of a second-story addition by the glow of a lantern that hung from the eave. As she approached the last pilings that anchored the jetty in the shallow bay, Harriet wondered why the impatient man didn't wait until morning, when the sun would provide all the light necessary, especially when she heard him exclaim as he hit his thumb.

"Dang it to heck!" came a familiar deep voice.

Harriet stopped short and contemplated turning around. She didn't feel like seeing Samuel—but the cheat owed her an explanation, she decided as she continued to the boathouse. She halted under the ladder.

Samuel reached into a pail that sat on the edge of the roof, withdrew something, and resumed hammering.

"Hey up there," she called, loud enough to be heard but not startle him.

Samuel turned cautiously, holding onto the ladder. He looked down. "Harriet," he said. She couldn't see his features in the shadow cast by the moonlight but heard a smile in his voice. "Stand back, sugar, and I'll come on down."

Harriet retreated two steps as Samuel descended the ladder with his hammer in the pail. "What's this place?" she asked as she took another step backward, out of arm's reach, once he'd gained the dock.

"My boathouse," he said. "What do you think?"

"What do I think? I think I don't know nothing about it."

"I got it off the tax rolls last month. It's one a them the Secesh abandoned. Commissioner Brisbane's letting me make payments. It'll be all mine by the end a the year."

"How you paying for it?" she asked.

"I been repairing old dugouts and selling em," he said proudly. "Dragged my first from the marsh. I think it got away in a storm. I'm here first thing every morning when we ain't scouting. When I sell one trus-me-Gawd, I find another."

Harriet shook her head with wonder. "You fixing to be a boat builder?"

"Yep. But my main idea is to start a ferry business. People need to get back and forth 'tween the islands. When the war's over, that gone be me. Ain't nobody rows faster. The packet to Sa'leenuh goes but twice a day. I'll take folk whenever they want. Gone train Jake to row. Sam can take the money."

"But why you working after dark? Why you down here fore we set sail?" She heard her voice rise. "Why you . . . leave this morning?"

Samuel cocked his head. "Oh, that's right. My noggin." He reached up and touched it tentatively. "I decided to get back to work. Found a medic. He said the wound looked dry. Walter stopped by after you left, so I knew he made it back after seeing Lucy. She's in on the plan, he said. The rock a Jesus, she is."

Harriet didn't know what to say. Of course his wife was a rock. She was there for Samuel's children. Harriet knew she should be grateful that Lucy Heyward was prepared to risk everything for their mission, but it was hard to hear her name.

"Why the hurry?" she asked. "Seems like healing up your head fore the raid is more important than this roof."

Samuel looked down at his pail. "I need to get it ready by tomorrow." His voice was no longer prideful. "I got to finish this for Luce and the boys. Especially now," he said as he reached out to touch her elbow.

"Why now?" she said.

"They gone live upstairs."

They. He'd said *they*, not *we*. He must be planning to live apart from his wife. Perhaps he was rushing to finish the roof to ease his guilt. An awkward silence grew between them. Three boys, she thought. Sam, Jake, and Abe.

"Nobody can say my boys want for anything. Nobody," Samuel added, as if nailing an argument and not just the roof. "And Lucy, she didn't want me to start with. She don't need me."

Harriet drew a deep breath. He was wrong and would see it once reality in the shape of a wife and three boys arrived, should they be lucky enough to get out. This was the world for which they were fighting: one where fathers and mothers weren't separated from their children. Where they lived free lives together under one roof.

She was glad it was dark so he couldn't see the cracks in her expression. "It's a fine boathouse," Harriet said, struggling to keep her voice even. "Don't let me interrupt. I jest passing by."

He glanced up at the roof. "Ain't much left. Another few rows." He looked down at her in the dark, his beard in silhouette. "What you doing?"

"Taking care a loose ends at the cookhouse." She adjusted her headscarf. "I best knuckle down. See you tomorrow. Montgomery says be there by noon."

He caught her elbow. "Not so fast, sweet girl. What about tonight?"

Harriet allowed her eyes to warm on the chance that he could see them in the moonlight, though she felt as cold as it was possible to feel on the eve of June in South Carolina. The shape of her solitary life was as clear in her mind as the family home on the dock. She hardly even knew what to think about Samuel. If he were a good man, he wouldn't leave Lucy. If he were a good man, he would be loyal to Harriet.

"We both got a lot to do," Harriet said. "There'll be plenty a time when this is over."

Samuel leaned close to kiss her, but Harriet drew back. "Not here," she said by way of excuse. "Get yourself some sleep."

"Yes, ma'am," he said. "Moses," he corrected himself with a chuckle. "I'll lay my head here tonight. Later, it'll be different."

Harriet retraced her steps along the road. She strolled at a measured pace, but once she'd passed the army dock, she broke into a fast, hard walk. The macadam road beat her thick soles. She wanted to get away from Samuel Heyward as quickly as possible. Put distance between their mission in the morning and the image of a woman and three boys eating supper alone under those eaves.

Tomorrow, and the next day, and the day after that would be

different from what they expected, as he said. But no matter what happened, if Harriet made it back alive, she wouldn't be the one who wrecked that home.

Harriet took an apron from the nail inside the door of the cookhouse and rolled it into a hard pillow. The humid air was blanket enough. She settled on the floor behind the worktable. Harriet closed her eyes, numb with fatigue, and was drifting toward sleep when Trouble emerged from the dark and nestled against her chest. She circled the cat with her arm to make a wall against the world and fell into a deep slumber.

In her dream, Samuel's hand gently traced the outline of her breast until his fingertips rested lightly on her nipple, which he pinched as delicately as a gardener testing a peach. Harriet's breath deepened, and she took in the warm smell of him, though she made no effort to assist his exploration. Instead, she waited, as patient as nature, allowing herself to experience what happened next. *Wait*, she told herself. *Wait, and he would come to her*, she thought as the sweet ache swelled. In the dream, his large hand traveled down her side, holding her entire hip between his thumb and fingers, until it slipped away, and she felt only the absence of fabric as he lifted her dress.

Harriet's head tilted back as Samuel parted her legs—as she wanted him to—but the apron-roll suddenly gave way to the hard stone of the floor, and she jerked, startled awake by the jarring bump.

Samuel slid up next to her. "Baby," he whispered in her ear, "Couldn't stay away. I don't want another night when we not together. Not one."

Still half asleep, Harriet wrapped her arms around him. She shut her eyes against the world that allowed her no love and the war that might kill them both tomorrow. Emotion and desire overcame every resolve. Even if it would never be right, she wanted him. She would have him.

CHAPTER TWENTY-FIVE

Damn the torpedoes, full speed ahead.
Admiral David Farragut, at the Battle of Mobile Bay

"HARRIET, YOU AWAKE?" AN ARM DREW her tighter. "Time to get up," Samuel whispered in her ear.

Harriet's eyes opened in the early morning light to spy the battered legs of the wooden table and a tin cup that had rolled under the Franklin stove. She turned over and looked up into Samuel's eyes. He smiled and brushed something—a speck of flour, perhaps—from her forehead.

"Morning, baby," he said. "Today's the day."

Harriet tucked her chin, shut her eyes again, and nestled closer. He felt so good. *Just five more minutes,* she thought as she pressed her cheek to the rounded muscles of his chest. She could sleep a week in his arms.

"Got to go," he said.

Harriet nodded but didn't open her eyes. "I know."

Samuel kissed the top of her head. "This time, someone gone be looking out for you."

They were the sweetest words she'd ever heard. They made her feel part of the world, rather outside looking in. Samuel had rowed back upriver for her, she mused sleepily. He truly had. Maybe freedom did mean they could choose one another. But wasn't that

233

yielding to temptation? Taking something that didn't belong to you?

The guilty thought woke her more fully, and she recalled what she had meant to tell him the day before. Harriet sat up. The awful news couldn't be postponed. "There's something we need to talk about," she said. "I would a told you yesterday, but you wasn't well—and then you left."

Samuel looked up at her with a half-smile that suggested he had a comeback for any objection she could throw at him.

Harriet forced herself to continue, despite the horror she felt creep over her as the images flooded back. Best to say it straight out. "When I was on the Lowndes Plantation night before last, that girl I told you about took me to Jacob," she said. "Pipkin has him in that jail a his."

Samuel sat up. "Jail? What for?"

"Jacob took a swing at Pipkin, the girl said. Jacob was defending her."

Samuel's mouth fell open. "You see him?"

She recalled the horrible odor. "It was too dark to see much, but he's bad off."

"What you mean?"

"Pipkin had him—" Harriet struggled with the words. Guilt thickened her tongue. "He . . . he had him strung up."

"Don't tell me he used his Teacher on my brother." Anger twisted Samuel's features. "Don't you say that."

"That's what Kizzy called it. She said Pipkin's letting him out soon. But Jacob gone have a hard time running." Harriet longed to reach for Samuel's hand.

"You should a told me, Moses," he said hotly.

Harriet and Samuel stared at one another as the likely outcome got its talons into them, and with one accord, they stood and tugged at their clothes.

Samuel buttoned his shirt and grabbed his hat. His bandage had fallen off in the night, but he didn't reach for it. "See you at the dock. Noontime," he said. His face was tight.

"Noon," she agreed. "We gone get him," she said.

"Hattie—" Samuel began, but then he just shook his head.

Steps sounded on the path. Samuel walked to the door. He threw a glance back at Harriet and then turned to leave. "Morning, ma'am," he said to Septima as they traded places in the doorway.

Septima set a basket of blackberries on the worktable with a loud thump and took her apron down from the hook. Eyes lowered, she poured water in the pewter basin they kept for that purpose and washed her hands thoroughly. Then she began picking leaves and stems off the dewy berries, which she placed one by one in a clean bowl.

"Morning," Harriet said. She slipped her arm behind what was left of the Sea Islander's waist. Septima's presence eased her heavy heart. The berries reminded Harriet that she should eat, and she took one. "Can I?" she said.

"You paying for em, Miz Harriet," Septima said stiffly. "I jest works here."

"Jest work here? You practically running the place." Harriet took a berry from the bowl and ate it. The room grew quiet.

Septima kept her eyes on her work. "Den why don't I know what's happening under my own roof?"

Harriet squeezed Septima's torso and laid her cheek against the high abdomen. An abrupt kick caused her to start back. Harriet put a hand on the dome just in time to catch the mysterious ripple. Septima held her breath and felt the other side of her taut belly. The two women laughed.

"You ketch dat backflip?" Septima said. "I fearing I got me another boy."

"Or a girl who never gone mind," Harriet said.

"Hmm." Septima shifted away and resumed sorting. "You know all bout dat, I 'spose."

"Samuel and I been helping General Montgomery," Harriet said.

"Dat what taking you clear to Hilton Head every other minute? Or have you finally gone sweet on somebody? Somebody like dat man?" Septima rested her purple-stained fingers on the basket. She looked at Harriet. Hurt clouded her eyes. "'Cause you don't need to sneak 'round me. We friends or not?"

Harriet bit her lip. She'd spent so much of her life dodging the law and avoiding the truth that it was hard to know how to answer simple questions. Lies sometimes sprang more readily to her tongue than the truth. She expected Septima to trust her, yet Harriet resisted doing the same. If one carried secrets, friends turned into strangers.

"A course, we friends," she said.

"Den why ain't you act like it? You don't tell me nothing."

"You know I help General Hunter some."

"And what bout dat man who jest left? Lookin' like a hound dog wit' chicken feathers in his mout'?"

"He's a scout."

Septima resumed her task. She pitched blackberry stems onto the worktable. "I heard dat one befo'."

Harriet wished she could explain, but they couldn't afford to lose the element of surprise. It took only one innocent slip of the tongue to alert a suspicious ear. One spy in a rowboat to deliver word to a picket on the Combahee. One picket on a horse to speed a telegraph message to the arsenal in Savannah. Just one.

Yet all Harriet had on Port Royal was one real friend. Just one.

"You might a seen them gunships down at the dock," she said. "I'm going with them. Samuel, too. Colonel Montgomery's in charge."

Septima looked at Harriet in surprise. Her curved eyebrows shot up. "Ki! To Florida, Miz Harriet? I hear dat boat captain got blowed clean out a de pilothouse last trip south."

Harriet ignored the part about Florida. "That's right. Poor man. Buried him at sea."

Septima used her hand to sweep the discarded stems into her now empty basket. She set it on the floor. "How long you be away?"

Harriet hesitated. "Couple a days."

Septima frowned. "Florida real far, ain't it?"

"Yes'm. Bout a hundred and fifty miles both ways."

"Dere and back in two days?" Septima said.

Harriet selected another fat berry from the bowl and popped it in her mouth. She bet the farmer had used dried molasses for fertilizer. "These gone make good pie," she said after a moment. "That crop finally hit its stride." Harriet brushed her hands together to clean them. "The crop on the mainland, it's ripe for picking too."

Understanding ticked across Septima's face. "De inlet where you found me 'n de boys. Dat ain't very far a'tall. Not like Florida."

Harriet didn't blink. "No, ma'am. That's much closer."

Septima crossed her hands atop her baby. "I got family scattered up and down dis devil coast, Miz Harriet. Most, I don't even know where dey gone. My sistah, though, she on the Nichols Plantation. Lawd knows I'd give anything—everything—to see Juno again."

Harriet thought of her own lost sisters and rose on her toes to kiss Septima's cheek. "I know jest how you feel," she said. "Don't you worry none. The Lord be watching over us both."

CHAPTER TWENTY-SIX

Our masters they have lived under the flag, they got their wealth under it, and [provided] everything beautiful for their children. Under it, they have ground us up and put us in their pocket for money. But the first minute they think that ol' flag means freedom for we colored people, they pull it right down, and run up that rag of their own. But we'll never desert the ol' flag, boys . . . and we'll die for it now.

Corporal Price Lambkin, 1st South Carolina Volunteers

HARRIET PULLED A SECOND HANDFUL OF bandages from the linen shelf in the hospital, concerned that she hadn't gotten enough the day before. As she did, she wondered if she'd left her sewing scissors at the boardinghouse. She might need them later to cut away clothing. Harriet set her canteen on the floor along with the bandages. She groped inside the satchel. A moment later, she felt the pointed tips. Relieved, she stuffed the bandages on top.

Doctor Durant poked his head in the doorway. "Harriet. Just in time. We're out of whiskey for pain. Can you hold a patient for me?"

"Sorry, doc," Harriet said as she struggled with the bag. "Ain't got time for surgery this morning."

"Won't take more than twenty minutes. It's a simple procedure. My Monday volunteer hasn't shown up."

Harriet pushed harder on the bulky bandages, shoving the edges down into the crevices until she managed to buckle the bag. "Jest can't, sir. Maybe Doctor Hawks can lend you someone."

Durant frowned, but Harriet kept her head down and made her way out the door with the satchel on one shoulder and a full canteen on the other.

The street was deserted. Horses and soldiers that had been outside when she arrived were gone. Alarmed, Harriet hurried down the avenue. Not until she turned onto Bay Street and heard the roll of a snare drum did her nerves calm.

Lined up in strict formation, troops of the 2nd South Carolina Volunteers waited in closely packed queues from the head of the wharf all the way up Bay Street. Sunlight flashed on their muskets and bayonets, arrayed like knives in a box across their bluecoated shoulders. The colored troops faced stoically forward while onlookers milled at the margins. Montgomery must be taking all of his men. Three hundred.

Townsfolk and field hands from across Port Royal Island had turned out to witness the launch of the 2nd South Carolina. Harriet spotted a woman selling lemonade from a folding table. A dog was curled underneath. A boy with a basket on his head hawked fruit on the crowded walkway. "Best peaches on de islan'!" the youngster called. Shopkeepers stood with their arms crossed in doorways, and two clerks in a second-floor window whistled down at a young woman walking by who ignored them, though a corner of her mouth turned up. A silent mother gripped the hand of a small boy on the corner. "Where papa going?" Harriet overheard the child ask his mother.

Harriet hurried by with the eerie sensation that every day of her life had been preparation for this one. It was the only day she couldn't miss. Without thinking, she moved faster. Two horse-drawn wagons blocked Bay Street for an instant, and she dashed around them with an irrational fear of losing sight of the ships and being left behind.

By the time she reached the dock, soldiers had begun to embark.

Officers directed the queues to their appointed transports while sutlers toting baskets hugged the edges of the wharf, working to deliver the last supplies. Harriet waded through the crowd until she reached the *John Adams* at the end of the dock, leading the flotilla, where a black officer checked his manifest and waved her aboard the main deck. She passed under one medium-size and two large tenders lashed overhead. Opposite them on the starboard side of the ship, four small rowboats swung on hooks.

At the foot of the ladder to the boiler deck, another officer checked his list carefully for Harriet's name, as did a third before admitting her to the hurricane deck and up another ladder to the square glass pillbox perched over the forecastle of the steamboat. There in the pilothouse, Colonel James Montgomery consulted the captain and a local waterman. The chamber had windows on all four sides. Beneath them, the wealthy town, marshes, and estuary looked like a drawing room mural. Seagulls fought over a fish on a piling far below.

Harriet stood in the doorway, waiting to be recognized. She noticed that Montgomery had finally shaved. His collar was open, but his missing button had been replaced, and the uniform had been ironed.

An enormous steering wheel dominated the pilothouse, which smelled of cheap pipe tobacco. A table and a captain's chair sat in one corner, next to freshly painted millwork and a sparkling new pane of glass. The sharpshooter's bullet that had shattered Captain Clifton's brainpan during the last expedition to Florida must have busted the window, too. Although the pilothouse had been repaired, the man's wife was still broken, Harriet knew. Whenever she passed Clifton's home, his widow stood at the window, staring onto the port as if waiting for her husband to sail in.

"What time will we approach the bar?" Montgomery asked the new captain, David Vaught. An older white man with a long, gray beard that brushed his chest, Vaught removed a corncob pipe from between his teeth and looked to the local pilot. Harriet had met

Vaught once before when leaving Hunter's office. He ignored her now.

"What time, would you say?" Vaught asked the pilot in a flat New York accent.

The Gullah waterman withdrew a watch on a chain. "Dat depend on when we leave, Cap'n." He glanced at the timepiece, then at the tidal straits of the Beaufort River swirling past. "Round one in de morning, I 'spect. We gone have to hang back some til de tide rises, sah. Nuf to take over us de bar."

Captain Vaught put his pipe in a dish, shuffled aside the map on the small desk, and withdrew a chart underneath. It appeared to be a tide table. "The flood should be sufficiently high around three," he told the colonel after consulting the paper. "But it's best to arrive early and not cast anchor until we can cross. The tide waits for no one."

Montgomery nodded, satisfied. "We should have a couple hours' leeway, then."

Captain Vaught cocked his head in Harriet's direction without looking at her. "What's a woman doing on board?" His voice was gruff.

Montgomery gave her his attention. "Moses, find yourself a corner. I won't need you for a while." To Vaught, he simply said, "Tell you later."

"Yes, Colonel," Harriet replied. "You want me back when we near the bar?"

"That instant. And bring Heyward, since he saw the torpedoes last. I want both of you up here once we're on the river."

"Yes, sir," she said.

Harriet made her way back to the hurricane deck, filling with soldiers and their gear. Bayonets were sheathed. Men stowed their canvas knapsacks on their laps and fixed their cartridge boxes on their belts. White officers circulated on deck.

Next to one of the twenty-pounders, two Rhode Island gunners hurriedly stacked scattered cannonballs. The ammunition piles next to the other cannons were arranged in neat pyramids, but something had upset theirs. Other crews waited in knots around the guns. "Cussed idiots! I told you keep your eyes open," an officer berated two white artillerymen as they restacked the cannonballs. "I turn my back one goddamn second—"

After the officer stomped away, a colored soldier with the insignia of the 2nd South Carolina approached and held out an iron ball. He cocked his head toward a water cask. "Dis one roll behind dat barrel."

A white artilleryman took the shell. "Thank you," he said, and then he placed it in the growing pile.

Harriet eyed the open space in the middle of the deck. Officers must be saving it for the contraband. She calculated that the space would hold at least three hundred people, and she wished it were bigger. The other decks might take another two hundred.

The old ferryboat had been stripped of all nonessential equipment. Ghostly screw-holes for missing passenger benches pocked the deck at regular intervals. Harriet found an empty spot on the deck with her back to the saloon where ladies took the shade in normal times. A cork life preserver still dangled from a hook above her head. The prospect of a long wait reminded Harriet how little she had rested in recent days and that she'd gotten less sleep than planned the night before. Now she'd be forced to sit still. It might be a few hours before they shoved off and several more before they crossed the bar into the Combahee.

Harriet took a packet of dried pork strips from her satchel. Her head felt woozy. From where she'd posted herself, she should spy Samuel and Walter the moment they came up the ship's ladder. Though hungry, she set the food in her lap while she retrieved Linah's button from the inside pocket of the satchel. Dyed brown to match her sister's dress, the polished-bone button had two thread holes. Harriet pressed it to her lips. "Tomorrow," she whispered, then she tucked it back into the deepest recess.

At last, she unwrapped her food, took the hunk of dried pork she'd brought for supper, and chewed slowly. She was determined not to use the boat's rations and hoped Montgomery had brought enough to provision the refugees on the long sail back to Port Royal. No one would starve, but they'd need something in the course of a day. Once finished with her meager meal, Harriet put her satchel behind her back for support and leaned against the wooden wall to wait. She took a tiny sip from her army canteen and grimaced at its metallic taste. The glare off the water was intense. She blinked—and closed her eyes without meaning to. The sounds of the dock ceased and the light went out.

A girl with pigtails clung to the white rail with two hands. "Auntie," she called excitedly over her shoulder as the wharf slipped away, "we gone see the ocean?"

"Aunt Harriet," she corrected the child. Harriet wanted the girl to remember she wasn't an auntie of the type black children had wherever they went, but that she was a real aunt, an aunt with a name.

"Aunt Harriet, is the sea big? Mama say it real big."

Harriet didn't want to answer but knew she must. "Your mama's right," she said. "The ocean bigger than anything else in the whole wide world."

"Is the ocean far?"

"Not too far, honey. At the other end a the Chesapeake."

"We gone see it soon?" Margaret asked. She wore a wide straw hat with a chinstrap on which she tugged. The nine-year-old seemed younger than Harriet recollected being at the same age, but she supposed that's what freedom looked like. White children struck her the same.

"Bal'more's at the top a the Chesapeake," Harriet said. "We gotta sail all the way south fore we come to the sea."

"Mama says we shouldn't go south. Not ever," the child said.

"Your mama wants you to have a good education, sugar. Up north," Harriet said, twisting the truth like a washrag. The child's *real* mama did want that, though Harriet's sister-in-law had wept when Harriet came through the back door and reminded Mary of her promise, at which she gestured to the home she had provided: glass in every window and a piano in the parlor. Harriet's former brother-in-law, Isaac, had driven off in what appeared to be a new carriage. The timber business must be good.

"You got your boy," Harriet said, her face set and her mind made up. "Margaret's my girl, and I ain't leaving her behind in the land a slavery, where she can walk down the street and see other children bought and sold in the middle a town."

"But when I gone talk to Mama?" the child now said. She hung from the rail with her shoes nosed against the decorative slats. Margaret had such observant brown eyes. Why didn't they know their own mother? When tears spilled down the child's cheeks, Harriet felt she would gladly walk from Maryland to Pennsylvania again to ease the pain. But this wasn't a hurt she could take away. She'd imposed it.

Rachel materialized at Harriet's elbow. Her sister's hair stood on end, uncombed. It had turned shock-white, though she was barely thirty. "Got my boys?" her sister asked and grabbed onto Harriet's arm. "You got Ben and Algerine?"

"You didn't tell me where they are," Harriet said.

But Rachel didn't relent. "Find em," she said. "We counting on you. Don't you let us down."

Harriet tried to throw off her sister's grasp. Not everyone could be rescued; Margaret didn't even want to be rescued. Harriet was doing her best yet must always do more. God had told her that again and again, though she wondered why He worked her so hard. Why her safety mattered so little to Him. A man like any other, she sometimes felt when He seemed not to listen.

The hold on her arm tightened.

"Moses," a voice said far away. Someone gently shook her.

Harriet woke from her nightmare. She passed a hand over her eyes. The ship's railing came into focus.

Samuel sat alongside her with his wide knees drawn up in the small space. Next to him, Charles Simmons and Walter Plowden stood with their backs to the wall, looking toward land. The ship under them vibrated. Night had fallen. A full moon hung over the river.

"You was out a while," Samuel said in a low voice. "You okay?"

"Thought I'd get some shut-eye fore things get lively," she said to ease his mind. She didn't want him thinking about her problem.

Harriet rose. Samuel stood as well. Only a few lights glowed from scattered cabins on shore. Men in uniform remained seated, but every neck craned to see the island slip away. Voices hummed with excitement as the boat's speed quickened. The spirit was infectious, the sentiment palpable: They were going for their kin. From the Beaufort River into the Coosaw, they were threading the maze of slavery, and this time they were armed.

A black sergeant strode into their midst. His heavy boots thundered on the wooden deck. "Quiet!" he said. "I don't want to hear a whisper 'til we reach our target. Your dang fool voices carry right across open water, and the colonel's counting on the Secesh to take us for a supply ship, not a troop ship. So don't let me see a single cheroot or pipe."

Montgomery appeared. He must have descended the ladder from the pilothouse. The crowd fell silent. The colonel cleared his throat, and men leaned forward not to miss a word.

"I'm saying this only once, soldiers, and then I need you to be absolutely silent. Not a hoot. Not a holler. We're on the most important mission of this war. This isn't just about attacking enemy positions. This is about fighting a way of life. We're going to show the world that evil men can no longer make money from treating people like beasts. You've been told we're headed to Florida. That plan's changed."

The colonel paused. Light from a lantern gleamed on his shaved cheeks. He had fastened the top button of his uniform. Standing tall, he looked fully in command. "Our brave scouts have found a way to strike closer to home," he continued. Montgomery nodded in Harriet's direction, and a few soldiers glanced her way. "We're headed up the Combahee, men."

"Yes!" a voice broke out.

"Praise God!" someone next to the ladder said. A buzz swept the ship.

"Shhh," the sergeant hissed angrily. The deck fell silent except for the splash of the side-wheels and chug of the engine.

"We'll be at the mouth of the river before morning," Montgomery said. "Some of you will storm the Rebel positions at Fields Point and Tar Bluff. Captain Apthorp and the men of the *Harriet Weed* will attack the Nichols place. Most of you, along with troops from the *Sentinel*, will continue with me to the plantations on the upper reaches of the river. You've trained for this, men. The fate of every man and woman on these shores depends upon your devotion to duty." Montgomery paused. Emotion colored his face in the glow of the lantern that an ensign held aloft. "Glory, hallelujah!" the former preacher added with feeling.

"Glory, hallelujah," went up the soft echo from men unable to restrain their voices. "Damn straight," came a call from the artillery. Several laughed.

A shrill boat whistle cleaved the moment in two. Montgomery froze, startled, then whipped around. He vanished up the ship's ladder. The whistle sounded again, and Harriet realized it came from one of the ships behind them, out of view around a bend. Three long whistles followed. The universal signal for distress.

"Quiet!" the sergeant barked before anyone spoke.

Every soul tensed. Harriet held her breath. What had gone wrong?

A moment later, the *John Adams*'s heartbeat chugged to a stop. The splash of the paddle wheels ceased, and the anchor chain clanged off its spindle. Montgomery and the colored pilot descended the ladder and continued on down to the lower decks. The earlier command of silence took on greater import. A profound hush fell over the deck. Everyone strained to hear what was happening. When a man coughed, three shushed him. Minutes passed, broken only by the sound of rowboats being lowered into the water. Time passed with unbearable slowness. An hour or more later, Harriet heard the crew clamber back aboard. The *Adams*'s engine roared to life. But instead of continuing on its voyage, the gunboat drew up anchor and began a three-point turn in the water, back toward Beaufort.

A soldier across from Harriet groaned. "Oh, Gawd, no. Turning 'round? My mama on de Cum'bee," he said to the man next to him, who put a finger to his lips.

Harriet felt like jumping to her feet. She must find Montgomery. They couldn't abort the mission. They couldn't turn back. Not now. The sergeant who had spoken earlier came up the ladder from the boiler deck to deliver the news.

"Everyone stay put, exactly where you is," he commanded. "The *Sentinel*'s hit a sandbar. They can't get her off, so the *Adams* and *Weed* are gone take on her men. We'll be underway again after that."

An artilleryman across from Harriet let out a whoop. Others moaned with relief.

"Damn *Sentinel*," a Rhode Islander said. Standing beside his howitzer, the white man spoke distinctly, though he kept his voice low. "Everyone knew she was a tub."

"Good thing Montgomery balked at putting guns aboard," another gunner said. "I'd hate to move those twenty-pounders in the dark."

Harriet calculated quickly on her fingers. Taking on the *Sentinel*'s troops meant at least an extra hundred soldiers divided between the *Adams* and *Weed*—fifty apiece—plus the loss of all the *Sentinel*'s passenger space. Possibly three hundred people, all told. Could she be right? "How many we gone lose?" she whispered to Samuel.

He knew exactly what she meant. "We down at least three hundred," he murmured in her ear. Three hundred contraband. Three hundred more souls left behind.

CHAPTER TWENTY-SEVEN

I have left my wife in the land of bondage; my little ones they say every night, where is my father? But when I die, . . . O Lord, I shall see my wife and little children once more.

Anonymous, 1st South Carolina Volunteers

BY THE TIME THE CREW FASTENED down the last tender and hauled up the anchor, they had lost more than two hours. Harriet guessed they wouldn't have to wait for the flood tide now. Trailed by the small *Harriet Weed*, the *John Adams* picked its way even more slowly through the Beaufort River, past the shifting sandbars. Once they gained the wider Coosaw, they sped up. The steam engines throbbed so loudly that Harriet feared a boiler might burst and burn them to the waterline. She'd seen a ship on the Hudson explode once. Sparks flew so high they looked like stars. All but three passengers died.

The sound of their engines bounced off the mainland. The paddle wheels swooshed steadily. Silent and tense, the soldiers kept their heads low. The full moon gleamed on the barrels of their smoothbore muskets. A few infantry—the better shots—had the newer Springfield rifles.

Although pinned between two men, Harriet felt only Samuel's leg and shoulder, acutely aware of his presence. He adjusted his position at one point to get more comfortable, and Harriet shifted

251

in response to let him know she was awake. When the ship took a small wave against the starboard side and briefly wallowed, the warm solidity of his hip against hers made her heart swell. He wouldn't leave her. If they didn't die on the Combahee, they would be with one another always.

At last, a shift in the breeze alerted Harriet that they had entered the Sound. Soon they would approach the bar that blocked ships from the Combahee at low tide. The moon had passed the high point. It must be near three in the morning.

Harriet slid her hand over Samuel's thigh, grateful for a last excuse to touch him. The fabric of his trousers was rough under her palm. She shook his sturdy leg. He nodded, and they rose together, stepped around the men propped against the saloon, and made their way up the ladder to the pilothouse.

Colonel Montgomery and Captain Vaught leaned over a map spread across the table, attended by a young ensign. The pilot was at the wheel. A candle in a hurricane glass lit the room. Montgomery straightened as they entered and looked at Harriet. He held a mug of coffee. "You say the first torpedo is in the channel on the blind side of the island, right?"

"Yes, sir," she said. "That's where our informant said they laid the mine."

"My brother," Samuel offered.

Montgomery swallowed the dregs of his coffee and set down the cup. "One of you confirm that with your own eyes?"

"No," Harriet answered. "We didn't have time."

The colonel frowned. "Wasn't that why you went upriver?"

Harriet couldn't tell him she'd been more anxious to find the mine near the ferry. There hadn't been time to comb the mouth of the river as well, especially with pickets guarding it so closely. "We jest couldn't do it all," she said. "But the location makes sense. Secesh want to sink us or force us into the open."

"Well, into the open we go," Montgomery said grimly.

The flat, dark marshes on either side of the waterway made

the river's mouth appear much wider than it actually was. The pilot set the ship's bow for a middle course as they approached the bar. Samuel dug in his pocket and pressed a piece of dried pork in Harriet's hand. "Eat," he murmured before he stepped outside to watch from the narrow deck surrounding the pilothouse.

Harriet chewed. The man never stopped thinking about food.

The ship sailed slowly in the moonlight. The engine sounded less burdened, though the captain appeared more strained as they approached the bar. The pipe clenched in his teeth had gone out. "Slow up," Captain Vaught told the pilot, speaking around the stem. Without taking his hands off the wheel, the pilot pressed on a treadle near his right foot. The stopping bell rang out. Somewhere below in the engine room, a sailor closed the throttle, and the ship shuddered. The vessel slowed almost immediately.

Harriet made herself small against the wall of the pilothouse. The captain kept checking the chart on the table and talking with the pilot, whose hands remained on the wheel. Vaught ordered the young ensign to sound a bell located outside the pilothouse to signal leadsmen on the main deck. "Make sure we're still at ten feet," Vaught told the junior officer, who dashed out the door, rang the bell, and hustled down the ladder.

A few minutes later, the young man ran up the ladder and back into the pilothouse. His chest heaved. "Still ten!"

"Tide ain't too rough here," the Gullah pilot said over his shoulder to the captain. "De bar stay flat."

Captain Vaught nodded, but fifteen minutes later, he ordered the ensign to ring the bell again to measure the channel's depth. The ship crept along. Montgomery kept lifting his binoculars. After a tense half hour, the captain drew an audible breath.

"Dere we go, sah," the pilot said at the same time. "We over de bar." Shortly thereafter, a small island appeared in the broad river. The experienced pilot navigated to starboard to pass into the channel.

Montgomery left when the hump of Fields Point appeared in

silhouette in the distance. His footsteps faded on the ladder. Two sharpshooters with Whitworth rifles came up after him and positioned themselves on the starboard side of the pilothouse, facing toward the Rebel post.

"Slow the engine," Captain Vaught ordered the helmsman, who again pressed the treadle of the stopping bell. "And don't take out that dock."

The gunship began its slow glide toward the landing. The dawn air was crystalline. Objects seemed sharper than normal, although Harriet couldn't tell if it was the light or her nerves. She studied the low dirt walls of the fort. No silhouette of cannons. But where was the shotgun that had winged Samuel? Where were the kepi caps and Confederate rifles?

She turned around to gauge the position of their sister ship. The *Harriet Weed* must have slowed its engine before they did, according to some plan of Montgomery's, because she now hung well back in the river to allow the *John Adams* to make landfall. The horizon glowed dully with the approach of dawn. The moon had finally set, and the sky overhead was gray.

Harriet left the pilothouse to join Samuel on the narrow walkway. Three decks below them, two crewmen leaped from the bow onto a rude dock. One landed on his feet. The other stumbled and fell to one knee but instantly jumped up to catch a line thrown at his head. Harriet tensed for gunshots from the fort, but the crew cleated the gunship to a piling without incident.

Someone pushed out a gangplank. A white officer armed with a sword and musket ran down the plank, followed by a small detachment of colored soldiers, their boots thumping hollowly. Harriet counted nine men, all with rifles aimed at the earthworks. The next moment, the two deckhands untied the ship and jumped aboard again. The engine roared, and the smokestack belched a black cloud that drifted over the fort.

As the boat pulled away on its upstream course, Harriet gripped the railing, riveted to the drama on shore. The soldiers rushed the weedy hill on which the Rebel picket station sat. One man tripped and fell as a gun went off. Harriet gasped. The soldier sprawled on the ground. He must have been hit. Then he sprang to his feet, grabbed his smoking musket, and continued upward.

In a moment, their advance troops had overrun the earthworks and were inside. Captain Apthorp waved his hat over the wall. Strangely, no shots had been fired other than the soldier's accidental discharge. The outpost must have been abandoned. Harriet wondered if the pickets had spotted the John Adams in the moonlight and gone for help.

"Right behind you, ma'am," a youthful voice said.

Harriet turned. The ensign held the chair from the pilothouse. He set it down, facing upriver. "Captain Vaught sent this," the young man said. "Colonel Montgomery informed him this was your plan, ma'am. Captain said you ought to have front row."

"Thank you, sir," she said. Touched at Vaught's gallantry, Harriet sat down. But she kept to the edge of the chair, careful not to get too comfortable. She couldn't afford to drop off.

The sharpshooters remained at their posts outside the pilothouse. Samuel scrutinized the murky river in the dim light. Below Harriet on the hurricane deck, two officers equipped with binoculars scanned the shore. The flood tide moved briskly now, and within half an hour, they had rounded the oxbow on the approach to the picket station at Tar Bluff. The fort appeared on the right, half a mile ahead.

Harriet got to her feet. "Samuel. You see the torpedo?" she called above the throb of the engine.

Without awaiting an answer, she stepped into the pilothouse. "Captain Vaught. You have the torpedo at Tar Bluff marked on your map?"

The bearded captain stood smoking his pipe over the chart table in the corner. He looked up, and then down again at the map. He gestured toward a coordinate with his corncob. "Montgomery says it's right here. On the near side of the landing."

Harriet studied the map that bore the same markings as the one she'd given Hunter. "Yes, sir."

Samuel put his head in the pilothouse. "Think we spotted it, Captain."

They followed him on deck. The sharpshooters had their rifles to their shoulders now, aimed at the fort on the distant rise. Samuel pointed downward.

The two officers with binoculars waved up at them from the hurricane deck. "There!" one of them called and pointed to a spot some yards ahead. A faint, diagonal-shaped ripple appeared in the water, in the pattern of an arrowhead. It didn't look any different from the trail made by a gator's snout, but the ripple didn't move in relation to the shore, Harriet observed, and it was in the right area.

Captain Vaught dashed back to the wheelhouse. "Torpedo ahead, starboard! Tack to port," he ordered the colored pilot. "Signal the *Weed,*" he told the ensign, who took up a wigwag flag from a metal cylinder next to him and signaled the *Harriet Weed* from the open doorway.

The large ferryboat glided to the left, around the danger. Harriet leaned over the railing as they passed the snag, but the girth of the lower decks, built atop one another, obscured her view of the waterline. The ship then pulled toward the right again, aiming for the makeshift dock at the foot of Tar Bluff. The sharpshooters trained their sights, the boat crew leaped to the pilings, and a small company rushed the fort some thirty feet above their heads.

Again, it was over in moments. Here, too, Confederate defenses were down. No rifle fire, no artillery, no guards. A buzzard, startled from its perch on the wall, winged its way overhead. The dusky river and primitive shore were so quiet aside from the noise of their ship that it seemed there had never been a war.

Colonel Montgomery came up the ladder. He went straight into the pilothouse. Harriet followed. She kept her back to the wall. Captain Vaught removed the pipe between his teeth. It had gone out again, and he stowed it on a window ledge for safekeeping. "I thought those forts were manned."

Montgomery lifted his hat and pushed back a hank of hair that had fallen across his forehead. "I'm sure glad they weren't."

"Might the Secesh be luring us upriver?" Vaught said. "Turning sidewheelers in a narrow channel is no easy trick."

"I don't think they knew we were coming," Montgomery said. "My hunch is they saw us and lit out for reinforcements."

Harriet thought of the Rebel army camped ten miles from the Combahee ferry. She prayed that Samuel's horse trick had cemented the guards' reputation for false alarms. If the Secesh got their field artillery down Stocks Road before the gunships escaped, their cannons would sink the wooden targets.

"Either that," Montgomery said, "or they've concentrated their pickets at the ferry for some reason. Let's hope we don't find an army upriver." The Kansas Jayhawker rubbed his hands together in an unsuitably eager fashion. Harriet pictured him on a raid with wild John Brown, caution tumbling behind them on the road.

"One problem at a time, though," Montgomery continued. "First, we've got to locate the torpedo on the approach to Nichols."

The captain nodded as if that at least conformed to his expectations.

"Then we'll proceed on past while the *Weed* commences the operation," the colonel said.

"Excuse me, sir," Harriet interrupted. "This mean the *John Adams* gone handle the Lowndes Plantation?"

Montgomery looked at her as if not quite seeing her. "We're aiming for the ferry," he said. "The *Adams*'s objective is to destroy the bridge across the river and take down the Heyward and Middleton Plantations." He turned to study the map on the table, talking to no one in particular. "But we still we need to get around the next mine."

Harriet felt a flutter of alarm. "We got people at Lowndes Plantation, sir. The man that helped us find the torpedoes."

The Kansas Jayhawker glanced up as if he had one second for

Harriet and nothing more. "Lowndes was the *Sentinel*'s mission, and she's sitting on a sandbar. We'll stop on the way back if we make good time. If we have room for more contraband," he said, and he turned back to the chart marked with various symbols.

Harriet's hands rolled tight. She stepped outside into the fresh breeze that had risen with the sun. It couldn't be much later than six o'clock in the morning. They should have plenty of time to reach the upper plantations and still raid the Lowndes estate, so long as they didn't encounter a Confederate force lying in wait at the ferry crossing. And that was good because Harriet would not leave Jacob and Kizzy behind.

Chapter Twenty-Eight

I stood on the river of Jordan,
to see that ship come sailing over.
Stood on the river of Jordan,
to see that ship sail by.
Spiritual

L USH RICE FIELDS APPEARED ON EITHER side of the river well
before Nichols's landing on the north bank. Low levees curved
with the river. Slave cabins above and beyond on the hills sat like
wooden blocks some careless child had scattered on a green carpet.
Dark heads dotted the fields, bent over and already hard at work in
the ankle-deep water, weeding the spring crop.

Suddenly, a small figure in a white turban around half a mile
away straightened in the middle of a verdant expanse. It must be
a woman, Harriet thought, since she wore a gray flour sack over a
long skirt. The slave shielded her brow against the bright sunrise.
She froze a long moment, and then she turned to someone stooped
several rows over. Harriet wondered what the woman was saying
and if she saw the Stars and Stripes flying from the mast. Would a
slave so remote from any town know the flag, or that it meant freedom? Had Charles's informant on the Nichols Plantation alerted
the right people?

A broad causeway dividing the wet fields ran toward a mansion
of modest size. The wooden house possessed a long, shaded porch

along the front, with a view commanding the river. A white man and a black servant stood on it, looking toward the ships. The white man raised what appeared to be a short telescope. He stood perfectly still with his spyglass trained on the *John Adams*. The black man was gesturing.

Harriet gripped the arms of her chair, and then she lifted her hand to wave in salute. She hoped the white man saw her in his telescope. She wasn't hiding anymore. *Now you know*, she thought. *I'm coming for you. I'm right here.*

The planter lowered his instrument. He said something to his servant, who disappeared into the house. The white man looked again through his spyglass before he ran inside, too. Was he going for his horse to alert the rebel army up Stocks Road?

The *John Adams* slowed as they neared the point on the river that Harriet had marked with a nail the week before. The second torpedo had to be nearby. She got to her feet on the narrow deck to get a better view of the muddy current below. An odd patch of berry bushes grew from the side of the levee. It would be a tricky place to pick fruit—but useful as a landmark.

"There!" she and Samuel called at the same time. He dashed to the pilothouse and was inside even before she. Harriet heard shouts from the hurricane deck as spotters below marked the torpedo, too.

"Captain. That bush yonder," he said, pointing. "Snag's thirty feet out from them bushes."

The pilot leaned hard on the spokes of the immense wheel. The ship lumbered slowly toward the south bank. They barely missed the triangular ripple. The ensign again waved his flag from the doorway, and the *Harriet Weed* mimicked their course. Colonel Montgomery disappeared down the ship's ladder, and Harriet stepped out of the pilothouse. On the hurricane deck below, she spotted Walter Plowden, who waved up at her. She waved back, and they both grinned. Harriet ducked back inside the cabin.

Captain Vaught spoke to the ensign. "Signal the *Harriet Weed* to land," and the young officer took up a different flag.

The *John Adams* continued its pace, still moving upriver but slowly enough to watch the other ship as she rounded the torpedo and steamed toward Nichols's landing. Captain Vaught reached for the cord of the ship's whistle. A deafening blast resounded across the river and rice fields. The *Weed* replied with a shrill toot of her own. A shout went up from the deck as soldiers waved and hollered at surprised slaves who looked up like startled deer from their work. Harriet broke into a grin at the signal to commence the operation. She hoped John Brown heard their whistle from his throne in heaven.

Harriet exited the pilothouse again and stood by her chair—too excited to sit—as they passed the Nichols mansion. The activity in the surrounding rice fields had changed. Voices filled the air as people called to one another. Dark faces headed in different directions. Some migrated toward the levee. Others streamed purposefully toward the mansion and cabins beyond. In the middle of one immense field, a man and woman argued as he tugged her toward the river and she pulled toward the cabins in the far distance. Harriet thought of Septima's sister Juno.

An overseer holding the reins of a spooked horse on the elevated causeway struggled to get his foot in the stirrup without letting go of his gun. He danced around the skittish animal but kept missing the swinging loop. The horse shied. The white man stumbled. His mouth worked as if he was cursing.

Samuel came to stand by her. He pointed at the faraway overseer. "Look at that Buckra," he said with a laugh. "Shitting his pants!"

Rifles cracked from the deck below. Two sharpshooters had fired at the white man. Just then, he swung up into the saddle, shot his own gun in the air, turned his horse toward the road that divided the rice fields from the forest, and galloped toward the Confederate encampment.

"Let's hope he don't reach the army," she said.

The *Harriet Weed* pulled neatly into the landing. Within moments, a regiment of colored soldiers sprinted from the ship with their muskets, led by a white captain. Four colored soldiers held torches they must have touched to the boilers at the last moment. Two others carried smoking metal buckets filled with hot pitch.

Harriet stepped around her chair to watch from the rear. The federal soldiers fanned out, running toward different buildings on the plantation. A sizeable group moved in the direction of the main road, perhaps to intercept Rebel pickets before they could reach the main army. A handful made for the barns and a rice mill with a grain chute. Two men with torches ran onto the wooden porch of the plantation house, followed by one with a bucket, who spilled the burning contents onto the floorboards. Harriet couldn't see what happened next as the *John Adams* rounded a bend in the river at that very moment.

Alone now, their ship glided alongside the low dike another mile or so, following the curve of the fields. Workers stared disbelievingly as the ship moved past, but some were already headed back toward their cabins. A few ran. One raggedy man climbed the dike and tried to hail the boat, but the vessel sailed on.

Harriet called across the water. "Get your people," she said and pointed in the direction of the Nichols Plantation. "There's another ship!"

The man kept waving. Sweat from the morning's labor coursed down his face. A boy and girl with bare feet stood at the bottom of the levee looking up at him. Samuel cupped his hands to his mouth and leaned over the railing. "The landing. Get to the landing," he yelled.

The man nodded, climbed back down into the field, and grabbed his children by the hand.

An acrid scent arrived on the water breeze. Harriet looked downriver. Three massive columns of black smoke rose over the Nichols

Plantation. The air smelled of burning timbers and scorched rice. Their troops must have found the storerooms.

The incoming tide continued to push strongly. The *John Adams* steamed upriver faster now. As they rounded an oxbow, Harriet wondered when they would reach the Lowndes property. They soon passed an inlet at the edge of a flat marsh, and she recognized the tributary up which Walter had rowed her a few nights earlier. Jack's Creek, he'd called it. Incredulous faces met them again as the levee reappeared on the other side of the reed-choked marsh. The workers must not have heard the commotion downriver, though they had likely caught the odor of smoke. Seeing colored soldiers, several people bolted toward the ship. A group of women weeding near the edge of the dike turned their faces in unison, like sunflowers.

Troops arrayed on the hurricane deck waited with remarkable stoicism at the railing for their turn to disembark and take up the attack, but one man suddenly lifted his rifle overhead. He shook the gun to attract the attention of someone on shore. "Ma," he shouted. His voice broke. "Ma—!"

Several women in the field started forward instinctively, and then they stopped. One took a few more halting steps before throwing down her hoe. She began to run. Her arms pumped wildly. She pelted forward without speaking. The man at the rail kept calling, "Ma!"

A trunk minder must have opened the gates the night before, when sweet water flowed past on the ebb, because the woman's skirt trailed and floated in the mire of the newly flooded field. She tripped more than once in the drifting grass. Just a few paces from the dike, her foot tangled with some weeds, and she sprawled headlong. Her face and dress were covered with mud when she scrambled up the levee on all fours.

By then, the *John Adams* had passed the spot where she jumped to her feet and waved her arms, but the troops on deck parted to allow the young soldier to run the length of the railing with his musket jiggling on his back. He looked ready to jump in the river and swim for her, but at the stern, he stopped. Mother and son appeared rooted, afraid to break eye contact.

Tears streaked the woman's face. "William!" she cried.

Other soldiers shouted and pointed, some downriver to Nichols, others upriver to Lowndes. The young man yelled back. "Downriver, Ma! Downriver."

Harriet turned her chair to face the bow, and she gripped the arms to steady her trembling nerves. It was hard to know if the woman would make it in time. *Godspeed*, she prayed, *Godspeed*. Only one thing was certain. If a Confederate force awaited them at the ferry, other mothers would soon be left on the bank.

Chapter Twenty-Nine

I was awakened in my bed by the driver, who rushed precipitately in my room, and informed me that two of the enemy's ships were in full sight.. . . . I arose, dressed myself with all possible speed . . . and, sure enough, there were the two steamers—one quite small, and the other very large, crowded with armed men in dark uniform. It seemed to me that I also saw women seated in chairs upon the upper deck of the large steamer.

Joshua Nichols, Combahee Planter

Colonel Montgomery ran up the ladder a while later and stepped inside the pilothouse. Harriet followed impatiently.

"How far to the ferry?" Montgomery asked Captain Vaught, who kept the unlit pipe clamped between his teeth.

The captain set the pipe on his chart table. He took out his pocket watch. "We're at three-quarters flood. Maybe half an hour. Six thirty at the latest. We've still got to pass the last torpedoes."

Montgomery nodded. "I want to land the two larger tenders just before that. We need to alert the contraband and commence operations against the dikes."

"You want me to go ashore, sir?" Harriet asked.

"No." The colonel stepped outside the pilothouse. "Samuel," he called. "Show me the location of the torpedoes again."

Samuel entered the cabin and bent close to the chart. He stroked his pointed beard, straightened, and tapped the map with his finger. "Right here. See where the Cum'bee takes a small, sharp

turn—hardly shows on the map—then narrows? A stand of tupelos grows right there. Within sight a the ferry. The mines are just
below the surface. The current's strong, so it's tricky. Normally,
you might hug the inside, especially since the high tide gone whip
us fast into that bend."

The river pilot, who hadn't said a word in hours that Harriet
recalled, looked over his shoulder. His weathered hands still
gripped the wheel. "How I sposed to know what to watch for, if
dem tupelos on t'other side?"

Harriet inhaled sharply. Samuel had scouted the mines from
the vantage point of the ferry. The meandering river that watered
the rice fields looked the same for miles. The gunship might be
around the bend before they spotted the trees and in danger of
veering too close to one bank or the other.

"We'll launch the tenders early. Get troops up on the dikes,"
Montgomery said rapidly. "Their view will be more open. They
can fire a signal."

"That's gone alert the pickets at the ferry," Samuel said.

"They'll see us soon enough anyway." Montgomery turned to
the captain. "Reverse the paddle wheels in fifteen minutes and
bring us to a stop so we can launch the boats. That's halfway to the
ferry by your calculations, correct?"

"That's about right," Vaught said.

"It better be right," he said. "Mark your watch, Captain. And
Samuel—keep your eyes open for torpedoes." He turned to Harriet.
"You watch from the other side. Spotters will be on the lower
decks, too. Be ready." With that, Montgomery vanished again
down the ladder.

Harriet and Samuel's eyes met. If they got past the mines, they
would make landfall soon. He looked as if there were a dozen
things he wanted to say. Instead, he stepped out of the cabin to
take his post, and Harriet brushed her fingers against his as she
passed behind him to the opposite deck.

Slaves in the fields on the south bank of the Combahee flocked toward the levee. Harriet thought they must be from the Middleton Plantation, which Walter had said was near the ferry and across from Heyward's. She turned around to glance through the cabin's large windows at the right bank once more. They must have been sailing past the lower portion of the Heyward estate for some time. The men and women she'd seen could be Samuel's people. Perhaps Lucy was among them, already risking a driver's wrath to spread the word. Harriet hoped the woman would be all right. The mother of Samuel's boys.

A horse's high whinny caught her attention. She turned around. Two white men galloped down a causeway toward the river on the Middleton side, brandishing whips and yelling at field hands to get back. One fired his shotgun over the heads of the fleeing workers. A furious pack of hounds followed. Their baying vied with the ruckus of the horses. The riders split once they reached the levee and rode in opposing directions to ward people away from the bank. The dogs were confused about which horse to follow, and they stopped at the end of the causeway to bark at men and women near the river. A yellow hound, yapping and snarling, broke from the pack and dove into the field when a man sprinted. The muscled dog leaped onto the slave's back. Its teeth closed on the man. The pack swarmed over the pair. The runaway vanished under the melee.

"No!" a soldier on the deck below Harriet called.

"Lawd a mercy," someone cried.

Harriet tore her gaze from the scene, unable to watch. There was nothing they could do except press on. A rifle cracked loudly and Harriet's eyes darted to the hurricane deck below. With a Springfield on his shoulder, a member of the 2nd South Carolina had broken rank. He stared to see the effect of his shot. The pack of dogs was in disarray. A scrambled mass on the ground possessed the hind legs of a yellow hound. The bloodied, half-naked slave stumbled to his feet.

"Hold your fire," a white officer yelled. "Save your ammunition for the Secesh army!"

The ship shuddered. Harriet grabbed at the railing. The *John Adams* must be stopping. Black water swirled upriver, bypassing her. The paddle wheel on the port side dredged muck as it churned backward. The vessel struggled against the incoming tide. A moment later, two large tenders with a handful of troops each passed off the bow of the ship. While the gunship trembled in the flood, men disembarked from the boats onto the bank. One waved an American flag as he strode up and down on the raised levee.

Other soldiers now reached down to pull slaves up onto the bank and push them toward the Heyward Plantation. Slaves farther afield were waved in the same direction. A man in the blue of the 2nd South Carolina blew a bugle. The thrilling notes of reveille sounded across the river, fields, and causeways. Then the paddle wheels on the *John Adams* reversed again, the smokestack belched black soot, and the ship steamed upriver once more, leaving the two tenders behind. A bend in the river beckoned. The gunboat slowed. Harriet felt they were drifting, though she knew the pilot maintained some degree of speed to operate the rudder. She leaned over the side and scrutinized the current with a hand to her brow to ward off glare. The bright morning sun dazzled the surface and obscured the depths. The torpedoes must lie just ahead.

Harriet gripped the wooden rail as they took the last turn. Concentrated on the danger to the ship, she barely felt the rail grind against her ribs as she leaned out as far as she could go. The bomb must be nearly underneath them. The Confederate regiment at the ferry would be right beyond it. But then the wide gunboat angled and straightened into another peaceful section of the river. Vast green fields spread out on either side. No torpedoes or troops. No stand of tupelos. Where were they?

A musket blast onshore was chased by another shot. Almost before Harriet realized it, the ship entered another turn. Faster. As they rounded the curving dike, she spotted a small brick ferry building on a rise far to her left with Rebel breastworks next to it. A moment later, six mounted Confederates thundered north across a pontoon bridge on the river beyond the building, headed toward the Heyward estate. At the same time, a cannon boomed so loudly that her ears rang. The reek of gunpowder filled her nostrils. Her eyes stung. She waved away smoke. They were under fire.

Harriet rubbed her eyes and frantically scanned the south bank for the hidden torpedo. The shore came into view dead ahead. A hundred feet away, a peaceful stand of green tupelos rustled along the swampy margins of the river. She squinted through the smoke. A large alligator rested in the shade of the reedy trees. When the reptile spotted the ship, it lumbered to the river. Water rippled outward from its lumpy snout as it dove and disappeared. Harriet couldn't see any other marks on the river aside from the normal dips and shifts of the rushing current. Then she spotted another arrow shape innocently wrinkling the surface. The alligator? She glanced at the trees and back at the snag. The pattern didn't move in relation to the bank. Harriet spun around and rapped on the window of the pilothouse. The captain was speaking to Samuel, who stood in the doorway pointing toward the opposite shore. Another cannon boomed loudly. When the pontoon bridge ahead splintered and shot upward in a blaze of smoke, Harriet realized the *John Adams*'s own guns were firing, not the enemy's.

The ship continued straight for the diagonal snag in the water. They would hit the mine. Harriet rapped harder on the window as a howitzer thundered. Samuel and Captain Vaught debated the far levee. No one heard her. She pounded the glass, which jiggled in the pane.

The pilot leaned heavily on the helm to turn the ship. At the last possible moment, he angled away from Harriet's torpedo. A moment later, he again threw his weight against the massive wheel and the ferryboat zagged in the opposite direction, back toward the ferry landing and away from the second torpedo. A flash caused Harriet to throw a hand in front of her face. She ducked her head against the glare, and then spotted a cigar-shaped mirror above the pilot's head. The man had been watching Harriet and Samuel in the mirror the whole time.

They had safely cleared the last mine.

The next minutes blurred together. The *John Adams* ran up to the ferry station on the south bank, shoved out a gangplank, and disembarked a host of troops with muskets and torches who marched toward the Middleton estate. Another company attacked the pontoon bridge with axes and saws, hacking away until the tide pushed large sections upriver, some ablaze with hot pitch. On the Heyward side of the bank, they landed twenty men who mustered into files and paraded north on the exposed causeway toward the retreating Confederate cavalry. When two Rebels turned around to fire, the Rhode Island artillery opened up, sending shells toward the horsemen, who vanished in the thick smoke.

The *John Adams* continued to advance upriver. They sailed a hundred yards past the ferry building, now consumed in flames, where the pilot made a laborious three-point turn in the narrowing channel and angled their bow downriver. They had traveled twenty-five miles into enemy territory, catching the Secesh unawares. At last, they tied up at Heyward's landing on the north bank of the river.

Harriet could contain herself no longer. *Montgomery doesn't need me to watch a docked ship,* she thought as she rounded the pilothouse. Samuel had already disappeared.

Harriet hurried down to the hurricane deck, then the boiler deck, then the main deck, catching sight of people on both sides of the river streaming toward the embankments. Tall columns of smoke poured from the trees in the direction of the Middleton Plantation.

Get to the gangplank, she thought on each step of the ladders. *Get off the ship. Get everyone on board.*

A sweat-stained man and woman rushed onto the *John Adams* as Harriet reached the main deck, already filling with a babble of voices. Dressed in little more than rags, the woman burst into tears. She fell to her knees and pressed her forehead to the deck. "Tank de Lawd!" she cried. "Tank de Lawd."

"Come on, baby. We safe," the man said, pulling the woman to her feet as others bunched up behind them. "Mas'r Heyward, he jest stan' lookun," the man reassured his wife as they passed Harriet.

"Gran'mammy! Gran'mammy!" cried a young boy who waved over the railing at a wizened old woman in the growing line to board the ship.

"Mos' dere, chile!" she called back with a toothless smile, before she lapsed into a coughing fit because of the smoke.

A rooster escaped from someone's grasp and flew, crowing, back toward land. "Wrong way!" someone called with a laugh.

Colonel Montgomery stood at the top of the gangplank. He held up a hand as Harriet ran toward him. "Stop," he said.

Harriet almost tripped over her feet.

"We've got contraband coming off both banks," he said. "There are plenty of soldiers on this side. I need you upstairs, Moses."

"But—"

"But nothing. Follow me. You're not needed here."

Montgomery brushed past. Tempted to disobey, Harriet turned with reluctance. What could she do from the deck? Harriet glanced over her shoulder as she reached for the rope banister of the ladder and took a last look at the Heyward side of the Combahee. Smoke streamed from the upper windows of a faraway mansion. Flames licked the gray sides of a storage barn. Troops carried bags of rice toward the dock. Walter Plowden, Charles Simmons, and Atticus Blake all had sacks on their backs. One soldier held the reins of a fine horse that he led toward the ship. Harriet supposed that Montgomery had decided to drive his point home in every way possible. Master Heyward would lose his prize pony, too.

In the hubbub, barefoot slaves clinging to every miserable possession came down the causeway. Ragged clothes afforded glimpses of bare torsos and thighs. A girl with a thin quilt ran behind a woman carrying a straw mattress on her back. One man toted a scrawny piglet under each arm. Two twins clung to the skirt of a mother who carried a cooking pot on her head and a toddler on her shoulders. The baby's legs were wrapped around her neck, and he hugged the pot with one arm. Harriet squinted to see better. Wide-eyed with surprise, the toddler dredged something from the tureen with his free hand and sucked his fingers clean.

Despite the chaos, Harriet laughed aloud. Joy coursed through her. Ecstasy tingled in her hands on the rope. They were getting everybody. Piglets and all. Glory, hallelujah.

She spotted a woman standing on a carved chair that belonged in some dining room. Its polished mahogany gleamed in the brilliant sunlight. Instead of running her loot down to the ship, however, the slave woman positioned the chair in the middle of the causeway. She wore an indigo headscarf and waved people toward the levee, commanding them to hurry. The woman was tall, like Septima. Even without the chair, she would be striking.

Samuel appeared in the smoke that drifted over the causeway. He carried a small boy close to his chest, with one hand under the child's bottom and another clasping the boy's head. The woman on the chair jumped down as he approached. Samuel handed off the child and grasped the hands of two other boys who ran up behind him. They would be Sammy and Jake. The baby must be Abe. Samuel's family.

Harriet pushed everything but the battle from her mind and ascended the ladder. Montgomery was right. She wasn't needed on this side of the river.

Chapter Thirty

O moaner, don't you weep,
When you see that ship come sailin' over.
Shout, "Glory, Hallelujah!"
When you see that ship sail by.
Spiritual

THE COLONEL STOOD ON THE HURRICANE deck, his field glasses pointed at the plantation across the river. "Any sign a pickets?" she asked.

Montgomery lowered his binoculars. "No. I think they all escaped over the bridge. Let's pray they don't reach the main army before we cast off."

Harriet nodded. She'd seen the four horses.

Montgomery put the glasses to his eyes once more. "But I'm concerned about the crowd in the trees. The ones coming down the far road." He lifted the lanyard over his head and handed her the binoculars. "We can only take so many without sinking."

A rutted dirt track led from the ferry landing to the estate hidden on a rise. Harriet aimed the glasses at the top of the road. Dense foliage obscured the wooded bluff and smoke further limited her view. The part of the road that came into focus looked deserted. Montgomery tapped her shoulder. "To the right."

Harriet shifted the binoculars. Pines, tupelos, and live oaks swam together in a green blur. She aimed the instrument downward to

273

find the riverbank. Oriented, she pointed the glasses toward the right-hand side of the hill. There, a smaller lane curved through some shanties on the bluff. Odd colors and shapes filtered past the buildings and through the trees. She followed the direction of their movement and picked out the spot where the lane ended down near the river. There, on a short dock built off the levee, a crowd of slaves awaited their turn for a trickle of rowboats that plied back and forth. A soldier at the landing coordinated the boarding process.

Harriet lowered the field glasses. Across the narrow channel, the group on the landing wasn't hard to spot. She noticed a young man with no shirt push around another boy his own age.

A thump sounded below. Harriet peered over the side of the gunship. Two decks down, a small rowboat bobbed against the ship. A pair of black hands reached across the watery gap and helped a woman climb aboard. "Lawd Almighty, a cullud sojer! Tank you, brudduh," she said before disappearing into the ship. The next instant, hands reached forward again and took another refugee by the wrists.

Harriet handed back the binoculars, and Montgomery slung them around his neck. She stared at the crowd, which didn't seem to be growing larger so much as more desperate. Crossing the river by rowboat was a slow process. Armed overseers couldn't be far away, and Rebel reinforcements would be right behind them. Harriet noticed a heap of cooking pots and blankets near the embankment. Someone must have told people they couldn't bring anything.

Another rowboat on the far side of the river loaded a group of slaves. The soldier on the landing raised his hands to keep too many from boarding at once. The dinghy cast off after a moment as another approached. The soldier caught a line thrown to him and knelt to cleat the craft.

The crowd surged around the stooping man. The boy who had pushed ahead of another clambered on board and took a seat in the bow. Others followed. The soldier stood. He put up his hands again. The onward rush slackened, but when the soldier leaned over to speak to a tiny woman who clung to a cooking pot, the fearful crowd surged again, and the dinghy swiftly filled. A refugee untied the line and jumped into the drifting craft. The oarsman steered the boat into the channel.

Harriet observed that the rower pulled easily. The man wasn't fighting the current. She wondered how much time had passed. The Combahee must be napping. Slack water had arrived. Soon the tide would turn.

Another rowboat made for the crowded landing. Harriet no longer saw the soldier on the dock, just a mass of people. Refugees were jammed so close together that she worried someone might fall into the murky river. The soldier on the dock reappeared when he reached up for a rope that came sailing across the water from the approaching dinghy. Several slaves grabbed for it at the same time, and the line fell uselessly into the stream. The rower pulled the dripping rope aboard and threw it again. This time, the soldier caught the line and tied the craft to the dock.

As before, the crowd pressed forward. Panic filled the air. Harriet could smell it—a sharp odor of fear and sweat. Men and women scrambled quickly into the rocking boat. Parents grabbed children onto their laps. A large, well-built man stepped aboard, and the vessel swayed wildly until a boy gave up his seat in the middle. The man pulled the child onto his lap. People shouted in Gullah from the dock to the rowboat. Soon, all the space was taken. Yet the skiff didn't move.

"Cast me off," the oarsman yelled.

The soldier on the dock cupped his hands around his mouth and called, "You clear!"

Yet the dinghy didn't budge. Harriet saw that its bowline dangled in the water. The vessel ought to be moving. Then she realized that refugees still on the dock had gripped the gunwales for fear of being left behind. The rowboat was locked in place.

Montgomery turned to her. "Moses," he said. "Do something. Calm your people, or nobody will get out. Tell them to take turns."

Voices on the far bank grew more tumultuous. "He'p! De Buckra coming," someone shouted. Harriet saw another man tumble onto the small craft. The rowboat dipped perilously low in the water. The dark Combahee almost lapped the gunwales. The soldier on the dock yanked the musket off his back, accidentally banging a woman behind him in the face. With the butt of his gun, he hit at hands clinging to the side of the rowboat, but when one person let go, two others grabbed on. "Hol' fast! Hol' fast!" a mother shouted to the boy alongside her.

Eighty slaves or more now crowded the landing. The lone soldier would soon be overwhelmed. The boat would be swamped, people thrown into the river. Where one alligator waited, there would be others.

Montgomery shook her arm. "Moses, call to your people!"

"Colonel," she snapped, angry at her own helplessness. "They ain't my people. They jest people."

A wild thought occurred to her. They were John Brown's people. Harriet cleared her throat. She began to hum. The notes stuck like dry breadcrumbs. She swallowed and started again. She could think of no other way to calm them. They needed faith.

"John Brown's body is a-molderin' in its grave," she sang hoarsely. Harriet drew a deep breath. "John Brown's body is a-molderin' in its grave," she sang louder and better. Heads on the dock turned in the direction of the tune. A woman looked up from the landing and waved at Harriet. The young boy holding her hand waved, too.

"John Brown's body is a-molderin' in its grave," she sang as loudly as she could. People gripping the boat looked up. "His *soul* is marching on!" she belted from the deck, and she clapped as hard as she could on the powerful word.

Tuneful voices across the water chimed in. "Glory, glory halle- lujah. His *soul* is marching on!" Others clapped, too, as the joyful sound gathered strength. The dory suddenly pulled away. Those holding onto the boat had let go to put their hands together. Miraculously, the crowd had calmed.

"Keep it up," Colonel Montgomery said as he moved to scan the opposite shore for Confederate forces.

Harriet sang on. An oarsman who had backed water in the middle of the channel now rowed toward the landing. The people boarded in an orderly fashion, still singing. The soldier on the dock cast off the line again without interference. A few minutes later, another rowboat pulled away, then another. The floorboards under Harriet's feet hummed. The ship's engine must have started. She sang and clapped until the last rowboat finally pushed off from the landing, loaded with a handful of bondsmen and the soldier from the dock. In the stern of the craft, he looked up wearily at the *John Adams*, then broke into a smile and saluted her as he came alongside.

The gunship shuddered briefly once it got underway again. Harriet kept her eyes trained on the green bluff. Some people worked too far afield to get to the dock. Flickers of light and color suggested movement between the shanties above. High tide had passed. Sweet water pushed back the salt, and the *John Adams* steamed alongside the charred ferry building. A blackened chimney guarded the smoking ruins. Harriet wondered which plantation Private Webster's assistant had been taken to the week before—and if the big-eared man had made it onto the *Adams* or *Weed*.

The Middleton landing receded. She continued gazing upriver. Something bright flashed among the trees at the margins. A second later, a man in a white shirt pounded onto the makeshift dock, followed by a woman. Each carried a child on the hip. The pair waved frantically. Harriet couldn't bring herself to wave back and admit she was leaving them.

CHAPTER THIRTY-ONE

The negroes, men and women, were rushing to the boat with their children, now and then greeting someone whom they recognized among the uniformed negroes . . . The negroes seemed to be utterly transformed, drunk with excitement, and capable of the wildest excesses. The roaring of the flames, the barbarous howls of the negroes . . . and the towering columns of smoke from every quarter, made an impression on my mind that can never be effaced. . . . My pleasant and comfortable house was in ashes.

Joshua Nichols, Combahee Planter

WHEN THE TUPELOS FINALLY DISAPPEARED, HARRIET turned her gaze downstream, looking for the two tenders they'd launched earlier. Not spying them, she surveyed the damage they'd wreaked. Brown lakes squatted in place of green rice fields wherever the floodgates had been destroyed. Harriet counted seven broken rice trunks on the north bank. Birds circled and dove for fish where slaves had weeded at daybreak. Fresh water now sluiced through the openings, too late to undo the damage wreaked by the brackish tide.

And Rome salted the Earth, she recalled Thomas Wentworth Higginson saying from the pulpit of his church. An unexpected sorrow swelled within her at the sight of the destruction. Africa's children had dug and planted and tended these fields with such pain and care. Would white and black both go hungry now? On the Middleton side of the river, where many of the water gates remained intact, groups of slaves from distant fields still hurried down the long causeways. Harriet's gut twisted as the *Adams* steamed past at least a hundred men, women, and children at one turn in the river. "Stop, brudduhs! Save us!" she heard again and again. Even if they had time to stop, there was no more room, accounting for the advance troops they had yet to retrieve.

Samuel stumped up the ladder behind Montgomery.

"—won't leave him, Colonel," he said. His furious tone suggested a threat rather than a promise.

"No one's got special call," Montgomery stated without looking around as they gained the deck. "We've freed at least four hundred already. We're over our capacity."

"There's room for one more."

"And we're bringing more aboard. The tenders might already have your brother."

"*Might* ain't good enough," Samuel said. "He's injured."

"We're not stopping for one man."

"Jacob showed us the torpedoes," Samuel argued. The men faced one another in the doorway of the pilothouse. Both were smoke-stained. Samuel's collar was open, and his face looked like a fist. He seemed a different person, remote and implacable.

"We've got to get downriver before the Secesh bring their guns to Fields Point," Montgomery said. "We'll pick up the tenders from the Lowndes raid on the way. Your brother will either be on them—or he won't."

"I won't leave him behind," Samuel said between gritted teeth.

Montgomery's lips blanched. "You'll do what you're told, soldier."

Samuel's hands balled. "I wear no uniform."

Harriet suddenly understood that Colonel Montgomery had ordered the tenders to take a run at the Lowndes estate. That must be why they hadn't yet reappeared. Perhaps the colonel hadn't mentioned his plan in order to focus Harriet and Samuel on getting past the final torpedoes. Samuel must suspect so. "Never met a reliable white man," he'd once said.

But they still had one tender left—and the troops who'd returned from the Heyward and Middleton estates.

Harriet stepped forward.

"This ain't jest bout Jacob, Colonel," she told Montgomery. "Our troops missed some a them rice trunks. Break every one and you stagger two counties." Her voice strengthened. "And that ain't all."

It took the last ounce of forbearance, but Harriet waited for Montgomery's question. They must get Jacob and Kizzy, but she wouldn't say that. She didn't want Montgomery to think it was personal.

Colonel Montgomery studied her face. Then he turned his back, ignoring the bait.

Samuel's dark eyes looked ready to swallow the Earth whole as the colonel disappeared into the pilothouse. Harriet tugged his sleeve. He stared through her. She tugged harder. He nodded, struggling for self-control, and they followed Montgomery through the doorway.

"We could spare only a handful a men earlier. Send that third tender now, and we won't miss a single water gate," Harriet promised the colonel.

"Lowndes is the cruelest plantation on the river," Samuel said. "It's hard to see from the river, sir, but there ain't no richer target. Bring it down, and every planter in Dixie gone get the message."

Captain Vaught watched the river over the shoulder of the colored pilot. He stroked his long gray beard and glanced toward the colonel. "We have a little time, sir. Not much, but some. You need to tell me now if you want the last tender."

Montgomery frowned. "How much time?"

The grizzled captain checked his watch. "It depends," he said. "The river is going to work with us. Though we'll reach the Sound quicker if we don't send another boat, of course."

"How much time exactly?" the colonel asked.

"Thirty minutes," the captain replied. "After that, we'll be fighting the tide to stay in place—and maybe the Rebs." He ducked his head to get a better view of the mottled sky. "I don't like the look of the clouds neither."

Montgomery turned to Harriet. He finally asked the question she'd anticipated. "What will it gain us?"

She launched into her answer. "Flood them fields and even Charleston won't have rice for supper, sir." The hated name bore repeating. "*Charleston*."

Montgomery paused, and then leaned onto the balls of his feet. He addressed Samuel. "Go along if you wish—but I won't hold up the ship for you or your brother. We're not stopping a second longer than necessary to destroy the rice trunks, and I'm not taking on more people than we can carry."

"Thank you, sir," Samuel replied. "Moses and I will fly like the wind."

"Just you," the commander said. "I need Moses on board to steady the contraband."

"I don't—" Samuel started.

Harriet spoke quickly. "Colonel Montgomery, with respect, sir, the folk on board ain't the ones needing help. I know every step a the way, sir, and I can do more good ashore in case the contraband grab the tenders again. On the *Adams*, I'll be out a sight."

Captain Vaught tapped the pilot on the shoulder. "Slow up some." The older man looked again at Montgomery. "We'll anchor here to rendezvous with the tenders. If you want to send the last one up Jack's Creek, now's the time, Colonel."

Montgomery drew out his pocket watch and glanced at it. "Follow me," he said abruptly and led the way down the ladder.

Minutes later, Harriet sat with Samuel behind a band of soldiers in the smallest of the tenders, headed up the short tributary. It wasn't long before she heard gunfire and smelled fresh smoke. As they approached, Harriet saw that rice trunks still held back the river from at least four large fields, although the gate on which she had waited for Walter stood broken and ajar. Green rectangles stood gap-toothed between dirty brown ones. Flames shot up from the rice mill she'd passed the night Kizzy took her to find Jacob.

A tender loaded with refugees had cast off from the small landing. The second boat was filling. Half-sheltered behind an overturned wagon, three colored soldiers pointed their weapons in the direction of the mansion while Union troops ran toward the boat. One fleeing soldier turned to fire into the trees, though Harriet couldn't see his target. Slaves ran down the path toward the creek. A storehouse burned out of control. Sparks jumped and twirled in the hot air. The world seemed on fire. Harriet's tender sailed toward the one that was headed downriver. Twenty to thirty people crowded atop full sacks of rice. She searched for Kizzy and Jacob among the joyful but anxious faces.

"You got a Jacob on board?" Samuel shouted at an officer stationed in the bow of the craft.

"There a Jacob here?" the officer cried as they came abreast.

No one answered. Instead, people shook their heads as the boats crossed paths. Harriet didn't see Kizzy. A man in the stern turned around to stare. He looked like he was trying to work out a puzzle.

"You de brudduh?" the contraband finally shouted across the widening gap. "Samuel?"

"Yes!" Samuel called back.

"Look jest like 'im. He too sick ta—"

The man's words were lost. A deafening blast rocked the plantation. The chimney of the steam mill exploded in a cascade of bricks. A wave of pressure numbed Harriet's ears, and smoke roiled up in a vast, expanding column. The mill's boilers had burst, Harriet thought as she felt—but didn't hear—the tender bump the dock. The shock obliterated every other sound.

Harriet stood up in the back of the boat. Troops wielding sledgehammers jumped off and ran in opposing directions to attack the remaining dikes hundreds of yards distant on either side of the tributary. She reached for the wooden piling, felt a splinter pierce her palm, and climbed up on the landing. She ran up the causeway, knowing Samuel was behind her. An instant later, he caught up.

They made it onto the path below the Big House. The wind vane shifted atop the mansion's copper cupola, high on the hill and safe thus far. The overseer had not been as lucky. His house on the neighboring rise roared with flames. The blue sash windows were no more. Two pillars holding a doorframe collided and collapsed in a red shower as Harriet and Samuel passed the ruins. The slave quarters stood directly ahead. The wooden tinderboxes remained untouched by the federal assault. They appeared abandoned. Harriet and Samuel ducked behind the shabby row. As they passed one of the cabins, she heard a voice urging someone to hurry.

Galloping suddenly thundered from the direction of the jail. *Lord God*, Harriet thought. Fear shot through her as she dropped to the ground behind a tiny shack that stood on blocks above the dank earth. Samuel crouched beside her, and they wriggled underneath, side by side. The thrum of hooves seemed to fill her head. A beetle scuttled over Harriet's hand. She shook it off and pressed closer to the dirt. *Let them pass quickly*, she prayed.

But the posse halted. Dust flew under the house. "We'll make a stand here," someone in authority said. "They won't be able to advance any farther."

"Lay an ambush, suh?" asked a man whose bass voice suggested someone of size.

"Yes. I want you in this cabin, McAfee. Southerland and I will take the other. Aim out the window. We'll set up a crossfire."

"Where do you want the horses?"

"Stake them 'round back. I don't want them seen."

Harriet felt a vise close. She looked at Samuel, who cocked his thumb toward the rear. She put up a hand to signal patience. If they inched backward now, the soldiers might spy them. Better to wait for the men to dismount and cobble their horses, then shimmy out as the men took cover inside. It was Samuel and Harriet's only hope of making it back to the boat. With Rebels staking out the slave quarters, their chances of getting Jacob were gone.

Samuel shook his head angrily.

"You making a stand *here*, Sergeant?" someone jeered.

Harriet couldn't forget that voice. It was Pipkin. A sweat broke out across her whole body, and she pressed closer to the dirt. The splinter from the wooden piling burned in her palm.

"Yes. Any closer and they'll blow our heads off," the officer said.

"We can at least grab the niggers," Pipkin said. "Yankees ain't stealing my stock."

"They're too well-armed," the sergeant insisted.

"Too well-armed? Maybe your troops are just too yellow. What took y'all so long? And where are the eight riders we started with?"

"I'll discipline them later," the sergeant said. "But if you insist on getting closer, we can't go with you."

"Are you *all* ready to turn tail at nigger soldiers?" Pipkin said.

Harriet heard the creak of a saddle. She could hardly believe the overseer might help them.

A man spoke in a low rumble. "Upon my honor, suh, no nigger soldier is driving me back."

"Reinforcements are right behind us," the sergeant said. "We're better off waiting here."

"All the same, suh, I'll take my chances with Pipkin," said the man with the bass voice. "With your permission."

"Go if you want," the officer said.

"This way," Pipkin said.

A whip cracked. Horses galloped down the lane in the direction of the causeway. A moment later, Harriet heard a lone mount canter back up the road. She wondered how close reinforcements actually were. The way was now open, but she and Samuel should retreat anyway. Harriet had a bad feeling about what lay ahead.

"Now!" Samuel hissed. He sounded more determined than ever.

As they wiggled out, she told herself they would give it one more try. Harriet arrived first. Breathing in gulps, with a stitch in her side, she stopped behind Jacob's cabin to peer around the cor- ner. If she saw anyone in the road, she was absolutely turning back. This was her rule. Live to fight another day. But the path between the last two cabins—and the yard beyond—was empty. She ran to the front and pushed open the creaky door.

A pregnant woman sat on the hearth with her head slumped on folded arms. Her shoulders shook with sobs. Jacob lay motionless on the pallet. His face seemed smaller than before. Harriet ran to the bed. Samuel was right behind her. She went down on her knees and put two fingers on the side of the man's neck. Samuel pushed her aside.

"No," he said. He shoved an arm under his brother's shoulders and propped him up. "Jacob," he said. "Come on, brother."

Jacob's head fell sideways. He made no effort to sit. The dull skin of his eyelids was grayish. Harriet turned to Jacob's wife, who had the swollen face of the last months of pregnancy.

"Help me," the woman said and put out her hands. "My baby—"

Harriet pulled the woman to her feet and hooked an arm under her left elbow. She was Harriet's height but at least thirty pounds heavier. "Baby gone be fine," Harriet said.

Cradling Jacob's shoulders, Samuel shook his brother. The slats of the bed creaked under his brother's uncaring weight. "Come on," Samuel said. "Don't leave, brother."

Mayline looked down at her husband. "He gone already. I seen him go," she said and sagged against Harriet.

"Samuel, we have to get back to the ship," Harriet said. "We can't miss it."

Samuel rubbed Jacob's cheeks and shook him harder. "Not now," he said as if explaining facts to a stubborn younger sibling. "We almost free."

"Samuel," Harriet said. She tamped down her growing panic. "We got to *go*."

Samuel lowered Jacob's body onto the pallet and stared at the dead man's face. Then he reached over the bottom of the bed where the blanket had slipped to the floor and drew the shroud over Jacob's head. He bent and touched his forehead to his brother's.

Samuel straightened a moment later. He took the pregnant woman's other arm without a word. Soon they were out the door and maneuvering down the steps.

Harriet stopped at the bottom. "Hold up."

She glanced at Samuel to make sure he had a firm grip on Mayline, and then Harriet took the steps of the neighboring shack. The door hung open. A gourd spilled water across a crude table, but no one was inside. Kizzy and her family had made it to the dock.

Harriet ran out. Samuel was already down the path between the cabins, guiding Jacob's wife. Harriet caught up. Ash filled the air of the besieged plantation. They began to run. The cry of a horse followed a burst of gunfire. The trio passed the overseer's smoking foundations. A briar snagged Harriet's dress, and her shoe caught the hem of her long skirt. The old fabric ripped along the bottom. Harriet kicked the sagging fringe out of her way.

They were almost at the causeway when shots rang out. Ahead, black faces scattered, some running downriver, some for the trees. Harriet spotted the overturned wagon. Behind it, a colored soldier with a Springfield rifle took aim. Another ducked out of sight to reload. Just out of range, a man in a dented bowler on the far side of the clearing held a smoking pistol skyward. He gripped a woman around the neck with his other hand. Pipkin's fleshy face was red with rage. The woman looked paralyzed with fear. He marched her by the throat toward a group that clutched odd household belongings next to a mounted Confederate.

Closer to the overturned wagon, but sheltered behind the torso of a dead horse sprawled on the ground, a Rebel soldier exchanged fire with the colored sharpshooters near the water. Tethered to the dock, the last tender was nearly full. The other had disappeared. The shiny current pulled strongly toward the sea.

The Rebel soldier on the ground rolled over to yank ammunition from his cartridge box as Harriet, Samuel, and Mayline entered the clearing. The fallen horse lay directly in their path. The Rebel looked up at them, startled, his blue eyes strangely bright in his dirty face.

Harriet jumped over the outstretched leg of the dead animal as they ran past, holding tight to Mayline's arm. Then they were beyond the overturned wagon, down the causeway, and onto the landing. A white officer waved them onto the boat. Samuel and Harriet helped the pregnant woman down and climbed in behind her.

The officer spoke to the two oarsmen. "Ready?" Harriet looked around for Kizzy but couldn't see her. Faces and bodies were crammed together. An infant wailed in an old man's palsied arms. Sweaty troops holding sledgehammers crowded close.

Harriet's throat tightened. Gunfire sounded again across the causeway. She looked up. Running down the path from the collapsed rice mill, a handful of slaves appeared out of nowhere. A colored soldier stepped from the broken wagon, exposing himself to fire to draw attention away from the fleeing men and women, and he opened on the Rebel sheltered behind the dead horse. The Secesh ducked, and a puff of dust flew up from the animal's hide. The small band kept coming.

"Retreat! Double-quick!" the captain on the dock yelled to the men behind the cart. The soldier who had discharged his rifle ran for the boat. The last two followed.

The small band of runaways neared the Confederate on the ground. A girl ran in front. She pulled the hand of an old man.

Pipkin charged forward, heedless of the Yankees. "Stop, niggers. Stop, or I'll shoot!"

The Rebel behind the dead horse pivoted to face the renegades, and then he fired. The old man spun sideways. His hands flew up, and he fell to earth. Blood gushed from his chest. Others halted in shock. The girl in front sprinted forward without her companions.

Braids that had come loose swung free. Her bare feet pounded the hard ground. A shell necklace bounced on her chest. It was Kizzy.

Harriet stood in the boat. "Run!"

Just then, numerous armed horsemen galloped over the rise behind the mansion. They dove their mounts down the path. Reinforcements had arrived.

"Stop, you goddamn nigger!" Pipkin shouted. He picked up speed, though age and bulk disadvantaged him against the girl. His derby tumbled behind him on the ground.

Kizzy soared over the fallen horse like a hare. She was on the causeway.

With the last troops aboard, the blue-uniformed captain jumped into the tender. A slip of water opened between the boat and the landing. "Wait!" Harriet cried to the oarsmen.

Kizzy's feet hit the landing. She was almost there. Pipkin stopped a dozen yards behind. He threw down his pistol and grabbed the shotgun off his back.

Harriet heard nothing. The world went silent as she reached out her hands to will the girl to safety. Kizzy pelted down the dock toward the tender, devouring distance.

A boom filled the air, and instead of flying forward, the girl collapsed, hands flat out. Her fingers fumbled on the rough surface of the landing, as if picking shelled peas.

The tender pulled swiftly into the river.

The overseer hauled Kizzy up by the collar. She wasn't dead, but a red stain spread across her right shoulder. He spun her around, and the wounded girl hobbled back toward the plantation.

Rebel horsemen jumped from their mounts, charged past Pipkin onto the landing, took aim, and shot. The guns blared loudly, but their bullets disappeared into the black water with barely a ripple as Harriet sank onto the bench and covered her face as the powerful current sucked the tender downriver.

Chapter Thirty-Two

Remembering the treatment that these poor people would suffer for their attempt to escape to the Yankees, it was hard to leave them. But it was impossible to take another one, and sadly we swung away from the landing.

Captain William Lee Apthorp, 2nd South Carolina

Minutes later a deckhand reached down to pull Harriet aboard the *John Adams*. Two other men held the tender to prevent the river from carrying away the lighter craft. The wind had picked up. Dark clouds gathered in the direction of the Sound. Just before, Samuel had guided Jacob's wife into the hands of a sailor, and the pair disappeared into the ship.

Harriet placed a foot on the main deck and allowed the sailor to help her up by the elbow. Her hands trembled with shock, yet she couldn't allow herself to think about what had just happened. They must still retrieve the advance troops at Tar Bluff and Fields Point.

"Where you sending the sick?" she asked the deckhand.

He reached down for the next passenger coming aboard. "Hurricane deck."

Drops of water from the hull of a tender overhead fell on Harriet's scarred neck as she ducked under the craft. Slaves they had picked up along the river sat and stood everywhere, all talking excitedly. Mesmerized young men studied the rifles of the colored soldiers who lined the railings. The racehorse was tethered near the stern. Harriet heard its whinny as a woman asked where her young daughter might relieve herself. "Thataway, ma'am," Harriet said, pointing toward the head, and she then made her way up the ladder to the hurricane deck. Someone had propped a bag of rice against the door of the saloon.

Pregnant women, old people, and children with eyes red from smoke sat on sacks of dry rice. A man with his leg in a splint was propped against a wall, eyes seamed against pain. The confusion was such that it took a few minutes for Harriet to spot Samuel. He balanced on one knee in the far corner, talking with Jacob's wife, who sat against the wall. A tall woman with a water jug looked down at the pair.

Harriet stepped over the legs of the wounded man to reach Mayline.

"She doing okay?" Harriet asked the woman with the jug, though as the words left her mouth, she realized it was the refugee who had stood on the chair at the Heyward Plantation. An arresting woman with deeply arched eyebrows, she wore the same indigo headscarf. Samuel's wife was a pretty woman.

"She look healt'y t' you?" Lucy said with a pronounced Gullah accent, not taking her eyes from Jacob's widow. She wiped away a tear as she spoke.

Samuel gazed up, his expression stoic. He must have decided that mourning would have to wait, though grief showed in the heavy lines that bracketed his mouth. He glanced from Harriet to the woman with the jug, then again at Jacob's wife.

Samuel tugged at a sack of grain to make space between it and the wall. "Luce," he said to the woman next to Harriet, "wedge that jug here, where Mayline can get at it. It ain't too too full, is it?" The directness of Samuel's inquiry suggested familiarity, and Harriet caught the echo of other questions across the years: When would supper be ready? Did they need more firewood? Where would they get shoes for the boys? Had Master Heyward said anything about being short of cash?

Lucy squatted to place the jug on the floor between the wall and the sack of rice. "I gots to get back to de chillun, Mayline," she said and arranged an army blanket that had slipped from her sister-in-law's shoulders. "You res' easy now. We gone take care y'all."

The pregnant refugee choked up. Tears glistened on her cheeks. "Can't b'lieve I made it. Can't b'lieve he didn't."

Lucy wiped Mayline's cheeks with her hand. "Me neither. But you and his baby here now."

Samuel rose. He looked at Harriet, then at his wife. "This is Moses," he said to Lucy. "She commands the scouts."

He had introduced Lucy to Harriet, not the other way around, Harriet noticed as she detected a shimmy under her feet.

Lucy stood. "You in charge? A de men?"

Harriet cleared her throat. "Yes'm. Jest when we scouting."

Lucy laid a hand on Samuel's arm. "Bless you for watching obuh dem."

"Moses planned the raid," Samuel said. "She found Jacob—" His fists closed, and he didn't finish the sentence.

Lucy's hand tightened on his sleeve, and she cocked her head sideways as if observing an odd phenomenon. "Ki. Leel gal like you?" she said to Harriet. "You must got a man's head."

Harriet recalled Lucy rallying the other slaves. She thought Lucy's head probably worked like hers. "Somebody got to give orders," Harriet said.

"Praise Gawd, you can git back to you own fambly now," Lucy replied. She looked at her husband and smiled. "Our fambly with my sistahs." Lucy shook his arm. "Coming, Pa?"

"Not now," he said.

"But de boys," Lucy said. "Dey can't take dey eyes off a you."

Samuel straightened as if the thought of his sons made him feel bigger. The lines in his face softened. "Hardly recognized Sammy, he growed so much."

"Tall like his daddy," Lucy said. She jiggled his arm. "Come see em."

Samuel shook his head. "Colonel Montgomery needs me."

Lucy dropped his arm and put her hands on her hips. She stood a little taller. "Dem boys need you."

Samuel frowned. "Didn't you say they with your sisters?"

Harriet now heard the echo of old arguments. She backed up a step. "Thank the Lord you made it aboard," she told Lucy. "I jest wanted to see Mayline got settled." Harriet turned away and closed her ears to the couple as she left the saloon. Only the mission counted, she told herself, and concentrated on the vibration that came up through her soles. The boilers were stoked, paddle wheels turning. The deckhands must have secured the last tender. The *John Adams* was sailing downriver. Into a trap, if the Confederates had finally mobilized.

Outside, the sky was darker than before. A rising wind had mostly cleared the ash from the air, but storm clouds gathered to the east. Harriet climbed the ladder to the pilothouse. The ensign waved from the doorway as she took the last steps. The chair he had put out for her earlier was gone.

"Captain Vaught doesn't need help scouting the torpedoes, ma'am. We charted them on the way upriver," he called.

"Colonel Montgomery with you?" Harriet asked.

"No, ma'am, he's on one of the lower decks."

Harriet backed down. She didn't see the colonel on the hurricane deck, so she continued below. She found him at the bow of the boiler deck, speaking with Samuel.

"—for now," the rawboned Jayhawker was saying.

"Yes, Colonel Montgomery," Samuel said.

Montgomery looked to Harriet as she approached. "Moses. You can help by keeping the contraband calm. We're stopping at Tar Bluff for Captain Carver and his men. The *Weed* will pick up Captain Thompson at Fields Point. Be ready for anything."

"Yes, sir," Harriet said.

At that moment, an officer from the 3rd Rhode Island Artillery elbowed his way through the refugees who crowded the railing.

"Colonel," the white officer said with a hurried salute, "we've got to clear the hurricane deck. My men need room to maneuver."

Montgomery nodded. "Moses," he said, "you and Samuel get busy. Spread out."

Over the next half hour, Harriet waved refugees coming down from the hurricane deck onto the jammed lower levels of the ship. She ran into Walter, whom she told about Jacob and Kizzy. His right eyebrow twitched, and he rubbed it with a knuckle. "Hanging's t-t-too good for P-P-Pipkin," Walter said.

At that moment, an old man behind them said to a companion, "Dis remind me when I come from de Congo. So many ooman die, dey only mens left by time we reach Cuba. Buckra jest pitch dem bodies overboard."

Walter shot Harriet a look. "Let's get folks to put their backs to the railing," he said quietly. "If they keep their eyes on each other instead a the riverbank, they won't be worrying about t-t-trouble ahead."

Harriet hardly noticed the river as she circulated among the refugees. "Face the smokestack," she instructed. "Hold tight to your chil'ren til the river goes so wide you can't see the other side," she said, realizing that few had ever spied the ocean. "It gone be a couple hours yet." When two young men balked at turning their backs to the view, Harriet explained that the colored troops needed help. The youths jumped at the opportunity to assist the uniformed men, and within short order, they had gotten those on the boiler deck seated and mostly quiet, except for the babies. Tension crept over the ship as everyone realized they weren't yet safe. An hour passed.

Harriet positioned herself between two soldiers at the portside railing, facing the north bank, and took tweezers from her satchel to worry the splinter out of her palm. When finished, she plucked at her collar to let air into her shirt. The humidity had thickened.

The Secesh must have finally learned what had happened. Their field artillery would be on the road to Tar Bluff or Fields

Point. It was baffling that the gunships had encountered so little opposition thus far. Could the Secesh commander be even more incompetent than they'd thought, or was he grouping his forces to smash them at the end? Harriet guessed that the *Adams* had only a mile or so before the first Rebel fort. The river still moved toward the sea, yet the black water had turned sluggish. It must be close to two in the afternoon. Earlier in the day, Captain Vaught had said the ebb tide would speed their escape until then. After two o'clock, the incoming tide would fight them—though it would also raise the water level to float them over the bar.

Harriet scanned downriver for the *Harriet Weed*, hoping Septima's sister Juno was aboard. She closed her eyes briefly. *Dear Lord, please let Juno be on the* Weed, she prayed. As if in answer, Harriet heard a faraway ship's whistle. The *Weed*. It must be near Field's Point. A moment later, another distant trill echoed across the marshes in the far distance. Then another. Three altogether. The signal for distress. The *Weed* had encountered Rebels.

The vibration under Harriet's feet increased. Two blasts sounded from the ship's whistle as the *Adams* gunned her engine. The river took another bend. On their left, the fort at Tar Bluff appeared. A Union officer on the dock urgently waved his hat. Troops clustered behind him.

"Hallelujah!" said a soldier standing to Harriet's left. He spoke over her head to a man on her right. "See dat? Didn't lose a single sojer!"

The *Adams* backed water at the last moment. They came alongside the dock so quickly that Harriet feared they were going to ram it. But the ship slowed in time, and a gangplank went out. As the advance guard ran aboard and vanished below, Harriet heard Montgomery. "Double-quick!" the colonel yelled. "Cast off!"

The *Adams* pulled away and picked up speed. Black soot from the smokestack filled the air. The ship's paddle wheels dug trenches in the slack tide. They sailed another couple miles. Clouds overhead grew ominous. They were closing on Fields Point: the end of the Combahee and last obstacle to freedom. When the *John Adams* rounded the last bend, Harriet spied the *Weed* treading water at the river's mouth. Puffs of gray smoke issued from her guns. The ship was firing at the road beyond the fort. On the landing, a white officer and a handful of colored soldiers stood with their backs to the river, guns trained at the promontory above. Just then, an enemy shell careened over their heads. It hit the slope next to the dock. Dirt flew onto the landing. The colored troops ducked, but they kept their muskets trained above.

Rebel field artillery had arrived. The Secesh were making a last stand. Trees obscured the road, and Harriet couldn't see how big a force they'd assembled, but a single shell in the wooden deck of either ferryboat would sink it. Everyone would go down.

Harriet leaned over the railing. Thunderheads towered above the estuary. A faraway curtain of rain blocked the light in the direction of Port Royal. Someone in the *Weed*'s pilothouse pushed a wigwag flag out the window to signal the *Adams*. A deafening boom sounded immediately from the deck above Harriet's head as a twenty-pounder opened up. All the heavy guns seemed to discharge at once. The *Adams* quaked with the concussion, and an instant later, an explosion erupted behind the Rebel fort on the hill. They had scored a hit. Other cannons boomed on the *Adams*, and debris again flew above the trees on Fields Point.

A cheer went up. "Give it to em!" Harriet yelled. A soldier beside her stamped his feet. Others shouted oaths. On their feet now, refugees strained over the railing. A woman covered her baby's face with a shawl and screamed, "Smite dem! Smite dem!" Harriet wished she had her musket. Just once, she wanted to kill someone. Draw blood. Strike down those who'd taken each and every one of her sisters.

Onshore, anxious Union troops crowded the landing while the *Weed* steamed forward and shoved out a gangplank. A boom came from the trees, and a fountain of water sprang up twenty feet from the portside. The spray washed the railing as the advance troops raced aboard. Moments later, the *Weed* sailed toward St. Helena Sound when thunder broke overhead.

Jagged lightning ripped across the sky like a root torn from the earth. The storm had arrived. Harriet felt the lift of the turbulent tide as a howitzer boomed above her head. Then, as the front wall of the Rebel fort erupted in dirt and stone, the *John Adams* steamed out of the Combahee and into the gale.

CHAPTER THIRTY-THREE

It took a smart nigger to know who his father was in slavery time. I just can remember my mother.

Elias Thomas, Slave

Dirty waves crested the bows of the flat-bottomed ships as they entered the Sound. Heavy clouds blocked the setting sun. On the *John Adams*, errant waters forced most passengers off the lowest deck and onto the boiler and hurricane decks where they sat hip-to-hip, terrified and soaked to the skin. Once darkness fell, not a glimmer of moonlight penetrated the clouds. Rain slashed the small flotilla, seemingly determined to wreck it on the enemy shore. President Jefferson Davis of the Confederacy might have sent the torrential storm.

Sometime after midnight, dead with exhaustion, Harriet struggled across the crowded deck with a sack of provisions. She had passed out most of the hardtack in her possession, but Harriet hoped to save some for morning, when it would be hard to calm the children's crying.

The storm had dampened her euphoria at victory and reminded her of all those she'd left behind, again and again. It seemed the cycle would never stop. Colored troops had triumphed, yet slavers still clutched their stolen flesh. A dark despair gathered in her mind. *No*, she thought. She would not let it engulf her. She would not think of Kizzy. Not yet.

299

The boat rocked sideways on a steep wave. Frightened passengers sent up a howl as the overburdened ferryboat bucked and wallowed. Harriet's shoe caught the torn hem of her dress, and she stumbled. She grasped at the slippery railing with her free hand. A lantern fixed to a pole threw a dim light onto the sea-foam twenty feet below.

The ripped dress was going to get her killed. If she slipped overboard, the waves would swallow her in an instant. Steadying herself, Harriet set down the bag and took up the sagging hem. To shorten the skirt, she tore off the damaged fringe at the bottom and threw it overboard. Her ankles now showed, but compared with the tattered refugees, she looked as proper as a Baltimore nun. For the first time in hours, a half-smile flitted across her face at the absurd thought.

Harriet felt a hand close on her ankle.

"Auntie, I hongry," a small voice said. A youngster whose age and sex were indeterminate in the dark looked up at her. Something told her it was a boy. His mother dozed sitting up, one arm tight around him even in sleep. The child's head was too big for his body.

"You got sumpin'?" he asked.

Harriet squatted, opened the sack, and withdrew two ship's biscuits. The wet burlap had moistened the rocklike bread. "One for you, one for your mama, hear?" she said as she handed him two pieces. Other hands reached out immediately. Harriet was too weary to resist. She gave out the remaining hardtack. "Pass it along," she said. "Share with your neighbor."

The child examined the biscuit. "Buckrabittle?" he asked.

"Buckra-what?"

"Buckra-*bittle*," the little boy said as if repeating the obvious. "White folk food."

"Jest food," she said before laying the empty sack on top of him to keep off the rain. Harriet stroked his head. She guessed his age at five. The boat pitched, and the child leaned his face into her hand. Tenderness swept her, and for once, she didn't resist. He was free—and always would be. This is what a free boy looked like. It made up for a lot.

"Everything jest fine," she said in her storyteller's voice. "We be safe and sound on Port Royal by morning."

"Dey plant rice dere?" he asked.

"No," she said, "cotton."

The boy took a small bite of his bread. "Mama and me work de field?"

"Your mama might. But you gone go to school."

The boy stopped chewing and tucked the biscuit under the burlap. "School?" His voice grew small. "Where dat? Cuba?"

Harriet placed a hand on his knee and shook her head vigorously. "No, school ain't Cuba. Your mama gone work during the day while some missionary ladies teach you letters. At a place called school. Nights, you and your mama be together."

The boy retrieved his bread and took a cautious bite. "We mos' dere?" he asked.

"Yes, we are," Harriet said. "You take care a mama 'til then."

Harriet stood and picked her way through the hunched crowd. She actually had little idea how close they were. They had planned to be in Beaufort before midnight, but that hour had passed long before. She hadn't seen Samuel since he took food for the contraband to the hurricane deck sometime after dark. She wondered if he was spending his boys' first night of freedom with them. He must be ecstatic for his children and devastated about his brother. It was hard to imagine how one heart could hold both feelings without tearing in two.

Harriet noticed families holding one another in the storm. One father had his long arms around a woman and at least four tiny children. At last, she found an open spot and propped herself against the outside of the boiler room. The motion of the waves seemed to cease the moment she folded her legs under herself. She was so everlastingly tired and wet. Harriet breathed rhythmically. The wind sighed, and she fell asleep.

A loud thunderclap broke overhead sometime later, waking her abruptly. A wave knocked the person next to her almost into her lap. She glanced at him. Samuel reached over and took her hand in his. "You awake," he whispered.

"How long I been out?" she said.

"A spell." He lifted her hand and gave the back a private kiss. "Jest glad I found you."

Harriet shifted closer. She didn't know how to ask about his family. "The boys all right? Everybody get something to eat?"

He nodded. "Yes, ma'am. They made short work a them biscuits. Downed em in a bite. Lord, it ain't been three months since I left, but Sammy's growed two inches."

"Lucy eat, too?" she said.

"Yep. She had some dried pork. Didn't want the biscuits, so I gave em to her mama and sisters." Samuel reached into the pocket of his old coat and drew out something that looked like leather. "Brought you a piece a the pork."

"Thank you. Got my own. You keep it for your boys," Harriet said, unwilling to take the woman's food. She reminded herself they had been forced to marry. Freedom should include freedom to love. Still, her conscience troubled her—and the grief she'd been ignoring welled up.

"Samuel, what about Jacob?" Her voice cracked. "And Kizzy?"

Samuel put his arm around her shoulder. "They in God's hands now."

Harriet thought of her sister Linah. "Seems I could've done more."

Samuel's arm tensed. "You could've told me sooner bout Jacob."

She didn't speak. What could she say? All the years of walking in front told her she had made the right decision. Years earlier, her brother Robert had called her cold. He'd been late for their rendezvous to escape to the North, when she'd had the safety of four other runaways to think about in addition to his. "I wait for no one," she'd told him. Robert kept up with the group after that but acted differently toward her once they got to Canada. "Your heart made a stone," he said.

But she wasn't made of stone. She was so human it ached.

Samuel's torso rocked as the boat hit a particularly large swell. "Seems like I been waiting for something bad to happen ever since mas'r sent him to Pipkin," he said after a moment. "Feels like someone cut off my right arm."

Harriet knew there was nothing she could say that would lessen the loss, but words were what she had to give. "I'm sorry," she said softly. "Real sorry."

He held her close. "I know, baby."

"Pa!" a voice called. Harriet looked up to see Lucy a few yards away, in the light of the ship's lanterns, following the railing toward them.

"Samuel Heyward, what you doing down here?" Lucy reached for her hair as the wind tore her scarf loose. "Yo fambly—"

The man on Harriet's right rocked against her as the ship slid down a wave. She braced her shoulder to keep him upright.

"No!" Samuel cried.

Harriet looked back at the railing. Splayed flat on the deck, Lucy clung to a heap of coiled line next to a barrel. The wind had whipped the indigo scarf from her head and blown it into the dark sea. One of her shoes had slipped through the slats in the railing and disappeared. Lucy looked ready to go overboard.

Samuel was at her side. He put his hands under her armpits and hauled her to her feet. "Where the boys?"

The howling wind picked up, and Harriet didn't hear Lucy's answer as Samuel helped his wife across the deck to the ladder. He didn't look back as he pushed her up the hurricane deck.

The ship bounced on the chop. It was a motion the ferry hadn't made before. The flat-bottomed boat slid sideways while its paddle wheels fought with the swell. The ship's bow seemed turned around. Harriet glanced fearfully toward the ocean in time to see a wall of water rise up. A giant wave hit them broadside, and the gunship tilted like a top.

Passengers skidded into one another. A woman screamed in terror. Harriet slammed against the boiler room. Her teeth clacked as her head hit the paneling. Then the ship crested the immense swell and heaved in the opposite direction. A loose rucksack sped past, bounced when it hit the railing, and sailed into the sea below. Harriet plastered her hands against the wet wood to keep from sliding downward. The overloaded ferry was ready to capsize.

She lifted her face to the rain. "Heavenly Father," she cried. "You saved your chil'ren from slavery. Take pity on us now. Send us home to Port Royal!"

The gunship entered a dark trough, and then it climbed the next wave. The vessel slanted backward, pinning Harriet against the wall of the boiler room yet again. At the top of the wave, the ship's rudder dug into the swell. The ferryboat shifted direction, and the bow turned. Rather than wallowing, the ship pitched.

Soon, they were riding the waves instead of hitting broadside. Harriet looked around, surprised to be alive. Passengers were crying, but no one had gone over.

The rain gradually slowed. The waves became longer, the water smoother, and the sky lighter. Pink showed on the horizon, and Harriet caught sight of a landmark on Lady's Island. Her legs felt wobbly, but she stood and gripped the railing to make certain. Yes, there was the oak split by lightening the year before. They were in the Coosaw at last, and everyone on board seemed awake. In nooks and passageways where they had found shelter, on open decks where others had clung to one another during the night, men and women got up to greet the first day of freedom. As the sun came over the horizon, refugees talked, laughed, hugged in astonishment, wrung out their shirts and scarves, and exclaimed at the approaching islands.

"What dat place called?" a stocky young woman asked a colored soldier at the railing.

The man smiled and pointed. "That one's Lady's Island. Maybe you gone be a lady there."

Harriet turned. She must find Samuel. A horse whinnied somewhere. Passengers hustled down the ladder from the hurricane deck to get closer to the gangway. At last, Harriet had an opportunity to ascend. She spotted Walter Plowden as she reached the top. The skinny scout and several other passengers stood looking down at a group huddled under the saloon's shallow eave. The crowd shifted, and Harriet realized that one of those seated was Samuel, who had something in his lap. A form wrapped in a gray army blanket. The still body of a child. Lucy sat beside them, one hand on the covering.

A cry escaped Harriet. She ran to the saloon, dodging around clumps of passengers. She pushed someone aside. "I'm a nurse," she said.

The crowd parted. Harriet fell to her knees. It must be Samuel's son. How could this happen? Not this child, too. Robbed at freedom's door.

"Samuel," she said.

He didn't answer her. Eyes anguished, skin gray, brow furrowed, Samuel looked as if this blow on top of losing his brother hours before had stripped him of reason. He wiped the face of the limp boy again and again. "We almost there, Jake, almost free," he said. "Stay with me."

"Wake up!" Lucy said frantically and shook the leg under the blanket.

"Come on, boy. Come on," he said, pleading with the inert child.

An older child spoke to a tall woman who gripped a toddler on her hip. "Mama said to wait, but Jake went looking for Pa. Jake always in trouble. Now he cain't wake up."

The unconscious boy appeared to be around six. He had a

bloody scrape across his cheek and an immense purple lump on his forehead. He lay absolutely still. Then his eyelids fluttered and he inhaled sharply. He looked up at his father.

Samuel bundled the boy closer. His voice broke. "I got you, son."

A deckhand set a tray with mugs of hot broth on the deck for the family of the injured boy. "This'll perk you up," he said.

The morning had dawned bright and calm. Lucy's sister had taken the other two children to watch the approach of Port Royal on the starboard side and to let their dazed parents rest. Harriet examined the tray. She didn't see the utensil she'd requested. With a concussion, the boy needed fluids. "Did you bring a spoon?"

The crewman reached into his top pocket. "Yes, ma'am."

Samuel leaned forward quickly. "Give that here," he said, and he took the utensil. They were the first words he'd spoken to anyone other than the child.

Walter reached down for the steaming mugs. He passed one to Samuel, then Lucy and Harriet. For himself, he took the last, which he sipped quietly. Hands wrapped around the cup, he glanced at Harriet before training his gaze on the deck, which he examined with pity.

Samuel dipped the spoon. "Here, Jake," he said as he lifted the broth to his son's mouth.

The boy sat against the wall with the blanket around his shoulders. He opened his lips, not taking his eyes from Samuel. Father and son gazed upon one another's features as if committing them to memory.

"The patrollers gone ask if I *seen* you, and I got to be able to say no," her own father had said when Harriet stole back to take her brothers north. So Daddy tied a kerchief over his eyes and entered the Maryland safe house blindfolded. He explored their faces with his hands as if molding a likeness before saying goodbye.

Samuel gave his son a teaspoonful of broth, then another. When the ship's roll caused him to spill some, Lucy dried the boy's chin with the hem of the blanket.

Harriet backed up. She sipped the hot liquid as quickly as she could without burning the roof of her mouth. It had no flavor to her.

Walter placed his empty cup on the tray. "Make sure you d-d-drink some a that yourself," he told Samuel. He looked at Harriet. "Coming? I think we 'most there. Colonel M-M-Montgomery gone want us."

Harriet set the broth on the tray without finishing it. "You all right?" she asked Samuel.

He nodded but didn't look up. Instead, he set the cup aside and put an arm around his son's shoulders to keep the slumped boy upright. Lucy rested against the wall, eyes shut and holding Jake's hand. The formidable woman looked spent. Walter touched Harriet's sleeve. "I'll be on the main deck, Moses," he mumbled and turned in the direction of the ladder.

"Samuel?" Harriet said. "You coming?"

Lucy Heyward opened her eyes, apparently alarmed by the question. She shook Samuel's leg. "Pa. You got to let other men do de sojering now. Me and de boys never been nowhere 'cept Heyward's place."

Samuel didn't speak, though he nodded once more in understanding.

Harriet felt as if the deck had tipped sideways again. The world seemed to slip away. She took a step toward him, pride broken. If only they could touch, he wouldn't leave her. No one saw that she was vulnerable, too. Never had she admitted it even to herself—especially to herself—but she needed someone just as anyone did. Rejection had turned her inside out years before, making her feel as if she was worth nothing, except in what she could do for others. She wanted to be loved for herself.

"Coming, Samuel?" she repeated, forcing out the words. "It's time."

Samuel finally looked up. His face was smudged with dirt, and indecision showed in his eyes. The light pulse in his neck beat fast. Harriet felt his longing from ten feet away. The engine purred, and the ship rocked gently on the tide. Harriet heard distant cheering from the shore.

Samuel seemed incapable of speech. His jaw bunched, and he tugged his son closer.

"All right, then," she said. "I'm going."

CHAPTER THIRTY-FOUR

Colonel Montgomery . . . penetrated the mainland for twenty-five miles, by way of the Combahee, with three companies, destroying large quantities of rice and cotton intended for the Rebel army, and burning a great many houses. He brought away 750 Negroes—men, women, and children, and threw the entire country into a panic. His forces behaved splendidly.

The New York Times, June 1863

Colonel James Montgomery stood at the head of Port Royal's long wharf an hour later. Colonel Thomas Wentworth Higginson and Sergeant Prince Rivers of the 1st South Carolina had positioned themselves alongside. Ticking the air with a forefinger, Rivers counted the refugees as they streamed toward Bay Street. Harriet assumed that Higginson's provost marshal took special note of able-bodied men, though she doubted Montgomery would let him steal a single one.

She lowered her head as she filed up the dock, grateful for deliverance yet numb with loneliness. By herself in the crowd, she felt she would never smile again. "Follow the parade, follow the parade," a white officer chanted to the contraband as they passed. "Everybody's headed to the church. Look for the church."

Harriet hitched her heavy satchel higher. She hadn't needed the bandages and would return them to the hospital on the way to the Savan house. Septima wouldn't want to work on a day of

309

celebration anyway. Harriet had confirmed that her sister made it out when a woman with catlike eyes disembarked from the *Harriet Weed* not long before.

"Juno?" Harriet asked.

"Yes, ma'am. Dat's right," the woman answered with a familiar quickness. Harriet told her where to find Septima, should her sister not be waiting on the dock.

One more family reunited, praise God. Even if they had lost Jacob and Kizzy, even if Harriet's own heart was broken, even if she'd let herself down by trusting Samuel, she was alive and so were her men. They had done the impossible and changed the fate of hundreds.

"Moses," Montgomery called over the crowd. From his elevated position at the head of the wharf, the silver eagles on his gold-braided shoulder straps glittered in the morning light. Harriet drifted behind a bunch of soldiers to avoid meeting his eyes. She needed time.

"See the look on that Secesh when his hoss throwed him?" a soldier in front of her said in a Tidewater accent. He grinned and clapped his companion on the shoulder.

"Like daddy done take out the paddle," the second man said. "That was my bullet. Too bad it missed his head."

"Your bullet? That one was mine," the first man said. "I jest glad it didn't hurt his hoss. Poor critter didn't have it coming."

Both men laughed, and the sun loomed brighter for a moment. Colored soldiers had earned their right to brag.

A messenger on a bay mare galloped onto the dock from Bay Street. He dismounted with a flourish to hand Montgomery a document. Harriet lowered her gaze to walk past, but steel fingers unexpectedly took her by the elbow. Though she tried to pull away, the man drew her easily out of line. "Colonel Montgomery wishes to see you, Miz Tubman," Sergeant Rivers said. She glanced up angrily at the difficult, exasperating officer. Rivers looked down

from his indomitable authority with an expression she didn't recognize. He smiled.

"Wait here, Moses," he said as he guided her to the flagpole.

Harriet turned to watch an egret pluck a blue crab from the
salt grass on the river's edge. She stared at the bank, hoping to
avoid seeing Samuel Heyward's face should he and his family pass
along the wharf while she stood there. Downriver, a large troop-
ship sailed into the estuary. Harriet wondered where it had come
from. Likely Boston or New York. The boat was still a ways off,
but she thought she saw uniformed men on deck. Wouldn't it be
something if Lincoln had finally sent reinforcements?

"Look a' dat," said a Gullah man who stopped behind her. The
refugee pointed toward the river. He had a hand on the ragged
sleeve of another escaped slave.

"Dang," said his friend. "Dem be sojers. Mo' cullud sojers."

"Maybe dey going back up de Cum'bee," the first man said. "I
got twenty cousins upriver if I got one."

Harriet squinted at the approaching ship. She saw the uniforms
more clearly now. The water's glare bounced off brass buttons.
Dark faces looked toward land. A man on the ship waved, and the
one next to Harriet waved back. "Brudduh!" the refugee shouted
in her ear.

A shooting pain above Harriet's left eyebrow caused her to
wince. Gore-splattered fields flashed through her mind. Soldiers
running muskets toward a fort. Red battlefields sowed with dead
men. She shook her head to clear the awful vision. Would the
next assault on Charleston end better than the last one?

Someone tapped her shoulder. Harriet turned around. James
Montgomery lifted his blue slouch hat and shoved a hand through
his dirty hair. The colonel's uniform was a mess again, rumpled
and sooty, with the lining poking through a tear in one sleeve.
"Our job isn't done," Montgomery said before restoring his hat. "I
need you at the church, Moses."

Harriet shook her head. "You don't need a scout," she said. "Won't be a single Rebel picket."

His blue eyes scrutinized her face for clues to her reluctance. "No. But you can help me recruit. That's why we went up the Combahee. To find men. Now they've got to sign up. They'll follow you."

Harriet gazed back at the estuary. At the moment, she loathed the thought of trying to persuade any man to follow her. She turned to him. "A course, Colonel. I'll head right over."

Harriet allowed her feet to follow the crowd. The weather continued to improve, and the sun shone strongly on her back. Within a block, Harriet's clothes felt drier, her spirit less stunned. A farmer stopped in the middle of the street to hand out oranges from the back of his wagon. "We'come, brudduh. We'come home," he said, grinning. The crowd grew as soldiers and contraband marched down Bay, turned onto Church Street, and trooped past the mansion where the war-hungry gentlemen of South Carolina had whipped up their rebellion half a million deaths earlier. By the time the parade wound through the Greek columns of the towering Baptist Church, Beaufort's largest building, it appeared that every man, woman, child, and dog in town had tagged along in awe.

A contraband preacher Harriet didn't know stood on the stage as jubilant refugees, mud-stained troops, and blackened artillerymen crowded onto the pews and balconies along with eager townsfolk, reporters, and missionaries. Shouts, cries, and laughter bounced off the thick walls of the building, amplifying the commotion. It was the largest crowd Harriet had seen since Emancipation Day five months earlier.

"Sit on down!" the preacher exhorted newcomers from a wooden pulpit on one side of a raised stage, though there were too many people for everyone to find a place in the pews. Hundreds lined the walls and stood in the aisles of the magnificent church.

More looked down from the balcony. Harriet wondered how the army would care for them all. No jobs, no homes, no land.

She stationed herself to one side of the portal to buttonhole men after the speeches ended. The recruitment office was a block away. An old woman in a dress so threadbare that Harriet was surprised it had not yet disintegrated climbed the stairs of the stage with the aid of two robust men. She recognized the trio from the shout. Once they began humming, Harriet smiled despite her troubled frame of mind. A moment later, she—and everyone else—hummed along. The stirring notes of "John Brown's Body" filled the church.

The crowd quieted and drew together. The warm alto launched into her solo. The new version of the old song, with lyrics that black units had recently adopted for their drills, reverberated in the nave and galleries. The singer's lone but powerful voice seemed to speak for all of them. Every soul in the grand old building hung on her words.

"*Mine eyes have seen the glory of the coming of the Lord,*

He is trampling out the vintage where the grapes of wrath are stored."

A man standing on the other side of the door from Harriet joined in. The row of soldiers in front of him sang, too.

"*He hath loosed the fateful lightning of His terrible swift sword.*"

Harriet and others who had known freedom even before yesterday's events, who had seen the war coming down the road and greeted it valiantly, lifted their voices.

"*His* truth *is marching on!*"

The walls rang as every single person clapped on the word. Down to the smallest child, each knew where the beat stood. *Truth.*

Harriet had wondered for years how planters could lie to the world. How they could pretend the color of their skin entitled none but them to liberty. How even whites who didn't own slaves could look away and tell themselves they had a free country.

When Colonel Montgomery strode down the center aisle at

last, most stood. The singers moved to one side of the wide stage, and someone handed up a piano stool for the old woman. There was little sound beyond the fussing of babies and Montgomery's resolute tread. It was as if the crowd wanted someone to explain what it all meant. Why this terrible tragedy had befallen them and where they would go next. How a man like him could become a friend.

The colonel walked up the burnished stairs of the stage, turned to the throng, and removed his hat. "Yesterday—"

"Jest yesterday!" a woman cried from somewhere in the middle of the congregation.

"Saved!" someone else said, before a chorus of shushes quieted them.

"Yesterday," Montgomery began again, "three hundred soldiers put a stop to one of history's gravest crimes. They spared the lives of 756 black men and women. And they saved the souls of millions of white people, too. Those who won't commit the sin of slavery once we end this terrible scourge."

The former evangelist paused. A sash scraped wood as someone lifted a window to admit a breeze. Random coughs echoed. Harriet heard someone still softly humming off to one side.

"This deed was accomplished without the loss of a single soldier. Not a single man," he continued, "and for that, we praise the Lord." Montgomery bowed his head.

A murmur rippled through the congregation. *"Praise the Lord."*

The weathered commander looked up. Strife and suffering had worn gullies in his face over the years. They deepened. "But not without the deaths—ones we witnessed with our own eyes—of at least four bondsmen whose only sin was to love the freedom that is God's blessing on every man. For that, we ask His forgiveness."

"Forgive us, Lord," the refrain sounded somewhat louder.

Montgomery lifted his chin. "Now we must ask Him for courage. Because for every free man and woman here today, there are thousands more still in bondage. We must save them. Help us, Lord!"

"*Help us, Lord!*" the crowd shouted back amidst clapping and stamping.

Montgomery raised a hand. When the sound died back like a wave against the shore, he continued. "Not all of us are given to know the right thing early on. It often takes a person a long time to see the path of righteousness. It takes a whole country even longer. But there is that rare person who knows the path from the start. They show others the way."

The crowd leaned forward. Harriet got an uncomfortable feeling. She backed up a foot, into the person of Sergeant Prince Rivers, who stood with his arms crossed in the open doorway. He looked down and shook his head.

"I was a latecomer," Colonel Montgomery admitted. "I had to be shown. And the person who showed me was a tiny woman who's known the path for decades and traveled it herself, mostly alone." He stared straight at Harriet. The pause was long enough that some turned their heads. A reporter across the aisle glanced at her and jotted something down. Montgomery waited until Harriet inclined her head.

"I've said enough," he concluded. "I want Moses to tell us what comes next. I want Moses to show us how we get to the Promised Land."

Some women now wept openly, and more than one man had call to use his sleeve. "Moses!" came a cry from somewhere in the balcony. Others took up the chant. "Moses!"

Harriet thought of all the white audiences she'd talked to in the North. All the times she'd stood in churches and lecture halls, sat in prayer meetings and sewing circles, to tell her story. She'd never spoken to an audience of black people, she realized, as the crowd parted again to let one person walk the length of the church. And that was because black people knew her story. It was their story.

Harriet heard the echo of her clumsy shoes in the large hall. She wished her hem wasn't torn and her ankles weren't bare. As she climbed the stairs to the stage in her ragged skirt, she wished she had her petticoat. And she wished, as she turned around to face her people—black and white—that she knew what story to tell them now.

Colonel Montgomery stood in front. Beside him was Thomas, her old friend. Farther back, she saw Septima, her best friend, whose sister held Kofi on her hip. The boy's runny nose needed attention, but he gave Harriet a shy wave. Above them, Walter leaned over the balcony and nodded. Others she knew well or not at all waited for her remarks. She looked for, but did not see, a man with clamshell ears. Near the center aisle, she spotted Samuel with his wife, three children, and widowed sister-in-law. Relief, sorrow, and devotion flickered across his face. Then he nodded, too, and she looked away.

"I'm not a preacher," she began. "I can't even read the Bible, for which I'm heartily sorry." She paused to study her hands. Well-made hands that had boosted people up the ladder. "But I can tell you a story. A story bout a girl."

Harriet raised her gaze to the audience. She sought the eyes of the men. "This child doesn't have no daddy. When a white over-seer took her to his bed, no man could stand up for her."

A man near the stage put his face in his hands. A mournful keening filled the church.

Harriet looked to the women before her. "When that man came for this child, her crippled mother had no way to stop him. No way a'tall."

Septima's eyes filled with tears. Two women in the aisle leaned against one another for support, their faces constricted in private agony.

"And when that child—that brave girl who should be with us today—tried to run away, that same man took his gun and shot her in the sight a God."

Harriet found her gaze drawn again to Samuel, on whose lap Jake clasped a small orange like he'd won a prize. For most folk, rescuing kin was enough. For a few, life would make sense only if everyone was free. Samuel had done right by his family, but Harriet would fight until not a single person was left behind. Then—if God was good, and He was—He might find the right man for her.

Earnest faces looked up for guidance. Most had been slaves only a day before. They were her people, eager for her words. She wasn't alone. They were with her.

"That's the girl we going back for. That girl and all the other girls. And our sons, and mothers, and fathers. That's our mission." She paused and held up two fingers. "Cause the Lord, He give us two choices. Jest two. Liberty or death. And I made my choice. Now you got to choose."

She looked toward heaven, where Rachel waited. Harriet lifted her hands. "But God don't mean us to fight by ourselves. No how! He brought us together for a reason. He gave us these hands—He gave us each other—to pull every last one a His chil'ren to freedom. Join me, and our chil'ren, and their chil'ren, and chil'ren all 'round the world gone say, '*That's* where black men and white men, black women and white women, stood up.' And they gone sing, as we did on Emancipation Day, 'My country tis a thee, sweet land a liberty!'"

Whistling, clapping, and shouts of "Amen" shook the old building until it seemed the foundation itself must shift. They were as loud as any horn Gabriel could blow. Judgment Day was coming. Men flocked toward the exit where Sergeant Prince Rivers waved them in the direction of the recruiting office. Harriet trembled with excitement and clenched her fists.

The Lord had spoken. Make a joyful noise. They were doing it.

AUTHOR'S NOTE

Col. Montgomery and his gallant band of 300 black soldiers, under the guidance of a black woman, dashed into the enemies' country, struck a bold and effective blow . . . without losing a man or receiving a scratch.. . . . The Colonel was followed by a speech from the black woman who led the raid, and under whose inspiration it was originated and conducted. For sound sense and real native eloquence, her address would do honor to any man, and it created quite a sensation.. . . . She is now called "Moses," having inherited the name.. . . . True, she is but a woman and a "nigger" at that, but in patriotism, sagacity, energy, ability and all that elevates human character, she is head and shoulders above all the copperheads in the land and above many who vaunt their patriotism and boast their philanthropy.

Wisconsin State Journal, June 1863

A WRITER OF NONFICTION CANNOT INVENT A single detail. Not a word, not a sound, not even a cloud in the sky. Readers must trust that professional historians will never present something as *known* when it isn't. Yet when I first read the quote above, I wondered what Harriet Tubman told the congregation that morning. So I decided to fictionalize the events noted in the report, which didn't even give the full name of the "black woman who led the raid."

The reporter's oversight isn't surprising. There are gaps in the records of even the most closely observed people. Historical evidence is always incomplete and often maddeningly fragmentary.

In previous novels, I have written about men whose lives were well documented. Even so, I sometimes quailed at my nerve. None of us can really know what went on in the heads (or beds) of men whose backgrounds, personalities, and times were so different from our own. Women are more challenging yet. Typically, their lives are lightly recorded. The letters of Elizabeth Schuyler, about whom I wrote in a novel on Alexander Hamilton, have been lost. Harriet Tubman was unable to pen one. When writing a nonfiction account of America's first women soldiers, I found that although their war records had been kept, they'd been ignored. In the past, chroniclers didn't think it was especially important to document women's deeds. Even now, we tend to assume they didn't do much and disbelieve evidence that they did.

Great women and men have much to teach us, however, so it is worth using our imaginations and the tools of history to see events through their eyes, as imperfectly as we shall. Fiction lights the dark corners of evidence. In the case of Harriet Tubman, I hope my portrayal will inspire others.

The epigrams that start each chapter of this book are drawn from original documents. I have relied upon extensive historical sources on the Civil War, American slavery, and Harriet Tubman. These include over two thousand oral history interviews conducted by the Federal Works Progress Administration in the 1930s that tell the story in enslaved peoples' own words and give insight into period language of the lower and upper South. The dialect used in this novel is based on these records and others, and on statements by Tubman that sympathetic friends, mostly Northerners, wrote down. To make the text less jarring to modern readers, I have streamlined the dialect and imposed consistent spellings.

As to the events themselves, I have followed the record as closely as possible while fleshing out bare facts with plausible fictions—from Webster's thievery, for example, to Pipkin's shooting of a nameless girl who bolted vainly for the ship. (Private Webster was found guilty in a court-martial at which Tubman and Plowden testified, and I created the story of Kizzy around the girl.) The danger posed by Confederate torpedoes was real. In an 1864 mission up the St. Johns River in Florida, the *Harriet Weed* sank in under a minute when it hit two underwater mines. As the *New York Times* reported, "She was literally blown to atoms."

We know from Harriet Tubman's candid testimony that her husband opposed her flight to freedom in 1849 around age twenty-seven. A year later, John married a free woman with whom he had free children. Tubman devoted herself after this painful event to bringing her own family and others to safety. Smuggling fugitives was highly illegal, so most people did not keep records, but we know from the secret logs of William Still of Philadelphia and Thomas Garrett of Delaware that Tubman guided close to one hundred people and possibly many more to freedom. In yearly raids, typically conducted during fall when nights grew long, she brought her enslaved brothers Robert, Ben, Henry, and Moses, her manumitted parents Benjamin and Harriet Ross, and various other family members to Canada along with countless strangers. When the Civil War broke out in 1861, she again courted danger to serve on the occupied Sea Islands.

Samuel Heyward and Walter Plowden belonged to a small group of scouts under Tubman's command. To make a living during the war, she sold pies, gingerbread, and root beer with the help of an assistant and set up a laundry in Beaufort to teach freedwomen how to support themselves. After the war, she married Nelson Davis, a veteran of the US Colored Troops who fought at the Battle of Olustee and was twenty years her junior. Harriet Tubman must have been magnetic. Both of her husbands would otherwise have chosen a peer as a mate. Someone younger. Someone free.

Nelson Davis and Harriet Tubman Davis lived in Auburn, New York, until Nelson passed away in 1888 in the house she had purchased from William Seward, Abraham Lincoln's political rival and secretary of state. She bought an adjacent parcel in 1896, where she built a shelter for homeless colored people, and where she lived until her own death in 1913, around age ninety-one. Harriet Tubman never knew her precise age since her birth was unrecorded, like so much else. William Seward wrote of her, "a nobler, higher spirit, or a truer, seldom dwells in human form." Colonel James Montgomery described her as "a most remarkable woman, and invaluable as a scout." General Rufus Saxton, supervisor of the contraband on Port Royal, recommended Tubman for a military pension as a "spy" who made "many a raid inside the enemy's lines, displaying remarkable courage, zeal, and fidelity." Despite disinterested testimonials on Tubman's behalf, and her own petition as "commander of several men," Congress nonetheless resisted granting a woman a scout's pay. Three decades later, the federal government retroactively awarded Tubman the lesser pension of a nurse. Congress granted Walter Plowden the pay of a scout.

Seven months after the Combahee raid, Rebel pickets had captured Plowden during a solo mission. He languished fifteen months as a prisoner of war in Charleston, until the 21st Infantry of the US Colored Troops entered the city. As indicated by Samuel Heyward's last name, he had likely escaped from the Heyward Plantation, since it was common for freedmen to be identified by the surnames of former owners. We know little else about the scout.

Nothing in the historical record describes his and Harriet's personal relationship. Tubman was a single woman as well as a canny military strategist. I don't accept the prejudice that a woman must be sexless to be virtuous, so I penned a love affair to reveal the individual behind the icon. War intensifies a yearning for sheltering arms, and it would be natural if Tubman sought them. Family reunification might well have precipitated a crisis. As historian Tera Hunter observes, one of the most challenging legal problems freed Americans faced was how to confirm or end relationships begun under slavery. Marriage and divorce were often the first civil rights they exercised. Readers who wish to understand the doubly difficult plight of enslaved women more generally—including its emotional costs—may wish to consult Deborah Gray White's seminal *Ar'n't I A Woman?*

On the subject of Harriet Tubman's family, historians speculate that a child she mysteriously took from a "brother" in Baltimore around 1858 was not her so-called niece but actually her daughter. Margaret Stewart physically resembled Tubman, and they were close until the older woman's death. In this novel, I have chosen to accept the best guess of biographers such as Catherine Clinton and Kate Larson. Since family lore holds that Margaret came from a "brother" in Maryland (though all of Tubman's brothers escaped to the North), I've depicted her as the ward of Harriet Tubman's brother-in-law.

Harriet Tubman suffered throughout her life from the brain trauma inflicted by an overseer. Her disability was documented by acquaintances who observed that she frequently lost consciousness when sitting quietly, only to wake after three or four minutes without losing the thread of a conversation. Tubman reported to her chosen biographer that strange dreams, sounds, and visions sometimes accompanied these episodes. Historians speculate that Tubman's original injury may have produced temporal lobe epilepsy, a seizure disorder that triggers loss of consciousness though not convulsions. The disability gave her increasingly painful headaches as she aged. In the 1890s, she sought brain surgery at Massachusetts General Hospital, where she underwent a procedure—without anesthesia—that moderated the condition.

Military accounts of the Combahee Raid are skimpy, as is common in war. The contribution of scouts was not documented and Tubman's name appears nowhere in the official record. For this reason, some historians question her leadership. Yet advance intelligence must have played a role. Plantation owner Joshua Nichols intuited that slaves had been forewarned as they did not evince the "slightest" surprise at the dawn raid, and he thought he spotted "women" (perhaps a lone woman) on the upper deck of the attacking gunship. Plantation owner William Heyward watched Union boats sail "safely" around torpedoes, as if their location was known. Harriet Tubman later recalled urging General Hunter to appoint Colonel Montgomery, and an eyewitness journalist wrote immediately after the raid that a woman named Moses "led" the expedition under the command of Montgomery, who himself called Tubman "invaluable." Although evidence doesn't paint a complete picture, in my opinion there is enough to substantiate the testimony of Tubman and the Wisconsin journalist, who had no reason to fabricate events and whose public reports no one contradicted at the time.

One of the last things about which we cannot be certain is how Harriet Tubman might feel about a white person writing this book. We do know she commissioned Sarah Bradford to pen her biography in 1869 and not Frederick Douglass, though he contributed a testimonial letter to the volume. Harriet Tubman advocated strenuously for women's rights, including the right to vote, and may have wished to give a female writer the opportunity. Today, she would undoubtedly be proud to have black authors tell her tale. Her long collaboration with white abolitionists suggests she would also encourage writers who share John Brown's skin color. I hope readers will be as openhearted, though some may not. The life-work of a historian is to reveal the experience of people from the past. For myself, I don't believe that gender, race, region, or time period make us unintelligible to one another. Harriet Tubman was a singular individual within her generation—or any generation—and wanted her story told widely. No one owns her. She risked everything to establish that fact.

Many people helped with this project. In Beaufort, Stephen Wise, Larry Rowland, Carolyn Lauvray, Reverend Kenneth Hodges, John Wharley, Grace Morris Cordial, and Larry Kooklin gave invaluable advice. I am indebted to Susan Meredith and her family for preserving the Maryland store where Harriet Tubman received the blow to her head and for finding the priceless runaway notice widow Eliza Brodess published when Tubman fled in 1849. Ashley Trujillo of the Museum of Miami helped locate relevant archives on the 2nd South Carolina. Jack and Bradley MacLean, avid fishermen of the Combahee, shared lore on tides, currents, and alligators. Historian Catherine Clinton provided guidance. Macke Raymond made hand pies. Lilly Golden of Arcade gave me courage, opportunity, and excellent editorial advice. Alexandra Shelley helped with writing craft while publicist Gretchen Crary supported the book with feats of legerdemain. Judy Beletti, Shelbee Cobbs, Sandra Dijkstra, Claudia Friddell, Michelle Gable, Maria Gomes, Khoi Le, Tina Lee, Christina Luhn, Michele Mattingly, Victoria Shelby, Stephanie Shelley, Susan St. Louis, Janice Steinberg, Victoria Wayne, and Iris Wyatt allowed me to see the prose through the eyes of discerning readers. Gregory Shelby and James Shelley allowed me to see it through the eyes of filmmakers. My first graduate advisor, Carl Degler of Stanford University, inspired my interest in slavery and the Civil War. Stanford's Hoover Institution, San Diego State University, and Texas A&M University provided research support, and I am particularly grateful for the generosity of Melbern and Susanne Glasscock.

Lastly, I wish to thank the first person who encouraged me to see the world through the eyes of a famous figure. "For Halloween, you should be Joan of Arc," my Aunt Diane told me when I was eight. "She was burned at the stake!" My aunt then made me a costume from cardboard, which, I note in retrospect, is a combustible material. Equipped with a wooden sword and dreams of heroism, I set out to collect my candy and save France. Yet even at that age, I sensed when historical details were wrong. My shiny suit of armor bore an embarrassing resemblance to a Tide box covered in tinfoil. So I removed the square breastplate and continued on the mission in leotard and tights, disappointed at my own cowardice. On the way home, I donned the armor once more, and my aunt was never the wiser. (Now she is.)

This book is dedicated to my friend and fellow historian Myra

Burton, who kindly read multiple drafts, offered salient perspectives as a person from what she calls "The Community," and cried with me at the end. With better attention to period costuming, it humbly honors an American leader who, like Joan of Arc, fought for her country and belongs to the ages.

Readers who wish to delve into the background of this novel may wish to consult the following original sources:

Scenes in the Life of Harriet Tubman (1869) and *Harriet, The Moses of Her People* (1886) by Sarah Hopkins Bradford

Army Life in a Black Regiment (1900) by Thomas Wentworth Higginson

Reminiscences of My Life in Camp with the 33rd United States Colored Troops, Late 1st South Carolina Volunteers (1902) by Susie King Taylor

The Letters and Diary of Laura M. Towne: Written from the Sea Islands of South Carolina, 1862-1884, ed. Rupert Holland (1912)

The Journals of Charlotte Forten Grimké, ed. Brenda Stevenson (1988)

A Woman Doctor's Civil War: Esther Hill Hawks' Diary, ed. Gerald Schwartz (1989)

Incidents in the Life of A Slave Girl (1861) by Harriet Jacobs

My Bondage and My Freedom (1855) by Frederick Douglass

Bullwhip Days, The Slaves Remember: An Oral History, ed. James Mellon (2014)

Slave Songs of the United States, ed. William Allen, Charles Ware, and Lucy Garrison (1857)

War of the Rebellion: A Compilation of the Official Records of the Union and Confederate Armies, United States War Department (1880-1901)

Award-winning novelist, historian, and documentary filmmaker, Elizabeth Cobbs is the author of eight books, including the *New York Times* bestselling novel, *The Hamilton Affair*, and *The Hello Girls: America's First Women Soldiers*, recently made into an off-Broadway musical. She holds the Melbern Glasscock Chair at Texas A&M University and is a Senior Fellow at Stanford University's Hoover Institution. The middle child of seven and married mother of two, she is grateful to live in the world Harriet Tubman helped make for American families.